MW00528891

Ain't Life Grand in Woodstock

Sally Cissna

Appleton, Wisconsin
2023

SuLu Press
1230 South Telulah Avenue
Appleton, Wisconsin 54915

Publisher's Cataloging-in-Publication Data

Ain't Life Grand in Woodstock/Sally Cissna
Paperback ISBN   978-0-578-25377-0
1. HIS054000 HISTORY/Social History
2. FIC008000 FICTION/Sagas/Family Sagas
3. SOC026000 SOCIAL SCIENCE/Sociology/Women/Religion.
I. Cissna, Sally. II. Ain't Life Grand in Woodstock.

Disclaimer: The stories herein are not factual accounts but rather flow from letters and the imagination and memory of the author. However, the general history of the families, the newspaper articles, and the era are as accurately represented as possible. These accounts are not meant to characterize or disrespect any person or group, past or present. While some words or ideas may challenge twenty-first century sensitivities, including the author's, these terms are true to the times and necessary to the story.

Cover design: The picture on the cover was taken around 1915 of the four Wienke children "enjoying" a day in the country. Is that the Woodstock's South Street Arch Bridge in the background?

Separators: The *** indicate a large amount of time passing between sections - days. Extra space but lack of *** means a little time passed.

News Articles: The news articles included herein are, to the best of the author's ability, exactly as they were printed. Spelling, grammar, and lack of cultural awareness is accurate to the day and paper, as is the editorializing regarding issues such as peace, war, and humanity.

First Edition

Dedicated
To
D. Edna Wienke (1906-1969)
who was

Assistant Librarian, 1925-1947
Librarian/Director, 1948-1959
Woodstock Library

And my aunt whom we called "Nenna."

Photo credit: Woodstock Library Archives, circa 1950,

AND to all librarians, bibliophiles, researchers, and avid readers who give us reason to tell stories, spin yarns, draft novels, voice opinions, articulate fantasies, and inspire generations to read.

Thanks

To Rebecca, my always-encouraging spouse and best editor and proofreader, for 30+ years of support.

To Liz, my cultural editor and cheerleader.

To Beta readers: Patrick, Joyce, and Debi.

To The Caramel Crisp Writers' Group
Patrick for holding the group together through thick and through thin.
Joyce for being a resource on early 1900s life and on multiple other topics.
Sandra for her fearless and educated critiques.
Connor for his friendly smile, sense of humor, and ability to help me see the whole picture.
Michael for helping me with German language (and Russian) and historical perspective.
Raiden for his youthful vigor and viewpoint.
To all of you, thank you for making time each week to support our novel expressions.

To the Woodstock Library for facilitating my research.

And thank you to all the readers who have waited so long to know if it's a girl or a boy.

Sally Cissna

Sally Cissna is an educator and history enthusiast. Sally lives in Appleton, Wisconsin with her spouse, Rebecca, two tiny pups, Maggie May and Pipa Jo, and a smarter-than-average cat, Clara Jane. Sally is honored to present these tales of her grandparents' and parents' lives.

In this the fourth book in the series *The Woodstock Tales*, readers not only catch up with the Wienkes and Clara Daring, but you also meet the other side of the family – the Cissnas of Southern Illinois. Watch for the fifth book, *At War in Woodstock*, late in 2023 or early 2024.

Happy Reading.

Other Books by Sally Cissna

Take Me Home to Woodstock (2019)
A Fine Grocer of Woodstock (2020)
I Will Fly to Woodstock (2021)

With Maryon Rasmussen Range

Fishing for Happiness (2020)

To read more about the Wienke/Doering/Cissna families, please follow my home page at sallycissna.wordpress.com or find me on Facebook @ Author Sally Cissna. I truly hope you've enjoyed this book. If so, a review is always appreciated.

John and Ida Wienke (circa 1913)

What Cha Doin' Mama?
(1912)

The gray sky began spitting flurries which fell wind-driven in a sparkling disorganized dance onto the bare ground. Low clouds moved fast from the northwest to the southeast. The smell of dampness was telltale even though it wasn't terribly cold. A big storm was brewing. Ida Wienke didn't need the weather forecast in *The Sentinel* to know. She had dressed eight-year-old Helen and seven-year-old Mamie warmly for their walk to school. Now she stood at the front window watching their figures recede into the swirling flurries.

"Whatcha doin,' Mama?" Dodi's voice was maturing. She was five years old now. She would be one of the oldest in first grade in the fall while Helen had been one of the youngest. Ida was going to miss Dodi's company at home.

"I'm just watching the clouds. It's beginning to snow."

"Oh, goody. Can we go play in the snow?" Dodi headed to the entry and began looking for her boots.

"I'm sorry, honey. I can't play outdoors just now."

Dodi stopped her search and returned to the parlor. She lifted her hands palms up in an incredulous gesture, and her face contorted in confusion. "Why not?"

"Because ladies who are going to have babies aren't allowed to go outside especially in bad weather."

"But you go outside all the time. You just went outside when we took the train to Oma's, remember?"

"Yes, but now a few weeks have passed, and my belly is getting too big to be out and about. It's…it's…unseemly."

"Why are you getting bigger?" Dodi's brow suddenly furrowed with worry. "Are you going to 'splode?"

"No-no." Ida stifled a laugh. "At least I hope not. You see the baby in my tummy is growing and because of that, so am I. When a lady who is with child gets to those last few months, no one needs to see them. They are supposed to stay at home and take it easy, so they don't upset the apple cart."

Dodi considered this. "Aren't the apple carts here in the summer? It's winter now."

This time Ida laughed. "You're right. Let me put it another way." What other way? "Um…we don't want the baby coming too early or too late. So, we need to keep an even keel until he decides to show himself."

Dodi's brow scrunched up in concentration. "What's that?"

"What?"

"An even keel?"

"Um, well, it's…I'm not sure what it is, but it means to keep everything calm and happy."

"Oh." Dodi looked at the floor still looking confused. "How does he show himself?"

"Okay, that's enough questions for now. I have a taste for bread, butter, and dill pickles. Would you, milady, like to join me in a pickle sandwich?"

"Yes! I love pickle sandwiches."

"Me too!"

They went to the kitchen and pulled out bread from the cabinet and butter and pickles from the icebox. Ida thought about how she was going to stand spending the next two months in seclusion. She had hand projects she was crocheting, and there was always the cooking and baking. Her beloved husband John had agreed to let the Chinese laundry off the square do the laundry for the next few months. All she had to do was gather it in bags. They even ironed John's shirts for her. She had refused his offer of a live-in helper even for a little while. Cooking and cleaning were easy and wouldn't hurt her or the baby.

She sat down at the table and started to make the sandwiches.

"I want sugar on mine," said Dodi.

"Sugar? On a pickle sandwich?"

"Maybe I don't want the pickles – just a sugar and butter sandwich."

"With cinnamon?"

"Yeah. That's good."

Ida rose to get the sugar and cinnamon. "Do you want it on toasted bread?"

"Yes, that's my favorite. Then the butter melts into the toast and the sugar and cinnamon taste so good together."

Ida smiled. One thing Dodi was particularly good at was describing food.

While she waited for the toast to brown on the cook stove rack, she said, "Dodi, what do you want to be when you grow up?"

Dodi laid her head on her arm on the table and waggled her hand, "I don't know? What can I be?"

"Well, let's see. You could be a wife and mother."

Dodi raised her head and shook it.

"How about a nurse?"

Dodi again shook her head.

"Um, a shopkeeper?"

"Like papa was? No, I don't think so."

"How about if the shop was a bakery?"

Dodi sat up straighter and her face brightened.

"That's what papa wants to have."

"Yes, it is. Would you like to work with him in his bakery? You already know how to bake bread and rolls."

"M-a-y-b-e." Dodi drew the word out. "But maybe I want to be a newspaperer like An' Clara. I could travel on the train and see things and write stories about them to THE *Woodstock Sentinel*."

"Hm. That's an interesting thought." Ida had plucked the toast off the wires and now was buttering it and sprinkling the cinnamon and sugar liberally on its surface.

Dodi's blue eyes sparkled as she watched the process.

Ida put the plate in front of Dodi, took her own chair and finished preparing her pickle sandwich, although the smell of cinnamon made her covet her daughter's choice. She took a bite. It needed cheese. She rose and took down the cheese cloth with the cheddar cheese. She sliced off a thin slice and put it on her sandwich. Perfect!

Dodi was working her way through the first piece of toast.

Before she took a bite, Ida asked, "Where would you travel by train?"

Dodi wiped her mouth with the back of her hand. "Effrywhere. London, New York, St. Louis, and Denison."

Ida laughed, "And Denison?"

"To see An' Clara and Unca Pearley. Remember their house is in Denison, Ohhiawa."

"Well, that is quite a list."

They chewed in silence for a bit, enjoying each their own idea of the perfect sandwich. Then Dodi said, "And Indian."

"India? Where did you hear about India?"

Dodi reached for her second toast. "Remember that book?"

"What book?"

"Helen said it was in Indian."

"What book?" Ida was still confused. John and she had gotten the girls ten books for Christmas. Of these they had read three before bed to everyone and the other seven Helen and Mamie consumed on their own.

"You know Lil Back Samblo. He's from Indian."

"Oh, you are right! I forgot about that book."

"It's so funny." Dodi balance the toast on one hand.

"Yes, it is." Ida's thoughts wandered to the night, now almost a decade ago, when she had seen John in blackface cavorting on the

Opera House stage as Prime Ursus, strongman of the County Fair. It was hilarious. "Yes, it is."

"When da tigers make butter for the pancakes. I like that part." She took a bite of the toast making sugary lips.

"So, you think you'd like to go to India?"

"On da train. For da butter. I like butter on pancakes."

"Oh, I see." Ida reached over and squeezed Dodi's shoulder. Her baby was growing up. But now she'd have a new baby to cuddle. She touched the wooden tabletop to prevent a jinx.

After their lunch, Ida and Dodi decided to lay down for a rest. Ida encouraged Dodi to go up to her own bed. According to John's plan, each girl had their own room, and the new baby would move into the fourth. As she arranged herself on the master bed in the downstairs back bedroom, Ida considered how John had thought of everything when he built this house.

At that time, he said, "In the new house, I promise, you will not have to go up and down stairs! And there will be four bedrooms upstairs for the children."

Having the master bedroom on the first floor was nice. She still had to climb the stairs to see to the children and go to the basement for laundry and canned goods, but she had long ago decided it was the thought that counted.

Her eyelids were as heavy as her belly. She wondered if Dodi was still awake – it was her last thought before sleep overcame her.

A loud crash shook the house. Or so it seemed to Ida who struggled from sleep to sitting up in bed. What in the world? She listened and heard Dodi's little sing-song voice.

> Ring around da rosy
> Pocket fulla posey.
> Ashes, ashes...

We all fall down.

Oh Lord, where had she fallen. Ida looked at the clock. Four o'clock! Can't be. The girls were home from school. She had slept right through their arrival.

She pulled herself over to the edge of the bed and slid off into her house slippers. Grabbing her shawl and throwing it around her shoulders, she quickly…well, quickly as an eight-month pregnant woman could…went to the kitchen.

Mamie sat on the floor with the cast-iron skillet between her legs. A white substance covered her head and shoulders, and floured chicken thighs were scattered on the floor. Dodi was dancing around, away from the mess, singing her rhyme.

"What happened here? Mamie are you all right?"

Mamie looked up with tears in her eyes. "I was trying to make dinner for you and then the pan went flying."

Ida went to her and decided that she was not going to be able to reach down and do clean up. "It's okay. Go ahead and put all the pieces back in the skillet. Did it hit you on the way down?"

Ashes, ashes…
And we all fall down.

Dodi fell to the ground, giggling.

"No," said Mamie. She looked miserable. She began to pick up the pieces of chicken and put them in the skillet. "I was holding it to put it on the stove, and it just flew out of my hands."

Ashes, ashes…
And we all fall down.

"Okay, Dodi. That's enough. Did you see what happened?"

Dodi put her index finger to her cheek and considered the question. "Well, we were making supper for you an' Papa an' Helen." She glanced at the stairs. "And Mamie was supposed to put the chicken on the stove and all of a sudden…." Dodi paused for effect. "She threw the pan up in the air and it almost hit her in the head coming down. It hit her arm, and she and the chicken 'all fall down'."

Ida looked at Mamie. She now had all the chicken pieces neatly packed in the pan. "All right. Can you pick it up now Mamie? Can you hand it to me?"

Mamie regained her feet and picked up the pan and handed it to Ida who placed it on the counter. Mamie started crying, and Ida drew her to her oversized belly with hands on her back. "It's all right, honey. Accidents happen."

"It wasn't an accident," Dodi broke in. Mamie shot her a dirty look. Dodi looked away.

Mamie buried her face and cried harder.

"Everything's fine. You did your best." Ida sank into a chair and lifted Mamie onto her lap. She rocked and cooed to her until the sobs reduced to only the occasional hiccup.

"You were very brave to try to cook supper, and I appreciate your effort," Ida said.

Mamie hiccupped. Dodi came and stood next to the chair and put her cheek against Ida's shoulder.

Ida smiled at Dodi and turned back to Mamie. "That is a very heavy pan especially when it is loaded with food."

Mamie nodded.

"How about we work together and make supper. Papa will be so happy."

Dodi patted Mamie on the shoulder. "You almost did it."

Ida smiled. "Shall we start over?"

***

Typewriters Given Away

The Emerson Typewriter company of Woodstock, Ill., have recently given away over 400 of the highest-grade, wholly visible Emerson Typewriters made in the world. They have gone into every state and territory of the United States. There may be some in your town. They are giving them away everywhere to men, women, and

boys and girls over 18 years of age on surprisingly liberal
conditions. If you could make any use of a $100.00
typewriter, providing it did not cost you even one cent,
then in a letter or on a postal card addressed to Frank L.
Wilder, President, Woodstock, Ill., simply say, "Mail me
all your Free Offers," and by return mail you will receive
their Free Offers, the names of over 400 who have
recently received typewriters free, and you will learn on
what easy conditions you can get one of their
typewriters right away. Many who have used the
"EMERSON" and other makes pronounce the
"EMERSON" superior to any $100.00 typewriter on the
market. It is a wholly visible machine, has every new,
up-to-date feature, looks like other high grade $100.00
typewriters, though it sells regularly for less and on
terms of $1.00 down and ten cents a day until paid for.
The "EMERSON" has every new improvement,
universal keyboard, back spacer, tabulator, two-color
ribbon, everything the best; is the ideal machine for
beginners as well as for the most expert typists and
stenographers; just the typewriter for the smallest or
largest office.

Woodstock Republican, January 25, 1912.

***

BIG CROWD WATCHES RACES

'The largest mid-winter crowd that has assembled in
McHenry in years' is how the McHenry Plaindealer
described the Ice Speedway races held Sunday afternoon
on the Fox River. It is estimated that nearly five
hundred lovers of the sport were in attendance from
Johnsburg, Wauconda, Richmond, Terra Cotta, Crystal
Lake, Ringwood, Spring Grove, and Woodstock.

All of the horses were in fit shape, and as a
consequence, those who turned out were not
disappointed but were given something to talk over.
The steeds entered in the different races were all owned
and driven by McHenry people, so more than a little

rivalry existed and as a result a few hundred dollars changed hands as soon as a race was over.

The Plaindealer claims that "the results of the day's sport have left no ill feeling and all who entered their horses are satisfied with the result, the losers taking defeat in a real sportsman-like manner."

Woodstock Sentinel, February 1, 1912.

***

"Bob would have liked this article," John said to Ida's back. It was early Friday morning and still dark.

Ida was looking out of the kitchen window at a slight glow to the east reflected in the neighbor's windows. She was preparing a breakfast skillet of scrambled eggs, summer sausage, and fried potatoes with onions. To that she added freshly baked bread with butter and strawberry preserves. The meal was one of John's favorites, and his mouth watered at the smell of the sausage sizzling in the pan.

"In what way?" Ida didn't turn. She had to stretch to reach the pan and still protect her belly from the hot stove.

"First of all, it is about horse racing."

"Ah yes, one of his favorite pastimes." John's younger brother Bob, dead now six years from the aftermath of rheumatic fever, had run a minor bookie business out of his saloon.

"And second, there was a good deal of betting on the winners. It says here a hundred dollars exchanged hands after each heat."

"A hundred dollars? Either high bets or lots of gamblers."

John smiled. "Lots of gamblers, I think."

Ida turned with two plates in her hands. She placed them on the table and sank heavily into her chair and pulled her plate closer to the edge of the table.

John reached for her hand, and they bowed their heads, and John led the prayer, "Gracious Lord, thank you for this food to make our bodies strong and ready for the trials of this day. Bless us and our children as we go out into the world in your service. Amen."

Before she took her first bite, Ida asked, "How can they be racing at this time of year?"

John chewed a bite and swallowed. "On the ice on the Fox River."

"On ice? Now that's something I'd like to see. Are the races over for the winter?"

John looked back at the paper as he consumed a hearty bite. "Says there's another one next week in Wauconda."

"Maybe we should go. The children would love it."

"I don't think this is a children's activity. And it isn't the kind of activity that a woman with child should be at either. What if you fell on the ice?"

"Don't you think we could park our sled close enough to watch without being out on the ice?"

"I don't know, and I don't want to travel all the way to Wauconda in the cold to find out with a pregnant wife who might just have to give birth on the ice of the Fox River."

Ida sighed, "Aren't you a wet blanket."

John gave her a steady gaze and decided she was not serious about going. He chuckled and shook his head. "You test me, woman."

Ida smiled. "But you are so testable. I would like to see it sometime. But maybe not this year."

"Or next? With a tiny baby?"

"We'd work it out. Let's make a date for next January if they are running again."

"Why do you want to go to a horse race?"

Ida put down her fork and looked at him. "I don't care if it's a horse race. I just want to go somewhere!" Tears suddenly welled in her eyes.

John wiped his mouth and rose to put his arms around her. "It won't be long now. Maybe you should ask some lady friends over for tea."

Ida wiped her eyes on her napkin. "Oh heavens! I'm okay. Just a bit bored, I guess. One can only make so many quilt squares before her eyes cross. I will call ladies from church to come for tea – I know just who. That would be fun. Thank you for the suggestion."

John tightened his hug slightly and let go, returning to his chair. She would be fine.

A sigh escaped Ida's lips. "But next year I'd like to see horses run on ice."

John rubbed is forehead, a smile playing on his lips. She would be fine.

***

Denison, Iowa
February 10, 1912

Dear Ida and John and children,

How are you, Ida? I hope you are taking it easy and not doing too much. You must think of the baby and yourself. We don't want a repeat of Mamie's perilous birth. I remember you said mid-March for the birth, right?

We are fine. Pearle is back on the road already, even though the snow continues to come off and on. If it snows, he lays low in the Watkins wagon for a few days. It's enclosed like a gypsy wagon and almost cozy. By that time, either the snow has melted, blown away or packed down on the roads so there is clear passage. He's only gotten stuck once all winter using that method. I truly miss him when he's gone, and when he is here it's lovely. And we continue to hope for a baby.

We were gratified to hear that Miss Dodi will travel to both London and Denison by train. We will welcome her with open arms at any time.

Helen seems settled into her schooling and I'm sure she is learning much. I'm so proud of you, Helen. Write me a letter when you have a chance. It will be a way to practice your penmanship.

And Mamie. Are you looking forward to seeing your little brother? I bet you are. Just think how tiny and sweet he will be. Oh, you think it might be a girl. Maybe. But the odds are against it. I love you, my little sweet one.

Is John jealous of Pearley Dear's freedom? Or is he too going door-to-door even in the winter? He must go door-to-door with his insurance products just as Pearle goes door-to-door with his Watkins products. Do you only sell in Woodstock, John? So, you can walk everywhere, or must you travel to other communities? I don't think I've ever heard how you do your work. Write and tell me about it. My sister only tells me about the children.

My biggest news is that I got a free Emerson Typewriter -well nearly free. I had to pay for them to ship it to Denison. But besides the shipping, they asked me to send a photograph of me using it. Taking the photograph wasn't the easiest thing to do. I lugged the machine, thirty pounds if it's an ounce, down to the photographer, and he made the picture for five dollars. I sent the photo and the endorsement for the Emerson back to them and they were so thrilled to have a female reporter using their machine that I won a new ribbon each year for five years! How are they making money on these machines? Seems like they will go broke if they keep giving everything away. Alas, I only paid for one photograph, so I can't share that with you, but you've seen me before. Now picture me sitting with my hands on a brand-new Emerson!

I suppose I better close and get back to 'All Things Denison.' I don't have a topic for this week so I must put on my tall boots and go digging. There must be news out there.

> *Our love to all of you,*
> *Clara (and Pearle)*

PS. Almost forgot to thank you for the Christmas box. The shawl is beautiful, and Pearle loves his socks. The jams and jellies came through fine. I loved the pictures from the children, and they hang on my wall right now.

***

Lemmers Lays Down Pen

C. A. Lemmers, publisher of the Woodstock Republican and engaged in newspaper work in this county longer than any other man now in harness, was taken Saturday to the M. W. A. sanitarium in Colorado Springs, Colo., suffering with tuberculosis. His recovery is considered doubtful. His brother Guy, publisher of the *Hebron Tribune*, has taken charge of the Republican, and will issue both weeklies from the Republican office.

Crystal Lake Herald, February 29, 1912.

***

John glanced up from his desk near the window of the Prudential Insurance office and saw his brothers Frank and Ed walking down Main Street. He got up and went to the door and stepped out, letting the door swing shut behind him.

John raised his hand and called out, "Hey!" Frank looked over and said, "Grass is greener, and straw is cheaper."

Ed smiled. "He's gotcha there."

John beckoned them into the office.

Frank and Ed entered stomping snow, fresh last night, off their feet.

Frank looked at John's worry-creased face, and his own smile faded.

"Have either of you talked to Ma since last Sunday?" asked John.

Frank and Ed looked at each other. "No," they said in unison. Frank continued, "Were we supposed to?"

"I tried to call her early this morning and couldn't get an answer. Maybe she was just sleeping soundly. You know old people sleep more, right?"

"Did you just try the once?" Ed asked.

"No, I just tried again a bit ago and still no answer. We should go check to make sure nothing has happened. Something may be wrong with the phone, but you never know."

"But we were on our way to lunch," said Ed.

"I know. I suppose I could go alone." John reached for his hat and coat and pulled on his galoshes. "But I'd appreciate the support. You know she'll feed you, right?"

"That's true." Ed rubbed his chin considering. "OK. I'd enjoy one of Ma's famous sandwiches for lunch."

John chuckled. "Always looking for the free lunch."

"Hey, little brother, watch out! I'm of a mind to let you go solo."

Frank laughed. "Come on, let's get moving so there's time to eat one of Ma's famous sandwiches."

As they moved out into the chilly air, John said, "What will we tell her about showing up without an invite?"

Frank looked at him. "Why the truth, of course. We were worried when we couldn't reach her. Don't worry she'll be glad to see us."

They walked briskly up Main Street and turned left on Washington. It was only two or three blocks depending on how you counted them. Many of the streets in Woodstock were not squared off, and Washington was one of them running northwest out of town toward Harvard. As they got closer, dread built in John's chest. He banged on the door and tried the latch. The door opened easily. "Ma? Your door is unlocked. Are you here?"

No answer...and then...was that a moan? The men looked at each other. John called out, "Ma?" They moved as one toward her bedroom. They saw the small round body under a light blanket. Another moan.

Ed went to the phone to call Ma's doctor. With luck he'd be at his office.

John knelt by the bed and said, "Ma? It's John. Can you tell us what's happening?"

Sophia mumbled something that John couldn't hear or understand. Her face looked slack and uncontrolled. "Oh no! A stroke!" he said under his breath.

From the other room, they could hear Ed's voice. "Yes, Doctor. Just now. I don't know. She's abed. Okay. Thank you. See you then."

"Doc's on his way," said Ed entering the room.

Sophia's right hand came up, and she gestured her boys away, speaking haltingly in faltering German that none of them could decipher.

John leaned close to the others and whispered. "Stroke, do you think?"

"Most probably," said Frank with a lowered voice. "Although she's moving quite a bit for a stroke. I've always heard that people can't move after a stroke." The three men looked at the bed. "Maybe I should call Anna to come," suggested Frank.

"Yes, yes," came the responses.

Frank left the room.

Ed said, "I'll go watch for the doctor."

John went back to the bedside and took Sophia's hand. "Ma. Can you tell me where it hurts?"

Sophia shook her head and shooed John away with her other hand.

"Ma, have you tried to sit up?"

Again, the shooing motion. We'll have to wait for the doctor. John didn't want to try to sit her up and make things worse.

Frank's wife, Anna, came hurrying in. She had dropped everything and came across the street with nothing more than her shawl against the frigid temperature. She moved John away and knelt by the bedside putting her hand on Sophia's head. "Maybe a bit of a fever." She took Sophia's wrist and felt for a pulse. "Good strong pulse." She lifted the hand John had been holding and let go. It dropped like a rock. Anna had concern written all over her face. "Ma, squeeze my hand." Anna looked at John and shook her head.

John put his hands to his face and turned away so the woman could not see his panic. When would the doctor get there?

"Ma, how long have you been here in bed?" Anna asked.

John turned back to see Sophia's answer. She held up one finger with the 'shooing' hand and then two fingers.

"One or two what," he said, his normally deep voice taking on a higher pitch. "Days?" Sophia shook her head. "Hours?" Sophia shook her head. What else was there?

"Nights?" asked Anna. Sophia nodded. "I bet you're starving." Sophia shook her head and closed her eyes.

The thump of a closing door signaled the arrival of the doctor. John heard Ed say, "…we think a stroke."

The doctor's friendly voice came with him through the door, "Well, Mrs. Wienke, what have we here?"

Ed pulled John out of the room by his coat sleeve, leaving Anna to help with undressing if necessary. "Call us if you need help lifting."

Six of the seven Wienke boys and their spouses sat around their mother's dining room table, all except for Charles and Minnie, who Frank had called, but had not yet arrived from Beloit. Anna and Ida bustled about to provide fixings for sandwiches.

The doctor had come and gone, agreeing with their lay diagnosis of a stroke. He described what they might expect in the next few days and weeks. "Provisions must be made for her care here at home. Taking her to the hospital would just put her in more peril of disease. I am encouraged by the motion on the left side and the verbalization even if it is hard to understand at present." He would come back tomorrow.

Now, those gathered were quiet. They looked at each other or the table and murmured thanks when Anna put the platters of meat and cheese on the table with two loaves of bread.

John said, as he made his sandwich, "Did you see by the paper that Lemmer's is done at the Republican... tuberculosis."

The others grunted that they had seen. Frank said, "I wonder where he got it?"

Ida took a dainty bite, chewed, and swallowed. "Do they even know how a person gets it?"

Emil's wife, Etta, sipped her coffee. "You're right, Ida. If they had figured out where it comes from, they'd know how to stop it. Right?"

Ed's wife Kate nodded in agreement. "They say it's spread by cows, don't they? I saw that in the paper."

William's wife, Lizzie paused before her first bite. "I saw that too. But Lemmer wouldn't have been out on a dairy farm."

"Maybe it stays in the milk from infected cows," said Emil.

The others looked horrified.

"Guess that means I'm switching to beer," said Ed.

Kate kicked him under the table, "You've already switched."

Smiles and nods supported her notion. Then only chewing was heard for a time.

John thought about how comfortable his family was to eat a meal together. That was all due to Ma and her Sunday dinners. What would happen now if she wasn't able to cook? He mentally slapped himself for the selfish thought.

The plates emptied, and hunger was satiated. Time for business. William pushed back from the table and spoke. "What are we thinking about Ma's care?"

The others were quiet for a spell, and Anna said. "She can come live with us."

Frank's head snapped toward her. "Anna?"

She patted his hand. "She can come live with us. She has taken care of all of us for so many years. Now it's time to repay that debt. Our children are not young, and we have room. And the trip across the street will not be as traumatic as those to other homes might be."

John looked from Anna to Frank. "Do you agree, Frank? It could be years of care, you know."

Frank looked down at his hands and back at Anna. "Are you sure, Anna?"

"Yes, I'm sure."

"Then I am, too. She can come live with us until she is able to resume a solitary life."

William nodded. "It's settled then. We'll move her tomorrow. What about this place?"

"This place?" Emil asked.

"Yes. The rooming house and its boarders. How many are there now?"

"Four," Emil said. "The Johnsons have the flat and there are three men in rooms above."

The group seemed stymied by the question.

Emil said, "We must hire a caretaker and cook, preferably a couple until Ma can come back. Do you think the Johnsons might be interested?"

John said, "Maybe. Let's talk to them first. Maybe the maintenance work could be compensated by lowered rent."

Frank nodded. "And we'll pay the Mrs. for cooking and cleaning. Sounds like that will work if we can find the right couple."

Nodding heads and sober faces ringed the table.

A moan came from the bedroom.

John pushed back his chair. "Do you think she can hear us?"

"I'm sure she can." Emil said. "She's always had acute hearing."

Anna rose. "I'll go. I made soup. I'm hoping to get her to eat a little."

John also rose. "I'll come too. We should see if she agrees with the plan."

William looked at the closed door. "What choice does she have?"

The next day Sophia left the house on Washington supine on a stretcher carried by four of her strong sons. They carried her across the street and laid her gently on the bed that Anna had made a place for her in the annex just off the parlor in their house on Dane Street.

***

365 Lincoln Avenue
Woodstock, Illinois
March 1, 1912

Dear Clara and Pearle,

I've had a letter from Emma. Mama is doing more and more poorly. She is having trouble remembering where she is and who Emma's family is. She talks endlessly about how Heinrich or Mr. Stoffel will take her back to Racine. Then Mama gets terribly upset when Emma or one of the girls unpacks her bag for the fourth time in a week or tells her Papa and Mr. Stoffel are dead. So, Clara, if you want to see her while she might remember you, you better come soon.

And then last week, Ma Wienke had a stroke. She is staying with Frank and Ann during recovery, but her it doesn't look promising. The doctor makes daily house calls, and they have a nurse during the night. We haven't seen her since they took her from her boarding house. John believes her boarding house should be sold to pay for her care, but the others are less certain. Emil especially doesn't want to sell it until we are sure she cannot resume her duties there. I do not have high hopes for that.

The girls are doing well in school and Dodi is taking good care of me as I approach the date of Jr.'s coming. We are all anxious for that day.

Not much else has happened since my last letter. Please let me know if and when you are coming. If it is before Jr. arrives, I won't be able to go to Jefferson with you, but if after I'm sure Jr. and Dodi will enjoy the train ride.

Ida

***

Ida looked around the basement. She had come down for something but then became distracted by a tin box about the size of a shoebox with two openings in the top on John's workbench. She peeked inside and saw a tiny platform on springs. She pushed down on a lever on the outside of the box. She heard the squeak of the springs, and looking inside, saw that the platform had lowered with the pressure. She worked the lever twice more watching the platform go up and down. What could it be? A book depository? Was it to keep your book safe from the elements and then you raised it with the lever when you wanted to read? Maybe. A folded piece of white paper caught her eye. Unfolding it she could see a drawing of the contraption with parts labeled. An arrow at the top said, "Bread in here." So, bread goes in the slots and the lever lowers it into the machine and raises it back out. She lowered the platform and looked inside. Black as pitch in there. She'd have to ask John.

Her trip down the stairs had been easy with gravity working in her favor. She had clung to the banister on each side. John had rebuilt the rickety stairs and railings earlier and had provided the sturdy newels, dug deep into the dirt floor, and the double railings.

Now why had she come down here? She felt foggy this morning, like she couldn't keep a thought in her head. The baby had been kicking up a storm yesterday, but now was quiet, sitting directly on her bladder creating a low ache which increased with intensity whenever he moved. Now she looked about in a daze. The most-likely candidate was canned goods. She moved over to the shelves. Yes, she remembered now. She had come down for peaches for supper. She would use the juice to make a glaze for the ham that was baking in the oven and then serve the fruit with the meal.

She picked up the glass ball jar and went to the stairs. She looked up. The steps stretched upward like the grand staircase at Gimbels in Chicago. She sighed and put her foot on the bottom step. A pain shot through her belly. The jar burst when it hit the hard packed floor.

"Oh, murder!"

Ida held on to the newel to keep herself upright and turned herself around to perch her bottom on the third step. She caught her breath. Just a foot to the ribs? Like Dodi, this one was a kicker. Ida hoped that didn't mean this would also be a girl. Four girls? She shook her head.

When she stood to see to the clean-up, she felt fluid running down her legs, soaking her socks, and filling her shoes. She sat back down.

"Oh dear, Junior," Ida said, "you picked an inconvenient time to come into the world, although I am glad to hear from you."

Ida put her head in her hands and thought about this predicament. No one else was in the house. Dodi had gone to spend the afternoon with cousins, Elizabeth, Grace, and Willie Doering. Mamie and Helen were at school, and John was...heaven only knows...at work...visiting his customers. Her mind was in a whirl. After a while, the pain passed, and she reminded herself that she had time before the blessed event occurred, but she needed...what...what did she need?

Ida shook her head. She needed to clean up this mess, get up the stairs, and call the doctor. She looked at the peach juice darkening the earthen floor. Most of the moisture had soaked in already. She stood and went to the laundry area for a broom and rags. She swept the glass and peaches into a pile. Another pain. Again, she reached to the newel for support, bent at the waist and waited it out...not too bad, but they shouldn't be coming so close together, should they? Had she just lost track of time?

She swept the detritus in a pile and looked down at it. She was not going to be able to lean down with the dustpan to pick it up. Maybe if I sat down on the stairs. She swept the glass closer to the bottom step and sat down heavily on the second step so she could reach the floor. She braced the pan against her foot and swept it full of glass and peaches. Best she could do.

Ida reached for the railing and pulled to get up but couldn't quite manage it. Another pain built and passed. Dear me, that was only three minutes at most since the last one. This baby is wasting no time. She tried again to rise but fell back to a seated position. Murder! She should have sat on the third step not the second.

Maybe if she turned around and crawled up the stairs. She turned on her side pushing with her feet on the now muddy floor. Her foot slipped, and she slid sideways, her belly lodged under the rail. She tried to turn back but seemed securely trapped under the rail. Breathless from the exertion she lay on her side on the steps to consider her dilemma. John had made the railing very sturdy with an upper banister and a lower parallel support rail which now cut into her protruding belly holding her in place. Could she raise her legs enough to bash the support rail out and escape? Possibly. She raised a leg and put it against the two by four and pushed. It didn't budge. She pulled her leg back and kicked the board. The railing shook but the rail stayed in place. John had done an excellent job.

What now? She would try to scootch backward to the other side of the stairs. She started to push with her foot moving her body toward the opposite side of the steps. They weren't very wide. She felt the step toe digging into her side. Then her back pushed against the opposite railing. Her belly was still slightly under the board. Great! Now all she had to do was flip onto all fours on the stairs. Another wave of pain washed over her, and she moaned and panted through it.

When it was gone, Ida pushed up with her knees and arms until she was face down on the stairs balanced on her belly. She hadn't tried to crawl with her extended body, and it seemed like this would be an impossibility. She also didn't want to hurt the baby banging his head on every step, so she pushed herself up into a kneeling position on the second to the bottom step. She felt the baby shift, hopefully, to a head down position. Was he confused by the rollover? She hoped he could figure it all out in the dark.

Standing upright, she looked up the stairs. It looked as long as the proverbial celestial stairway to heaven. She grabbed the rails and pulled herself up one step. She could do this. Slowly, she mounted the stairs stopping after each step to catch her breath. Eventually, she came out into the kitchen and closed the basement door behind her and leaned back on it to rest a moment.

She walked over to the steps going up to the landing accessed from either the kitchen or the front foyer. Clever man...no wasted space in John's house. She had to go up at least one step to reach the phone hanging on the kitchen wall above. No railing here to pull on. She pulled over a kitchen chair and wedged it between the hot stove and the edge of the stairs...just for a moment. She pushed herself up two stairs and slid the chair away from the stove – only a slight melting of the material on one side.

Now...who to call? First the doctor and then her sister-in-law Bessie. Bessie could call her brother Herman, and he could find John. She hoped Herman would be willing to leave his store for this errand. He had once said to her that he had done enough for the family. But, in an emergency, she was sure he would help.

After the two calls were made, another pain left her panting. She better start timing these. She sat on the fourth step and unpinned her broach watch, a Valentine gift from John, and noted the time.

Was the front door unlocked? They had put a lock on it when they moved in, motivated by brother Bob's gambling connections with the Chicago mob. They could throw the lock when needed to keep riffraff out. She doubted she had locked it after Bessie and the children picked up Dodi, but she couldn't swear to it.

She went to rise, but the pain in her back sat her back down. She looked at the watch - six minutes. Six minutes!? She widened her eyes to make sure she was seeing the watch clearly. Closer to six and a half.

"You better wait until others get here, Junior, or I may have to drop you here on the kitchen floor."

Ida's thoughts went to stories she had read about women working in fields, who pause, have the baby, and go back to their work with the babies slung on their backs. It seemed impossible. She pushed herself up, gathered bath towels from a closet in the bathroom, and made her way to the front door. Yes, unlocked. She went to the back bedroom and threw back the covers. She spread two towels on the bed. The others she put on the stool in front of her dressing table. She undressed, removing her skirt and shirt, and replacing them with a nightgown.

Pain. Ida doubled over and held on to the bedstead until it passed. This pain was longer and felt more urgent like she should push, but she knew to hold back. She sat on the edge of the bed.

Was it better to be sitting or lying down if one is to deliver one's own baby? She reached down to see if she could receive the child standing or sitting. Seemed like sitting would work best. She decided to lie down and rest until the time came. She piled the pillows and lay back on them, pulling up the sheet to cover her legs.

When the pains were coming about four minutes apart and more severe than the basement cramps had been, Ida felt the need to push. She did everything she could to keep from doing so. Someone surely had to come soon.

When the contractions were coming three minutes apart, she panted through the pain and felt an increasing pressure "down there." Closing her eyes waiting for the next pain, it occurred to her that she should sit up because this baby was coming, ready or not. She pulled the pillows up behind her and scooted back against them as best she could. Now she could reach the baby should he appear.

A knock at the front door took her attention away from the task at hand. She heard a voice call out, "Mrs. Wienke?"

"Back here, doctor,' Ida called out through gritted teeth.

Doctor Windmueller walked in confidently with a big smile, "Well, well, well, what hav…." The smile fell from his face as he astutely measured the situation. He dropped his bag, removed his coat, throwing it haphazardly on the floor, and rushed to the bedside. He pulled back the sheet and looked under her nightgown.

"Oh my! The head is crowning."

"Yes! I know." Ida gasped.

The doctor headed toward the door. "I must go wash my—"

"NO!" Ida shouted.

The doctor turned back, "But I must!"

"No! Come here!" Ida indicated the clean towels on the stool. "Cover…your…hands…use…those," Ida panted.

In one quick motion the doctor grabbed a towel and stationed himself between Ida's legs.

The pain, the push and the baby slid out into the doctor's towel, not even hitting the bed.

The little one let out a squall at the cold indignity of it all, and the doctor gathered the child into the towel for warmth.

"Well?" said Ida.

The doctor, who had been so flabbergasted that he had not looked, peeked under the towel before laying the baby on the bed to deal with the umbilical cord. "A boy," he said and broke into a large smile.

"Thank you, gracious God," prayed the tired lady on the bed. "Doctor?"

"Yes?"

"When you are done cleaning him up, can you go check the ham in the oven. Make sure it's not getting too dark on the skin? If not, add a couple sticks of wood to keep the heat up."

In just under an hour later John ran up the front porch stairs with Dodi in tow. He had recognized the doctor's automobile parked along the curb in front of the house, and he heard a cry from the back bedroom. He smiled. That cry meant good news; he was sure of it.

He came to the bedroom door and peeked in, Dodi pushing in front of him to yell, "Mama, did you get a baby?"

The adults chuckled, and John picked Dodi up so she could see. Ida pulled the little one from her breast where he had been sucking noisily and covered up.

"He is learning to eat." Ida looked at John while using the male pronoun.

He! A boy! John turned to Dodi with a big smile. "You have a little brother."

Dodi clapped her hands and struggled to get down on the bed.

"It's OK," said Ida. John let her down, just as the back door banged open and Mamie called out, "Mama?"

John called, "Helen, Mamie. We're in here."

Mamie ran to the bedroom and climbed up onto the bed. "The baby! Is it a brother?"

Helen lagged. "She had the baby!? Why didn't someone come get us?"

Ida smiled. "There wasn't time, and yes, it is a brother." She held the little one up, and he looked at his family for the first time with eyes wide open, and his tiny face crumbled. He started to cry.

Helen stared at the baby. "His face is so tiny."

Mamie added her two cents. "And so cute."

Dodi would not be left out. "And so loud." She put her hands over her ears. The others laughed. Dodi had always hated loud noises.

Ida cradled him back in her arms, rocking slightly, and the crying stopped.

John looked around. "I'm not sure he liked what he saw."

The adults chuckled.

Dr. Windmueller picked up his coat and bag. "Just so you know, John, your girl here practically delivered him without me. I was here for only one great push and the catch."

John's eyes bulged. "Indeed."

Dodi laughed. "Ready, set, push!" And her hands flew up in a V. "Hurrah!!"

"I could have used you a few hours ago, Dodi." Ida squeezed Dodi's hand.

The good doctor took his leave, letting himself out.

Mamie hadn't taken her eyes off the baby. "What will we call him?"

"Why Junior, I think," said Ida.

John cleared his throat. "No, I think not."

"No? I thought we agreed on a name long ago. John Francis Wienke Junior."

"I think it should be something just a bit different. How about John Robert Wienke?"

Ida looked at the little face. "John Robert Wienke. I like it!"

Mamie said, "Can we call him Johnny?"

Her father put his hand on her back. "No, he will be Bobby."

Ida nodded, but then her face turned red, and she looked up in a panic. "Oh, good gosh, John. Go check the ham, I bet it's burnt to a crisp."

The ham had very dark skin on the outside, but the inside was slow cooked to perfection. John cut off the skin as he sliced it onto a platter, covered it with a cloth and put it back in the cooling oven to stay warm.

Ida had said there was a mess in the basement and to bring up a jar of peaches and a jar of green beans to round out supper. He had accomplished this mission.

Ida came into the kitchen in her robe holding Bobby. "Wait, John, not that pan for green beans. The smaller one there to the right."

John hesitated and stared cluelessly into the cupboard.

"Here come sit and hold your son. I'll do it. Where's the ham?"

"In the oven."

"It needs more time?" Ida's eyes were large.

"No. Just staying warm."

John sat, and Ida put the swaddled sleeping baby into his arms. Perfect fit, John thought.

As Ida pulled the pan out and poured the beans into it, she called out, "Girls, come set the table. It's about time to eat."

***

Woodstock Growing

Our erstwhile Prudential Insurance agent, John Wienke is handing out cigars in celebration of his first son, John Robert, born April 26th and weighing in at a robust twelve pounds.

Woodstock Sentinel, April 31, 1912.

***

John laughed loudly. Twelve pounds? Where did this editor get his information? He had dropped off the announcement of the birth of a son but had not included any particulars about weight. Twelve pounds?

"Says by the paper that your son weighed twelve pounds at birth."

Ida looked up from her crocheting. "But he was just nine pounds last week at his first check up at the doctors. That paper always exaggerates the greatness of Woodstock." She assumed a lower and more emphatic voice. "Our children are robust, our women are strong and beautiful, and our men are the smartest on earth! Woodstock! Heaven on earth!"

John chuckled. "You mean you don't feel that way?"

"I don't know. It's a fine place to live, and I love the church and our friends and...well...I suppose it might be heaven on earth. Who knows? I've only lived four places on earth so far."

"I've only lived here in Woodstock, so don't look at me for an answer."

"I am very doubtful that Bobby weighed twelve pounds at birth. I think I would have noticed the boy walking out of the womb on his own."

John smiled at the vision. "You must remember; he almost did. Did Dr. W. say he was healthy?"

Ida looked over at him. "I guess he did. Maybe the paper got that story from a worthy source." She went back to her work. "Yes, Bobby is the epitome of a healthy, bouncing baby boy."

"Great." John returned to his paper. Yes, life in Woodstock was grand. The men were strong, the women were beautiful, and the children were bouncy!

***

THE LADY COMETH
Titanic Coming to New York

April 14, 1912. [From the New York Times]—The White Star liner Titanic, which, for a year at least, will be the largest vessel in the world, is due to arrive in New York on Wednesday afternoon at the end of her maiden westward passage of the Atlantic. The tonnage of the Titanic is 46,328 tons.

When the Titanic steams into the Hudson this week New Yorkers will see a ship that is more than four city blocks long, and which, if stood on end, would be 181.7 feet higher than the Metropolitan Life tower and 270 feet higher than the Singer Building.

If it were possible to drop the Titanic into Broadway, for instance, at Thirty-eighth Street, she would occupy a space more than 92 feet wide, her rudders would be about opposite the Knickerbocker Theatre, while the point of her stern would extend about 80 feet north of Forty-second Street into Times Square.

Inter Ocean, April 14, 1912.

***

Ida took a sip of her tepid creamy coffee. She didn't mind when coffee cooled off. Seemed like she had drunk it somewhat cool or iced, as often as she had hot. John and the older girls were gone to work and to school, Dodi was visiting her Oma Wienke, the baby was asleep for a few precious hours, and she was enjoying yesterday's *Times* with a second cup of coffee or was it a third?

The article about the coming of the Titanic made Ida's mind wandered back to the trip she had made so many years ago from Germany to America with her parents, brother, and sister. She had been only six years old, and the voyage had been so exciting; it was unforgettable. She remembered racing with Herman along the deck during the time that they were allowed above board. The crisp ocean air stung her nose and left her lips salty. Ida licked her lips and smiled.

She wondered if they had taken the same route as the Titanic. She did remember the noise of the engines which never stopped, a roar that could barely be heard on deck, but that increased with each step as they approached their cabin three decks below. They were lucky to have a cabin at all. Most immigrants could only afford general accommodations in the lady's and men's salons, and all slept on the floor *'gepfahlt wie Holz'* (stacked like wood), as Oma would say. At least Mama and Papa had berths. She and Emma slept at one end and Mama put her head at the other with a blanket over the middle covering them all. Papa and Herman shared the second, although Papa often tried to get Herman to take the floor.

Ida shook her head. How had Papa afforded those accommodations? How long had they saved so that they didn't have to sleep on the floor? She wished she had asked Mama more questions about their journey. She would have to do that on her next visit to Racine.

The paper lay, still clutched in her hands with a picture of the great ship emblazoned on the first page. Ida looked closer. No masts. That must be a new thing on these modern ships. She would prefer to have the option of wind power as their ship, the SS Katie, had had on their trip from Stettin, Germany to New York.

As she looked at the ship in detail, a feeling of dread came over her. She imagined herself on the upper deck while all around her passengers were running and screaming. She looked out at the sea, but it was calm as a spring day. The sea air washed over her with its salty, fishy smell. Someone bumped into her hard, and she almost fell over the rail. What was wrong with these people?

Ida shook herself and came back to the kitchen table. Now she looked with concern at the gigantic ship in the picture. So many people, so far from land with very little to protect them. She was suddenly glad that she was not on that ship no matter how decadent it was. She would stay on terra firma, thank you very much.

***

DISABLED TITANIC UNDER TOW AFTER HITTING BIG ICEBERG
Wireless Brings Steamships to Scene of Disaster, and Passengers, Including Many Notables, Are Transferred to Carpathia and Parisian.

NEW YORK, April 15.—The Canadian Government Marine Agency at 4:15 A.M. received a wireless dispatch that the Titanic is sinking.

White Star line's office reported by authenticated wireless that gave account late this afternoon that the liner Titanic, which was in a collision with an iceberg 400 miles off the Newfoundland coast at 10:25 o'clock last night, was badly disabled and is being attended by three big steamships for the safe transferal of her passengers.

The line office said late this evening that all the disabled vessel's passengers had been put aboard the Carpathia, Parisian, and Virginian.

Shortly before noon the first official news of the fate of the Titanic since the flash of the disaster fourteen hours before was received from Cape Race, Newfoundland, in the following wireless dispatch from Capt. Haddock of the Olympic, Titanic's sister ship:

"Parisian and Carpathia in attendance on Titanic. Carpathia has already taken off twenty boatloads of passengers and Parisian five. The Baltic is approaching. Olympic 260 miles from Titanic."

Vice-President Franklin of the International Mercantile Marine declared in making public his message from the Olympic that the Titanic would be safely towed to port and that her passengers would be landed at Halifax on Wednesday.

Vice-President Franklin of the International Mercantile Marine assured the throngs of relatives and friends of passengers aboard the Titanic who clamored for news at the White Star offices that the great steamship could not sink, no matter how bad the collision.

Another report of an unofficial character received at Montreal at 8:30 o'clock this morning stated: "The Titanic is still afloat, and her engines are working. At this hour she was reported crawling slowly in the general direction of Halifax and toward the Virginian.

Chicago Evening World, April 15, 1912.

***

"I knew it!" Ida let her hands holding the paper fall to the tabletop. She closed her eyes and said a prayer for those people pulled from lifeboats or out of the sea to safety.

Again, she was transported momentarily to the deck of the ship. People were running and screaming. Panic wafted over her as she felt the ship listing to the side. She started to slide toward the rail.

She imagined the hysteria of that deck. She saw mothers clutching babies. Men in tears. Little boys and girls lifted hand-to-hand across into lifeboats. Stewards running, offering strong drinks to passengers. Her feet slipped toward the rail. She handed Bobby across to outstretched arms, and the lifeboat began to lower.

Ida mentally slapped herself. "Stop it, you fool!! You weren't there, and you have no idea what it was like." With earnest effort she sought to turn her thoughts to brighter visions. The garden in summer, the city square at Christmas, the church choir singing *Rock of Ages*. She hummed along.

> Rock of Ages cleft for me
> Let me hide myself in thee…

Tears ran down her cheeks. She opened her eyes, folded the paper, and reached for her ever-ready hanky. Luckily, disaster had been averted. No one had died. It was time to do up the breakfast dishes and straighten the parlor. No rest for the wicked. And Bobby started crying.

(Toplady, Augustus M. "Rock of Ages," 1776. *Evangelical Lutheran Hymn Book,* 1912.)

***

LINER TITANIC SINKS; 1300 DROWNED, 866 SAVED
Women and Children Saved

Boston, April 16.— (2 a.m.)—A wireless message picked up late tonight, and relayed from the Olympic, says that the Carpathia is on her way to New York with 866 passengers from the steamer Titanic aboard.

The Olympic dispatch in full follows:

"Carpathia reached Titanic position at daybreak. Found boats and wreckage only. Titanic sank about 2:20 a.m. at 41:16N; 50:14W. All her boats accounted for about 675 souls saved, crew and passengers included. NEARLY ALL SAVED WOMEN AND CHILDREN. Leyland liner Californian remained and searched for the exact location of the disaster. Loss likely to total 1,800 souls. Grave fears are felt for the safety of the balance of the passengers and crew."

Chicago Tribune, April 16, 1912.

***

Ida shook her head in an attempt to clear it. What? She reread the headline. No! That's not what the paper said yesterday. This must be a misprint. They can't say one thing, and the very next day, change it, can they? One thousand three hundred people dead, frozen in the cold water or drowned or both? It must be a mistake. A cruel joke.

Ida's mind rushed back to the day that a steamer with Clara and friends on board broke down and was blown out into Lake Michigan and the panic that had gripped her. Mama began crying when word had reached them and went to bed, mourning the loss of her youngest child. Later in the day when word spread that the boat had been towed into harbor, Ida had raced to the docks only to find Clara calling out orders through a megaphone from the deck of the ship.

That's likely what will happen here. The fear mongers are doing their best to have us throw up our hands saying all is lost and go hide under a quilt. She thought about going to the bedroom and hiding there, taking a nap with Bobby, and all would be well when she woke up. Instead, she picked up the phone.

"Prudential Insurance. Thank you for calling the Rock," said an unfamiliar voice.

"Good afternoon. Is John Wienke there?"

"No, I'm sorry. He has appointments all afternoon. Is there some way that I could help you?"

Ida considered that. She cleared her throat. "Would you happen to know if the Titanic sank?"

"The Titanic? I don't think we insured that."

"No, I mean yesterday the paper said the boat didn't sink, but this morning in the *Tribune* - we get it delivered - they said it did sink."

"Well," the man said slowly. "I'd take their word for it if I saw it in the *Tribune*."

"But how can that be? How can it not sink one day and sink the next?"

The silence on the line stretched.

"Hello? Are you still there?"

The speaker at the other end of the line cleared his throat. "Well...I'm not sure. Why are you calling an insurance office to ask about this, rather than a newspaper office?"

"Oh, I hadn't thought about calling the newspaper. That's a good idea. Thank you."

Ida hung up. He was most likely right that the *Tribune* would have the true scoop. And if that was the case, what a terrible tragedy. All those families, believing they would see their members again, only to have their hopes dashed. Just awful. Grief gripped her as tears leaked from her eyes. Then panic. Did she know anyone on the ship? Were any of them from Woodstock?

Ida perused the newspaper, looking for a list of lost, but found nothing. She thought about calling the insurance office back and asking that friendly colleague of John's if he knew but decided against it. Oh, those poor people. Her mind flitted back to the deck of the Titanic as the ship turned on its side dumping everyone in the water. NO! Stop that! She would not go down that road again. She had Bobby to protect.

Would they know anyone on the list? Ida hoped not. Was that an unchristian thought? She looked skyward. "Sorry." Then, while she was at it, she sent up another prayer for the families of those lost and for the safety of her own.

***

DISASTER REPORT HELD
FROM PUBLIC

NEW YORK, April 17.—For eight hours before public announcement was made that the Titanic had gone down with many of her passengers, it was known in this city and carefully guarded as a secret, according to the statement of an official of the Cunard line owners the Carpathia and close friend of J. P. Morgan, Jr., Thomas J. Stead. It is rumored that J. P. Morgan called at White Star offices on Monday and demanded

the suppression of the extent of the disaster until after
the market closed.
                                        New York Times, April 17, 1912.

***

Ida stared out the front window and rocked the baby. His
tummy was full, he had burped, and he was now examining his
hands with those dazzling blue eyes. Bobby had been making eye
contact with his family over the last week as if to say, who are all
these people? Dodi had even gotten what might have been a smile
from him last evening.

While Bobby was trying to figure out the world, Ida was
having trouble concentrating on anything except the Titanic
disaster. As it turned out, John recognized one of the names on
the list: a businessman he had dealt with in Chicago. Ida only
knew the names of the famous people lost, including American
businessman Benjamin Guggenheim, Isidor and Ida Straus of the
Macy's department store, and Thomas Andrews, the architect that
designed the Titanic.

Ida imagined what it would be like to have designed the ship
and then feel it dropping out from under her. Once again, she was
on the ship's deck this time as it slid downward into the abyss—

Helen banged in the back door from school and called out. "I
need all the papers from the last two weeks."

"Not a proper greeting. Where are your manners?"

"Good afternoon, Mother. I hope you are having a lovely day. I
need newspapers from the last two weeks."

"Good afternoon, Helen. I hope your day has been pleasant
also. What are you going to do with old newspapers? Papier
Mache?"

"No, not art. I'm doing a report on why the Titanic sank."

"You better go retrieve them from the basement. I put the
whole stack down there last night for your father to use to light
the fire."

Helen went to the basement door and trotted down the stairs.
"Found them!" she called up to her mother. She brought the stack

of papers to the kitchen table, spread them out, retrieved a pair of scissors, and began cutting out the pertinent articles.

Ida brought Bobby into the kitchen. He was fussing a bit, having been abruptly awakened by the banging of the door. Ida began warming a bottle of milk in the reserve at the back of the stove.

Helen didn't look up from her labor. "You should save the papers from now until it's over being investigated. Just give them to me, okay?"

"Okay. How was school today?"

"Fine. But when I said that I was going to do my English report on why the Titanic sank, Freddie Strehlow started laughing and said, 'It hit an iceberg, dummy.' So now I'm dedicated to finding the whole story."

"Hm. So you think it went down for reasons other than hitting the iceberg?" Ida was curious about what else could have done it.

"Hitting the iceberg was the last straw. You'll see. I'm no dummy."

"I never thought you were a dummy."

"I mean, I hope that Freddie will see the truth and be amazed."

"Okay. I'll save the papers for you."

Ida looked at her oldest child as she arranged the articles in chronological order. In some ways, Helen reminded her so much of Clara at that age. Clara, who was now running about the wild west solving mysteries as a reporter, would get so focused on one thing that all else fell by the wayside. Will that be Helen's fate? Reporter, teacher, scholar? Who knew? But everyone knew Helen was no dummy.

***

America's War Aircraft Few

Although officially the army and navy of the United States are credited with 15 and 11 aeroplanes respectively, the total of effective strength for both branches of service is actually 10 machines. Of the

army aircroft flying, all by four were suspended by an
order of the War Department in February, owing to the
dangerous qualities of eleven of the machines. The four
retained in active use were Burgess tractors, built by the
Burgess Company and Curtis of Marble head. In
addition to these four, a Curtiss tractor is now
undergoing alterations and repairs at San Diego where
the other machines are stationed.

Crawford County Courier, April 22, 1914.

***

BLUNDER CAUSED LOSS OF
MANY LIVES ON TITANIC
Lookouts Thrice Warned Officers on Bridge
Before Vessel Struck

New York, April 22.—First Officer Murdock, on the
bridge of the Titanic, racing to New York for assistance
in quenching a fire that had been raging since the day
the liner left Southampton, passed unheeded three
warnings from the lookouts of the iceberg ahead. The
ship struck and then the wireless operators blundered.

Three Warnings Given

Three warnings that an iceberg was ahead were
transmitted from the crow's nest of the Titanic to the
officer on the doomed steamship's bridge 25 minutes
before she struck it, according to Thomas Whiteley, a
first salon steward, who now lies in St. Vincent's
hospital with frozen and lacerated feet.

Whiteley reached the Carpathia aboard one of the
boats that contained, he said, both the crow's nest
lookouts. He heard a conversation between them, he
asserted, in which they discussed the warnings given of
the presence of the iceberg.

Titanic Operator Blunders

The impatience of Phillips, the wireless operator on
the Titanic, with the receiving ability of the operator on
the North German Lloyd steamer Frankfurt, the nearest
ship at the time of the disaster and the first to answer

this stricken liner's call for aid, caused Phillips to the tell the Frankford operator: "You are a fool; keep out." And might have prevented the saving of many more lives from the wrecked liner, admitted H. S. McBride, second wireless operator of the Titanic, pain-wracked and sitting in an invalid chair, under the fire of cross-examination before the senate committee investigating the disaster.

J. Dilley, fireman on the Titanic, stated that a fire had been raging in the coal bunkers since the day the Titanic left Southampton, that 12 men had succeeded in making no headway against it, and that the talk among the stokers was that the blaze would not be extinguished until the aid of fireboats in New York Harbor was receive.

"No, sir, we didn't get that fire out. But in the end, we didn't need such help. It was right under bunker No. 6 that the iceberg tore the biggest hole, and the flood that came through that rip put out the fire that our tons and tons of water hadn't been able to.

"It had been necessary to take the coal out of sections two and three on the starboard side forward," he said, "and when the water came rushing in after the collision, the bulkheads would not hold because they did not have the supporting weight of the coal."

Early Messages Held Up

Mr. Franklin told the committee how he had asked to have the earlier reports of the Titanic disaster held up to avoid unnecessary alarm. He denied any knowledge of the message signed by the White Star line and addressed to Representative Hughes of West Virginia about the ship's being towed to Halifax and that all passengers had been saved. Mr. Franklin acknowledged that he had issued reassuring statements when he had no facts on which to base them.

Inter Ocean, April 25, 1912.

DENIES FALSE REPORT ISSUED
Captain of Olympic Did Not Say Steamer
Virginian Was Towing Titanic

London, England, April 22.—Captain Haddock
of the White Star line steamer Olympic denied, on
arriving at Plymouth from New York, that the
Olympic had sent out a wireless report that the
Allan liner Virginian was towing the Titanic and
that all the latter's passengers were safe.

Passengers of the Olympic, which is a sister ship
of the ill-fated Titanic, subscribed $7,000 to the
relief fund for the survivors.

McHenry Plaindealer, April 25, 1912.

***

"So, Helen. Have you solved the mystery of the Titanic?" her
father asked. Utensils clinked against dishes as the Wienkes settled
into a family-style supper.

Ida seemed to have gone all out for the fare tonight with
Fischbrötchen—crispy bread rolls filled with pickled herring,
onions, pickles, and creamy horseradish sauce. Cooked carrots in
brown sugar sauce and tiny, boiled red potatoes in butter rounded
out the menu. Each member at the table made their sandwich
differently. All started with the freshly baked roll. John included all
the traditional ingredients; Ida included all the ingredients except
the pickles; Helen left off the pickles, also, but added tomato and
lettuce; Mamie kept the pickles and added tomato; and Dodi left
off the herring, the onion and the sauce and added tomato and
lettuce to her pickle sandwich. As she built her sandwich, Helen
explained her dilemma.

"The newspapers kept changing their stories."

"What do you mean?" John took a big bite of his first
sandwich. He looked at Ida. "Yum!" he said through the
mouthful.

"Well, let's see. First there was the question of whether the ship had actually sunk or not and—"

"Yes," interjected Ida, "that was very confusing and disheartening when the truth was known."

Helen shot her mother a stern look. "…and…then there is the question of why did the company withhold the information for a day or even lie about the fate of the ship? Can you pass me the horseradish sauce, please?"

Ida reached for the sauce boat and passed it to Helen. "Yes, I found that very upsetting. The story changed so much from one day to the next, I knew that something was amiss." Helen's steady gaze caused Ida to take a bite of her sandwich.

A baby's cry came from the adjacent bedroom. They all stopped chewing and waited. No further crying commenced, and Ida smiled at her well-trained family. She picked up her fork and tried the carrots. Perfection, if she did say so herself.

Helen put the top of the roll on the sandwich and pushed it down, squishing all the ingredients flat so it would fit in her mouth. "And there were the reports that a fire was burning during the whole voyage, and some say that would have eventually made it sink even without hitting an iceberg."

John choked a bit, pushed the bite into his cheek. "On fire? And no one knew? They didn't call for help? They didn't evacuate?"

"Nope!"

"Well, I never!" John went back to chewing.

"Another thing," Helen was yet to take a bite, "is that another ship was very close to the Titanic when they sent out a message for help, but they just sailed away. The Senate decided that the ship's radio room was closed for the night, so they didn't hear the call. But other people say that the radioman on the Titanic for some unknown reason sent the rescue ship away." She picked up her sandwich trying to keep everything inside the bread and took a bite. Sauce squeezed out and landed on the tablecloth by her plate.

"Ew," she gasped. "How am I supposed to eat this!"

Ida got a wet towel from the kitchen and wiped at the spot. "I think it will come out. I'll soak it as soon as we finish eating." She handed each girl a dishtowel. "Use them like bibs. Tuck them into your collars. Do you need one, Papa?"

"No, I'll take my chances." He took another big bite and was able to get it all in his mouth.

Dodi laughed. "Papa has a big mouth."

"Dat, I do," said John around his mouthful.

After a moment or two of chewing, Helen took a drink of her milk. "And finally, there is the design of the ship which seems to have been awful. Instead of being able to block incoming water into two or three compartments after the iceberg crushed the hull, the water just ran in and filled the bottom of the ship making it sink."

"Didn't they have a hand pump or buckets to throw the water back into the ocean?" asked Mamie. She was yet to attempt a bite of sandwich focusing on the carrots and potatoes.

Helen shook her head. "No, it was too big a ship for that to work."

"How big was it?" Dodi had finished her pickle, lettuce and tomato sandwich and was working on the carrots one at a time with a fork that seemed too big for her hand.

"Big!" said Helen.

"How big?" Dodi popped another carrot piece into her mouth.

Helen tried to think of something to compare to the Titanic that Dodi could understand. "If you put the ship on Lincoln Avenue, it would be longer than the whole street."

Dodi's eyes grew round.

"And it would be about five times as high as the houses. Of course, about half of that would normally be below water. And it would take up more space than is between our house and Clancey's across the street. Probably both houses would get squished."

"Wow." Dodi seemed at a loss for words.

"Wow is right!" said Mamie.

Helen continued. "More than two-thousand people lived on it while it was crossing the ocean or trying to cross the ocean. Dodi, do you know how many people two thousand is?"

"No." A round red potato disappeared into Dodi's mouth.

"It's like twenty Grace congregations on Christmas morning. Think of twenty churches lining Washington Street from our church down to Oma's house with all the pews packed in every church."

Dodi squinted her eyes now as if trying to imagine. "I can see them."

"Holy cats!" John was also squinting his eyes in concentration.

"So how many of those people died?" Mamie had eaten about a fourth of her sandwich and finished the vegetables, and now sat with her hands in her lap.

"Died?" parroted Dodi.

"Oh, we don't have to talk about that, do we?" Ida wiped her mouth before speaking to make sure horseradish sauce wasn't running down her chin.

Helen wasn't to be stopped. She glanced at her mother, and said, "About fifteen congregations of the twenty died."

"Fifteen?" Dodi was blinking back tears. "Children, too?"

"Yes, fifteen, but only a few children. Most of the children were in the lifeboats."

Dodi had stopped eating. "If they had lifeboats, how did people die?"

"Helen." Ida tried again.

Helen was not to be deterred. "There weren't enough lifeboats for everyone to be saved. Some people jumped into the sea which was like ice water, and they froze solid. Others stayed on the ship and went down with it into the dark, dark sea."

Now a tear trickled down each of Dodi's cheeks.

Helen wrapped up the story on a high note. "But remember five churches survived by getting into the lifeboats that were rescued after the ship went down even though it was nighttime, and the rescuers had trouble seeing the Titanic."

Dodi stifled a little sob. "Was it dark?"

"Helen—"

"Yup. The middle of the night. Once the lights on the ship went down to the depths, there wouldn't have been a light to be seen for miles."

"Miles?"

"That's right, miles. It would have been so dark that you couldn't see your hand in front of your face." Helen held up her hand in front of Dodi to demonstrate.

Dodi hiccupped.

Mamie was staring at Helen. "Were there dogs on the ship?"

Helen's eyes shifted from Dodi to Mamie. "Hm. I don't know. Maybe. But there was a car."

"A car. There was room on the boat for a car?" Mamie's eyes were now big and round.

"I told you how big it was."

Ida looked over at John who was smiling and looking at Helen as he chewed.

"Okay, girls." Ida claimed center stage. "Let's eat our sandwiches so we aren't here all night."

"In the dark." Dodi still had tears on her cheeks.

"Waiting for the ocean to splash over the top of us and pull—"

"Helen! Let's not give little sisters nightmares."

Helen grinned, nonchalantly picked up her sandwich, and bit into it. Squish! Sauce squirted out and down the front of her smock.

Mamie started laughing, and Dodi followed suit. Soon, Ida and John were unable to hide their smiles.

Mamie, still giggling, said, "You didn't put on your bib!"

Helen looked down. This wasn't funny at all. She had ruined her smock.

Ida took the unused towel and wiped at the stain. "I'll set it to soak with the tablecloth." She sat back down, took up her fork, and looked at her oldest daughter. "Thank you for the stimulating table talk, Helen."

Helen looked smug. Her lips pursed, turning her smile into an upside-down horseshoe. She was no dummy.

***

All Things Denison
By Clara Daring

How much do you laugh each day? Do you go days without feeling happy with your lot in life? Do you feel too exhausted after a day of work to participate in the pleasures of life?

Now you can change your feelings of despair to "true ripe happiness." At least according to Mr. Frances Gable who lectured last Friday evening at the opera house under the auspices of The Women's Federation. The lecture was a benefit for the Denison hospital, always a worthy cause. Frances Gable is a hometown boy who has made a name for himself lecturing on his invented philosophy of well-being. And I must say that the lecture was one of the best I have heard for a long while with its original ideas and material. The very well-presented lecture was entertaining for the near capacity crowd.

While Mr. Gable's lecture was not a humorous one, he had a good sense of humor, eliciting laughter from the crowd from time to time as he enunciated his "Laughilosophy" which is 'a philosophy of living that makes a man glad that he is alive.' He called his procedure the cultivation of 'serious cheerfulness' because it searches out the causes of that inward satisfaction which gladdens the hearts of men.

Laughilosophy, as presented, provides a recipe for a happy and useful life in a logical way. The first step is to get it into your heart and head and into your religion that it is not only fine to enjoy things, but that enjoyment is right of all men. The second step is to make a full and fair catalog of all that God has given you to enjoy. In other words, count your blessings. Gable's third step is to learn the happy art of enjoying things. He was a bit vague on exactly how to do this except to emphasize experiencing happy times. And the fourth step is to realize that the greatest of all joys is the joy of a benevolent life; living to make others happy. "It is not a sin to enjoy things; Our heavenly father is a God of love. Every person has the desire to be happy, and God wills it so," were some of the assertions coming from the happy man's mouth.

It is a good contention that finding joy in life, even if one must dig deep to find it, makes life more bearable and satisfying. We could all use more joy and satisfaction in life. So how much do you laugh each day? Is it time to make a new habit?

Crawford County Courier, April 26, 1912.

***

april 28 1912
denison iowa

dear ida,

ive tuned over a new leaf. Im going to stop feling sorry for myself about be barren and start ~~cao~~ counting my blesings. im to 38 blessings i won't list them all here because im also trying to figre out this typwriter machine i wukk start b=lessons nxt week i hope she show us hos to get al the extra characters and capitals

Okay. I tried, but if I'm going to get this note to the train today, I better switch from typing to handwriting. As I said, I've turned over a new leaf. I was really taken with Mr. Gable and his Laughilosophy. I've been feeling so down and blue because we have not been blessed, as yet, but then look at all else that has transpired since we came to Denison. We have everything we could want. A cozy home, our health, for the most part, and my reporting is going strong. While I'm sure that a child would be a wonderful addition to our little family, I should not put all my eggs in that basket. There may be a problem with my womb or with Pearle since his accident. Who knows. If I want to be near children, I suppose I could volunteer to help at the school, I'm as qualified to teach as the girl they have teaching now. She is only 17 years old and has only one year of high school. The teacher can't be married so I cannot apply for a teaching job, but I could volunteer to work with the children on their reading and writing skills. Maybe. But then I don't know. There is a difference if children are your own or someone else's, don't you think? And I wouldn't know them from babe in a cradle through adulthood. That is what I yearn for. So, there I go, already failing the positive thinking. This is harder than you think.

Do you and John do this kind of positive thinking? I think you must, in order to have such a happy family. If it will dispel even one day of brooding for me, I must try it. But enough about that.

Tell me more about Bobby. Oh, how I wish I could be there to hold him and rock him to sleep. I bet John is just bursting his vest buttons with pride? Your, embellished, I'm sure, story of his birth was hair-raising. I would not have had the faintest idea of what to do and would have fainted dead away in the basement, where they would have found me and the babe at the bottom of the stairs. And then to have him almost bounce out into your own hands! I hope the men involved were duly impressed. I was. But Bobby. Does he have blond hair, dark hair, or saint's preserve us, red? Is he chubby or slim? Does he look like he'll be tall like John? I can't wait to meet him. I count Bobby and my talented nieces as one of my greatest blessings.

Time to get out and beat the bushes for another story. I had a great lead on the whereabouts of some train robbers who stripped passengers of their watches and rings and melted them down to chunks so they couldn't be identified. I thought it was correct to tell the police what I knew, and wouldn't you know it, they beat me to the hideout and arrested them all before I had a chance to talk to them. Not only that, but they gave the story to a man reporter from the Denison Review. I'll not make that mistake again. I will pursue the facts and let the police fend for themselves. I was so mad.

Guess I better get a move on. Wish you were here for tea. We send our love to each one of you.

Clara and Pearle

PATRONS ARE REQUESTED TO FAVOR THE COMPANY BY
CRITICISM AND SUGGESTION CONCERNING ITS SERVICE

CLASS OF SERVICE This is a full-rate Telegram or Cable- gram unless its de- ferred character is in- dicated by a suitable sign above or preceding the address.	# Western Union	SIGNS DL=Day Letter NM=Night Message NL=Night Letter LCO=Deferred Cable NLT=Cable Night Letter WLT=Week-End Letter

NEWCOMB CARLTON, PRESIDENT J.C. WILLEVER, FIRST VICE-PRESIDENT

The filing time as shown in the date line on full-rate telegrams and day letters, and the time of receipt at destination as
shown on all messages, is STANDARD TIME.

MRS. CLARA DYE. WU N004 DL PD F213 DENISON, IOWA
WUX JEFFERSON, WISCONSIN. MAY 15 800A=

MAMA HAD STROKE YESTERDAY [STOP]
ASKING FOR YOU [STOP]
COME QUICKLY [STOP]
                                    EMMA

***

Called Home

Mr. and Mrs. P. F. Dye were called to Jefferson,
Wis., Saturday morning by the serious illness of her
mother. Word comes from there later announcing the
death of her mother Sunday morning.

Denison Review May 22, 1912.

***

Sad Occurrence

Mrs. Louisa Doering Stoffel, mother of H. C.
Doering and Mrs. John Wienke died in Jefferson, Wis.,
on the 19th after a short illness with paralysis. Preceding
her in death was her first husband Henry Doering and a
second husband J. Nicholas Stoffel. Besides the two
well-known citizens of our fair city, the deceased had
two other children, Emma Fisher of Jefferson, Wis and
Clara Dye of Denison, Iowa. Attending the funeral in
Wisconsin from here were Mr. and Mrs. H. C. Doering
and children Elizabeth, Grace, and William and Mr. and

Mrs. John Wienke and children Helen, Marion, Dorothea. and Robert. Burial took place in Watertown, Wis. on the same day.

Woodstock Sentinel, May 23, 1912.

***

The son and three daughters of Louisa Ardelt Doering Stoffel stood in the Fisher's living room in Whitewater, Wisconsin, receiving the condolences of friends and neighbors. Ida noted that there was a contingent who had traveled out to Jefferson by train from her mother's church in Racine and others that she still recognized from years ago when the family was a part of the German Lutheran Synod of Southeastern Wisconsin. Lena and Al Wienke came from Beloit by carriage. To be hugged by an old friend on this sad day was comforting.

The funeral service had been in the old style of German Lutherans with everything said and sung in the mother tongue. Ida preferred the more modern services of Grace Lutheran in Woodstock but found the drone of the not understood voices was in a way soothing. She knew her mother would have approved.

The children of Louisa stood from oldest to youngest. Emma was the first to greet the visitor who she passed on to Herman. When it was Ida's turn, she shook hands as a greeting instead of curtsying, a politeness that was going out of style. And last was Clara who had been complaining that her feet hurt for the last twenty minutes. The line dwindled, and they were free to mingle or sit as their soles demanded. Bobby was with his father and started crying as soon as he heard Ida's voice.

Clara placed a hand on Ida's arm. "Let me."

Ida smiled and nodded. Killing two birds with one stone. She shouldn't think such a thought after a funeral. "Let me know if he seems hungry."

Clara bustled away.

"Ida," a deep voice said near her ear. Herman.

Ida turned to him with a small smile on her face and looked at him full-on. He was still very handsome although his face and body had 'filled out' as a successful businessman should. He was a good head taller than she. Now his face was florid, and he had tears welling in his eyes. She reached out, and they hugged for a long moment, then she led him out to the porch swing. They sat and rocked back and forth for a bit in silence.

"Herm—"

"Id—" They spoke at once but then both cut off.

Ida said, "You first."

Herman lowered his eyes. "I'm sorry that things have been somewhat strained between us. I didn't think we'd lose her quite this soon."

Ida didn't lower her eyes. "Well, I remember telling you that both Emma and I were worried, but you didn't have the time for it. I was so angry with you. And it hurt to hear the things you said about our family."

Herman looked up as if he had not expected any reprimand for his behavior over the last year. "What did I say?"

Now Ida looked away. She reached up and pulled at the high lace collar of her mourning dress. She hated the thing and would be rid of it as soon as allowed. "I don't want to get into all that again. Water under the bridge, I say. I'm only glad you believed that you should come to see her this time. It's the way I want to die; with the family gathered all around the bed."

Herman sighed and shook his head. "Not me. I want to die in a dirigible crash."

Ida looked at him and chuckled. "In truth? Have you ever flown in a dirigible?"

"No, but someday I will. I just figure I'll make *The Sentinel* if I go out that way."

Time stood still for a moment as each considered the numerous ways to die. Ida broke the silence. "I think a stroke seems like a horrible way to die unless it takes you quickly like with Papa Stoffel."

"Yes." Herman slapped his thighs. "You know I have yet to meet young master Wienke."

"How in the world have you and he not crossed paths thus far?"

"I don't know, but I believe that is our young sister coming our way with the boy in her arms."

Clara looked out through the screen and a look of relief crossed her face. She pushed out onto the porch. "There you are. This young man is looking for you. He says he doesn't like bread or ham or lemonade. It's only mother's milk for him."

Ida took the baby and turned to Herman. "Bobby, meet your Uncle Herman. Herman, please meet the youngest member of the Wienke Clan, John Robert."

Herman widened his eyes and made a funny face at the child, who began to scream.

"My thoughts exactly," said Clara. "Don't worry I won't let the big bad man get you."

"I will leave you two to work this out, I must to the bedroom retire and ease this boy's suffering," Ida called out over the frantic cries as she adjourned back into the house.

"Did you make up?" Clara asked as she watched the screen door slam.

"I think so...maybe."

"I'm glad we both made it back. I felt like it was a very peaceful passing."

Herman sucked in breath. "I suppose."

Clara punched his arm lightly, "When did you get to be such an old curmudgeon?"

"Herman!" A high voice came through the screen door. "What are you doing out there? There's someone from Racine, I want you to meet." Bessie.

"Who is it?"

"Just come in!" The voice fell into a whine.

Clara was looking at her feet with a smile playing on her lips.

His eyes on Clara, Herman called out, "I'll be right there, darling."

Clara covered her mouth with a hand to stifle a laugh. And it was Herman's turn to bump her with a fist on the shoulder. "Quiet, young'un. Happy mama, happy home. I'm sure Pearle does the same."

"I should say not! He does everything for me from the goodness of his heart."

Herman laughed and gathered his little sister into his arms. "It is so good to see you."

"Herman! Where ARE you!"

Clara disengaged. "You better get a wiggle on."

Herman, still holding her by the arms, harrumphed, but then let go and turned toward the door. "Such a wiseacre."

"That's Mrs. Wiseacre to you," she called to his retreating back.

***

DAWSON WINS 500 MILE AUTO RACE IN 6:21:06, SETTING WORLD'S RECORD

INDIANAPOLIS, Ind., May 30.—After leading all the way from the start to the 198th lap, Ralph de Palma's Mercedes developed engine trouble, and Joe Dawson's National came up from six laps behind today and won the second international 500-mile sweepstakes automobile race in record time.

Teddy Tetslaff's Fiat was second. The Stutz company protested the awarding of third place to Hughie Hughes Mercer, contending the car, driven by Charles Mera, which was announced as fourth, won the position.

Twenty-four cars, the pick of American, German, English, and Italian factories, started.

A Lexington, driven by Harry Knight, the hero of last year's race, who deliberately wrecked his car to avoid running down the driver of another car who had fallen on the track, was the first to quit, dropping out in the seventh lap.

David Bruce-Brown was the next to leave the track. When he found his National was out for good, he broke down and wept on the shoulder of his mechanician.

There were only ten cars to finish.

Inter Ocean, May 31, 1912.

WILBER WRIGHT IS DEAD AFTER A LONG STRUGGLE FOR LIFE

DAYTON, Ohio, May 30.—Following a sinking spell that developed soon after midnight, Wilbur Wright, the father of the great new science of Aeronautics, died of typhoid fever at 3:13 o'clock this morning. Wright had been lingering on the border for many days, and though his condition from time to time gave some hope to members of his family, the attending physicians... maintained throughout the latter part of his sickness that he could not recover.

The aviator was stricken with typhoid fever on May 4, while on a business trip in the East. On that day he returned to Dayton from Boston and consulted Dr. Cocklin, the family physician. He took to his bed almost immediately, and it was several days before his case was definitely diagnosed as typhoid.

Wilbur Wright, who with his younger brother Orville, made flying in a heavier-than-air machine possible, was born in Millville, Indiana, in 1847, and a short time later was taken by his parents to Dayton, Ohio, where he had since resided. He was the son of the Rev. Milton Wright, a Bishop of the United Brethren Church and came from Puritan stock.

Inter Ocean, May 31, 1912.

***

"He's truly dead?" Mamie's face had a look of wonder upon it. She had listened as John read the article announcing the death of her dear aviator, Wilbur Wright.

"Yes, I'm afraid so," said her father.

Mamie looked down, "But how will I ever meet him then?"

John drew Mamie to his lap. They were in the parlor, and it was evening. Time for bed.

"You will not be able to see him in this life," said John.

"Then in what life?"

John looked at her. "No, I didn't mean…well, there sort of is…I mean, you may see him in heaven."

Mamie considered this. "So, I have to wait to die to meet him?"

When had she gotten so smart? John didn't like where this conversation was going. "I suppose that's right. But you needn't worry. He'll wait for you. He'll be at the head of the line when you come to the pearly gates."

Mamie looked him in the eye. Was he being serious? "Maybe. But I was looking forward to meeting him in this life."

John hugged her. "I know you were. We can try to find a way to meet his brother Orville."

Mamie murmured into his shoulder. "It's not fair. Wilber was the best one."

"I know. I know." John rocked a bit hoping his bear hug was soothing.

Ida walked into the parlor and took in the hugging pair. "What's going on here?"

Mamie pushed back to look at her mother. "Wilber Wright died." And she burst into tears and went back to her father's hug.

John did a quick head shake to Ida to let her know it was under control.

"I'm sorry to hear that," said Ida. "I'll be in the kitchen."

She retreated to the kitchen table and sat down. She was tired. Ida rested her head on her folded arms on the table. It had been a long day, and she dreaded tomorrow when she would go to Racine to hear the reading of Louisa's will. Herman would be her escort, and Bobby would go with them while Bessie took the three girls for the day. She wondered what Bessie would do with the six children all day. Ida knew that Helen would pitch in to organize playtime, but still, dealing with six children was much to ask. How she missed the doting of Ma Wienke.

John stopped every other day on his rounds to see his mother who had made surprising progress. She could sit up and even stand but had no strength on the right side to walk, yet. She could talk. Her speech, while slurred, was very demanding in her desire to "Go home!"

Anna was doing a wonderful job occupying her with cooking chores and other activities, but it must be exhausting. Now that Bobby was three months old, Ida thought maybe she should relieve Anna once a week. She'd talk to John about that when she got back from Racine.

Racine. She was anxious to have this meeting over.

John came into the kitchen. "Mamie's gone up."

Ida straightened in her chair and nodded.

"Good. How'd you like to read a story tonight?"

"I can. You look bushed."

"I am, and I have to get ready to go to Racine tomorrow morning."

"Oh, that's right. I'm glad Herman will be with you and Bobby."

"Yes, I must admit that he has stepped up a bit since the funeral.

John leaned down and kissed her on the cheek. "Why don't you put your things together for tomorrow and feed the littlest Wienke, and I'll go read to the girls. What story were you on?"

"I don't remember. Helen will know," said Ida in a soft voice which made John stare after her as she left the room. Was she okay? Should he offer to go to Racine with her? Being a good husband and father was NOT a walk in the park.

***

NO PICTURE OF PA?

Father really ought to have his picture taken—he hasn't had a photograph since that funny looking one in the cut-away coat that he was married in. ('Twas a noon wedding you know.)

Yes, mother says 'twas a good one of him as he looked then, but really for the sake of the family, there should be one of him as he looks now.

Herbert B. Medlar
The Photographer in Your Town
214 Dean Street   Phone 274-R
Woodstock, Ill.

Woodstock Sentinel, June 3, 1912.

COMING! TODAY!
Two Performances: Afternoon and Night

Not a Dramatic Show but Real Cowboys, Indians, and Cow Girls of the Far West.

Don't Fail TO SEE The Rough Riders, The Tribe of Sioux Indians, The Bucking Broncos, The Fancy Rifle Shooting, The Trick Riding, The Lariat Throwing and Roping, The Holdup of the Stagecoach, The Cowboy Sports and Pastimes, and The Quadrille on Horse Back.

WATCH FOR THE BIG STREET PARADE
PRICES 25 AND 35c
Show Lot Corner East and Lumber Streets

Woodstock Sentinel, June 22, 1912.

WOMEN TO STUMP IOWA

Des Moines, June 3.—The leader in the women's suffrage movement in Iowa will stump the state in the interest of suffrage. The executive committee of the state suffrage association has mapped the state for automobile tours to be made by women, who will address outdoor audiences from the machines or make indoor addresses in the smaller towns where the state executive committee has made appointments for them.

A number of automobile owners thru-out the state have offered to the committee the free use of their machines for these speaking tours.

Crawford County Courier, June 3, 1912.

***

First publication June 24, 1912
H. G. Smieding, Attorney
STATE OF WISCONSIN,
RACINE COUNTY COURT

Notice is hereby given that at the special term of the county court in and for said county to be held in the courthouse in the city of Racine, in said county on Tuesday, the 30th day of July, A. D. 1912, beginning at 9 o'clock in the forenoon, the following matter will be heard and considered:

The application of Herman C. Doering to admit to probate the last will and testament of Louisa Stoffel, late of the city of Racine, in said county, deceased, and for the appointment of Herman C. Doering as executor thereof.

Dated June 24th, 1912.
By order of the Court,
MAX W. HECK,
County Judge.
Racine Journal, June 25, 1912.

***

PRESIDENT TAFT RE-NOMINATED
WITH SHERMAN
Roosevelt Claims He Was Cheated of
Nomination

William H. Taft for president and James S. Sherman for vice president are the results of the big Republican National convention in Chicago last week.

The contest between the friends of President Taft and the supporters of former President Theodore

Roosevelt was very bitter, the result hinging largely on the decision of the contested delegate cases.

No attempt will be made by us to recite the history of that eventful convention, which has now passed into history. The recital of the events which has appeared in the "trust" newspapers has been unfair and dishonest toward President Taft and his supporters, as we believe the people will recognize in time, when the true facts are placed before them during the coming campaign.

The present attempt of Theodore Roosevelt to rally around himself a new party, of which he shall be the dictator, we believe, will fail and as the sober judgment of the American people has time to develop, they will recognize that the noise and bluster, roughneck work and riot of the Rooseveltians was nothing more than a desperate attempt to snatch victory from defeat. In the same way the organization of a new party, to be made up of sore heads and disappointed office seekers will fail to inspire any considerable support.

Meanwhile the Democrats are having troubles of their own in their convention at Baltimore, where it seems to be a battle royal for control of the convention between the radicals led by the thrice defeated presidential candidate William Jennings Bryan, and the conservatives, as represented by leaders like Governor Harmon of Ohio, Representative Underwood of Alabama, and Judge Alton B. Parker of New York.

The latest reports indicate that Bryan is gaining in strength and while he is not himself a candidate for the presidential nomination many predictions are heard that he will again be named to lead the Democratic hosts to defeat.

Woodstock Sentinel, June 27, 2012.

***

WILL CLOSE UP AND ENJOY
BIG DAY IN WOODS
STORES AND OFFICES CLOSE AT NOON

The Woodstock merchants and professional men are planning for a big Stag Basket picnic, to be held in

Sandow's woods, one mile south of Woodstock, next
week Friday.

For this event all the stores and offices will be closed
at noon and remain closed for the balance of the day,
while the proprietors with their clerks and friends go to
the picnic grounds for the afternoon's festivities.

Dr. E. Windmueller has been named by the
committee in charge of the affair as chairman of the
day....

The Oliver Typewriter Military band has been
engaged for the afternoon and plans are being made for
a ball game, all kinds of races and games and a good
time generally.

The picnic will be of the basket variety, or in other
words, each participant will bring his own lunch.

Woodstock Sentinel, June 30, 1912.

***

Ida Doering Wienke looked out of the train window as it
wound through the hills of Walworth County. The trees were lush
with summer fullness and Lake Geneva sparkled in the late
descending sun. Bobby stirred in her arms, but then settled back
lulled by the rhythmic clack of the rails and the sway of the car. It
was a mild day, and the train was neither too hot nor too cold, and
Ida thought that it was the most decadent way to travel. Sitting on
velvet seats with the coachman checking on her well-being every
now and again. Herman had seen her onto the train after the
reading, and John would be there to pick her up at the station in
Woodstock.

The day had been sad, but predictable. Mama had the house on
Huron Street and a nice sum of cash to pay for her coffin and
burial. Herman would also receive pay for being the executor of
her will. The only surprise of the day was a piece of property in
Racine which was deeded to Mama and Herman. Ida and Emma
had agreed to sell the Huron house. Herman would contact Clara
with details and to get her consent. Herman would keep the
unimproved property. The proceeds from the house and any

leftover cash would be split between the three sisters after paying bills. It wasn't quite an equitable agreement, but they could work out the actual amounts once the house was sold.

Ida closed her eyes, remembering her sweet mother and how hard Louisa had worked after her husband died. She hadn't skipped a beat. No long mourning face for her although she did dress as custom demanded for over five years in black. She had worked as a clerk and then a stenographer – she always had beautiful handwriting – for a German company in Racine. After Ida came back from her sewing classes in Chicago, she and her mother started sewing. Ida remembered that even though she was the one with the credentials, she had learned so much from Louisa about tailoring – a skill Louisa always claimed came with a German baby from the womb.

Ida smiled. It was that sense of humor that Ida would miss the most. And Louisa had absolutely loved John. All other disagreements faded into the past as the train pulled into Woodstock.

"There you are!" John's outstretched arms reached for his son before Ida could even attempt to climb down the stairs with her arms full. She handed off the now squalling child and grabbed up her carpet bag as John steadied her with one hand down the steps.

"Hey, big fellow, what's going on?" John cooed at the red-faced child who recognized love when he heard it and stopped his howl, focusing on his father's face.

"He's fine. Needs a change and is, I suspect, a bit hungry. He slept the whole way and awoke when I got up and started gathering things. Luckily, the coachman came to my aid."

"Glad you're both home. I missed you."

"Oh, go on with you. I was gone for less than 18 hours."

"Seemed much longer."

"No surrey?"

"No. I thought, if you were up to it, we'd walk. It's such a pleasant evening."

"And if I'm not up to it?"

"Then I guess I'll have to carry you."

Ida laughed at the very picture of John struggling up Lincoln Avenue with her over his shoulder and the babe in the other arm. "I'll walk. I've been sitting for a long while."

They began their journey the couple blocks up Washington Street to the Catholic Church, left on Tyron one block to Lincoln, then right toward home. Ida carried the carpet bag and John bounced and sang to his son as needed.

"So, how'd it go at the reading?"

"Mm. Nothing new except for one property she and Herman had purchased several years ago. He will take ownership of that, and we three girls will split the proceeds from the house. I don't expect it to be much."

"That's it?" He bounced the baby a bit.

"Why John, are you disappointed?"

John's face reddened. "No...I...not real—"

"I'm just teasing." Ida put the bag in her left hand and took his arm with the right. "There was some cash, but not a lot. Enough to pay Herman back for the funeral expenses, and of course, there's also the pay he gets as executor. If there is any left, Emma will get it for taking Mama in these last six months. She deserves it."

"So, Mama chose Herman to be executor," John guessed.

"Of course, she did. I think Emma would have been a much more logical choice being the oldest and living in Wisconsin, but Emma is not a man, so I expected that Herman would be named."

"Did Emma seem fine with everything?"

"Yes. I suppose so.

"Mama wanted everything sold and split four ways after expenses. But Herman doesn't want to sell the land. I think they both had their say, but it's Herman's decision as executor. So, who knows what will happen in the end."

They arrived at 365 and the door flew open, and Mamie and
Dodi rushed out. "Welcome home!" they called out as they
danced around Ida.

"It's as if I'd been gone for weeks but thank you for the
wonderful homecoming."

"Where's Helen?"

"I'm here," said Helen through the screen door. "Glad you're
home. Now I can stop watching the little ones."

"Who's a little one?" Mamie, offense written all over her angry
brow.

"You are."

"Am NOT!"

Dodi chimed in. "I'm not either!" and she stamped her foot on
the porch.

"Girls, let's let your mother in before we try to settle this
argument."

The three girls glared at each other for a few seconds. Crickets
chirped in the dust.

"Okay, fine!" Helen backed up allowing entry.

John looked at Ida. "Welcome home."

***

LOCAL INTEREST

The Square has been upgraded to accommodate
farmers with hitching rings. Sixteen beautiful pillars
mark entrances and adorn corners of the park's electric
globes on those pillars just in time for the Fourth of
July celebration.

Woodstock Sentinel, July 1, 1912.

***

July 15, 1912
Denison, Iowa

Dear Ida, John, and children,

Look at me type. Just three lessons I'm ready to type a full
letter. Once they put my fingers in the righ paces, I can pretty mush

do it. A natural, the teacher said. Of course, practice makes perfect. Worst part about typing is fixing mistakes. I have two choices cross through it or just leaf it.

I've heard from Herman regarding the will, and I know more about Mamaas assets than he does. She actually had a bank account at the First National Bank. Maby, he knew too. She got the account before Papa Stoffel died, and he put it in her name so the Stoffel boys couldn't take it from her if ~~someone~~ (oops) something happened to him. Herman said you and Emma agreed to let him handle the whole thing and he wants my approval. Did you agree? Did Emma? I'm sorry to throw a monkey wretch into the works. I havn't answered him yet. I wanted to hear your side.

My writing is doing okay. Nothing big but steady. I feel the need for a scandal to solve. Ha !@ I keep my eyes open.

Pearle is having a good year with Watkins so far. His wagon has held up well and our horses are still young and spry. In the good sumer wether he is gone for a couple of weeks at a time until he gets bak past here. Then he swoops in for a few days to pick up supplies which come from Chicago by train. I take a cart down to pick them up about once a week. I miss him, but he likes the fredom.

If Herman is trying to pull something, what can wej do? Ask John. He'll know.

It's been very hot and dry this summer in Iowa. Makes me somtime smis the lake with its cool breezes and beaches. I've talked to Pearle about coming back closer to all of you, maybe Indiana, but he says there are no positions for horse drivers. Maybe he's right. Indiana is probably much more modern than Iowa is. No horses, just cars. I asked him what he has against cars to deliver Watkins, but he just smiled. What is that supposed to mean? I guess like the baby bird, I beter bee satisfied with where I landed.

See I made it through a whole letter. I hope you can read it. Typing is fun and I'm getting so much beter than I was at first.

Much love from the sticks,

Clara and Pearle

***
PRINCESS THEATRE
If our films are not up to the mark of excellence you demand and leave you kicking that prices are not fair, our practices have at least gained for us a reputation. But we don't care as long as we are able to offer MOVING PICTURES that win your appreciation. Just now, we have some new films that are more than usually interesting. Better see them before we change again. Films keep moving all the time here you know.

Now Showing
FRIDAY AND SATURDAY
August 2 and 3
"PATHE'S WEEKLY REVIEW"
Current events from All Over the World
"THE GUN SMUGGLERS"
A page out of Mexican History
"LENA AND THE GEESE"
Biograph Comedy
SUNDAY
August 4
"DAYS OF TERROR"
Vitagraph Historical Drama
"THE CHOIR OF DENSMORE"
A Beautiful Lubin drama
"CHASED BY BLOODHOUNDS"
A Vitagraph Comedy Featuring John Penny, the Funny Man
MONDAY AND TUESDAY
August 5 and 6
"LINCOLN'S GETTYSBURG ADDRESS"
A Patriotic and Inspirational Feature Film
"DERBY DAY AT CHURCHILL DOWNS"
The Life of a Race Horse, S & A Sports
"KATCHEM KATE"
Biograph Comedy

Woodstock Sentinel, July 30, 1912.

***

Too Late for Last Issue

Mr. Dye, the Watkins Medicine man, met with quite a loss Friday, when his team became frightened and ran away, breaking the wagon and otherwise damaging his outfit. Mr. Dye estimates his loss at about $40.

Denison Review, August 7, 1912.

***

BAPTISTS TO FEED THE MULTITUDES

The ladies of the Woodstock Baptist church will have charge of the dining hall at the McHenry County fair.

McHenry Plaindealer, August 14, 1912.

***

ALL THINGS DENISON
By Clara Daring

What a wonderful adventure to ride in the auto caravan of the suffragists across the wide prairies of Iowa. This reporter has just now returned from just such an adventure and wishes to report on the events in first person.

The automobile, a brand-new 1912 Pope-Hartford Touring Model 27, was as shiny as a mirror, at least at the beginning of the jaunt in Omaha. By the end in Des Moines, both it and we were dust covered but happy with the day of 'stumping.' We stopped at little towns along the way where the suffragist, Miss Mary Garrett Hay, would place her soap box on the corner and draw a crowd of ten to twenty citizens. She would talk for five or ten minutes and then we would move on with great fanfare, having a traveling four-piece brass band in the car behind.

Miss Hay is the president of the New York Federation of Women's Clubs, and it was an honor to ride by her side through the dusty roads of Iowa. Our proximity also gave a chance to interview her about what she sees as the future for suffrage in the United States. She had said in a report by a prominent New York newspaper that she thinks that the millennium is here. Why does she believe this?

"I believe this because of the way the National Progressive party is kowtowing to women. I was considerably surprised by what happened at the Chicago convention. When I heard of men whom I had begged on my bended knees for the privilege of addressing some political gathering for five little minutes simply falling over themselves to let women take the lead, that's when I knew, 'The millennium has come!' The T. R. party has taken up women because it saw it had to. Much of their strength lies in the west and women are strong there."

"Governor Wilson has stated that he is 'on the fence' about suffrage. Others say that he is afraid to say what he believes because it might hurt him in the southern states. What about the Democratic Party?" this reporter asked.

"Wilson?" said Miss Hay. "He's – academic. I'm afraid he'll be elected, though."

And so, there is the prediction for the Democrats in November. We won't know until then if Miss Hay's crystal ball is right or wrong.

Crawford County Courier, August 20, 1912.

***

NEIGHBORING NEWS AS CHRONICLED BY OUR ABLE CORPS OF CORRESPONDENTS

Come to the great McHenry County fair August 27-30, 1912. General admission, 35 cents. Season ticket, $1.50 for man and wife or $1.00 for one person.

Several hundred dollars have been added in the premiums for educational and boys' and girls' farm production departments. Get a premium list from Theo Hamer, Sec., Woodstock, Ill.

McHenry Plaindealer, August 22, 1912.

***

Ida heard the front door open and close.

"Papa, papa, papa," the chorus echoed from the parlor.

After a moment, John appeared in the kitchen doorway. "Hello."

Ida bustled over and gave him a kiss on the cheek. "Glad you are home. I have a question for you. You are down at the Square every day, right?"

John was slow to answer "Right?" He drew the word out to a question.

"Why didn't you tell me that it was unpassable."

"Unpassable? I pass it every day."

Ida spooned mashed potatoes into a bowl. "Mamie, Dodi come help with the table. Helen, get Bobby, he should be awake and change him before supper which is ready. I'm dishing up."

"Unpassable?" John persisted.

"Yes, Dodi and I went down to get groceries at Austin's which, as you know, is at the opposite side of the square from us."

"Yes."

"And we couldn't get across the square. We had to retrace our steps and go in on Washington past the depot to get there. What in the world is going on?"

"Obviously, you haven't looked at today's paper."

Ida stopped mid scoop of creamed peas and looked at John blankly.

John shifted weight and said, "No, of course, you haven't. Here let me help you with that."

Ida called out, "Girls! Schnell!"

John took the peas and potatoes to the table and returned. "We are at long last paving the square."

"Paving?" She took a deep brown beef roast out of the pan and sliced six slabs. "Looked to me that they were digging, not paving."

John chuckled. "They are taking away the unstable dirt and replacing it with gravel and sand and then paving the street with bricks."

"Bricks?" Ida handed the platter to John and undid the tie of her apron. Helen appeared at the top of the landing with Bobby and descended into the kitchen handing him to Ida. Ida smiled. "Thank you, Helen." With her free hand, she picked up the bread and butter and handed it to Helen. And they went to the dining room. Already seated were Mamie, Dodi, and John. Ida slid Bobby into the highchair and put a piece of bread before him in the tray. He pounded on it with a fist before trying to pick it up.

John said, "Whose turn?"

Helen said, "Mine."

They folded their hands and bowed their heads.

"Dear Father, we give you thanks for this our daily bread. Amen," Helen intoned.

The others replied, "Amen."

They passed the serving dishes and platter around to each person with Ida helping Dodi as necessary.

"Your father says that they are paving the square with bricks." Ida opened the dinner conversation.

"We see'd it," said Dodi.

"Saw it," said Helen.

Dodi glared at Helen but then became distracted by the mashed potatoes Ida ladled onto her plate.

"Yes," said Ida. "We did saw it." Helen rolled her eyes and started cutting her meat.

"It was a big mess," said Dodi as Ida selected a small piece of meat and cut it into bite-sized squares. "Big piles of dirt and men digging and horses. We couldn't get to the grocery store."

Mamie looked up from her peas, "Were there many horses?"

"Yes, many," confirmed Dodi.

Mamie's eyes sparkled. "I wish I could have seen it."

John cleared his throat. "Never fear little bears, it will take a good while for them to finish. We will all get to see it."

"If we want to," Helen amended.

Ida looked at her morose daughter. "Helen, why would you not want to see them working on it? Those bricks will last a lifetime."

John swallowed and looked at Ida. "I'm not sure—"

"I don't care about those things. Where is the educational benefit from seeing men laying bricks?" Helen put a piece of meat into her mouth and began chewing.

John tried again. "I'm not sure that—"

"You don't care about how the streets are made?"

"No," said Helen around her food.

"I do," said Mamie. "I will go and see."

John took a breath. "I'm not sure that these bricks will—"

"I want to go too," said Dodi. "I like to walk around the square and look in the windows. It's my favorite."

"I'm not sure that these bricks will last a lifetime," John blurted out.

"Oh, I was just being metaphorical," said Ida.

Suddenly it was quiet with only the sounds of spoons and forks against china.

"On another front," John ventured, "the McHenry County Fair is only three weeks away. Is anyone planning to exhibit?"

A chorus rang out, "I am" which only left out the men in the family.

"All of you?"

"Yes," said Ida. "Girls, tell your father what you will be submitting. Helen?"

"A watercolor painting that I did in school."

"Mamie?"

"My vegetables I grew in the garden. Cucumbers, tomatoes, and radishes."

"Dodi?"

"Um." Her eyes welled up. "I can't remember."

"Oh honey, don't cry. Remember you are going to bake rolls."

Large tears rolled down her cheeks, but Dodi's face was all smiles. "Yes, rolls. Good German rolls."

"And you, Ida?" asked John.

"An apple pie and a jar of sauerkraut with caraway seeds. And maybe my German chocolate cake if there is time."

"Prudential is having a booth at the fair, so I'll be working from there at least part of the time when the fair is running," said John.

"Then we will see you there!" Mamie clapped her hands and Dodi followed suit.

Bobby chose that time to squeal and smile.

They all laughed. "I think Bobby is glad he'll see Papa there also," said Ida.

Bobby squealed again.

"May I be excused?" asked Helen.

"You didn't eat very well," said Ida.

"I ate some of everything."

"But all of nothing. Don't you want dessert? I made chocolate pudding."

"No. I have homework."

They all looked at her as she realized that school was out for the summer.

"I mean I'm reading something important that might be homework next year."

John raised his eyebrows and drew in breath. "Okay. You may be excused."

Helen got up to leave, but Ida stopped her, "Take your plate to the kitchen, please."

Helen picked up her plate and silverware and took them to the kitchen, and they heard her run up the stairs.

John looked at Ida with a question furrowing his brow. Ida shook her head just a little to say, 'not now.'

"So, Mamie," John directed his attention to his second daughter. "You are taking vegetables. What will you put the vegetables in?" He looked back to Ida. "The display is as important as the product, right?"

"Yes, but we haven't talked about that—"

"Is it time for pudding yet?" Dodi sat with her spoon clinched in her fist.

John chuckled.

"You bet it is! I'll be right back," said Ida.

***

Attend the Great
McHENRY COUNTY FAIR AND RACES
WOODSTOCK, ILL.,
AUGUST 27, 28, 29, 30 1912
$10,000 in Premiums and Prizes
The Greatest County Fair in
Northern Illinois

Speedy Horse Races, Exciting Motor Cycle Races, First Class Ball Games, Elegant Music, Splendid Free Attractions and Fine Exhibits of Horses, Cattle, Sheep, Swine, Products of Farm and Garden, Handiwork, Manufactures, Art, Textile Fabrics and School Work. Take a day off and bring your families.

General Admission, 35c
SPECIAL TRAIN SERVICE
For Premium Lists and information
Address at Woodstock, Ill.

Ben Throop, President.   Theo. Hammer, Secretary.
Dr. W. W. Lichity, Supt. of Speed.

Woodstock Sentinel, August 22, 1912.

***

SCHOOLS BACK IN SESSION
This school year opens with 110 beginners and 875 in the grade school. High school has 132 students, including one postgraduate.

Woodstock Sentinel, September 1, 1912.

***

Cornell's Seven Wonders
The physical department of Cornell university was asked some time ago to name seven wonders of the modern world selected from a list of 57 outstanding inventions and structures. The faculty, graduates and seniors in the Physics seminary balloted, the award of this voting going to wireless telegraphy, synthetic chemistry, radium, antitoxins, aviation, the Panama Canal, and the telephone.

Woodstock Sentinel, September 12, 1912.

SAVE YOUR MONEY

You can always paint for a less price than Devoe Lead and Zinc; don't do it; save your money. Less price probably means less value, short measure, maybe, or cheap quality. "Cheap" paint takes more gallons than Devoe; and that means more hours of work. The cost of painting is by the gallon, poor paint costs most because more gallons.

Better Get Devoe Lead and Zinc.

MURPHY & DOERING,

Agents.

Woodstock Sentinel, September 12, 1912.

PAPER CURRENCY TO BE REFORMED
Plans to Reduce Size of Old Notes by One-third will Affect Big Savings.

The size of all United States currency and national bank notes will be reduced by one-third and their designs revolutionized for the sake of economies to the government, convenience to the public and safety against counterfeiting. This decision has practically been reached by the secretary of the treasury, Mr. McVeigh. It is proposed to make the dimensions 6 by 2.5 inches. The paper money now in circulation measures 7.28 by 3.04 inches. The designs of all paper money – United States notes and certificates and national bank notes – would be systematized and made uniform for every denomination.

This move is expected to save the government about $900,000 annually and the national banks, which pay for the plates for their notes and part of the cost of redemption, about $200,000. The economies would be affected in less steel for the plates, in paper, and in labor.

Eighteen months would be required to effect the change by the preparation of the designs, engraving of the plates and printing of the notes. To meet the objection that for a time at least there would be two sizes of currency in circulation it has been suggested that the government print in advance a sufficient quantity of the notes of the new size to be exchanged at the subtreasuries and national banks on a fixed date. The change could be substantially accomplished within a few days, treasury officials believe. There are now nineteen different designs of currency. The change would reduce these to nine. Each denomination would be characterized by a distinctive American historical portrait engraved in the center of the note. In time the portrait would be a distinguishing feature of each denomination.

The department is considering using portraits as follows: $1 note, Washington; $2, Jefferson; $5, Lincoln; $10, Cleveland; $20, Jackson; $50, Grant; $100, Franklin; $500, Chase; $1,000, Hamilton.

Woodstock Sentinel, September 12, 1912.

***

Suffragette Minstrel Show

"The Suffragette Minstrel," a ladies' minstrel, will be given in this city by local talent in the near future, under the management of Mr. C. E. Jones. Mr. Jones has devoted many weeks to the preparation of this minstrel and a pleasing entertainment is anticipated. The date will probably be in October.

Woodstock Sentinel, September 14, 1912.

***

Silver Medal Contest Program

To be held Thursday evening, Oct. 3, at the German M. E. church, 7:30 o'clock.

Hymn......................... "The Fight is On."
Scripture—Isa. 5:11-22 and prayer—Rev. Wiegaud
"A Bartender's Dream"......Katherine Albrecht
"Religion vs. Politics".................Bertha Rucker
Vocal Solo..................... Miss Ruth Trimble
"Little Blossoms"....................…......Lena Sloan
"The Three Homes"...............Zenia Nicholson
Vocal Duet.....Misses Anna and Margaret Rinkel
"Christian Patriotism"................... Lena Taylor
"The Reason Why"......................Zella McNeely
Vocal Solo.....................Miss Anna Schwinn
"Lizzie's Divorce"........…................Alice Byers

"The Question of the Century.... Lillian Cissna

Offering
Presentation of Medal
Benediction
Boonville (Indiana) Standard, September 27, 1912.

***

Women Buy the Model

Mrs. C. W. Hart and Mrs. W. H. Shipton have purchased the Model restaurant in the basement of the Bird block. It is stated that the place will be closed up for repairs for a few days and when re-opened will be conducted as a cafeteria.

Woodstock Sentinel, September 30, 1912.

***

No Racing on Sundays

Mayor Donovan refused to give permission for an airshow on a Sunday and friends of Mayor Donovan defended his action on the claim that the aviation events, and especially the automobile and motorcycle races would have been a desecration of the Sabbath. On Sunday evening Rev. Truman R. Greene warmly defended the mayor, in his sermon at the Methodist Episcopal church.

Woodstock Sentinel, October 3, 1912.

***

Monday, October 14, 1912
Milwaukee, Wisconsin

Young Frank Wienke had defied his father by coming to Milwaukee. William was forever preaching to him about staying away from the progressive side of Republican beliefs. But the progressives were modern, and their candidate was none other than the great Theodore Roosevelt. In his younger days Frank had relished the stories about Teddy the Rough Rider charging up the hill without care for the Spanish bullets whizzing past his ears. Tonight, Frank would hear him speak, and if he were lucky, shake his hand. The idea was very exciting. He willed the train to move faster.

Frank was old enough to make his own decisions. He had been living apart from his family for five years, working for a mercantile store based in Richmond. When he heard that Roosevelt would give a speech in Milwaukee, he was obsessed with going. He needed to hear the fellow firsthand, so that he could decide if he would pull away from the Republican party to join the progressives.

Frank had often talked with his Uncle Emil about the McKinley assassination that made Teddy the President the first time. Emil had been in Buffalo in 1901 for the Pan-American Exposition and had seen the whole thing. T.R., as he was known, had taken over and run the country so well after an assassin gunned down the beloved President McKinley. Beloved at least to his father. Now here was Teddy Roosevelt running again for President from the Progressive Party.

Frank stood at the front door of the Hotel Gilpatrick in Milwaukee next to the car that would take the great man from the hotel to the auditorium to make his speech. The crowd chanted, "Ted-dy! Ted-dy!"

Then out walked THE Teddy Roosevelt. He was broader and shorter than Frank expected but walked with a brisk assured gait. Fashionably dressed in a brown wool pinstripe suit and brown western style hat, Frank wished T.R. had on his Rough Rider khakis. Even without them, T.R. still cut a fine figure of a man's man. Perched on his nose were his signature spectacles, and he carried leather gloves in one hand.

A cheer went up, and Frank stepped forward to get a handshake. Shaking Teddy Roosevelt's hand would be his claim to fame. Roosevelt moved down the walk shaking outstretched hands toward the open door of the car. When he came to Frank, he briskly shook his hand, squeezing hard enough that it almost hurt and moved on. Close up under the brim of his hat, Frank could see his disarming blue eyes, cleft chin, and bushy drooping mustache under a large nose. Not exactly what he expected such a famous man to look like, but it was very close to the cartoon caricatures that Frank saw daily in the papers.

As Roosevelt reached the car he turned and lifted his hat in a farewell wave at the crowd. The crowd roared and again began the "Ted-dy" chant. Focused on T.R., most people didn't notice a man who rushed forward hand outstretched, but Frank saw him. He doesn't want to be left out, Frank thought and stepped aside for him. Teddy paused before turning to the car and reached his hand toward the young man.

Crack!

Teddy toppled backward into the waiting car, most likely killed by an assassin's bullet. Frank reeled back, caught himself, and took a step toward the shooter. He was only five feet away and was still pointing the gun at the car. Two men jumped the would-be assassin, shoving his hand skyward. *Crack!* A second shot rang out.

The driver jumped from the car, grabbed the gun from the man's hand, and the three men wrestled the assassin to the ground. They began beating him with their fists and choking him. Frank got his feet under him and backed away. The crowd closed in around the man being held on the ground, screaming, "Kill him!" "String him up!!"

A powerful, but strangely high-pitched voice boomed from behind Frank, "Don't hurt him. I'm all right!" Frank swung around and came face-to-face with Teddy Roosevelt who had risen like a phoenix from the car. All action had stopped as the company stared at the Roosevelt.

The driver had stopped his pummeling, and now pushing Frank aside, rushed to support the former President who sat down again in the car. The Milwaukee Police arrived with their whistles shrieking into the tumult. Two officers stepped in to separate the would-be assassin from the others, and the squad dragged him into the hotel away from the crowd.

The driver resumed his place and the car started. President Roosevelt waved his hat out of the window and called out "My good friends, I'm not hurt. I'm going on to the hall to speak. Good luck!" Slowly the car moved away from the curb, parting the crowd.

Frank watched the car pull away. He passed his hands over his face and took a deep breath. His mind whirled. What had he just witnessed? An assassination? A resurrection? Was T.R. the messiah? Had the bullet missed?

He shook himself and brushed street dirt from his pants and jacket. If he was not going to miss this speech, he had better get moving. He turned and took off running down the street toward the auditorium.

Frank pushed his way into the standing-room-only crowd at the arena. He could just hear the announcer saying that Roosevelt was shot. The crowd gasped, and a loud wail went up. The emcee quieted the crowd and pulled them back in to tell them that the great man had insisted on coming to the auditorium to speak even in his distress. The crowd murmured, and a cheer went up. Frank stood on his tiptoes and saw the man of the hour striding across the stage to the podium. He looked robust and healthy, his face ruddy and smiling.

As the cheering subsided, Teddy stepped to the edge of the stage. "Fellow citizens of Wisconsin!"

The crowd went wild, people threw things up in the air, hats, and newspapers and programs. The cheering was deafening. Frank was jostled and slapped on the back and pushed and shoved, but he kept his feet. During the celebration, Frank was able to move forward until he could easily see the stage. People filled every seat and packed the aisles, shoulder to shoulder. Frank looked around at the mass of people and hoped that there wouldn't be a fire.

Roosevelt went to the podium and reached in his breast pocket removing an eyeglass case and a thick sheaf of paper folded lengthwise, unfolded it on the podium, but then moved around the podium and addressed the crowd. "Ladies and Gentlemen, I don't know whether you fully understand that I have just been shot, but it takes more than that to kill a Bull Moose."

A gray-haired woman near Frank called out, "You're a child of destiny!" And again, the crowd cheered.

Returning to the podium, T.R. began his speech by lambasting Wisconsin's own Fighting Bob La Follette who had expected to be the progressive candidate. With the ascendance of Roosevelt, LaFollette had turned his allegiance to Democrat Woodrow Wilson. The candidate from the progressive Bull Moose Party spoke forcefully in crisp, clipped cadence, gesticulating and pounding his fist in the air or on the podium for emphasis.

After a half hour of speaking with the vigor and volume he was known for, Roosevelt clutched at his side. "Please Mr. President," someone yelled. "Go see to your injury. We will wait."

Teddy's face became serious and then maddened by the calls that he surrender the podium. "Now, this is a trivial affair. Anyone who knows me must realize that I would not stop for a thing like this. I have a right to feel sore with a bullet in me. But if you saw me in battle leading my regiment you would not want me to stop. You would expect me to go ahead, no matter what happened." Frank shook his head. What a Mensch!

Continuing for over an hour longer, stopping only once for a sip of water, Roosevelt concluded his remarks with "Now, my friends, I want to thank you for your forbearance. You have listened patiently to me. Thank you and good luck."

The cheer that went up was deafening. Two men rushed in and escorted Roosevelt off the stage.

Frank felt the crush of the crowd and let it carry him to the lobby and out of the auditorium. What a speech! What a day! What a story to tell Uncle Emil! This would be his claim to fame.

***

November 8, 1912
Denison, Iowa

Dear Ida, John, Helen, Mamie, Dodi, and Bobby,

How are all of you? We are fine and busy with battening down the hatches for winter. Wasn't it an exciting election? It's all anyone in journalism has been talking about. Wilson winning was not a surprise, but I would rather have seen Teddy. Ah well, he'll run again next time.

I believe I sent you my August column where I had the chance to ride with Miss Mary Garrett Hay while she stumped for suffrage. I've had a letter from her inviting me to Washington – can you believe it – for a women's march the day before the inauguration. They are trying to get women to come from every state and every county where women's suffrage is allowed or being sought. And I am going! Pearley and I talked it over. He will be out on his rounds so there is no reason I can't make the train trip to Washington. Isn't that exciting? I can't wait to see the monuments and be a part of such a noble cause.

Are the girls looking forward to the holidays? I sent my box early this year so that you have it by Christmas. Write and tell your Aunt Clara about your lessons. I'm especially going to Washington for you girls. I wish I could take you with me, but I will be too busy to be watchful. I want to get interviews with all the prominent advocates for suffrage and bring that information back to Iowa. Hopefully, we can convince the legislature here that they should vote for the amendment to the state constitution so that you girls will be able to vote when you come here to live. Ha!

And what is young man Bobby up to. He will be walking soon, right? How are you keeping up with everything, Ida? Remember that you need your rest also. Sleep when the baby sleeps.

That's about it from the prairie. I will let you know my plans. If I can arrange it, I will stop for an overnight in Woodstock either going east (to pick you up?) or coming back. It will be great fun to see you all.

Love to each of you,
Clara and Pearle

***

PEOPLE'S COLUMN

If your Victor Talking Machine or Victrola needs maintenance. Will oil and adjust or repair. Call 169-J.

Woodstock Sentinel, November 10, 1912.

***

Purely Personal

Rev. W. C. Cissna, of the local M. E. circuit, has been transferred to Wayne City, Ill., and left for his new station Tuesday.

Boonville Standard, November 15, 1912.

***

CITY COUNCIL

City grants petition to allow movie screenings on Sunday if they are clean pictures depicting historical, educational, and biblical topics and only from 7 to 9 p.m.

Woodstock Sentinel, December 1, 1912.

***

A short man and a tall fat man pushed through the saloon door into the crisp twilight. They were drunk and seemed glad to be.

"Happy Newss Years!" one of them shouted to the square.

Ida, who had been walking down Cass with Helen and Mamie toward Hoys Drug Store, stepped back away from the loud men pulling the girls back by their coat sleeves.

"Well, well, well. What haf we here, Shorty?" said the other man, the taller of the two. He doffed his winter cap. "Tree fine young ladies. Where you off ta dis fine evening?"

Ida put her arms protectively in front of the girls, pushing them behind her, but said nothing in return. She glanced about for other people who might save her. No one.

In a soft voice, she said to the girls. "Run to your father's office. GO!"

The girls darted past the men and Shorty shouted, "Hey, where're ya goin.' I was gonna buy you a drink." He reached out to grab Helen's arm, but she snatched it away and ran.

The men looked at each other. "Well, dat weren't very polite, were it, Slim?" Shorty took a staggering step toward Ida.

The taller was still looking after the girls. "Ah hell. They's too young anyways." His eyes swung toward Ida. "But dis one's fully formed, ripe for the picking."

"Stay away!" Ida shouted. "My husband will be here in a moment. You better be on your way." Ida's voice shook a bit but was loud and strong. Hopefully, someone would hear her and notice her plight.

The men laughed. "Your husband is coming?" They looked around but saw no threat and focused back on Ida.

"Yes. Right now, look." She pointed down the hill.

The men swung around ready to defend themselves against the empty street. Ida saw her chance and ran back up Cass Street as briskly as her skirts would allow. They caught her just as she was stepping off the walk toward the new jail house. So close.

Slim grabbed her from behind, one hand around her middle and the other covered her mouth and jerked her around into the doorway of John's old store.

"Where do ya think youse goin'," he growled.

His hand smelled of oil of some kind. She tried to scream but was unable. Oh, John. Where are you? She kicked her feet back and came down on the man's instep.

He grunted and loosened his grip enough for her to jerk away and again face them.

Shorty laughed. "Dis one 'snot going down easy. She bite you?"

"Nah, just tapped my foot. I wonder how many petticoats dere is under dat dress." He reached down to pick up the hem and Ida kicked out as hard as she could, catching Slim in the chops and knocking him back onto the concrete walk.

Shorty thought this was hilarious and bent over as he laughed at his friend's disgrace. Slim regained his feet and advanced on Ida with more anger than lust. She readied herself for a blow.

Out of the corner of her eye she saw John round the corner from Main Street, look up and down Cass, and come up the hill more slowly. Oh Lord, he can't see me, thought Ida; a dull panic clutched at her breastbone.

"Don't touch me," she screamed and slapped Slim's hand away as he attempted to grab her chin so that he clutched her arm instead.

"My husband is coming."

Shorty laughed again. "Damn, girl. You thinks we's stupid. We turn to look an' you run away again." He took a step closer still laughing.

John was tearing up the block.

Ida almost smiled. "Yes, I guess you are that stupid," she said as John reached them. He shoved Shorty off the walk facedown into the street.

John turned to Slim. "Get your grubby hands off my wife!" he yelled. He grabbed the man and twirled him around.

"What the fuc—"

John hauled off and smacked him in the jaw with a tight fist. "And watch your mouth around a lady!"

The blow sent Slim reeling backward. His heel struck a joint in the concrete walk, and he sat down hard. His hand went to his face.

John held out his hand to Ida. "Come on."

John and Ida hurried away as the confused men attempted to right themselves.

At the entrance to John's office, the two girls ran out and threw their arms around their mother.

"Mama, are you all right?" Concern etched Helen's face.

"Mama, we were so scared." Mamie hugged her close.

"Where were you going?" asked John.

"To Hoy's."

"At this time of night?"

"It's only four thirty."

"But Ida—"

"Don't! Just don't." Ida's eyes filled with tears. "It was frightening enough without a scolding." She fished in her coat pocket for a handkerchief. John offered her his.

Ida wiped her eyes, blew her nose, and tucked the handkerchief in her sleeve.

John drew her into his arms and hugged her tightly. The girls joined them in a public display of affection right there on Clay Street.

"Let's get my coat and hat and walk with you to Hoy's. It's cold out here and time to go home anyway." John held the door as they trooped in.

***

John took a sip of his tepid coffee and made a face. He and Frank were discussing a plan to get Sophia to a bedroom upstairs so that Frank and Anna could have their parlor back. The stairs were not steep, but the ceilings were high so the trek to the top was beyond Sophia's abilities.

"We could put her in a chair and pull it up each night," said Frank.

"And during the day? Would Anna have the strength to do that?"

"No. I guess not."

"Too bad there isn't a way to put an elevator in a house." John looked at his coffee cup again.

"Hm. Hadn't thought of that. I wonder if that would be cheaper, if it could be done, than building on a room for her."

"Maybe, but most likely not. Seems like anything that is new is expensive. I think adding a room at the back like I did with our house would probably be the easiest and quickest solution. We have lots of builders in Woodstock, and since the demand for new housing has dropped off, they are looking for work."

"How would we arrange payment? I don't want to assume anything." Pink rose in Frank's cheeks.

"No. You should ask. There are two options I see. One is for all the brothers to throw in to pay for it. Or we can take the money from Ma's account. She would agree to that, I'm sure. Or she could sell the rooming house. Seems only fair that she uses some of the profit for this."

John lifted his cup again and sipped. His lips puckered. "Anna? Is there any hot coffee?" he called to the kitchen.

John heard his mother's voice. "I vill take to him."

And then Anna's, "No Ma. It's hot. You bring the cookies."

Anna entered with her apron over her hand, using it as a hot pad for the tin coffee pot. Behind her Sophia came slowly, eyes on the cookie plate grasped in her left hand, her right hand hanging useless at her side. She had made great progress in walking, but her right leg still dragged as she walked, and she needed her cane to transverse any long distance. She set the plate down heavily on the table and the ginger cookies slipped to one side and one fell over the edge onto the tabletop.

"Dat's mine," she said.

The others chuckled.

John snatched up the cookie before she could reach for it and popped it into his mouth.

Sophia chuckled and waved her hand in a go-on-with-you gesture.

Anna filled John's and Frank's cups and two more for herself and her mother-in-law, and the women sat.

"So, all is well at Grace Lutheran?" asked Anna.

John and Frank looked at each other. Frank shrugged. "As good as can be expected, I suppose."

They all sipped in silence.

Then John asked, "Did I tell you about the other day on the square?"

"On da square?" said Sophia.

"Ida and the girls were down there shopping, and two men confronted her on the walk."

"Did she know them?" asked Anna.

"No. She said they were strangers to her, and she couldn't describe them well. They had on coats, hats, and boots, and called each other Shorty and Slim, but that's about it. And they were drunk."

"Did she say anything to them?" Anna again.

"Say to dem, 'go to hell'," Sophia said loudly, cookie in hand.

They all looked at Sophia. She shrugged and took a bite.

"She didn't respond to them at first. She told me she just looked down at the walk and tried to put herself between the girls and the men."

Anna put her hand to her heart. "Oh. How frightening."

"She distracted the men and told the girls to run to the office to get me. Which they did. But you know it's blocks to the office."

"And what did they say?" Frank's brow deeply furrowed in concern.

"Just the normal 'Ain't this one sweet' kind of thing."

Anna sipped her sweetened coffee and stared at the tabletop, "Yes, that's the way of these terror seekers. Scare a person and disappear into the darkness again."

"I ran all the way up to the square - pretty good for an old man, eh? - and knocked them both in the street."

"Oh, my hero!" said Anna.

"*Blöder Lappen!*" said Sophia.

They all looked at her. Stupid rag? John sipped his coffee and considered her upset.

"To change the subject," said John. The others nodded. "Ma, have you gotten your chair with wheels yet? Maybe Anna and you in the chair could accompany Ida to do Christmas shopping."

"Ach, I stay. No need wheels. Anna, you go." She looked at her daughter-in-law. "I give list."

Anna smiled. "We'll see." She looked back at John. "I'll see what we can arrange. One of the girls might be able to accompany them of an evening or one of the other sisters-in-law. Maybe Kate."

"I'll leave it up to you then." John wiped his mouth on his napkin and rose. "I best be getting on home. My bride will be wondering what happened to me."

Frank stood also. "Do you still lock your doors?"

"Yes, at night to protect the children...and Ida...from the hooligans."

"*Hooligans fahren zur Hölle*," said Sophia staring straight ahead. Hooligans go to hell.

Anna put her hand on Sophia's shoulder. *"Mach dir keine Sorge. Hier sind Sie sicher."* Don't worry. You are safe here.

"Not worry. Need bat by bed."

John chuckled. "Ma, you are not to worry. Frank will lock the doors."

As they walked to the door, John whispered, "I'll get her a bat."

Frank smiled and nodded.

***

In the parlor, John and Ida sat close with his arm around her shoulders. It was nearing midnight, and both were having trouble staying awake in order to kiss the new year in.

"I forgot to ask," said John. "What did you do this afternoon?"

"Went to Frank's to give Anna a day off. Bobby fell asleep in his Oma's arms. Dodi and I did some baking – bread and such – to save Anna some work. Helen brought a book along to read to Oma, and Mamie had her drawing kit and made several colorful drawings for her to tack up. It was a nice day. Ma was so happy to be holding a sleeping baby."

"I bet she was. She's doing better and better, isn't she?"

"Mm. I guess I don't see much change over the last few months. Her right arm is still unmoving, but she's a stubborn woman. She pushes herself to move. She seems to have settled into Frank's household well, and Anna encourages her to do as much as she can."

"Mm. I thought she was better the other night. Feisty."

After a comfortable pause, Ida said, "This has been a busy year, hasn't it?"

John nodded.

"Ma's stroke. Mama passing." Ida's voice caught a bit.

John continued the list, "A new baby boy. All three girls in school. My sister-in-law turned into a rabble rouser."

Ida smiled. "Turned into? She's always had an ear for trouble."

"You aren't thinking about going with her to Washington, are you?"

"Hm. Hadn't thought about it. What would you and the girls do?"

John pulled back and looked at her. Fear and anxiety creased his brow, and his eyes were wide in surprise.

Ida laughed and punched his leg lightly. "Gotcha!"

"You are such a tease. We'd do just fine." John pouted for a moment but continued the list of the year's events. "Young Frank was almost shot by an assassin."

"And Clara got a typewriter."

Now it was John's turn to laugh. "Think she'll ever master it?"

"Oh, I'm certain she will. She must, if only to keep up with the times. According to her, it won't be long until reporters will be required to type up their articles."

"I wonder if insurance men will soon have the same requirement. Seems a little far-fetched that businesses would require their office workers to type."

"Maybe I should learn, so I can help out in your office."

"Dearest, you have a new baby and a household to run, don't you?"

"Well, yes. Right now, but once Bobby is older, he could come with me to the office."

"Maybe. It's a possibility."

They heard the bells begin at St. Mary's down the block, ringing in the new year.

John leaned down and kissed Ida properly on the lips, lingering just a bit.

"Nineteen thirteen," said Ida. "Doesn't sound like a lucky year. Maybe we should bring those sweepers back."

John laughed at the memory of the chimney sweeps sweeping away Mamie's bad health. "Well, it worked then, maybe we should."

"But now we should be off to bed. Bobby and Dodi will be up early. Happy New Year, John."

"Happy New Year, my girl. Here's to a new year filled with family and only good news."

Lacking champagne, they sealed it with another kiss.

Mamie and Bobby;
Dodi and Dolly (Spring 1913)

Don't Call Me Dodi!
(1913)

112 DOCTORS TO FIGHT EPIDEMIC IN CITY SCHOOLS
Rapid Spread of Contagious Diseases Is Blamed on Dry Weather

January 4, 1913—[Chicago Examiner]—With a force of 112 doctors, seven medical supervisors and seventy nurses, the City Health Office will launch a vigorous campaign against scarlet fever and other contagious diseases when the public schools reopen tomorrow.

For several weeks there have been epidemics of scarlet fever, diphtheria, and measles in the vicinity of many of the largest schools in Chicago. In some of these school districts not less than thirteen cases of scarlet fever and from four to seven cases of diphtheria or measles have been reported.

A case of smallpox was reported yesterday, Michael Harriet, 6527 Ingleside Avenue, who came to Chicago a few days ago from LaSalle, Ill., where the disease prevails, was the victim. He was taken to the Isolation Hospital.

"The present epidemics are serious, but not as alarming as the statistics would seem to indicate," said Dr. Herman Spalding, first assistant to Dr. George B. Young, the Health Commissioner. "The unusually dry weather, without the usual snow at Christmastide, is regarded as the principal cause of the increase in scarlet fever and diphtheria as compared with 1911 and other years. The whirling dust in our streets gets into the nostrils and throats of children. As this dust is laden with disease germs, it was to be expected that there would be an increase in the diseases of children. Our reports for December show an increase of more than four hundred per cent in measles, and more than one hundred per cent in scarlet fever cases as compared with last year.

"We are ready to wage a brisk battle against those diseases when the schools reopen. The worst zones of fever and diphtheria are in the school districts of the Northwest and the North Side and the Ghetto. More than half of the school districts have diphtheria, measles, or scarlet fever cases, but the situation is nothing like it was in 1907, when the new cases increased to 400 a day. The milk was then blamed, but I don't think the milk is to blame very much, if at all, at present."

Chicago Tribune, January 5, 1913.

***

Ida dropped the paper like it was a diseased rat. Her chest tightened in panic. She fought back the urge to drop everything, bundle herself and Bobby up, and march over to the school to withdraw her children. The article said the diseases were spreading to the northwest of Chicago which was where Woodstock sat. At the very least, she should get Mamie. Mamie might not survive another bout of scarlet fever. The girls, now in first, third and fifth grades, had said nothing about sickness at school, but the Chicago paper was rarely wrong as she had discovered when they published the truth about the Titanic.

Ida looked at her watch pendant – three o'clock. She sagged into a chair with relief. They would be home in a few minutes. Best to just continue making dinner and talk about it with John tonight.

Ida took leftover bread that was now stale and broke it up in a large bowl and added two cups of room temperature water. She covered it with a cloth dish towel and set it to the side.

She took out her grinder and brought in a small, uncooked pork roast and beef roast about a pound each. She attached the grinder to the edge of the counter, screwed on the grinding blade, and placed a chair with a catch-bowl beneath it. Cutting the roasts into thick slices, she fed them into the grinder as she turned the crank. The grinder transformed the pink and red slabs of meat into a mound of fresh-smelling ground meat in the bowl below. She covered that bowl and dismantled the grinder, putting it to soak in the dishpan.

Ida thought again about the article on disease. Spread by the dust of the streets? That dust would be over everything and everyone. She picked up the bar of lye soap and scrubbed her hands well.

Going back to the first bowl, she added the meat to the now softened bread, added two eggs and a large pinch of dried parsley, salt, and pepper. With damp hands, Ida kneaded the mixture until well combined. When the mixture felt right to her hands, she made seven meatballs, one for each of the girls and two for John and two for herself. She flattened each ball slightly, her hands working automatically, to make a rounded, oblong disks of meat – somewhat the shape of footballs.

The front door banged open, and the chatter of girls' voices filled the house. Ida placed the 'footballs' into the cleaner bowl and covered them again.

"Mama?"

"I'm in the kitchen. Do you need a snack? We are eating early tonight. Papa has a church meeting."

Two faces appeared at the kitchen door while Helen stopped on the landing on the way upstairs. "I'll wait for supper," she said and continued up the stairs.

Ida smiled at Mamie and Dodi, and they smiled back. "How about you two?"

"Dodi has a problem." Mamie came in and sat down at the table.

"I'll have a snack," said Dodi. "Can I have cereal? Corn flakes?"

"What is your problem, Dodi?" Ida was curious. "You aren't sick, are you?"

"No."

Ida got a bowl down and the milk bottle from the icebox, and Dodi climbed up on a chair and brought down the giant box of Kellogg's Corn Flakes.

"Mamie?"

"No. I'm not hungry yet. What are we having for supper?"

"*Buletten* and boiled potatoes." Ida indicated the covered bowl.

"Meatballs! Yummy!" But Mamie remained at the table.

Ida set an empty bowl in front of Dodi who put a healthy portion of flakes into it. Ida poured milk over the flakes and took the bottle back to the ice box.

Ida sat down at the table with the girls. "Okay. What is the problem?"

"Today, we were playing at recess—"

"Inside or outside?" Ida was still thinking about children breathing contaminated dust.

Mamie looked at her. "Inside. We weren't playing like running around, but we were coloring pictures that Teacher put up on the walls."

"Okay."

Mamie looked at Dodi, as if hoping she would assume the storyline from there, but the chubby little girl focused her attention on eating the flakes before they got too soggy.

Mamie came back to Ida. "Then these third-grade boys started whispering bad things at Dodi and calling her Dodo."

"I thought your teacher called you Dorothea?" Ida directed the comment to Dodi who looked up and nodded, her mouth full of flakes.

Mamie continued looking contrite. "Teacher does, but I may have called her Dodi sometimes by mistake."

"Oh."

"She did," said Dodi around soggy flakes not looking up. She made a face and stirred the cereal with her spoon.

"So, what did your teacher do?"

"Nothing," said the girls at the same time.

"Nothing?"

"She didn't hear them because they were whispering." Mamie clarified. "I didn't hear them either. I was on the other side of the room."

"Then what happened?"

"Then Dodi stood up and yelled at them to stop. But Teacher was busy, so they didn't stop but just talked louder. Then I heard them."

"And what did you do then?"

"I got up and went over there to see if I could make them stop. But then...."

Dodi put down her spoon and looked at her mother. "Then they started saying terrible things about Mamie too. Like she's a 'skinny-so' and 'a gawk' and...I can't remember what else."

"A gawk?" Ida looked at Mamie.

Mamie nodded, not making eye contact. "I'm clumsy."

"So, a gawk?"

Mamie nodded again. "And they kept calling Dodi, Dodo. Do you know it's a bird?"

"Yes, I know that."

"A stupid bird." A little sob escaped from Dodi. "They said 'The Dodo should be more like her sisters.'"

"And then what happened."

"Teacher heard them then and came over and told them to stop, and they did."

"Well, that's good."

"Yes, but while we were walking home Dodi told me that they didn't stop even after Teacher told them to. Whenever they were close to her one or another of them would whisper 'dodo.'"

Dodi pushed out her bottom lip and stared at her bowl now with leftover milk and a few soaked flakes of corn. Ida reached over and put her hand on Dodi's shoulder, and Dodi burst into tears and came into Ida's arms.

Between sobs she said, "It wasn't the first time. They do it all the time. I hate my name! I hate Dodi! I hate Dorothea!! I hate those boys and I hate school! I want to just stay here and cook with you like we used to." Tears spilled down her cheeks wetting Ida's apron bib.

Mamie looked at her sister and shrugged. "Now you know." She got down and slowly climbed the stairs. "Let me know when Papa gets home, okay?"

"Okay." Ida held Dodi whose tears were still coming hot and heavy. "Oh honey, there's nothing we can do about our names. You need to just ignore those boys. When you give in to teasing and get mad, it just makes the teasers want to do it all the more."

"I'm not a dodo!" Dodi's face was flushed with anger. "I hate it. I want a new name!"

"A new name?"

"Yes, I don't want anyone to call me Dodi ever again."

"But—"

"Never! Never again!"

Helen peeked around from the stairwell. "What's going on?"

Ida held Dodi close. "Dodi is—"

"Don't call me DODI!" Dodi wailed.

Helen came down to sit on the steps that extended into the kitchen.

"Well, how about Dorothy or Dot? Dodi isn't the only nickname for Dorothea," Ida suggested.

"No!" Dodi pushed away from Ida. "No! Don't try. Do not. Not Dorothy. Not Dorothea! And not Dot! The boys would love to call me other punctuation marks."

Helen, who had been taking in the scene of her hysterical little sister, giggled. "Like comma or asterisk or—"

"SHUT UP, HELEN! It's all your fault being so smart and beautiful." Dodi's face was scarlet with anger.

"Don't say 'shut up' to your sister, Dodi," Ida admonished her.

"I'm beautiful?" A tiny smile tickled at Helen's lips.

"Yes, and smart and no one ever forgets to remind us! It's 'Helen was much better at this' or 'Helen never had trouble with that.'" Dodi said in a singsong. "All the time. Just ask Mamie...I mean...Marion."

Ida sputtered. "But...but...Helen can't help that she is talented."

Ida went to Helen and put her arm around Helen's shoulders and squeezed.

Helen smiled. "It's okay, Mama."

Turning her attention back to Dodi, Ida noted that while Dodi's tears had abated, there was still fire in her eyes aimed right at her mother. Ida let go of Helen, sat, and gently pulled Dodi to her. "But sweetie, what will we call you?"

"You can call me Edna!"

"Edna?"

"Yes! Edna. Tell my teacher." And with that the small girl named Dorothea Edna pulled away, turned, and ran up the stairs.

"Edna?" Ida turned the name over in her mind.

"Edna," said Helen.

"I guess that would be a unique name in the family. Dorothea is a name from Oma Wienke's family."

"The Fisher girls use their middle names," Helen reminded her.

"Yes. But Aunt Emma planned that from the beginning. I remember her saying even before she married that she was going to do that because it was a German way of naming. You gave a child two or three names and they are known by their middle name, not their first."

"So, I should be Frances?" Helen stuck out her tongue. "Do they get to pick which one they want when they grow up?"

"I suppose. But most people, both Americans and Germans, keep the name that their parents gave them."

"I prefer Helen over Frances, thank you."

Ida smiled, "Me too."

"So, it wouldn't be so strange for Dodi to be Edna then, would it?"

Ida thought for a moment. "I suppose not. It wouldn't take long for us to get used to 'Edna;' do you think?"

"I'm already used to it. And if it would stop the boys—"

Ida broke in. "I doubt it would. Dodi...er...Edna is very teasable."

Helen snickered.

Ida shot her a look and looked at the stairs. She hoped D...Edna wasn't eavesdropping. "She'll just have to get over it. If she doesn't show it bothers her, they will stop teasing. I will talk to Miss Nelson when I tell her about the name change. But she has her hands full with three grades. If she steps in too much, the other children will take offense and tease D. Edna for being the teacher's pet."

Helen nodded sagely in agreement. "She needs to stand up for herself or else just ignore them."

The hubbub over the name had pushed the sick children in Chicago out of her mind. She thought now of asking Helen if there were sick children at school but looked at the time – 4:15. "Will you run up and make sure Do...Edna has stopped crying. Tell her what you just said. Give her some big sister advice. I must get supper ready so your father can make his meeting."

"Okay," said Helen. "Do you need help?"

Ida smiled at her oldest daughter. "Not this time, if you can talk to Edna...there! I said it."

Helen turned and mounted the stairs. Ida heard her say "Edna?" as she reached the top.

Ida pulled the cast iron frypan and a saucepan out from under the counter. After placing the saucepan on the stove, filling it with water and peeled potatoes, she added one stick of wood to the fire and put a large dollop of lard in the frypan. When it had melted, the Buletten went into the pan to brown. Here was the part of cooking that she loved; the smells that said something good is in the wind.

When the meat was brown on all sides, she added a quarter cup and a little bit more butter and put the lid on the pan, moving it off the hotspot so the Buletten slowly cooked through. Ida's mouth watered. This is the smell that will bring her family to the table.

Fresh, fist-sized rolls went into a basket and on the table as did a salt cellar, pepper grinder, butter, and mustard.

The front door opened and closed. Right on time – both the good husband and supper.

***

WOMEN FIGHT AT REVIVAL

Columbus, Ohio, Feb. 3.—Twenty thousand women battled with each other, battled with policemen, and were beaten, bruised, and crushed in an effort to get into the tabernacle here where Rev. W. A. Sunday, the baseball evangelist, is conducting a revival, in which more than five thousand persons have been converted. Their goal was to stop the preaching.

Women fought with umbrellas and with hatpins, policemen used their clubs. A score of women fainted, and hundreds suffered injuries in being jostled against each other and against the building, and a dozen policemen were nursing scratches and bruises. One cripple was badly hurt.

Stuart Advocate, February 6, 1913.

***

Chicago Suffragists Who Will March at Washington

A suffrage speaking campaign from the rear platform of a train is being planned by the Illinois delegation of suffragists who will make the trip from Chicago to Washington, D. C. for the big parade in the capitol March 3. The delegation will have a special club car and its "spellbinders" will make short speeches at every stop along the route.

Chicago Tribune, February 20, 1913.

NO HOPE FOR BALD REDHEADS?

Hair tonic – all the hair tonic in the world cannot restore red hair. Especially is this true when the hair is a particular shade and style of that which long ago decorated the shining dome of Policeman Burke.

That's what Municipal Judge Skully announced yesterday. A year ago, Feb. 19, 1912, the judge heard the case of Miss Kate C. Houlihan, then living at 45 East Thirty-fourth Street, against F. F. Gonzales, hair tonic manufacturer at 4223 Indiana avenue, claiming that his tonic had no effect on her husband's red receding hairline.

There were many strange features to this case, and the court was puzzled until the judge's speculative eye fell upon Policeman Burke's shining bald pate.

"I'm going to set you free on a peace bond," he said
to Gonzales, "for one year. During that time, I want
you to decorate Mr. Burke with a beautiful roof. At the
end of the year come back and I'll decide the case."

Several months rolled by and Gonzales, tearful and
discouraged, presented himself before the judge once
more.

"I have used gallons of tonic upon Burke's scalp," he
said "yet not a red blade has sprouted. My tonic would
grow bristles on a mountain. It would put hair on an
asphalt pavement, but upon Burke's head – O, judge,
have mercy!"

Judge Scully shook his head and sent the
manufacturer back upon his hopeless experiment.
Several times later Gonzales has reappeared in court,
saying the policeman's thatch had disappeared forever
like his own boyhood days.

Yesterday the court decided Gonzales had suffered
enough for his misrepresentation of the tonic, and he
was given his liberty and Burkes' head was abandoned
to its fate.

Chicago Tribune, February 20, 1913.

***

John laughed. "Ida, did you see this story about the hair tonic
trial in the *Tribune*?"

Ida came from the kitchen wiping her hands on her apron.
"Yes, I did. You know Clara and Pearle sent some Watkins hair
tonic with those samples at Christmas. Do you want to try it?"

"I was taking it more as a joke and feeling glad I don't have red
hair."

"So, you want to try it then?"

"I don't know. What do you think?"

Ida shrugged. "It's up to you."

"I'm not troubled by my shiny dome." John ran his hand
across the top of his head.

"Me either, but if you want to try it, we have it."

John considered. "Runs in the family, you know."

"What does that have to do with it?" Ida's hands came up to
rest on her hips.

"Well, I'm just saying that if any head would be reluctant to the tonic, it seems like it would be one with bald brothers."

Ida nodded. "Was your father bald?"

"Nope."

Ida's brow creased, considering. "That's strange, don't you think?"

"I suppose."

"I mean, if it runs in the family."

"I suppose. I'm just glad I don't have red hair."

"Me too." Ida started to the kitchen but stopped looking back. "So, do you want to try the Watkins tonic?"

Now John shrugged. "Why not? Couldn't hurt."

***

February 26, 1913
Denison, Iowa

Dear Ida, John, and children,

Tomorrow is the big day when I will board the train for the east. Ten of us are going from western Iowa – eight women and two men – so I will be in good company. The two men are husbands who are turning their shops over to underlings so that they can see the spectacle. Has it been in your papers? Maybe not. The Republicans are ignoring the march for obvious reasons and the Wilson Democrats are not acting much differently. I don't know if Teddy will be there, but they say we will be led up Pennsylvania Avenue by Inez Mulholland. Do you know of her? She is called the "most beautiful suffragist" and she will ride her horse named Gray Dawn astride down the avenue parting the crowd if necessary. We are all to dress in white for the march, and I've made a wonderful traveling suit of white wool, so I'll stay warm. We are hoping our parade will outshine Wilson's Inaugural procession the next day. Washington doesn't know what's coming.

The procession will be on March 3. I'm not sure what time it will start, but I'm very excited to get underway from this end. My plan is to go directly to Washington with my colleagues and after the events, I will come home via Woodstock to see all of you. I can't *believe it's been almost a year since Mama's passing. This visit will be a happier occasion.*

I do understand, Ida, why you say you cannot be with us in Washington. Bobby is young and needs his mother's milk, but he is also old enough to eat other food. One of your sisters-in-law surely could take him for five days or a week. Maybe Anna and Ma Wienke would enjoy having a baby around for a few days. This is an important event – once in a lifetime. Just a thought. But I do understand that you couldn't bring him to Washington with you. So, I'll abide by your decision.

Plus, there is the possibility of troublemakers attending which could get risky. I have been impressed by the suffrage organization thus far, so if the police do their jobs all should be well.

I will be in Woodstock on or about March 6. Can't wait to see your shining faces.

Love,
Clara

***

Clara stood looking up at the ceiling of the new Union Station in Washington, D. C. The building was enormous, larger than the Chicago station or any of the stations along the way. The arched ceiling was painted cream trimmed in gold, like looking into heaven without the angels. The cacophony of voices, trains bleeding their brakes, and announcement of leaving trains – "Two o'clock bound for Phil-a-delphia, Tren-ton, and NEW York City now loading at gate twelve" – was deafening. The crowd pushed this way and that to gain the correct platforms for their travels. Clara gaped at the international garb: men in top hats and tails stood near men in the robes of Arabia; women in colorful hats with plumage rising two feet above their brows; a woman and man in Asian kimonos and wooden shoes clacking by; a man in an actual sombrero with a lasso tied to his belt. Clara smiled and wondered where he'd left his horse. Clara had to push forward just to hold her position against the tide.

Hanna, Clara's newspaper friend from Marshalltown, leaned close and yelled, "Which way?"

Which way? Clara stood on her tiptoes to look over the masses. She yelled over her shoulder and pointed, "Sign. Trolleys."

Hanna nodded, and they pushed their way toward the exit. As the doors closed behind them, the world quieted. Trolleys stood waiting in the circular drive, each with the destination above the front windows in tall white letters. Two were bright yellow and one was lime green. The colors made for a gay atmosphere as people of every color and dress mingled searching for the proper livery. The women wore the latest fashions including frocks with skirts nearly too tight to walk comfortably and many of the men wore evening dress – or at least what Denison, Iowa, or Racine, Wisconsin considered evening dress.

Once they were away from the rush at the doors, Hanna put down her carpet bag and adjusted her straw hat which had become skewed in the crush. "Let's wait for the others, shall we?"

"Good idea. What's the name of our hotel?" Clara rummaged in the courier bag where she had stowed all the literature about the march.

"Oh my! Look!" Hanna's voice, which had taken on an air of wonder pulled Clara away from her paper search.

The two women in their modest, slightly out of fashion dresses and straw hats stared awestruck up the hill to the United States Capitol building three blocks away. Clara was the first to come to herself and close her mouth.

"We wondered where you two had gotten off to." A jovial man approached them with a quick step, the rest of the entourage scurrying after him.

"Hank." Clara and Hanna said together. "Thank goodness."

"I'm so glad we found you. Wasn't it a madhouse inside? A bit too much for our bumpkin ways, wouldn't you say?" Hank looked a bit overwhelmed by the experience.

"We are glad you found us also." Clara held up a piece of paper. "We were just trying to figure out where we are staying. I remember seeing it in one of the announcements you distributed."

Hank reached into his breast pocket and pulled a slip of paper out and read from the advertisement. "'The Afton House. 1123-25 13th St., corner Massachusetts Avenue – A select boarding place; centrally located; excellent table; convenient to all car lines; transients accommodated. Phone North 3136.' We have reservations there for all ten of us for a week starting tonight."

"It sounds lovely." Clara stuffed the papers back into her bag, zipped it, and stood up, ready to take off. "I hope they have a bathhouse nearby."

Hanna looked aghast. "Nearby?"

"In the building, I hope." Hank looked troubled by the idea that they would have to walk to a bathhouse. "I'm sure there will be inside plumbing, and we have reservations for five rooms."

Hanna blanched. The other ladies who had caught up and gathered around the three began to murmur to each other.

"Ladies, ladies. It is a highly reputable house. We mustn't worry until we see it. Then you can complain. Let's find out which of the lines will take us there – yellow or green."

They moved off toward the trolleys with hope in their hearts that a hot bath was in their future after three days on the train.

The group stepped off the trolley and walked the block and a half to the Afton House with Hank in the lead. At the door he went in first and Jonathan, the other man in the group, held the door as the women entered.

The house was – fine, Clara decided after a moment's consideration. It was tastefully decorated with wallpaper with plate-sized chrysanthemums in pinks and purples against a background of dark blue. To the right was a large dining room with a pine plank table sized to seat fifteen or even twenty people on benches to each side. This corner room was well lit with sheer cream curtains on either side of the four six-foot windows. On the walls, delicate paper with bunches of forget-me-nots and several Victorian landscapes had created an old-fashioned but tasteful air. Clara turned to the other side of the entry to see a parlor furnished with a light blue velvet covered settee and heavy mauve drapes. Hank stepped forward to the front desk. He gave one clap of the hand bell that sat on the desk.

A late middle-aged woman scurried out from the back and took stock of the large group that was choking the entryway. Her graying hair strained a tight bun, with strands that had escaped to each side of her face purporting a busy day. "Can I help you?" she said, in her New England accent.

"Why yes, my fine lady. We are the group from Denison, Iowa, here in your fine city to take part in the suffrage march three days hence. We have a reservation."

"Name?"

"Name…oh…er…my name is Hank Olsen. Or do you need all our names?"

"No Hank Olsen in the book. Who made the reservation?"

"I was the one who wrote you." Hank's wife stepped forward. "Harmony Olsen." Harmony put out her hand. "Howdyado."

The landlady tentatively took Harmony's hand with just her fingertips. "Nice to meet you. I'm Mrs. March."

"As you can see there are ten of us and I reserved five rooms."

Mrs. March looked over her glasses at the group as if counting. "There will be no commingling in these rooms."

Harmony blushed. "Why no. Of course, not…well except for husbands and wives."

Mrs. March shook her head. Another strand broke its bond and sagged forward. "No ma'am. None. Unless you brought your marriage licenses."

Hank looked helplessly at Harmony and shook his head.

"Well, alright then." Harmony took charge. "Looks like the two men will have one room. The rest of us must partner up. Line up, men first in this case and come forward with you and your partner to get a room."

Mrs. March looked dismissively at Harmony. "Did I say we have rooms?"

Harmony wilted. "You don't have rooms?"

"Well, this is an extremely busy week with all of you…ladies…coming for the great march and the inauguration, ta boot. I've had over a hundred requests for rooms."

Clara saw the housemother lift her lip as she said 'ladies.' She stepped forward. "We have reservations. Please look in your register." Her voice was strict, and she sounded much like a schoolmarm addressing an unruly child.

Mrs. March looked a bit taken aback, eyes widening as she took in the crooked straw hat and self-made gray woolen cape. All concerned held their breath. She acknowledged Clara with a curt nod. "Let me look at the book and see if we have any rooms left." Mrs. March pulled a two-by-two ledger from under the desk and began to page through it. "Here we are. March 30. Well, you are in luck. Whoever answered your letter blocked off five rooms for you on the third floor."

A loud sigh escaped from everyone on the customer's side of the desk. They scampered into a double line. Clara and Hanna were right behind the men. As soon as the matron had doled out the rooms, the tired travelers mounted the two flights to the third floor where they found exactly five rooms with a shared bathroom at the end of the hall. One of the women rushed to use the facilities but turned grinning before closing the door. "There's a tub!"

***

Clara looked up at the sky – sunny and bright. The day had been warm by Denison standards – 58 degrees at noon when the first marchers arrived at the Peace Monument behind the Capitol at the beginning of Pennsylvania Avenue, but as the day had progressed, the temperature had dropped a bit. In her white traveling suit, the plainswoman was not cold.

The Denison contingent walked down the still stationary parade. The marchers formed a serpentine line twelve across around the circle behind the Capital building and disappeared down a side street.

Hanna's eyes bulged. "Look at all the people. I can't see the end of the line. Oh listen. I can hear a band. Is that *Stars and Stripes Forever?*"

"I think it is." Clara pulled her reporter's notebook out of her courier bag slung over her shoulder and began making notes.

They stopped and watched as Grand Marshall Jane Walker Burleson mounted her horse at the head of the line. Beside her was a large bell on a pushcart.

Clara's turn to be bug-eyed. "The Liberty Bell."

A woman nearby heard her comment. "No ma'am. They wn't let us have it. Made one up ourselves, we did."

"But it looks—"

"Exact replicer, crack 'n all."

Clara smiled at her accent, but hurried to catch up with the others who were standing looking at a white horse and its rider. Herald Inez Milholland and Gray Dawn!

The herald's pale-blue cape covered the horse's flanks and down over her stirrups. Under it, Clara could see the white suit most likely made just for the occasion, just like hers had been. The horse stood calmly waiting with a feed bag covering its face. The banner Milholland held as she waited read "Forward Into Light!"

"Isn't she magnificent!" Hanna exclaimed.

"Yes, she is!" Clara could hardly wait to tell her readers about the beautiful woman astride the white horse with the cape flowing behind her, leading them all to victory.

"We Demand An Amendment To The Constitution Of The United States Enfranchising the Women Of This Country" screamed a nearby float.

"And that is what this is all about," muttered Ella, the youngest woman from Denison at seventeen, and she shouted, "We demand the vote!"

"Yes!" The Iowa and other women within earshot called out and started cheering.

Next groups representing the international community – nations where women already had the vote.

"Are you joking? Norway, Finland, Australia, and New Zealand have already given women equality. What's wrong with the United States?" Harmony said in a loud voice over the din.

"Exactly!" "Truly!" "We shall find out." Voices from women all around them chimed in.

Clara wanted to just stand and stare at the colorful scene so she wouldn't forget any of it. But also, not wanting to be separated from her friends in the crowds, Clara struggled to observe and keep up. They walked briskly past floats with scenes depicting the suffrage victory moments, ending with a float representing today – 1913 – which had a tableau of women inspiring a group of girls to join the cause.

Hanna leaned in close. "We should start a suffrage club at the high school. Maybe call it the Young Women's Voting Club."

"Great idea—"

"Write it down." Hanna indicated Clara's pad. "So, we don't forget."

Clara smiled and wrote, thinking about her own recent recruitment. This movement had already lasted 70 years. How much longer would they have to wait?

A horse brushed by Clara. "Coming through," a deep female voice said. "Look lively, coming through." Clara stepped to the side. A mounted brigade of women all riding astride beautiful black horses walked forward into formation.

"How beautiful." Clara sighed. She'd always wanted to ride astride a strong horse. The mere thought made a tingle start at her toes and move to the top of her crown. She blushed and stumbled just a bit.

"Are you okay?" Hanna said, taking her arm.

Clara drew in a long breath and smiled. "Never better. Just thinking about riding one of those beautiful stallions."

Hanna shivered as they walked arm-in-arm. "I see what you mean. A bit frightening."

Clara smiled. Not exactly what she was thinking.

Hanna pointed. "Oh my! Look at that."

Clara followed her extended arm to a scene presented on a flag draped buckboard wagon. A man held the government on his shoulders in the form of the Capital on his back while a woman stood helplessly at his side with her hands tied in front of her.

"What is—"

"Don't you see?" Clara broke in. "Total responsibility for the running of the government is on the back of men as they keep the women tied to the cook stove."

Hanna nodded slowly. "It isn't fair to either of them."

"Exactly. He needs help but can't bring himself to ask for it from a female."

"Tha's a lota readin' into a simple scene, little lady." A man in a black cowboy hat, black suit and bolo tie stood on the curb next to the two women.

Clara looked at him. "Are you for suffrage, sir?"

"I'm fer women, ain't that enough?"

Clara considered. "And I assume you are for freedom and equality as the Constitution requires?"

The cowboy smiled, "Fer sure."

"Well, then you must be for women's suffrage. Good day to you."

The man in black tipped his hat as the two women hustled away.

Where had the group disappeared to? Clara looked in the direction they had been heading but they had melted into the sea of white. She felt a bit of panic which passed as fast as it had appeared.

"Where'd they go?" Hanna's eyes scanned the endless procession.

"Don't worry," Clara assured her. "The Iowa delegation can't be too much farther ahead. We just must look for the sign."

More floats materialized out of the mass of humanity: nurses in uniform, mothers pushing prams, homemakers carrying pans and wooden spoons — the caretakers of the nation — and women in less-traditional careers such as librarians, lawyers, artists, teachers, and businesswomen.

A giant Bill of Rights floated by as the procession began to move down the street. But where was Iowa?

Hanna pointed to a banner that Clara recognized as an Abraham Lincoln quote: "No Country Can Exist Half Slave and Half Free."

As the procession moved, Clara realized that they didn't have to keep walking. All they had to do was stand still and watch the Iowa delegation. She pulled Hanna up on the curb and they ducked under the police rope taking a place in the spectator's gallery.

"When we see Iowa, we'll just jump in."

Hanna looked skeptical.

The crowd lining the street had a predominance of gray and black suits and men's hats. They stood at least ten deep or more and lined the route for as far as the eye could see. Many of the catcalls from the sidelines were vulgar, and the mass strained the police ropes.

The state delegations began to troop by. Has no one told them about alphabetical order? As she watched the banners, a man pushed up against Clara's back and whispered, "Does your husband know you're here?"

Clara's skin prickled. She stepped forward into the rope. The crowd moved forward into the space behind her. She could still feel him leaning into her.

The procession moved past her unseeing eyes as she trained her attention on the pressure from behind. She stood very still, slowly put her notebook and pencil into her courier bag and said over her shoulder. "Please, back away from me."

The man chuckled. "Oh, you do have a voice. You must be one of those women who doesn't like men much. I can fix that."

The basso murmur was close to her ear as his hands came around her waist.

Just then Hanna said, "There's Iowa!' and she ducked under the rope and ran into the crowd marching by.

Clara tried to follow her, but the hands at her waist held her back. She struggled but he held her in place.

"Jus' ten minutes, and I'll make a woman out of you, Missy," his voice hissed.

Clara turned as smartly as she could in the crowd and yelled, "Unhand me, you rogue!" and with both hands, she shoved the man backward. He stumbled, but the mass of people behind him caught him and kept him upright, but it also held him back.

Clara slipped under the rope and into the parade. She didn't know whose delegation she was joining at that moment, she but began proudly marching away from the man.

As the procession turned onto Pennsylvania Avenue, Clara walked on tiptoes for five or six steps trying to see. Thousands of women struggled to make their way down the avenue to the Treasury building where the ladies would present a tableau of Lady Liberty, and Helen Keller would speak.

Clara could see that the spectators had taken to the streets between them and the Treasury, closing in on the marching women, blocking the way forward. The horse brigade of women had moved forward trying to clear a path down the avenue, but hatless men in suits and ties pulled riders from their saddles, throwing them to the ground.

Where were the police? For the first time, Clara felt afraid. Yes, as far as the eye could see, violence was breaking out, pitting spectators against women wheeling signs. A cry spread up the ranks in the street. A cry of disbelief, frustration, and yes, fury.

"Miss, have you lost your group?" A young Black woman dressed in a black academic gown was marching beside her. Clara looked at the woman – tall with a straight back, hair pulled up in a tight bun with nary a hair out of place under the mortar board firmly pinned atop her head. The hem of a brown and blue gingham dress showed beyond the robe. She carried a sign which read, "Delta Sigma Theta Demand the Vote."

Clara looked around and saw that all the women surrounding her were Negroes in cap and gown. "Yes, I guess, I have. I'm Clara Daring from Iowa." She held out her hand.

The other woman shifted her sign to her left hand, and they did a quick firm shake. "Bertha Pitts Campbell of Delta Sigma Theta sorority, Howard College, and Colorado."

"You are a graduate of Howard?"

"I will be graduating in three months." Bertha moved her sign up and down as they walked, switching hands when her arm got tired.

The bystanders began a chant: "Women! Back to the Kitchen! Women! Back to the Hearth!" which made conversation difficult.

"I'm a journalist from Denison, Iowa," Clara shouted over the din. "Is this the colored delegation?"

Bertha looked at her sharply. "No! This is the college graduate delegation. I only knew you weren't one of us because you didn't have on a cap and gown."

Bertha was right, of course. On further inspection, Clara found that the group was quite integrated, although there were many colored graduates. Negroes graduating from college was something that she had never thought about.

They had walked by the chanters and the crowd noise diminished.

"Sorry. I should have noticed all that academic attire. Are you all from Howard?"

"Oh no. Thirty of us are in the Delta Sigma Theta sorority - that's a colored sorority. But others are from all the finest colleges for women in the country." Bertha continued to hoist the sign as they walked. "We had heard that colored people wouldn't be allowed to march. And if they did march, they would have to do so at the very end of the procession. The sisters talked it over and said, 'Hell, no!'"

Clara smiled.

"We waited until the line started to move and just walked off the curb and joined the collegiate marchers."

Clara nodded. "Brave."

"Not so much. Our academic sisters joined arms with us so the 'parade planners'," Bertha made little quote marks around parade planners to express her disdain, "couldn't do a thing about it without causing a ruckus. The last thing they want is a ruckus."

They had walked three blocks down the avenue and the pace was noticeably slowing. Again, Clara walked on tiptoes to see what the problem might be. The group in front of the 'University Women' sign came to a halt, and Clara practically fell over the woman in front of her.

An older white woman – a professor? – turned to look at her. "Watch your feet, young lady."

"I'm so sorry!" Clara said at once. "I was trying to see up the street to see why we were stopping."

The woman looked Clara up and down. "You are in the wrong delegation, my dear."

"Yes, I know. I stepped in here to escape from a scallywag at the edge who wanted to make me his wife. As I'm already married, I ducked into the parade. Reporter Clara Daring from Denison, Iowa." She stuck out her hand.

The older woman looked at Clara's hand. Slowly, she presented her own hand to be shook. "Ella Riegel, Bryn Mawr, Class of '89."

"How do you do," the women said together and disengaged.

"A reporter, eh?" Ella looked impressed.

The procession moved fifty feet. The crowds on the walks seethed. Clara heard "black bitches" and "mammies go back to the plantation" and other color-oriented shouts.

Clara thought this might be the time to play her 'I-know-someone-you-know' card. "I rode from Omaha to Des Moines with Miss Mary Garrett Hay last year in the suffrage caravan."

"I know Mary Hay. A lovely woman," said Ella.

"Yes, she is."

"And you are now marching with us?" Ella took a few steps forward with Clara at her heels.

"Only for a moment. I'm looking for Iowa."

Bertha and Ella chuckled. Ella recovered first, "I believe Iowa would be 'that away' as they say where you come from out west." She jerked her thumb toward the front of the procession. "Since we have stopped, you might be able to walk along the side and find them."

"That's a fine idea." Clara smiled at the women, and to Bertha she said, "Let's try to find each other at the end. I want to hear more."

Clara skirted the gowned delegation and moved along on the left side of the stopped procession. Men catcalled to her or anyone who'd listen.

"Hey baby, I've got something you'd like."

"Well, looka dat Georgia Peach showing off her stuff. I'd like to get a bite of that."

"Where ya goin' little girl. Where's your daddy?"

Clara kept her eyes straight ahead where she could see that a massive crowd still blocked the way forward and covered the procession route at 9th Street two blocks away.

"It looks like we've hit an impasse." A tall man said, falling in to walk between her and the crowd.

"An impasse?" Clara hoped he was a supporter.

"Looks like the crowd has blocked the procession."

"Yes, I can see that. I wonder why there aren't more mounted officers along the route?" Clara's tone was tense.

"Nothing to do but wait and see, I suppose."

Clara looked around at the ugly, angry faces of the men held back by the police ropes stretched to the limit. "Not me, I'm going forward. Waiting to see is not my style." She sped up her strides leaving him behind.

Why are they all so mad? What are they afraid will happen if women gain permission to go to the polls? Why do women even need permission? Aren't they citizens just like the men?

She was now adjacent to the state delegations. She moved further into the middle of the marchers, walked through a wall of Wisconsin women, and made her way until she spotted the sign, "Iowa for the Vote," slowed, and saw her friends.

"Clara! Thank God," Janet from Denison said, crossing herself.

"Where have you been!" Hank said angrily, as he rushed over to her, his hand tightening around her upper arm. "If you are wandering off, would you please do me the very small courtesy of telling me before you go. I would never be able to face Pearle if something happened to you."

Clara looked at him steadily. "When did you become the boss of my actions?" Clara's voice was calm, but she wasn't about to allow this man to patronize her. "I'll wander if I want to wander. You are not my husb—" Clara cut herself off, realizing what she was about to say.

"No, I'm not, but I am responsible for your safety."

"Says who? I believe, good sir, that I am responsible for my own safety." Her eyes went to the hand which still held her arm.

Harmony came over and physically removed Hank's hand from Clara's arm. "Hank. She's back. No foul."

Hank harrumphed, his face scarlet. "The only reason that William and I came on this trip was to protect you ladies from.... them." Hank pointed at the loud crowds on both sides of the street. "We promised your husbands!"

Hanna had also come over, and now she shook her head. "Hank, thank you for being here with us, but Clara is a bona fide reporter, and she needs freedom to discover the story." She turned Clara on her heel and putting her hand through Clara's arm, she pulled her away to protect Hank from himself.

Hanna leaned close, "What have you found out?"

"Good smart women, both colored and white. Good marching men and ugly, angry men screeching from the sidelines. The procession leaders tried to keep colored women from marching, but they marched anyway. But what I want to know is why are the spectators angry enough to attack the women in the procession? It seems to go against all decency and decorum. It just doesn't make sense to me."

A horse pulling a police paddy wagon came slowly clopping down the street pushing between the bystanders and the marchers. On the other side a horse-drawn ambulance did the same. The white-clad driver of the ambulance called out through a blow horn, "Is anyone hurt?"

"Don't cha worry," someone called out from the sidewalk crowd. "Der'll be someone hurt fer sure!" The masculine crowd laughed and surged forward again, this time the rope gave.

The crowd swarmed around the ambulance and infiltrated the women pushing, shoving, and slapping women who didn't cower before them. One woman fought back, kicking a man in the shin. A burly man grabbed her from behind, lifted her into the air, her arms and legs flailing, and threw her to the ground where she lay crumpled. A team in white rushed in to pick her up and place her in the back of the ambulance.

The Iowa delegation crowded together in a circle facing outward. The marchers brandished signs and umbrellas to keep the rioters at bay. William and Hank pushed the men who got too close, taking blows themselves.

"Traitor!" A man in a nice business suit and bowler hat yelled into Hank's face. Hank decked him with a nifty fist to the jaw.

Just when it seemed that the marchers had lost the battle, eight large men in blue wearing bell shaped helmets emerged without haste from the back of the paddy wagon each with a Billy club in hand. They began to use their clubs to back the crowd up and accomplished two or three feet of separation before retreating to stand near their wagon.

Without warning, the procession began to move again. With the police threatening the irate crowd to "stand back or else," the women grabbed the hand of the believer to either side and began again walking up Pennsylvania Avenue.

***

300 PERSONS HURT AS WOMEN MARCHERS BATTLE WITH MOB

[By the Associated Press]

WASHINGTON, D. C., March 3.—Five thousand women, marching in the women's suffrage pageant today, practically fought their way foot by foot up Pennsylvania avenue, through a surging mob that completely defied the Washington police, swamped the marchers, and broke their procession into little companies. The women, trudging stoutly along under great difficulties, were able to complete their march only when troops of cavalry from Fort Myer were rushed into Washington to take charge of Pennsylvania avenue.

No inauguration has ever produced such scenes, which in many instances amounted to nothing less than riots. Three hundred or more persons were hurt in the crush along Pennsylvania avenue, according to hospital estimates tonight.

Later in Continental Hall, the women turned what was to have been a suffrage demonstration into an indignation meeting, in which the Washington police were roundly denounced for their inactivity, and resolutions were passed calling upon President-elect Wilson and the incoming Congress to make an investigation and locate those responsible for the indignities the marchers suffered.

The marchers had to fight their way from the start and took more than one hour to make the first ten blocks. Many of the women were in tears under the jibes and insults of the mob that lined the route.

Although stout wire ropes had been stretched up and down the length of Pennsylvania avenue from the Peace monument to the mall behind the White House, the enormous crowds that gathered early to obtain points of vantage overstepped them or crawled underneath. Apparently, no effort was made to drive back the trespassers in the early hours, with the result that when the parade started, it faced at almost every hundred yards a solid wall of humanity.

On the whole, it was a hostile crowd through which the women marched. Miss Inez Milholland, herald of this procession, distinguished herself by aiding in riding down a mob that blocked the way and threatened to disrupt the parade. Another woman member of the "Petticoat Cavalry" struck a hoodlum a stinging blow across the face with her riding crop in reply to a scurrilous remark as she was passing. The mounted police rode hither and yon but seemed powerless to stem the tide of humanity.

When the cavalry appeared, there was a wild outburst of applause in the reviewing stand. The men in brown virtually brushed aside the mounted and foot police and took charge. In two lines, the group charged the crowd. Eventually realizing that they would be ridden down, the mobs fought their way back. When they hesitated, the cavalrymen, under the orders of their officers, did not hesitate. Their horses were driven into the throngs and whirled and wheeled until hooting men and women were forced to retreat. The space was quickly cleared.

The parade in itself, in spite of the delays, was a great success. Passing through two walls of antagonistic humanity, the marchers for the most part kept their temper. They suffered insults and closed their ears to jibes and jeers. Few faltered, although several of the older women were forced to drop out from time to time.

Chicago Tribune, March 4, 1913.

***

Ida's eyes widened as she read of the events two days earlier in Washington, D. C. No wonder Clara hadn't telegraphed that she was all right. She could be one of the three hundred fallen.

"How hard would it be to pop into a telegraph office and send two words, 'I'm fine. Stop!' I knew she shouldn't have gone. What if she is dead in the gutter somewhere, the hoity-toity Washington buggies splashing mud all over that white travel suit. Lying there dead with no family to bury her," she said aloud to an empty house, except for Bobby who was playing quietly in the Parlor.

"Ma!" Bobby called out.

She called out to him. "Mama's here. Don't worry." She lowered her voice to a grumble. "What was she thinking? Not about her own safety, that's for sure, and would she be happy to have me lying beside her dead as a doornail?" She raised her voice so Bobby could hear. "And who would you call out to then, son? No one. You'd have no one, that's who." Her voice became even louder. "And now she's gone. I just know that no one in Washington cares one iota about a woman from Iowa lying in their gutter when there are so many more important people. The senators and the President and.... Well, it serves her right! She is so pigheaded."

"Ma!" Bobby started to cry.

Ida rubbed her face with her hands. She must be strong for the children. This news was not going to be easy for them to take. Look at Bobby already crying. She rose from the table and went into the parlor. Bobby had scooched his way under one of the sofa side tables and was stuck. She grabbed his feet and gently pulled him out.

"There, there, little one. Mama's here. Don't cry about Aunt Clara. She loved you—"

"Ida?" A call from the front door. A woman's voice.

Ida's heart skipped a beat. Couldn't be, but in walked Clara.

As Clara stepped into the foyer, Ida felt as if she would swoon.

"Oh, there you are." Clara dropped her carpet bag. "And little Bobby! Oh my, how you have grown!"

Bobby sniffled, looking at this strange lady who he hadn't seen since he was two months old. Clara reached out, and Bobby hesitated just a bit and went to her. She hugged the ten-month-old to her and spun around. He giggled.

Ida put her head between her knees.

Clara stopped. "Ida. Are you all right? You aren't having a stroke, are you?" She tickled the baby, and he laughed again.

Ida slowly sat up, stood, and opened her arms to her not-dead sister. "You are not a ghost because you are holding my baby. Ghosts can't hold babies."

"A ghost? Why would you think I'm a ghost?"

"The march. The dead...three hundred women."

"Oh, come on. No one died. I'm fine. Here," Clara reached out, "touch my hand."

Ida's hand extended and touched Clara's hand, and she burst into tears. "Oh! Thank God, Clara! Thank God you are alive!"

"Ma!" Bobby began crying again.

Clara gathered her sister and nephew into her arms. "Of course, I'm alive, and I have so much to tell you."

They sobbed together for a moment, then Ida pushed back and wiped her tears with her sleeve-hankie. "The paper said that three hundred women were injured during the march. I was sure—"

"Three hundred out of ten thousand."

"Ten thousand? The paper said five thousand."

"Ten thousand. Five thousand. What does it matter? Women as far as the eye could see. It was marvelous." Clara swung Bobby around again, and he squealed even as the tears were drying on his face.

***

Later, as they sat in the dining room with Bobby down for his nap, Ida poured hot tea into two glasses, added milk, and asked, "Now really. Were you in danger?"

Clara considered. "Yes, I suppose I was, but sure strong women were all around me, and we just kept walking. When the antis blocked the way, the women on horseback and eventually the horse soldiers pushed them back, and we just walked through them. It was inspiring, and I am so glad I went." Clara's eyes were sparking gold amongst the brown.

Ida looked at Clara in a motherly fashion, her eyebrows drawn together in a faux scowl. "I had hoped for a telegram saying you were fine and when you'd arrive. But none came. Then again, why didn't you stay a few days to enjoy the sights?" Ida shuddered to think of what might have been a longer delay with no word. Surely, she would have had a nervous breakdown not hearing.

Clara looked at her over the glass not looking one bit chagrined. "Sorry. I should have thought of a telegram. As for not staying, the city was a madhouse after the parade, and with the inaugural the next day, transportation was going to be difficult, so we left as soon as we could and earlier than planned…going out while everyone else was coming in. I wanted to get back here to see you, and of course, home to Pearle to draft my story. We were there for five days. It was enough time to see everything. If you had been with me, I might have stayed longer."

"I'm sorry that I couldn't come, but I'm just not sure if I care that much about women voting."

Clara placed her hands on the table and half rose, leaning toward Ida. "Don't care? How can you not care, mother of three girls?"

"I know, I know. I do want them to have the vote."

Clara relaxed into her chair. "Until they do, things aren't equal between the sexes."

Clara couldn't help preaching, Ida thought. "Oh, I don't know about that. You can do pretty much anything you want to do. Pearle supports your endeavors, your writing, your independence. What more could you want?"

Clara considered. She did have more freedom than many women. "I don't think I'm a good example. I don't have freedom simply because Pearle LETS me do things—"

"I said 'supports.'"

"Same thing."

Ida shook her head, but Clara didn't allow her argument.

"I have more freedom because I don't have children. As you told me, you couldn't come to Washington because Bobby was too young, right?"

Ida didn't know if she should feel offended at the charge that she had used Bobby as an excuse not to go. "But some suffragists have children. How do they manage?"

"I have no idea." Clara's brow creased as she thought. "I guess, if you are strongly for the cause, you will be willing to leave the children and your husband to fight for it. That doesn't mean you don't miss them and aren't glad when you get home. There must always be sacrifice to achieve change. Men do it all the time. Look at Pearle. He leaves me for several weeks at a time to make a living for us. Or how about when there is a war, the men go off to fight and are gone for months or even years because they believe in the cause. Why wouldn't women do the same?" Clara paused to take a sip of tea. She was warming to this argument.

"True. But—"

"No buts. Women will not be equal until they are full voting citizens. Everyone doesn't have to travel to a grand procession to support suffrage. Most women do it in their own towns. Doesn't Woodstock have a Suffrage society?"

"I don't know. But—"

"We have many little things that we can do to remind men of our skills and importance in the world. Suffrage groups earned money to come to the march by selling pies or other baked goods on the street corners. One group in Tennessee called it 'One Pie in the Eye for Suffrage.'"

Ida smiled. "Clever."

"And that's just one example of what women are doing to keep the subject front and center locally. You could write letters to the Congressmen and President. You could perform in a pageant in the park in the square—"

Ida blushed. Her hand went to her mouth. "Oh, I could never—"

"Of course, you could. Maybe your Ladies Aid could find a way to make…oh, I don't know…let's say cookies and put a little paper sticking out of each one saying, 'Give Women the Vote.'"

"How would you stop the papers from burning up in the oven?"

Clara's eyes widened and she chuckled. "See. You are already looking for solutions."

"A lot to think about. I bet Helen would love to hear your encouraging speech. She's our child who loves causes."

"I will have a discussion with her while I'm here. We are on the verge of universal suffrage in the United States. Do you know who I met in Washington?"

Ida thought for a moment. "The President?"

"No, not a man."

"Susan B. Anthony."

"She's dead…oh never mind guessing. You'll never guess. Nellie Bly."

Ida's face had no reaction. "Nellie who?"

"Bly. You don't know who Nellie Bly is? Well, I suppose that's understandable. You don't live in New York, and you aren't all that interested in journalism."

"I read the paper. She's a reporter, I'd guess. What paper does she write for?"

"The New York Evening Journal."

"Never heard of it."

"Nellie was one of the people riding her horse as one of the heralds at the front of the procession, while I was walking closer to the end. Part of the way I walked with the University Women and met a very nice woman from Howard University who let me interview her. You'll see more about that in my articles."

"Okay. Back to Nellie."

"Yes, Nellie. You should have seen her riding togs. Her whole outfit was gray tweed with little specks of emerald-green, even her riding cap. And she wore TROUSERS! So, she could ride astride her mount like a man does. Her boots came to just below the knee and were of shiny black leather, and the tails of her coat were long, almost touching the top of her boots. But she said that while this procession and the tenacity of the women present was impressive it was still going to be at least 1920 before there would be nationwide suffrage."

"1920? That's years away."

"Well, yes, but only seven years away. Only seven years. Just think of it. How old is Helen now? Ten years, right? When she acquires voting age, she will be able to vote and so will Mamie and Dodi—"

"Wait, we no longer have a Dodi in this household."

Clara stopped, confused. "What...what happened."

"She is now D. Edna Wienke."

"Dee Edna?"

"D like the initial D. She doesn't want anyone ever again to call her Dodi."

"Why?"

"Boys teasing her at school."

"And she doesn't think she'll get teased with Edna?"

"I guess not. Helen is coaching her on how to handle the teasing. So, we'll see."

Clara sipped her tea. "That's a big change. Edna. I'm never going to remember. Okay, Mamie and Edna, you and I will be able to vote and so will Emma and her girls. And Herman's girls. Think of the impact all those voting Deutsche will make. We alone will be able to change the world."

Now Ida was laughing. "Clara, you are so dramatic. How could anyone talking with you not join the cause? But now I need to finish dinner. I could use your help if you are willing."

"Of course, I'm willing. What are we having?"

"Rinderroulade und Kartoffelpuffer."

"Oh my. You make my mouth water. Beef Roll and Potato Pancakes are my favorite."

"I know."

***

Clara rummaged in her pouch. "I brought you girls something." They were sitting at the dinner table having just finished a dessert of *Kirschmichel* – Cherry pudding – which was also one of Clara's favorites.

"You did?" said Mamie. "Thank you."

"Don't thank me quite yet. You may not like them." Clara pulled out three picture postcards from her pouch. One was of the U. S. Capitol, one was of the White House, and one was of Union Station. "Let's choose by age. Helen, which—"

"Helen always gets to go first," complained Edna in a whine, her lower lip protruding.

"Okay." Clara reached for her pouch and pulled out a page of blank paper. She ripped three pieces off the big sheet and gave one to each girl. "Each of you write down your first and second choices. We'll put them in order 1, 2 and 3: Capitol, White House, Union Station."

While the girls worked on their choices, Ida leaned over to Clara and said softly, "You are so smart."

John smiled. "Did you hear the one about the neighbor lady who came to visit. The woman and her homely daughter welcomed her into their home. After the gossip wound down to a close, the neighbor lady put her hand comfortingly on the woman's arm and whispered, 'She isn't very P-R-E-T-T-Y, is she?' The little girl looked up and said, 'No but she's very S-M-A-R-T.'"

Everyone laughed except Edna. "I don't get it. What did she mean? What does it spell? Why was that funny?"

Her questions just made the others laugh harder and Edna glowered more intensely at them. Especially she scowled at her sisters. Mamie leaned over and explained the joke.

Edna shook her head. "I don't think that's funny at all."

And that sent another spasm of hilarity through them.

Clara wiped her eyes on her napkin. "Okay. Let me see your choices." Edna had picked in order the White House and Union Station. Mamie had picked the White House and the Capitol. Helen had picked the Capitol and Union Station

The loving aunt looked over the choices. She picked up the White House and presented it to Edna. Edna's puckery face bloomed into a wide smile.

Mamie got the Capitol, and Helen got Union Station. They all were smiling now, and said almost in unison, "Thank you, Aunt Clara."

"And for Bobby." Clara returned to her bag. "A picture of the Lincoln Memorial to hang in his room so he doesn't forget me." She showed the picture to the baby who was peacefully sitting in his highchair teething on a gingersnap. He looked at the picture and at his aunt and smiled, his two front teeth glinting in the light from the chandelier.

Helen smiled. "He likes it, Aunt Clara. Maybe he will let me borrow it if I do a report on Abraham Lincoln."

"Maybe. Are you planning to do a report on Lincoln?"

"Now I am."

***

"Clara, what did you learn in Washington?" John blew cigar smoke at the porch ceiling as he, Clara, and Ida enjoyed an unusually warm evening for March and a nightcap of hot cocoa. The women sat with thick sweaters and lap blankets for warmth. John, still in his wool business suit, sat without an additional wrap. He enjoyed the coolness of the air. *Gutes Schlafwetter* - good sleeping weather - as his mother, Sophia, always said.

Clara set her cup down on the white wicker side table and looked at him. She seemed to be weighing if she should tell the truth. "I learned," she said slowly. "I learned that men can be real 'poor fish' and that women can stand up to anything, even sharks."

Ida face broke into a grin. "Spoken like a writer!"

John had a very small smile. "You think men are dullards?"

"Not all men." Clara backpedaled. "But the ones I saw in Washington, attacking women physically and slinging vile insults at them for no reason that I could discern, were without a doubt poor fish. Do you not agree, John, that that behavior is uncouth?"

"I see your point." John's turn to pull back a bit. "But weren't the women stup...ah...unwise to take their cause to the street? Weren't they just asking for the attacks?"

Ida looked up sharply from examining a loose button on her sweater. "Asking for—"

"Asking for the attack?" Clara broke in, her voice rising with passion. "You've got to be jesting! When does a woman walking down the street ask for any of the crude attention that men give her? When does a woman ask for a strange man to whisper propositions in her ear or push his body into hers in a crowd? When does a woman ask to be manhandled or accosted when simply going about her business? Asking Congress for the vote is every citizen's right, even women's right. That is all we were ASKING for!"

"Bravo!" said Ida thinking about her near assault last fall right on the Woodstock square. "Women have every right to walk down the street unmolested no matter where or when."

John tapped his cigar on the porch railing to dislodge ash. He looked at Ida with raised eyebrows. "So, you approve of the march, Ida? Even though your little sister could have been hurt?"

Ida's hands played with the loose button. "You know I was worried, but Clara has convinced me that women are stronger than men think, and that she can take care of herself."

"Indeed." John took a drag on the cigar and blew the smoke away from the ladies. "May I ask, Clara, were you actually accosted?"

Clara took a sip of cocoa and looked John unflinchingly in the eyes. "Yes, John, I was 'actually accosted.' The crowd was ugly and vulgar and chanted and catcalled all sorts of rude things at the women. The crowd especially attacked the colored women verbally. I had a man offer to save my womanhood if I would only...." She paused, "If I would act like his wife for the afternoon. Well, what, he said was he could fix me in ten minutes."

Ida gasped, her hand going to her mouth, her face reddening.

"And that was a mild proposal compared with other phrases shouted from Mr. Anonymous in the crowd calling us Jezebels, Georgia Peaches, and even traitors. The men told us to go back to our kitchens, to stop walking the streets like 'whores,' to go home because our children were dying. And worse things that I can't repeat."

John flinched at the use of such language in polite company. He looked down at the porch deck as she spoke and shook his head, nursing his cigar.

"These fine gentlemen broke down the police ropes and charged into the street, ripping women from their horses, and slapping and punching them. And when women fought back, it was a signal that the man could attack with full force. With my own eyes, I saw women picked up off their feet and flung down on the concrete, women punched in the face and the stomach. I saw a man lift a woman over his shoulder and carry her off saying what he was going to do to her. No one in the crowd of bystanders tried to stop him. No one. It was up to the women to chase him down and retrieve the woman. He didn't fare well."

Again, Ida drew in breath, her eyes wide with shock.

John looked at her. "Now are you glad you didn't go, Ida?"

Ida turned to him. "If anything, it makes me wish that I could have been there. What awful men and brave women."

Clara smiled slightly and returned her attention to the man on the porch. "And that happened because women would like to ease men's burden of being the main decision makers for the nation. That's another thing I learned. It isn't fair for intelligent women to place the burden of governance solely on the shoulders of men. Those of us who are able should step up and assume half the yoke."

"Even if you are not asked to?" John mumbled, eyes on a black carriage going by. He raised his arm and waved at the neighbor and received a wave in return.

Clara laughed and took a sip. "When do men ever ask for help? They think they can do it all and take care of everyone. Show no weakness, especially in front of other men. They think that women will teach their children morals and Christian living, but children are always watching their fathers' actions. The boys, especially, learn from their fathers how men should act in the world. Wouldn't it be wonderful if the men taught their boys that women don't have to sequester themselves to be safe."

John considered this argument. "I'll agree that men do respect other men more than women. Some do not respect single women of any age, because women gain stature through their husbands…and, of course, their abilities as a homemaker."

"Thank you," Ida broke in, nodding.

John took that as encouragement. "So, men are to protect the women through custom and culture. When women break with that custom, when they destroy that culture, men are not going to react well."

Now it was Clara's turn to look at the porch floor. "I met a colored woman named Bertha at the march. She'll be graduating from Howard in three months. Should she limit her talents to only motherhood and homemaking?"

Clara felt Ida stiffen. She looked at her sister and placed a hand on her arm. "Now Ida, before you jump to the defense of motherhood, you know I realize that some women are fulfilled and happy being homemakers." Still looking at Ida, she softened her tone. "You know I would love to have children, but since that doesn't seem to be in the cards, should I hide my light under a basket, sitting in Denison, waiting for my husband to come home?"

"No, of course not." Ida patted her hand and lifted her own cup to her lips.

"Exactly. Very few of the women I met in Washington put all their eggs in the nest of homemakers and mothers. Some women said that they don't want to marry. Some said that they are hesitant to bring children into this turbulent world. Others felt that they can be mothers, wives, but still have other options. No matter who I talked to, one common thread came through: Women as citizens, have the right to vote. They should not be silenced or ignored under the guise of protecting them." Clara stopped and took a deep breath of the cool air.

Ida looked at John who was re-lighting his cigar. He puffed and realized the conversation had stopped. He saw a place to get a word in.

"It seems to me," he began, "that getting the vote will lead many more women to enter the profane world. Are you not afraid that the coarseness of the world will lead to women neglecting their children's education and thus lead to delinquent children? Won't the adoption of men's more irreverent nature coarsen women making them less attractive? Won't women be putting themselves in a world where murder, mayhem, and yes, rape are always at their doorstep? Would it not be better for them to stay away from the ruthless, uncouth men of the secular world?"

Clara and Ida looked at him for a long moment. Clara found her voice first. "You know John, women are told to do many things for their own safety; they are told to stay home; to travel only with an escort; to bypass saloons and public houses; to avoid mean-looking men. They are treated like little girls who shouldn't have a care in the world if they have a strong man by their side."

Clara paused to take a breath. A horse clapped along the avenue pulling a coal wagon. They all watched it go by. "But…have you, John, or any other man for that matter ever thought of telling men to stop making the world unsafe for women? Have you ever thought about telling men, or better yet boys, to stop treating their mothers and other women as delicate flowers one minute and hussies the next? Have you ever thought about telling men that just because a woman is alone, doesn't mean she wants or needs a man's attention? It's time for a fundamental change in these obnoxious attitudes toward women. It's time that men kept their lips and flies buttoned." Ida choked on a sip and began coughing. "It's time that women got respect as people and as equals with men. Giving women the vote is the first step toward establishing that equality."

Neither John nor Ida could meet Clara's determined stare. Ida coughed again. John's cigar had gone out. The silence stretched.

Clara rose and gathered her empty cup. "Now I believe I will retire to my bedchamber." She smiled at the stunned couple. "Good night. Sweet dreams of a better world."

"Good night, Clara. Sleep well." Ida sent her off with a half-smile.

They heard the screen door thump closed and steps on the stairs. John looked at Ida and reached over and took her hand. "I love you and just want you to be safe."

Ida smiled. "I love you too. You are a good husband and father. Times are changing I guess, but don't worry, I'll always want you by my side."

He brought her hand to his lips. "It's getting too chilly. We should go in."

John held the door for Ida as she brought their cups inside. Once there, he turned, closed the inner door, and locked it securely. "I just want you to be safe," he said again in a hushed voice, but Ida had already gone to the kitchen.

***

Personal Mention

Miss Lillian Cissna of Wayne City, Ill., a pupil of our
high school, left for home, Wednesday, on account of
the illness of her mother, Mrs. William Calvin Cissna.

Boonville Enquirer, March 14, 1913.

***

"Thank you for your wonderful hospitality, John," Clara said
sincerely two days later as she boarded the train back to Iowa. She
stood on tiptoe to hug him. "Ida, I think it's your time to come
visit me." She hugged her sister tightly for a long moment. "I will
miss all of you. Especially you." She softly pinched the chubby
cheek of her youngest nephew.

"Oh, that was so much like our old aunts from Germany," Ida
declared. "Remember how they'd pinch cheeks...hard."

Clara laughed. "I remember alright, why do you think I hardly
need rouge?"

Ida hugged her sister around Bobby and kissed her on the
cheek. "Have a great ride home. Be careful."

Clara smiled at the phrase. "I'm always careful."

Ida lightly slapped her shoulder. "You are not! Remember the
ferry trip to the middle of Lake Michigan?"

"That wasn't my fault. I—"

"All aboard." The conductor made his last call, and Clara
stepped up onto the train just before it started moving.

Ida walked with the movement down the platform. "Write to
me."

Clara's lips formed the words "I will" as the train's whistle
sounded mere steps away.

Ida stopped and blew a kiss. "Wave bye-bye to Aunt Clara,
Bobby." Bobby looked after the train, raised his arm, palm toward
his face, and wiggled his fingers.

"What shall we do with the rest of the day, Kind Sir? Shall we
go up to the square? Hm? Maybe we should stop in to see how
your Uncle Herman is doing after talking to Aunt Clara. That

could be interesting, right?" Bobby nodded. Ida kissed him on the cheek and put him back in the baby buggy and headed toward Murphy and Doering's department store.

A dark-complected man doffed his straw hat and held the door so Ida could roll the buggy into Murphy and Doering's unimpeded.

Ida smiled, inclined her head, and said, "Thank you, sir."

"Not tat all," he replied with a lilting accent she couldn't place.

"Good afternoon, Mrs. Wienke. How are you today?" The girl at the front counter always greeted customers by name.

"Good afternoon, Jane. Is my brother in?"

"Yes, I do believe he is. Do you want me to run back and tell him you're here?"

"No. That's okay. I'll just roll back and surprise him."

As Ida moved toward the offices at the rear of the store, she found herself impressed as always with the clever layout. None of the merchandise was out of reach of the customer. She stopped to look at some nice red and white dotted Swiss material. A dress for one of the girls perhaps. She turned back to the front and called out, "Jane?"

"Yes, mum."

"I'll take three yards of this dotted Swiss."

"Anything else?"

"I'll let you know." Ida smiled at the helpful young woman with her shiny black hair down on her shoulders and caught a family resemblance to the man who had just left the store. "May I ask, are you related to that man who just left?"

"Yes, mum. My brother."

"He sounded so exotic. Where are you from?"

"The Bahama Islands, mum."

"How do you like Woodstock?"

"Oh, we love et here, mum." Suddenly Jane had the Island accent that Ida loved to listen to. "Da people are friendly and kind, and America is full of da freedom. And I haf dis lovely job with the Misters."

"Where does your brother work?"

"He is at da hotel cookin'"

"Indeed. We will have to go sample his work."

"I be tellin' him you are coming."

Ida turned and began moving again toward the back.

"I will have this ready for you when you are done speakin' wit your brother." Jane's accent had all but disappeared.

"Ida! And Bobby! What a surprise. I thought I heard your voice out here." Herman came toward them down the aisle. "What can I find for you?"

"Hello Herman." They faux embraced and kissed each other on the cheek. "We aren't shopping today, but I'm going to take some of your material with me since it is on such a nice sale. Jane is cutting it while we talk."

"Talk? About what?"

"I just put Clara on the train back to Denison. I know you and she talked about Mama's will, and I would like an update."

"Oh. Well, c'mon back. We'll have a chat."

He looked down in the baby buggy. "Bobby, you are getting so big!" Bobby smiled at him, and he reached down and ruffled the little boy's hair. "Won't be long and you'll be running up and down the aisles like Helen did."

Ida smiled at the bitter-sweet memory of John sweeping Helen up into his arms before she could reach the glass canning jars at Wienke and Doering's grocery. "I don't know. He is a much calmer baby than Helen was."

"Wasn't Helen walking and talking plainly by his age?"

"Walking for sure but talking and reading came a bit later."

Herman led the way to his office and took the seat behind the desk while Ida sat in one of the less comfortable chairs across from him.

She peered over the desk. "You and Clara discussed her discoveries about Mama's estate?"

Herman didn't answer. He seemed to be considering what he should reveal.

Ida broke into his thinking. "She told me about it also."

"Well then." He cleared his throat. "I'm not sure that it changes anything."

"Truly?"

"The money she found under the mattress will become part of the estate. It was about $900.00. So, each of us will get an extra...." He slid a pencil and paper to him and did a quick calculation. "An extra $225 approximately. The surprise account in Mama and Clara's names...what was it?" He pulled out a sheet out of his top drawer. "The $4,582.93 is different. I must check with the lawyer to make sure, but I think it might all go to Clara. If not all of it, then half of it at any rate."

"Half? Why only half?"

"It depends on who opened the account. If the account was opened by Mama and if Clara was listed as her beneficiary, then Clara owns the whole amount. If Mama and Clara opened it together as a household account, then each of them owns half the amount and the other half will be split four ways."

"I see." Ida put on her most thoughtful face.

Herman put down the pencil and raised his eyebrows. "I'm perturbed that she is bringing this up only now. She should have brought this forward last fall when we were discussing this with the lawyer. Keeping things from the judge can have severe consequences."

Ida wanted to argue for her little sister. "Did Clara know you were discussing it with the lawyer?"

He considered and shook his head. "I'm sure it was obvious that I would be talking to the lawyer. I'm the executor."

"I don't remember knowing." Ida looked down and straightened her skirt letting silence fall. Without looking up she said, "Have you considered just letting her have the money since she took care of Mama those years after I left? Her money from the laundry paid the bills."

Herman stared at her for a moment. "No. I didn't. We all helped take care of Mama over those years, especially Emma."

Ida's head snapped up, and she examined Herman's face. He was serious. "All of us? You and I did the bare minimum, don't you think?"

"We were just starting our own families and—"

"And Mama understood that, but we still DID much less than Clara and Emma."

"They were closer. And Clara did nothing from Denison after she left."

It was Ida's turn to shake her head. "I can't believe you. It's all about the money, isn't it?"

Herman looked down at his desk and was silent for a few moments. Then, "She'd have to itemize her expenses over those years."

"You know they lived on Clara's income—"

"And Mr. Stoffel's donations."

"Yes, once Mama and he were married for sure. It was complicated, but I don't think they kept records of who paid what. She wouldn't be able to provide receipts, I'm sure."

Herman shook his head. "Then legally it goes into the estate."

"But the lawyer and the judge don't know anything about it at this point. She didn't have to tell us, you know."

"Yes, she did. The law requires it." Herman's voice was strident and his complexion ruddy.

"If the law knows about it." Ida held her ground. "She could have just put the money into her pocket and said nothing to any of us."

Ida let a minute or two pass to give him time to think.

Herman's face went from red to pink as he ruminated. "So, you think we should just give the money to our baby sister when she has a husband to provide for her?"

"Don't we all…I mean…Clara, Emma, and I. And you seem to be providing well for your family. Pearle has struggled with his health ever since his accident. But even though he isn't in the best of health, he goes out into the country in his Watkins wagon and sells his wares. Clara must work to put food on the table. They are anything but well-to-do."

"She didn't say anything about Pearle. She just rambled on about suffrage. I had to continually bring her back to the issue at hand."

"She was enthusiastic about her trip, wasn't she?" Ida smiled.

Herman harrumphed. "That's what she'll do with the money. Give it to the suffragettes."

Ida thought about that. She would hope not, but maybe.

"I don't want our money going to pay for women on soapboxes." Herman puckered his lips in distaste as if he had just bitten into a persimmon.

A tiny smile turned up the corners of Ida's mouth. "Is Bessie pro-suffrage?"

"I don't know. We don't talk about such things." Herman picked up the pencil and twiddled it between his thumb and forefinger.

The silence stretched between them. Bobby had fallen asleep in his carriage. Ida looked around the room. She didn't blame Bobby. The peaceful décor of the room was soothing.

She gathered herself to stand. "Well, you think about it. I am in favor of letting Clara have all or most of the money. You'll have to ask Emma what she thinks. Generosity breeds generosity, they say." She stood.

Herman stood and came around the desk. He looked at the sleeping boy. "I think he's going to be a football player."

Ida chuckled. "That's what John said, too. I'm not sure how you can tell, but he is tall for his age. He's pulling himself up and will be walking soon. Then we'll see how coordinated he is.

Thanks for the information and for listening. How are the girls and Willie?"

"Everyone's fine. Looking forward to Easter." They began the journey to the front of the store. "You are all coming right?"

"Miss the Doering Easter Egg hunt? Mamie would never forgive me. She's been talking about it since Christmas."

Ida felt at peace as she walked the baby around the square. Many people greeted her and she, them. Herman had seemed less driven than she had seen him in years. The store must be doing well. As she made her way past the courthouse, she looked at John's store and tears welled in her eyes. She had loved being the grocer's wife, and John had not been quite the same since he gave up the business. Maybe when Bobby goes to school, she would have more time, and they could do something like that again. Maybe a bakery with Mama's money if there was any coming her way. Don't count your chickens, she reminded herself.

***

All Things Denison (And Beyond)
By Clara Daring

As my readers know, I have just returned from the Women's Suffrage Procession in Washington, D. C., and I am now here to tell you that it was a rare, once-in-a-lifetime experience. The wonderful feel of the mild mid-Atlantic weather in early March was only exceeded by the pageantry of the parade from start to finish. The women in the horse brigades wore riding styles that included trousers or knickers to allow a full-saddle mount, including Herald Inez Milholland (known as the most beautiful suffragist) who led the procession astride her beautiful white horse, Gray Dawn.

Behind Milholland came at least fifty delegations from all corners of the globe and all walks of life. Women, young and old, colored, and white, in academic gowns and mortarboards, in nursing caps and homemaker's babushkas were truly a remarkable sight indicating women going into every career available. The procession stretched from the Capital to the Supreme Court Building where women put on a patriotic and feminine diorama starring Lady Liberty.

Of course, what made the papers were the spectators, the, for the most part, men on the sidelines who tried their best to intimidate and shame the woman marchers into quitting their trek. Some threw insults while others brazenly came right into the parade formations and assaulted women who chose to be cheeky in return. This reporter was accosted twice during the ten-block march but continued to proudly push forward to the end. But the rude behavior of the spectators was not the story.

The real story is women's struggle for equality and the vote. We must not allow the naysayers and critics to stop progress. I have promised my beautiful and intelligent nieces that before they don the cap and gown of high school graduation that they shall have the vote. So, we must push on as sisters united because 1921, when my first niece will move to adulthood, is only a few years ahead. Now is the time for Iowan women (and men) to take up the cause of suffrage because here we believe in equality and freedom.

Crawford County Courier, March 13, 1913.

SOCIAL SETS

With pulpit and press bitterly denouncing the snuggling, sinuous, rackety American "one-step" dances, there nevertheless, has been fixed for April 3 at the Savoy Hotel, London, an "all ragtime" affair, a program to include all the extravagances of the turkey trot, bunny hug, tango, chicken flip, Texas Tommy, and the crocodile clutch.

Chicago Tribune, March 16, 1913.

***

Reports of Fever Greatly Exaggerated

The reports of forty-one cases of scarlet fever in Algonquin have apparently been greatly exaggerated, as we are informed that later developments showed only four or five actual cases of the disease. It is claimed that

most of the illness was measles. The school was closed
last week. A surprising lack of knowledge of the actual
facts was exhibited by the Elgin papers, which
contained garbled accounts and, with their usual
disregard of the truth, made a mountain out of a
molehill.

Crystal Lake Herald, March 27, 1913.

***

"April Showers bring May flowers," Mamie chanted as she
picked another purple violet from the grass along the concrete
walk at the front of 365 Lincoln Avenue.

"Those won't last in a vase you know." Helen said while not
looking up from the book in her hands. She often chided her
sister for being too sentimental.

"I know, but I will press them in a book, and I'll have them
forever."

Helen shook her head. "Not a great use for a book, I'd say."

"Of course, you would." Mamie smiled. "But I can think of
only one better use…well except possibly for defense."

"What are you going on about?"

"At recess yesterday, Tyler said that the Huns are going to
attack America."

Helen laughed. "The Huns?"

"Yes. So, when we got back to class, I asked teacher if it was
true."

"And what did Miss Nelson say?"

"She said that the best defense against war is a book and
children who can read it."

"What did that mean?"

"I'm not positive, but maybe the book would protect the
holder from a saber."

Helen laughed. "What do you know about sabers?"

"The boys play sabers with sticks all the time at recess." Mamie
jumped to her feet and struck a pose – one arm over her head and

the other holding a pretend sword. "On guard," she said, pointing the non-existent sword at Helen.

"You play with the boys too much. Women don't do sabers."

"They do too. Miss Nelson said so." Mamie sat back down on the walk and began arranging her violets in rows from biggest to littlest.

Helen shook her head at the notion. "I still don't see how a book would save you from a saber or a Hun."

"Well. The Huns will have sabers, right?"

"The Huns are not coming to America."

Mamie looked up from her work. "They might. If we don't stop them in Germany."

Helen looked at her sister for a long moment...eye to eye until her sister blanched.

"Anyway," Mamie went on going back to her flower arranging, "if the Huns do come to America and if they do have sabers then when they go to stab you, you can hold your book up and they will stab the book instead, and it will save your life."

Helen had continued to look at Mamie.

Mamie looked at her laid out flowers. "What is a Hun, anyway?"

Helen shifted her position on the step sitting up straighter looking up to the right to remember. "A Hun is a warrior who lived in Asia and was very mean. They rode horses and would sweep down from the hills," Helen made a large swooping motion with her hands, "and completely destroy a town, people and buildings and animals. Most famous among them was Attila, the Hun." Helen's eyes returned to Mamie.

Mamie was wide-eyed, one violet drooped in her fingertips. "How would they ride their horses to America?"

"They couldn't unless the ocean froze over."

"Like when the Titanic sank?"

"The ocean was only half-frozen then. I don't think it can freeze over completely like a pond."

"Maybe it can, and maybe that's what the Huns are waiting for – winter."

Helen looked skeptical. "I don't think so."

Mamie jumped up and took the 'en-garde' position again. She slashed at her invisible enemy saying, "You dirty Hun. Go back to Germany where you belong."

"Mamie!" It was Ida's stern voice from the front door.

Mamie dropped her pretend saber to the ground. "Mama?"

"I don't want to hear you saying things like that! The Huns were not from Germany."

"But...but...that's what Tyler said at school."

Ida shook her head. "It's not true. The Huns are Orientals."

Helen looked confused, but before she could say anything, Ida said, "It's time to wash-up and set the table."

"Okay, Mama," the girls chorused.

Mamie gathered up her flowers into a wilted bouquet and as they mounted the steps toward their chores, Helen seemed to hold her book protectively against her chest.

***

Personals

Ray Wienke of Woodstock passed the latter part of last week as a guest of McHenry friends.

McHenry Plaindealer, June 5, 1913.

***

John was cutting across the park from the courthouse to the Church Block when he recognized his oldest brother sitting on a bench near the artesian well.

"William, what are you doing here? Taking the waters? Are you not well?"

"Ach, no. Just enjoying a day off and away from the house. How are you and Ida?"

John took the seat next to William. "Good. We are good. The girls are glad it's summer. They are social butterflies these days. They go to more parties than we ever did when we were young."

William looked at John with his mouth hanging open. "Truly your advanced age has led to forgetfulness. We could have gone to a party every night, the way I remember it."

John chuckled. "Not in grade school! Do you remember any parties in grade school?"

William's eyes scanned the square. "A few."

"That's what I'm saying. They each have a party every week and with three of them…. What are you looking for?"

"I was hoping to see Frank coming or going."

"Ah. Don't you see him at home?"

"Not much. He is working long hours at the Factory. My off time and his don't match up very often. Lizzie sees both of us, but…."

"But it's not the same, hearing second hand."

William looked at John with a weak smile. "Yes."

"What do you hear from Ray?"

"He's doing well. Second year at Kent now, don't cha know."

"They grow up fast, don't they? Is he still thinking of taking the bar and coming back here to practice?"

"I think so. I don't get to talk to either of them enough. And when they do have time off, they gather with their friends in McHenry or Hebron. I think Ray has his eye set on a girl from McHenry. He hasn't said so, but he's there all the time, if one can trust the paper."

William again scanned the square but did not see his wayward son. John took out a cigar and offered it to William, who declined.

After the ritual lighting, John asked, "Are you worried about a war?"

William's eyes snapped to John's. "What war is that?"

"I guess I should say, 'the rumors of war' in Europe."

"In Europe? What has that to do with us?"

John puffed and blew a stream of smoke into the sky. "Nothing, I suppose. As long as America can stay out of it. But if we go in—"

"We won't. Wouldn't make any sense. What can we do over here…cheer them on?"

"Maybe we'll end up ferrying troops over there to fight." John knew he was egging his brother on.

"Why? What difference would that make in the whole scheme of European affairs, except get us on the wrong side of the winner. We should stay far away from any fighting. Our sons are not going to die for Kaiser Wilhelm."

"I'm not sure that is the side that America would join. Maybe the British."

"The British? Didn't we fight a war or two with them already? But I can't imagine the *Kohlköpfe* over here fighting the *Kohlköpfe* over there, can you?" William's eyes were no longer scanning for Frank, but rather were shooting daggers at John.

"You're right I suppose 'cabbage heads' would not want to fight their cousins in the Fatherland. But if we join the war, boys like Frank and Ray will be expected to fight on whichever side we join."

"Won't happen." William's clipped words exposed his worry. "The populace won't stand for it."

John was like a terrier unwilling to give the topic up. "Then maybe Mexico."

"No. They are fighting themselves unless it bleeds across the southern border." William was staring at John who nursed his cigar with a slight smile on his face.

William shook his head. "You sure know how to get this old man going."

John smiled. "You are your father's son."

William leaned forward, elbows on knees and looked at the ground. *"Kein Krieg ist ein guter Krieg."* No war is a good war. "I remember Pa saying that many times."

John nodded and drew on his stogie. "I'll have to agree with that." John looked around the square. Business was booming in Woodstock. The sidewalks were busy with people scurrying here and there, from Stafford's Furniture to Murphy and Doering's to

Hoy's Pharmacy, and to all the other shops on the square. The traffic moved counterclockwise around the park about one-half horse-drawn conveyances and one-half automobiles. He watched the jockeying for open road and stopping places. The situation in Europe, whatever it was, was not impacting America in any way that he could see. He hoped it would stay that way.

William clapped his hands on his knees and stood.

John stood also with his hand outstretched, and William shook it warmly. "My best to Ida."

"And to Lizzie."

John puffed his cigar a few times to get it burning smoothly and watched his brother walk away toward Main Street. He could see the toll that the last few years of hard labor had taken on his stature. John envisioned his brother as he had been the year Pa died...was it 27 years ago?

William, muscular and lean, had given up his butcher shop in Rockford and come home to manage their small farm. Once he put the farm in order and under the control of the younger boys, he applied for a town job as trimmer for the new power plant. Ma was so proud of him. Then two years ago, a political disaster knocked him out of the city engineer's position after twenty years of humble service. His present factory job had taken its toll. Slightly hump-backed now and with a slight limp in his right leg, he was surely looking his age. That didn't mean he was about to slow down.

"God bless you, William Wienke," John said under his breath, and turning, stopped for a sip of water at the well using the tin cup that hung there. He crossed Benton Street and made his way south toward the Woodstock Dry Goods Store in the Church Block and an appointment with Mr. W. F. Weaver regarding insuring his premises in case of theft. Weaver already had a policy with John in case of fire, but John hoped to convince him that theft and even political reprisal should also be major concerns. John thought back to when brother Al's Saloon was shot up and the renovation came from Al's pocket because he had little or no insurance. John himself had had no insurance on his grocery. But the world was changing, and disaster seemed always to be on the horizon. It was time to buy insurance against all dangers, and John was ready to sell Weaver a new policy. John smiled as he stubbed out his cigar on the building's wall and placed it in his breast pocket for later.

The bell above sounded as John came through the front door of the business, and a swarthy-complected tall man with slicked-back black hair and a large, hooked nose turned to greet him. Dapperly dressed in a gray wool suit with blue broad-cloth shirt and matching breast pocket handkerchief, it was Mr. Weaver himself.

John wasted no time. "Walt, good to see you." He stretched out his hand and clasped the other man's firmly, continued, "The world is changing, there are rumors that war is on the horizon. It's time you were in the capable hands of Prudential."

***

DOERINGS RETURN
FROM GERMAN TRIP

Oscar Doering, proprietor of the Doering hotel in Doering, Wis., and his wife have returned to the city after a trip of nearly three months in Germany with the Milwaukee Singers' German Traveling association. Two hundred and seven delegates of the association from Milwaukee and other cities in Wisconsin, left Milwaukee on April 29. During the time spent in the old country the society sang in most of the principal cities, including Berlin. They had intended to give a performance before Kaiser Wilhelm but found that he was not at the capital while they were there.

La Crosse Tribune, August 22, 1913.

***

Personals

Mr. and Mrs. Frank Wienke and Clayton of Woodstock were guests of relatives in Crystal Lake over the weekend.

Crystal Lake Herald, August 28, 1913.

***

PERSONAL MENTION

Isaac Cissna spent the later part of the last week with his brother, Will Cissna of Wayne City, Ill.

Boonville Enquirer, September 5, 1913.

***

A FAMILY REUNION

On Sunday, Aug. 31, the family of Rev. W. C. Cissna, pastor of the M. E. church at Wayne City, Ill., held a reunion at the parsonage. The children were all present after a separation of a number of years. Thos present were Rev. W. E. Cissna, pastor of Simpson M. E. Church, Chicago; Elmer Cissna, Boonville, Ind; C. E. Cissna, traveling salesman Richardson Lubricating Co., Quincy; Mr. and Mrs. Herbert Massie and son, Everett, of Evansville, Ind.; Mrs. Joe Brown and daughter Lucile, and son, Gaspard, of Dale, Ind. And an only brother Isaac G. Cissna of Boonville, Ind. These and the two children at home, Roy and Lillian, together with several friends spent the day enjoying many good things to eat, singing the old-time songs and social concourse. At night Rev. W. E. Cissna preached to a large audience at the church. His subject was, "A Clean Life." It was a forceful message portraying the value of a clean, pure life and its necessity to accomplish the best service for God.

Boonville Standard, September 12, 1913.

***

All Things Denison
By Clara Daring

Are you ready to celebrate!!? The Lincoln Highway celebration is only a few months away. Patriotic citizens from each of the first thirteen states of the union will be driving their automobiles the length of the Lincoln Highway to celebrate its completion, and they will be passing through Denison in just three weeks on Friday evening, October 31st. The group will start in New York and going the whole length of this magnificent road, they will end up in California creating a strong new bond between east and west in our fine country.

Programs are to be arranged in every city, village, hamlet, and crossroads, either on or adjacent to the route. Denison has been asked to mark the route with stars and stripes, bunting other patriotic decorations. Also, the official flag of the Lincoln Highway association is to be prominently displayed somewhere in the village.

Thus far there are plans for a parade lead by a good old-fashioned torchlight procession meeting the caravan at the city limits and leading it downtown where the main street will be alive with people. There will be a civic barbeque of Iowa beef steaks, a band concert and speeches about the great Abraham Lincoln and the Lincoln highway.

This highway will be open to everyone and every kind of vehicle, from farm equipment to sporty cars. The Good Highway association promises that it will be 'open at all seasons of the year, smooth, dustless, operated without toll charges. The Lincoln Highway will be a level, long-lasting roadway, enabling drivers to touch the scenic grandeur of our country.'

School children will assist in our fair city as well as other towns and villages accommodating the highway by planting trees along its length next spring on Arbor Day, 1914.

Denison should prepare for the influx of tourists coming our way due to this beautiful road. Make plans today to attend the October 31st program.

If you are interested in supporting this grand cause, either through the purse or the person, please contact the *Denison*

Review or the *Crawford County Courier* for information. I'll see you there!

Crawford County Courier, September 24, 1913.

***

A Dinner at Isaac Cissnas

Those that spent Sunday, October 12, with Isaac Cissna and family and enjoyed a delicious dinner were: Rev. and Mrs. W. C. Cissna and son, Roy, of Wayne City, Ill., Mary Massie and sons, William Lutz and William Agbert of Evanston; Joe Brown and family of Dale, General York and wife, Elmer Cissna and family, Will Skelton and family, Mary Brooner, John Foster and wife, Sally Gray, John Baker and wife, Robert Rogers and wife, Joe Davis, Samuel Gasaway and family, Florence Miller and Luia Skelton, of Boonville. All had a good time. Isaac Cissna had a stroke of paralysis recently but is recovering nicely.

Boonville Standard, October 17, 1913.

***

"Whoa!" Pearle pulled back on the reins and the white mare, Peaches, came to a halt along the side of the street. "We can watch the rest of the parade from here."

"Great! I'll take notes. Maybe this would be a good column. I'm glad we got the third spot to show off the wagon."

Pearle and Clara sat on the front seat of the Watkins wagon watching the many types of vehicles roll by on the Lincoln Highway or what they called Main Street in Denison.

Clara had that morning received a letter from the executor of her mother's will...her brother Herman. The letter was full of surprises. The court had decided that one-half of the money in the secret account was Clara's plus one-fourth of the other half. In addition, Emma, Ida, and Herman had decided not to mention to the court the money Clara had found in the house after her mother's death. They did this to pay Clara for the several years that she was breadwinner of the household. What the court didn't know, didn't matter. Clara had reread the letter with her mouth hanging open in shock tears in her eyes.

Now, Pearle asked, "How much are we talking about?"

"A little over three thousand dollars."

"Three thousand dollars?" Pearle's face gave away his shock.

"See." Clara cuddled up to his side. "I told you to stick with me."

Pearle laughed and put his arm around her shoulders. "You were right."

"What shall we do with it?" Clara cooed.

"That's for you to decide. I'm just along for the ride."

"I was thinking that maybe we could go to Akron for Christmas."

Clara felt Pearle's body stiffen at the suggestion. "Don't you think it's about time I met your family?"

His tension eased a bit. A large steel-wheeled combine rattled by leaving wide wheel tracks in the roadway as it ground along. He looked down on Clara. Their eyes met.

"Christmas, eh?" He smiled. "They would like that."

The parade continued. Everyone was taking their first ride or stroll on the new highway that led all the way back to Ohio.

***

LOCAL & GENERAL NEWS

Rev. William Everett Cissna of Chicago has received a merited promotion and is rapidly going up the ladder—Hurrah for Brother Cissna; his many friends in Warrick county, will rejoice at his success. We copy the following from the official bulletin of The Young Men's Christian association of Chicago. William Everett Cissna, the new Secretary of General Religious

Activities at Central Department, was born near Heilman, Ind., taught in public schools for five years. He is a graduate of Normal School, Moor's Hill College, and College of Liberal Arts with a degree of B. L., 1910; graduated from Garrett Biblical Institute with degree of B. D. in 1913. For the past three years Mr. Cissna has held student pastorates in Dalton, Ill., and at Simpson M. E. Church, Chicago. He was identified with the Student Association during his college life and for two years was directly connected with C. & E. I. Railroad Department at Dalton.

Boonville Enquirer, November 7, 1913.

***

Suffragist Hits Ignorant Vote

Madison, Wis., Nov. 20.—"We have been defeated, voted down by the ignorant, vicious, drunken, or foreign elements in the community," the Rev. Olympia Brown of Racine declared yesterday, speaking of the twenty-two times the subject of woman suffrage has been submitted and defeated in various states at the opening of the state suffrage convention here.

Before the convention adjourns strong resolutions will be demanded that at the next election every party platform include a plank pledging the enactment of a woman's suffrage law.

Moline Dispatch, November 20, 1913.

***

Of course, Clara and Pearle didn't take the Watkin's wagon on the Lincoln Highway to Akron. That would have been too long and too dangerous in the winter. They had heard many stories of robberies when autos didn't arrive at safe havens before dark. And then there was the unpredictable weather. Clara and Pearle took the train.

They splurged for a compartment with a berth. And rode in total comfort overnight to Chicago where they took in the sights for two days before going on to Akron. They decided they would stop in Woodstock for a layover on the way back.

The Akron Union Rail station was located next to the tracks in an industrial part of Akron. It was a square brick building with a red slate roof which looked festive against the fresh snow. A long concrete ramp allowed horses and buggies and other vehicles to rise from the station to the street level. Clara had never seen such a set up and wondered about the slipperiness of the ramp in winter. She was about to comment on it to Pearle when a loud voice declared, "Look what the dogs dragged in! Can you believe it, sister?"

"I truly cannot, brother! I never thought I'd see the day!"

Clara turned toward the voices, and Pearle dropped the valise he was holding and rushed forward, all of them laughing their joy at seeing one another.

Pearle hugged the woman and held her at arm's length. "Oh, Sadie, don't you look fine, almost like a refined woman." The woman faux-slapped his shoulder, but also blushed.

"Will." Pearle held out his hand, but the man pulled him into an embrace.

"Good to see you, my man!" They assessed each other top to bottom.

Clara slowly approached the threesome until Pearle noticed her there.

"Oh my." He took Clara's elbow and pulled her to his side. "Will, Sadie, this is my wife, Clara. Clara, this is my sister Sadie...er...Sarah..." Clara put out her hand which Sadie grasped warmly. "And my brother William." Again, Clara and William exchanged handshakes rather than bows and curtsies.

Will leaned in sotto voce, "Well done, little brother!"

Clara blushed slightly. "It's good to meet both of you."

Sadie snaked her hand through Clara's arm, turning them toward the exit. "You better wait a while before exclaiming how good it is to meet us. There are more of us to come."

The men laughed, Will more spontaneously than Pearle, Clara noted. A fleeting worried look passed over Pearle's continence, but it was quickly replaced by a jolly good fellow.

The ride from the station to the house was chilly – no worse than the cold of the train, but on the train, they had huddled together in the berth under a blanket staying warm. In the carriage there were no foot warmers or blankets, and Clara was glad when she felt Will pull the horse to a walk after forty-five minutes of trotting.

The horse pulled up in front of a Victorian house painted light green with a dark green roof and shutters. In the late afternoon twilight of December, the yellow light streaming from the windows looked welcoming or at least warm. They disembarked with Sadie again taking Clara's arm while the men managed the luggage. An elderly Black man came out wrapping a scarf around his neck. Will handed the horse and carriage over to him with only a "Thank you, Jim." Jim inclined his head and climbed to the driver's seat.

At the door, Sadie paused. A look passed between her and the men. She took a deep breath and opened the door. "We're back," she called lightly.

A gray-haired woman came bustling from the kitchen laughing and saying, "Pearle! Oh, Pearle!" She threw her arms around his neck, and he had no choice but to drop the cases and hug her back. The hug continued for quite a spell while the others looked on smiling. They parted, and the woman pulled a handkerchief from her bosom and blotted her eyes. She turned toward Clara.

Pearle took a step toward Clara and put his arm lightly around her waist. "Mama, I want you to meet my wife. Clara." Turning to Clara, he continued, "Clara, this is my mother, Delila Dye."

Both women curtsied and said almost in unison, "Very nice to meet you." Clara tried to make hers just a little deeper bend than the old woman.

Delila's face held a genuine smile of delight. "I trust your train trip was pleasant."

Pearle answered, "It was fine. Such improvements they have made in comfort. We even had a bed to sleep in."

His mother blushed slightly, and she looked at the floor while Sadie and Will stifled a giggle. Pearle wished he had reconsidered his example of comfort.

"Well, how nice," Delila said, regaining her composure. "Will, you see to the luggage. Sadie, will you change for dinner?"

"No, Mama."

"You go oversee the kitchen then."

"Yes, Mama."

Delila eyes landed on Pearle as she brushed the others away with shooing gestures.

"Your father is waiting for you in the study. He's asked to see you alone."

"Mama...I—"

"No, you need to go deal with this."

"I will show Clara to your room where she can freshen up after your long trip."

Delila put her hand to Clara's elbow and smiled. "Come along, my dear. It's just up the stairs to the right."

Clara cast a fleeting glance at Pearle, who looked so forlorn and abandoned she could not bear to leave him. She tried to pull away to return to his side, but her mother-in-law was relentless in her grasp, and they climbed the stairs.

Pearle took a deep breath and blew it out. He had done all he could to avoid this day. As much as he felt joy at seeing his mother, brother, and sister, at this moment he was sorry he had agreed to come.

"Pearle!" A harsh, baritone voice emanated from the adjacent room. "Come here!"

Pearle looked at the floor. He was going to have to comply or walk out leaving Clara upstairs. Nicely played, mother dear.

Pearle set his bowler on the peg by the door and removed his coat, hanging it beside the bowler. He rubbed his hands together so they wouldn't be icy for the handshake and took small steps toward the parlor door.

"Come here, I say!" Pearle could hear his father's cane stumping on the floor for emphasis. John Ely Dye had served in the Civil War, and according to his wife, had come back changed. He was only eighteen when he enlisted and by the end of the war, he was a respected Sergeant in charge of a brigade of men most of whom died. He had survived, but his leg had not, and his good nature had turned surly. He ruled over his wife and children with an iron fist that often found its mark.

"I know you are there, come in here this instant!" The impairment of age had not sweetened his disposition.

Pearle pushed open the cracked door and stepped into the room. "Hello, Father," he said, trying to sound calm and strong.

John Ely burst into laughter.

Pearle looked down at the floor feeling weak and angry.

"Came back with your tail between your legs then? You look like a dandy in that suit. What is it, pink?"

Pearle looked down at his suit. It was a wool vested suit in brown as much as he could tell. "I think it's brown, isn't it?"

"Looks pansy purple to me." The old man again laughed as if he had made a funny joke for all to enjoy. He had an uncombed, uncontrolled shock of white hair which stuck out at all angles from his rather large head. He sat in a wheeled chair designed for him and his girth. In his hand was his cane which he used to gesture, to threaten, to point, and to emphasize.

John Ely was suddenly serious. "Why are you here?" The cane bounced off the floor with each word.

"I came back to introduce you to my wife."

"Your wife? You have a wife?" The white head again fell back, but his disdainful laugh turned into a coughing spell, wracking his body and lungs in great heaving barks followed by wheezes that challenged the sound of the north wind.

Pearle crossed to the side table and poured two shots of Kentucky whiskey into a cut glass highball glass. He returned to the old man's side and handed it to him.

John Ely nodded. Was that 'thanks'?

When the cough had subsided, Pearle said, "Yes, Father, my wife."

"What business do you have taking a wife?"

"Father, I—"

"You had a wife and son right here in Akron. Do you think you can perform better this time than the last?"

"No, I don't…I—"

"You know we still see her and your son. Have you told 'your wife' about the boy?"

Pearle sank into a chair as if cut off at the knees.

"Father, the boy is not—"

"Oh, for God's sake, don't you dare pretend you didn't know."

"Didn't know what?"

"That you have a son."

"I don't have a son."

Then who is that boy who comes around?"

"Father, won't you listen to the truth?"

"THE TRUTH?" John Ely thundered. "I KNOW THE TRUTH!"

"No, you don't. If you'd just—"

"Here's the TRUTH. You ran away from your responsibility and now you come crawling back with 'a wife.' I'm ashamed to have ever sired you."

Pearle looked at the clenched hands in his lap. He wanted to get up and walk out and never look back, just as he had done to avoid his father's raving five years ago. "I see you have not changed your mind about me. You have no idea what was going on. Winnie was—"

"Pregnant. I know that. And you walked away from that fine young lass. How dare you show your face in this house again after shirking your responsibility."

"I did not shirk anything. I—"

"Well, what would you call it? Going off for adventure? I call it running away. I call it leaving your woman and son to starve."

"I am not married to Winnie and the boy is not mine."

"Really?"

"Have you asked her? What does Winnie say?"

"She doesn't say anything. She brings the boy to see us. You know, she has another child."

"I know."

"And HOW do you know that?"

"Friends."

John Ely began laughing, squeezing out, "Friends?" before the coughing overtook him again. He reached out for the whiskey glass but couldn't find it with his hand. Pearle rose and on shaky legs crossed to him and put the glass in his father's hand. As the spasms subsided, John Ely wheezed, "You still have friends here?"

A knock at the door and a quarter opening. A male voice said, "Dinner is served. I'm to wheel you to the table, Mister John."

Between Pearle and the caretaker, Tom, they were able to move the wheeled chair from the parlor, down the hall, to the dining room without mishap.

As they came in through one door, Clara passed through the kitchen door with a bottle of wine which she handed to Will. She smiled at Pearle, hoping he had weathered the meeting with his father. He was pale as the white woodwork which adorned the dining room.

Clara set down the bottle and came to him, taking his arm. "Are you alright?" she whispered.

Pearl gave a curt nod and a weak smile and patted her hand.

After John Ely was settled at one end of the table, Pearle took Clara's hand and led her forward. "Clara, I would like you to meet my father, John Ely Dye. Father, this is my wife, Clara Doering Dye."

Clara curtsied low and said, "How do you do, Father Dye."

John Ely looked her up and down and snorted. "Too much woman for this man, I'd say."

"Father!" several voices chorused.

"John Ely!" Delila spoke his name as if a mother were disciplining a child. "You will be civil in my dining room!"

John Ely looked at Clara who stood with eyes downcast and back at his wife. Without breaking eye contact with Delila, he said, "I do apologize, Miss Clara. I am glad to meet you."

Clara looked up and smiled, but she found that she had lost his attention.

Pearle moved her to a place along the far side of the table. Tradition would have put her next to his father as his sister sat across the table, but Pearle seated her next to his mother across from his brother and he took the seat next to his father. John Ely scowled at the arrangement, but before he could voice his objection, Delila said, "John Ely, will you ask the blessing on this food and thank the Lord for bringing Pearle and Clara home safely."

Everyone bowed their heads. John Ely cleared his throat—a pregnant pause—then with disdain in his voice, he muttered, "As the wife said, Lord. Amen."

Near the end of the meal, Delila announced, "It's Christmas Eve. We will be going to the watch service."

Pearle blanched slightly. "Oh Mother, we are so tired from our trip. I don't believe we'll be attending."

"What? But you must! I've told all your friends that you are coming. And all my friends. What will I say? You must come. Clara, my dear, are you a church going lady?"

"Why yes, Mother Dye. I'm Lutheran."

"Well, there, you see, Pearle, your wife wants to attend. We leave at 10:15. It isn't far, but dress warmly. The air is brisk tonight."

***

John pulled his sheepskin coat's collar up against the brisk north wind. He was leaning on his snow shovel watching the wind sweep the tiny crystalline cloud along the cleared walk-in front of 365 Lincoln Avenue.

Looking at the action of the snow in the wind, John decided that the walk would be drifted over by the time he walked to the stable to stow the shovel. Well, he'd done the best he could. Nature was, once again, totally in control. He'd have to do the front walk again after church.

The lights danced in the window of the house as Ida and the girls prepared an early supper. Santa would be coming while they were at Christmas Eve services, and the Wienke household tradition was to open presents tonight before bed. The wind gusted, and John shivered. Time to sup.

John went to the back porch, stomped his feet free from snow, and hung his coat and hat in the cold but dry atmosphere the enclosed porch provided. As he came in through the back door, the swirl of smells made his mouth water. Anticipation crackled in the air and soup bubbled on the stove. The kitchen table was set with soup bowls, and Ida was cutting a loaf of white bread for dipping. John made his way around the table and into the dining room. Garland and decorations covered the tabletop. Strings of popcorn and colorful paper loops fell in haphazard piles. Bobby was pulling one of the popcorn strings down and eating the popcorn along the line. John scooped up the almost two-year-old and took the string out of his mouth.

"We won't tell anyone," John whispered in his ear. John held him at arm's length toward the ceiling and let him drop...catching him at shoulder height.

Bobby squealed. "A-gin!"

John repeated the stunt two more times with the same result each time. "A-gin!"

"Oh, I think that's enough. Your old Papa's arms are tired from shoveling snow, and I might drop you."

"A-gin!"

Instead, John let the boy slide toward the floor, grabbing his hands just before his feet touched.

"A-gin!"

John grabbed his feet and turned him upside down, holding him out in front of him.

Bobby laughed and flailed. John returned him to a standing position, the popcorn forgotten. Bobby pointed at the tree shining with the light of forty bulbs. Helen and Edna circled the tree with the brightly colored garland. Mamie was gently hanging ornaments, many handmade, saved from year to year in the attic off of Edna's room.

John clapped his hands appreciatively and called out "Bravo, ladies! Bravo!" Bobby clapped his hands, too.

John and Bobby joined in to help Mamie with the ornaments. John showed Bobby how to put on the ornaments so they wouldn't fall off and break. But Bobby was more interested in taking the ornaments off than putting them on.

The last ornament was always the star, and for the last few years, John had held Edna up to place it. This year, he gave the star to Bobby.

"Mama!" called out Helen. "The star is going up."

Ida bustled from the kitchen wiping her hands on her apron just as John lifted his son to the top of the tree, the star clasped tightly in Bobby's right fist.

"Put it on, Bobby." Edna was a bit impatient because she could have done it easily, and now, they had to wait for the baby to figure it out. "Just slide it right on the top."

Ida smiled at the sight of her family gathered around the tree, their faces reflecting the light it gave off. Bobby put the star on sideways, and it looked like it was going to slide off. "Edna, climb up on that stepstool and show him how to do it," Ida said.

Edna beamed. She climbed two steps up and on tiptoe took the star and set it upright on the top spire of the tree. "See Bobby, then it won't fall off. Isn't that pretty?"

"Pity," said Bobby. "Gimme. Mine." And he plucked the star off and clutched it to his chest.

Edna reached over and tried to take the star, but he wouldn't let go. She pulled harder, and it slipped out of his hands. Edna windmilled a few times until Helen reached up and righted her on the stepstool. Bobby started to whimper.

Helen, always pragmatic, said "Papa, take him down. He's too little. Maybe next year. Edna, you put it up."

Edna smiled again and decisively placed the star on the tree. Bobby sniffled a little and pointed up, "My 'tar."

John hugged his son. "Ja, da purdiest 'tar in Woodstock."

Ida shook her head. "He's going to learn to talk that way, you know."

"I know." John kissed her cheek.

A little smile played across her lips. "Come on then. Soup's on."

***

In the upstairs bedroom, Pearle paced. The room was somewhat smaller than he remembered it – only three strides across. "I don't want to go to church."

Clara sat on the edge of the bed, smoothing warm woolen leggings up her legs and attaching them to her garter belt. "Is religion why you left?"

"Yes…er, no. Not completely."

"Well, I think for at least tonight, we must go. I packed your high collar and black suit in the trunk. We can discuss your religiosity at another time."

She rose and caught him up as he walked past. "Besides," she said with her arms around his neck and her lips near his, "You are going to look so handsome in a proper suit." She kissed him long and hard, and his hands began to stray down her back to her back side.

She pushed him away, "We don't have time for that now, but maybe, if you can stay awake, when we get back."

"I have to wait until Christmas Day?"

"Of course. We must be pure of heart to go to church," she teased. "Plus, it will give us something to look forward to."

"Okay. I'll go...for you. I will be proud to have you on my arm."

Clara kissed him again and pulled up her petticoat and fastened it. Curiouser and curiouser, as Alice might say.

Twenty minutes later, they came down the stairs together and looked stunning if Clara said so herself. She had chosen the deep burgundy brocade dress that hit her just at the ankle. Its high collar and black piping and embellishment was in the Victorian style. She would not usually dress like this for church to avoid seeming prideful. But tonight, she was meeting the rest of the family and Pearle's friends. In addition, the dress was warm on this frosty night.

Delila clasped her hands over her heart. "Oh. What a fine couple you make. What a beautiful dress."

"Thank you." Clara dropped her head and eyes in acknowledgment of the compliment.

"Clara's family comes from a long line of dressmakers and tailors," Pearle bragged.

Delila gasped. "You made this dress?"

"Yes ma'am. Every stitch." Clara blushed with pleasure.

They walked toward the front door where their wraps hung.

His mother caught Pearle's arm part way across the foyer. "Why are you limping? Are you all right? Did something happen on the train on the way out?"

Clara looked at Pearle: "You never wrote to her about your fall?" Pearle looked a bit panicky.

Delila demurred, "Well, we haven't time right now. Jim brought the carriage around. Can we all fit in? Father has declined to come."

"Sadie and I will hang on the back as footmen." Will doffed his cap and made a low bow.

Sadie giggled. "I'll be a lady-in-waiting. You may be the footman."

Delila agreed. "And the lady-in-waiting rides inside the carriage not hanging off its back end."

Will held the door, "Milady."

As they walked up the aisle to what seemed to be the Dye's usual pew, Clara could hear the whispers. The prelude had already begun so there was no time to greet people or exchange introductions before the service.

The service had all the normal rituals Clara expected: the songs, the children, the tree, the nativity scene acted out as the congregation sang Silent Night. At the end, the minister came to the middle of the chancel. He raised his hand, the white robe falling back to reveal a black cuff. "The Lord bless and keep you. The Lord make his face shine upon you and be gracious unto you. The Lord lift up his continence and give you peace. In the name of the Father, the Son, and the Holy Ghost. Amen."

The deacon stepped forward. "In peace and love, go and serve the Lord...."

The congregation responded, "Thanks be to God."

At the sound of the first notes of the Postlude, before Pearle and Clara could rise, people from every side rushed in. Clara looked at Pearle with more than a bit of concern. He took her hand, and they rose to meet their fans.

"Well, look who has graced us...who is this beautiful...when did you get in...." Too many voices to answer them at once. The men clapped Pearle on the shoulder and back and the girls threw their arms around him in warm embraces. Clara stood back letting the chaos happen around her.

She noted that Pearle's family had removed themselves a few pews away to make room for the well-wishers. A huge smile lit Delila's face. Clara examined her in-laws, which now included Pearle's brother Corty, sister Bertha, and brother Andy. There had been hurried introductions before they entered the church. From the expressions of pleasure, the whole family, sans John Ely, was enjoying this homecoming. The crowd suddenly quieted, and she looked back to Pearle.

His flushed face had gone pale, his smile vanishing. Clara looked around to see what had happened. Approaching the group was a tall, thin woman with chestnut hair pulled back from her face, but left long in back, like a schoolgirl. She wore a flowing white dress that rippled as she walked. Clara recognized her as the choir director for the program. As she came closer, as if in slow motion, Clara could see her large green eyes, petite nose, and bright red lips.

The company parted, making a path directly to Pearle.

"Pearle," she purred.

"Winnie," said Pearle.

She stretched forward and hugged him, but he did not bring his hands or arms around to hug her. The crowd pulled back giving them a modicum of space but no privacy. Clara held her place at his side.

The handsome minister, now in a black suit and clerical collar with his thick blond hair and deep blue eyes, appeared and reached out a hand toward her husband.

"Pearle. Looks like your homecoming is outshining the coming of our Savior."

"Reverend." They shook hands.

Winnie had a hand on his sleeve. "You and your family are coming to the reception at the rectory, aren't you?"

"Of course, they are. Right, Delila?" The minister's eyes locked on Mother Dye.

Delila blushed. "Oh Reverend, we wouldn't miss it for the world."

"I'm afraid that my wife and I are much too tired from traveling to join you." Pearle turned and drew Clara up beside him.

Delila flapped her hand at him. "Nonsense! You've come this far for Christmas, you must come and let your friends fill you in on their adventures while you were away. And allow them to get to know Clara."

Voices from the crowd encouraged a positive response.

Pearle looked at Clara. She shrugged and whispered, "It's up to you."

Pearle, still looking at Clara, said "Okay. For a little while."

A cheer went up, and the gathering dispersed.

The minister put his arm around Winnie: "Well, my dear, we need to beat the hordes home." She smiled up at him, and they, too, left.

Pearle slouched. Clara was not aware how stiffly he had been holding his body, but it was as if the air had just flowed out of him. He sat down in a pew and retrieved his handkerchief to mop his forehead. His face was an odd shade of gray.

She sat down next to him with her hand on his shoulder. "Are you alright?"

Before he could answer, a voice rang out from the Narthex, "Pearle, Clara. Your carriage awaits."

They stood and made their way down the long aisle.

"Dearest. We don't have to go. We can drop off your mother, brother, and sister and have Jim take us home. It's not that far. Jim can come back to fetch them later." Clara clutched his waist under his jacket, giving, she hoped, some physical support.

"I'll be all right. This was why I didn't want to come to see them together like that." Pearle's right arm was around Clara's shoulders. She could feel the tremor in his right hand and his limp seemed accentuated.

"What do you mean?"

They had reached the carriage, and the 'footman' held out his hand for Clara to ascend. Pearle smiled and squeezed his brother's upper arm as he climbed aboard.

His mother began even before they had settled into the seats. "Pearle, isn't Winnie still so beautiful? We were so pleased when Pastor and she married. They make such an inspiring couple for our congregation."

"Mama!" Sadie's tone was one of warning. Delila pursed her lips and looked out at the snowy night.

Pearle said nothing.

As the silence stretched, Clara reached over and took his hand.

It was a short ride to the rectory. As the horses pulled up, the 'footman' ran around to place a box so that they could dismount. Delila descended first followed by Sadie.

Clara leaned toward the door opening. "Mother Dye, I think Pearle is much too tired to be social tonight. If we may borrow Jim to drive us home, we will see you in the morning. There will be other times, I hope, for meeting everyone."

Pearle squeezed her hand.

"Well, of course, my dear." Delila peered in at Pearle. "He does look exhausted, and socializing has always been a bit of a strain to him. Will, you take them home and then return to fetch us. Come, Sadie."

Clara smiled, attempting to make it genuine. "Thank you for understanding."

They rode home cuddled in the back seat with a wool blanket over their legs. When they reached the residence, the gracious 'footman,' who had ridden inside the coach on this leg of the journey, offered Clara his hand to descend. Clara turned on the cobbled street, and both she and Will steadied Pearle as he stepped down.

"Shall I assist you up to the bedroom?" Will seemed concerned.

With a quick headshake, Pearle indicated he didn't need help, and Will bounded back to the carriage and was off to the awaiting party.

Slowly Clara and Pearle climbed to their second story room and removed their togs. After visiting the water closet, they fell into bed and slept the sleep of the dead until morning. Clara woke first and heard the pots in the kitchen. She rose and slipped her feet into felt bed shoes, put on a dressing gown, and stole out of the room.

Time for a little investigating. She would discover the secrets or...or what? Dye trying? She giggled. Maybe an exchange of information. I'll tell mine if you tell yours. That could work. It had before.

***

DEPENDENTS FIND
YULETIDE CHEER
Catholic Orders Give Christmas Trees for Young and Old in Institutions.
FETE AT HULL HOUSE

The spirit of Christmas hovered in many parts of the city yesterday. No one class had a monopoly of its presence. From nursery children to the aged in old people's homes there were presents and trees to bring down the Christmas cheer.

There was an entertainment for the children of St. Mary's Training school at Feehanville in the form of a minstrel show, in which members of Daniel Dowing and Commodore Barry councils of the Knights of Columbus took part. A Christmas tree party for children was also given at the clubhouse of the Calumet council, Knights of Columbus.

There was a German tree in the coffee room at Hull House for fifteen nationalities of children, and there was a tree in the nursery of St. Mary's settlement at 656 West Forty-fourth street. Two hundred old men and women in the Little Sisters of the Poor home at Fullerton and Sheffield avenues had an eventful day.

The tree that stood in all its twelve feet of whiteness in the coffee room at Hull house was said to be ideal in the way it brought out the Christmas spirit. For fifteen years, Miss Amelie Hannig supervised the erection of the Hull house tree.

Chicago Tribune, December 24, 1913.

Tree on Church Lawn

An ecclesiastical rival to Chicago's big municipal Christmas tree delighted the public gaze yesterday on the lawn in front of the Immanuel Baptist church. It was illuminated last evening.

While an electrician was arranging the bulbs, he was espied by a passerby who thought him a thief. A policeman was unearthed and, pistol in hand, commanded the workman to descend. Explanations followed.

Chicago Tribune, December 24, 1913.

***

SANTA TO USE AN AEROPLANE.
Corning, N.Y., Hires Pilot to Fly Low Over City and Drop Presents to Boys and Girls

Corning, N. Y., Dec. 21 – Santa Clause will come to Corning by aeroplane tomorrow. The Corning Business Men's association has hired an aviator from Bath to fly to Corning dressed as Santa and distribute gifts to children of the city from his aeroplane as he flies low over the streets.

Chicago Tribune, December 24, 1913.

***

Clara came into the kitchen where a slight, colored woman had coffee boiling on the stove and was preparing to fry bacon and eggs for breakfast. The woman startled at the intruder, but then regained her poise and mumbled "G'd mornin'." And went back to the preparations.

"Good morning. I'm Clara!" She shot out her hand to the woman, who didn't take it, but rather she did a little curtsy and said, "Jane…da cook."

"It's nice to meet you, Jane. That coffee smells wonderful."

Jane looked over at the tiny glass knob on the top of the percolator. "Ain't done yet. Needs five more minutes."

"I'll wait."

Jane looked anxious, but then said, "Sit dare at da table whilst you wait. I'll get on wid da eggs."

"Deal!" Clara pulled out one of the wooden chairs and sat down at the kitchen table. She looked around the large room. Along one side were windows that gave a view of the backyard, more like a field. It was hard to tell how deep the snow was as the yard fell away from the house. Not one boot mark flawed the perfect surface. She brought her eyes back inside. Herbs hung from a line in front of the windows, high enough so men's heads wouldn't be in danger of an herbal shower. Clara recognized Thyme and Rosemary and Parsley.

The room was square with good cupboards and a wooden countertop that had the plentiful scars of past meals. Clara smiled, very clever - no need to protect it from sharp knives. Off-white paint covered the walls and other vertical wooden surfaces, doors, woodwork, cabinets, but the doors of the cabinets had glass inserts so one could see the products within. Very clever, indeed.

"Good morning, Clara. How did you sleep?" The voice of Delila brought Clara to her feet.

"Good morning, Mother Dye. I slept very, very well. I don't think either of us moved a fraction of an inch after we hit the sheets. May I help in any way with breakfast? I'm afraid it will be lunch for Pearle. I haven't seen him that tired since the acc—" She cut herself off. "How did you sleep?"

"Not bad, but too short. But then, I'm a morning person. I shall take a rest this afternoon. No need to help Jane, she often cooks for large groups. Did you say accident? What accident?"

They moved into the dining room and sat in the plush, padded chairs. "I should let Pearle tell it."

"I doubt he will." Delila rose and began rearranging the sideboard in preparation for the arrival of food. She found serving utensils in a drawer and closed it with some force. "He would never admit weakness, even as a child. Never a tear. Never an admission of pain."

"That's the Pearle I know and love. I know the signs, however, and won't let him get away with it."

"So, what accident? We know nothing about an accident. You should have written to us about it."

Clara felt her cheeks burn and stammered, "I didn't know you – I didn't – I didn't have your address. I knew Pearle was from Akron, but other than that, he never talked about his family."

Delila sank into a chair. Her hand came up to cradle her forehead.

Clara went to her, lightly touching her shoulder. "Are you alright?"

Delila waved her away, "Yes, yes. I just didn't know he hated us so."

"Mother Dye, he doesn't hate you." Clara shook her head and returned to her seat just as Jane emerged with two steaming cups of coffee, cream, and sugar on a tray. She placed the cups in front of each of them and the small pitcher and bowl between them on the table and disappeared back through the swinging door to the kitchen.

Delila took a spoonful of sugar, put it in her coffee and stirred vigorously. Then laying her spoon back on the tray, she breathed deeply.

Clara followed suit but added only cream to the cup and stirred it well.

Delila took a small sip and smiled weakly at Clara. "Thank you for bringing him home to us. I know it was your doing. After he left, for quite a spell, we didn't know where he'd gone. Then he wrote from Wisconsin that he'd met you and that you were to be married. I can't tell you how much it eased my mind to know that he had found someone. Especially after what had happened here."

They sat across the table from each other, these two women who loved Pearle. Delila's eyes, deep brown in weak winter light, filled with sadness and something else. Guilt perhaps.

Clara sipped her coffee. Good, strong, and hot. "What did happen?"

"I'm sure Pearle has told you all about it. He broke our hearts." Delila said, her gaze fixed outside at the snow piles.

Clara nodded, keeping her eyes on her mother-in-law's face.

"First it was Pearle and Winnie. It was always Pearle and Winnie from fifth grade on. That's where they met when Winnie moved from the country school out at Twin Corners to the school here in Akron. Pearle came home after meeting her walking on clouds, and he was that way from then on. They did everything together, walked to school, went to events, sat on the porch swing for hours. I don't believe she was ever more than a thought away on into high school. They made each other promises, and everyone, including the two of them, assumed that they would marry the day after graduation. And at Christmas during their senior year, Pearle and Winnie announced they were engaged."

Delila paused for a sip of coffee, and Clara nodded her encouragement. The whole idea of their engagement was distasteful, but she had to know what happened.

"That spring when our old priest died, the synod found a seminarian to come and fill the pulpit, and we loved him and called him after his graduation. He's so smart and those beautiful blue eyes shining from the pulpit could convince anyone to love Jesus. Who could resist? All the girls went gaga for him except Winnie."

Clara was surprised. Had she not just seen them together as husband-and-wife love birds last night? "Not Winnie?"

"Right, Winnie pretty much ignored him...well, at least in a way. She was nice to him but did not fawn over him. I was so pleased to see this because I knew that Pearle was still head-over-heels in love with her, and preparations were being made for a June wedding. And as far as I could tell, she felt the same."

Clara sipped her coffee now looking at the tablecloth, a beautiful white linen with a subtle pattern. "What changed?"

"The Reverend asked her to lead the new choir he had formed. She is a talented musically, and we were all glad that he had noticed her skill."

"Of course. I could see that last night." Clara tried to be gracious to this young woman, her competition.

"So, she began leading the choir with rehearsal once a week. You must remember that Pearle and Winnie were still in high school at the time. They saw each other all week at school and on weekends, and that was enough, in my opinion. Over this time, Pearle became less and less supportive of the assignment she had been given. They began to bicker. I remember assuming he was a bit jealous of her time with the Reverend, I mean, what man wouldn't have been. But they always made up and as graduation and the date for the wedding grew closer, everything seemed fine."

Clara nodded and took a big gulp and another. She mused at how quickly unattended coffee cools. "Better drink that, it's getting cold."

"I'll get Jane for a warmup. Jane!" Delila called out toward the kitchen door.

Jane poked her head out.

"Could we get a warmup for the coffee?"

"Yez, ma'am!"

She returned with the pot held with a dishtowel. She filled their cups and asked, "What time's breakfast gonna be?"

"Anytime you're ready. We'll do it buffet style with the warming pans."

"Yez, ma'am." Jane looked at the cups, once again steaming, seemed satisfied, and headed back to the kitchen.

"Thank you, Jane," Delila called after her.

They sat in silence as each worked at preparing and drinking the hot beverage before it chilled again.

Delila sipped and set her cup down. "As the great day approached, I could tell Pearle was troubled. I sat him down and tried to have a talk about the duties of a husband...John Ely was not of a mind to do so although he was not against the marriage. Pearle listened but didn't seem to enjoy the ideas I put forth. He asked a few questions about finances and told me about their plans...to live as a tenant on Winnie's parents farm while he went to school to be an electrician. It all sounded fine.

"The wedding day was glorious. Blue sky and they were a stunning couple—"

Clara cleared her throat, and looked down at her cup, taking a long breath.

"Oh, my dear, I'm sorry...I got carried away in the memory."

"It's okay, but maybe we could just move on. Did the Reverend do the service?"

"Yes, he did. He was very attentive to them, especially Winnie. I did wonder a bit, but what did that matter? They were married, and I thanked God for that."

Clara finished the last of her coffee. "Sounds like a match made in heaven," she said without a smile.

"Would you like more coffee?"

"No, I better eat something before I drink anymore."

As if she was listening at the door, Jane brought in the first chafing dish of eggs, followed by skillets of fried potatoes and bacon, gravy along with toasted bread and a bowl of sliced peaches.

Delila stood. "Well, let's go ahead. Looks like the rest of the house is sleeping late this morning."

Clara wasn't sure how much she was going to be able to eat, but it would give her something to do with her hands. She rose and followed her mother-in-law to the buffet.

They brought plates back to the table, where Jane had already furnished fresh coffee, and sat down to finish the story.

They ate their breakfast for a few minutes, each entertaining their own thoughts. Then Delila pushed away her plate and continued. "They were married three days, when I opened the front door to a knock, and there stood Winnie."

Winnie had looked at her mother-in-law's questioning face and burst into tears.

"Winnie? What is it? Has something happened?" Delila looked around. "Where is Pearle?"

"That's what's wrong. I don't know." And she rushed into Delila's arms.

"There, there, my girl. What's happened? Come in, come in. Let me get you some water." She hurried to the kitchen, spoke to Jane, and rushed back to Winnie's side.

John Ely rolled his way in from his study. "Who was at the door? What's all this?"

Winnie sat sobbing into Delila's proffered handkerchief. Delila shook her head at John Ely.

As the sobs subsided, Winnie blew her nose. Dabbing at her eyes as tears still trickled, she looked at the concerned faces staring at her. "He's left me. Is he here?" she managed and buried her face in her hands sobbing.

"Left you?" John Ely's voice was shocked and angry.

Delila was more pragmatic. "He hasn't left you. You've just had a bit of a row is all. Can you tell us about it?"

Winnie looked up and seemed to consider. Her beautiful face was lined with grief and fatigue. "I kept something from him, and he was not understanding."

"Oh, I can hardly believe that. He loves you so."

The tears started anew. John Ely shifted in his chair which creaked under his weight. He rolled a bit closer and patted her hand.

Once again, Winnie seemed to attempt to pull herself together. At that moment, Jane brought in the water in a carafe with three glasses. Delila motioned her away and poured one glass. Winnie took a sip and then drank nearly the whole glass.

"Maybe she needs something a bit stronger," John Ely said. "I surely do."

Delila left the room and returned with two glasses half-full of amber liquid. John Ely greedily accepted his and took a big gulp. Winnie waved the drink away. Delila looked at the glass, took a healthy sip, and set the glass aside. Winnie seemed much calmer.

"Okay. Tell us what happened," Delila encouraged.

Winnie took a long shaky breath. "Yesterday...." She cleared her throat. "Yesterday, Pearle brought up how he wanted to go to school to be an electrician so he could support me without the help of my folks or you—"

"He'll get no support from here." John Ely's voice was gruff and his speech slightly slurred.

Winnie looked at him but continued. "I said that I thought he should work for Daddy for a while and build up some savings so that when he went to school it wouldn't be so austere. That he needed to support us now and not just in the future."

"Us?" John Ely now had a belligerent look about him.

"Yes. Me, himself, and...the baby."

"The baby?" John Ely's stick came down to the floor with a crack. "The BABY?"

"It's okay, John Ely. They are married." Delila tried to soothe the beast.

John Ely looked confused. "What has it been since you said I do? Three hours? How can you already have a baby?"

Delila turned her attention back to Winnie. "You mean should you have a baby in the near future, right?"

Winnie looked miserable. Her head hung down and she wouldn't or couldn't make eye contact. "No. I mean when I have the child, six months hence."

Delila felt her breath stop. This couldn't be. After the mumps had almost killed Pearle, the doctor said that he wouldn't be able to sire children. It was a miracle, unless…

"I'm sure he was thrilled with the idea of being a father." Delila worked at keeping her voice calm, leaving the hysterics to her husband.

"That's just it. I thought he would be thrilled, but instead he was furious. He called me a harlot and a cheater. He threw dishes at the wall and smashed one of our chairs. I thought he was going to hit me, but he didn't. Then he went quiet, wouldn't speak. Then…" A sob escaped. "Then he packed a bag and left."

"When was this," asked John Ely.

Winnie looked up at him. "Day before yesterday."

"And he hasn't been back or messaged you?"

"No." Winnie sniffled and blew her nose again.

John Ely took a deep breath. "I must ask, did you consummate on your wedding night?"

"No. We were so tired that we just fell asleep in each other's arms."

"So, it wasn't a marriage yet at the time he walked out. That's good. It will be easier to get out of your vows. He always was namby-pamby. Weak, sickly, and emotional. I never thought he'd marry, and he didn't. You are better off without him."

As he spoke, Delila's color had come up. "John Ely! That is our son you are talking about. I won't have you speaking ill of him to his wife."

"Yes, you will have it. I've put up with enough from him and his sissy ways. Good riddance is all I'll say." John Ely turned his chair in a half circle and rolled back to his study. The door slammed.

"Thing is," Delila said to Clara, "Pearle WAS a sickly boy with weak nerves. And of course, there was the concern that he would never be able to have children. John Ely believes if one cannot sire children then one isn't a man."

Clara reached over and got her cup and gulped the last of the cold coffee. She swallowed hard and drew a shaky breath.

"I didn't mean to upset you."

"It's okay," Clara said. But she wasn't.

"When did Winnie and the Reverend marry?"

"The marriage was annulled, which happened quickly, the Reverend must have pulled some strings because the child needed a father, so about three months later they were married, and four months after the wedding, Charlie was born. I'm sure some looked askance at his timing, but no one made a formal objection. You see, we all love the Reverend and were proud of him for stepping up when he was needed. So, no one questioned, and Pastor and Winnie seemed so happy."

"I see." Clara pushed back her chair and rubbed the back of her neck. Thank goodness, she didn't have her corset on.

"Jane! Bring us some water please and the smelling salts?"

Jane scurried in and poured a glass of water for each of them, leaving the smelling salts on the table. Without looking at Clara, she bustled back to the kitchen.

"Truth is, Winnie fessed up, the bickering between Pearle and her before the marriage was because of the amount of time with the Reverend being 'counseled.'" Delila put quote marks around the word counseled. "Of course, Pearle didn't know why…until she told him the second day of the marriage that she was pregnant."

Delila looked up at Clara and she nodded to go on.

"Now, even if Winnie and Pearle had been playing at marriage beforehand, I'm sure he didn't believe it was his child. He had had mumps as a teen, and they had gone to his…um…man parts…he's maybe told you all this. He was a very sick boy. The doctor said that it was likely that he would never be able to have children."

Clara stared at her mother-in-law. "He can't have children?"

Delila shook her head. "So, the question was whose child was it? Clara? Clara, dear?"

Clara felt the room spin and Delila's voice faded. She saw the blackness swirling in. Fireworks went off behind her eyelids. She thrust her head down between her knees and took some long deep breaths while Delila waved a cotton ball beneath her nose. Slowly the flashes and the dizziness subsided, and she accepted a glass of tepid water.

Delila's worried face loomed over her. "Let me get one of the men to help you back to your room so you can lie down."

"No!" Clara said a little too sharply. She drew in breath. "No, I want to know. Whose child was it?"

Delila looked Clara over, "I'm reluctant to continue. This seems to be a very upsetting story for you, as well it might. Pearle must have told you some of this?"

"Please finish the story. I've...uh...wondered for so long."

"Okay, but then you must tell me about the accident."

Clara nodded.

Delila took up the story again. "Well, let's see. By the end of the summer, the Reverend and Winnie were married. The baby came and wouldn't you know it, he had blond hair and blue eyes. Well, if we had wondered before, there was no denying it. And now at almost four years old, he is the perfect likeness of his father."

Clara put her head in her hands, elbows on the table. "The Reverend's child?"

"Yes. Of course, Winnie continues to bring him over as if we are his grandparents. John Ely dotes on Charlie. He's a sweet boy. But he doesn't have either Winnie's or Pearle's coloring. I'm sure I know the truth. I'm sure everyone knows the truth."

"But they say nothing?" Clara reeled. How could he do this? How could he lie to me like this?

"What is to say? The couple is happy; the boy is happy and now you and Pearle are happy. It has all worked out for the best."

Clara looked down at the tabletop, at her half-eaten breakfast, and her cold coffee and drew a long shaky breath. Investigate, indeed.

"Now tell me your story. I'm sure it is a happier tale. How did you meet? How did you end up in Iowa, of all places? And what of your family?"

Clara drank a bit more water and tried to get the fog from her head. She tried to smile but it didn't reach her eyes.

"Well let's see. Where to start? I met Pearle in Racine and knew at once that...that...." Her hands flew to her face. She stood and looked at her mother-in-law. Tears spilled down her cheeks. "I knew at once that he was the one with whom I wanted to have babies." She turned and ran from the room and up the stairs to the water closet.

***

MAY ADD ANOTHER MONTH
TO YEAR

New Year's Day, when the calendar prods us into personal reforms of one kind or another, is an appropriate time to be reminded that there is a steady trend toward reform of the calendar itself.

Sooner or later, we will abandon the ancient system of twelve months, and divide the year into thirteen months of twenty-eight days each. The New month would be put in between June and July. In leap year there would be one extra day, an international holiday at the end of June.

The best reason for believing that this plan will eventually be adopted is that business interests want it. Time units are highly important to the orderly management of business. By our eccentric calendar, pay days and meeting days come at irregular intervals, and statistics comparing one month's business with another are often deceptive.

March, for example, has 10 to 20 percent more working days than February. Holidays fall at inconvenient times. Easter, in particular, wanders about so queerly that it disrupts the business of style industries, railways, and resorts, and sometimes has even caused unemployment.

Julius Caesar let us in for all this trouble. His notion has been given plenty of chance. It's about time to change.

Woman's Home Companion, Dec. 1913.

***

Ida read a second time the article from Women's Home Companion reprinted in *The Sentinel*. What a stupid idea! Why would anyone want to rearrange the year? It had been this way forever, hadn't it? And to blame Easter, of all things, was ridiculous. Easter had to come in the Spring when the tulips were blooming.

Br-ng! Br-ng! The turning of the doorbell.

"Oh, I bet that's them." Ida removed her apron and walked to the front door.

"I knew it was you! Come in, come in out of that cold. Are you frozen solid? This snow just won't stop."

"Pretty much," said Pearle. Ida saw how pale he looked, not ruddy, the way many people's faces get when out in the cold.

"Here darling, let's get you out of that heavy, wet coat." Clara began pulling at Pearle's sleeves. She shot a worried look at Ida. "He's not been well in Akron."

Ida raised her eyebrows. "I'm so sorry to hear that. Let's get you dry and in bed. Some chicken soup will be just the thing."

"That sounds just ducky, doesn't it, Pearle?"

Pearle nodded. "Just the thing."

Clara looked at her husband. He was white as the snow they had pushed through to get from the train station to 365 Lincoln Avenue. He looked like an old man, bent over at the shoulders holding the newel post for support. They had had it out on the train between Fort Wayne and Chicago.

"I just don't understand why you didn't tell me." Clara's back was to Pearle as she adjusted the bags on the overhead shelf looking for lap shawls that would provide a modicum of comfort in the cold compartment.

Pearle didn't answer. Clara glanced around. He was crouched along the wall of the car fussing with a valve. A hiss ensued as the steam line to the generator bled its air. When the hiss stopped, he stood swaying with the movement of the train. "That should help. What were you saying?"

"I was asking. Why didn't you tell me about Winnie?"

Pearle sagged into one of the seats. He looked up at her and shrugged with one shoulder. "It didn't seem important. It was over and in the past. I never thought I'd have to see her or even my parents again. Why bother you with it?"

Clara stepped down off the seat with the two shawls. She spread one across Pearle, tucking it around in back so it would stay put, and sat down opposite him, covering herself with the second. She sighed.

He was looking down at the wrap. "Thank you. That's much better."

"I would think that a previous marriage would be something you would want to explain to your second wife, especially when we are about to go into the lion's den."

"That marriage wasn't a real marriage. I had hoped that it had all blown over – and it had, hadn't it? Well, except for Father, but then—"

"No, it hadn't. And there I stood without a single notion as to what was going on. I had to hear it from your mother and see the pity in her eyes and listen to your father berate you for God knows what...I'm not sure I still understand what he was going on about."

Pearl managed a humorless smile. "Me either. He didn't look at all well, did he?"

"Don't change the subject. I don't understand why you didn't tell me about them. I asked you a hundred times why you didn't want to go back."

"It was too complicated to tell." Pearle's voice had acquired a hard edge. "I don't even want to talk about it now."

"Well, too bad. You are going to. We have hours to spend before Woodstock. We need to talk this out."

Pearle threw his head back and looked up at the black ceiling of the car. "What else is there to talk about? You now know the story. You now know my sordid past. I don't see what else there is to talk about."

"Babies!" Clara blurted out loudly.

Pearle looked at her hard. "Babies?"

"Yes! Tell me about having babies." Clara felt her suppressed fire rise into her face.

"Um. Well, when a man and woman make love, they—"

"Don't get smart with me!" Now the fire was in her voice also.

"Clara, I don't know what you want me to say."

"I know you don't, and that's the problem. I don't understand why you didn't tell me about not having children. You knew how important that was to me and still is." Clara clinched the blanket in her fists.

Pearle seemed to try to pull his thoughts together. He looked miserable. His face was drawn up as if he would cry at any minute. His hair was windblown and standing up, and he hadn't shaved for several days. He shrugged. "I just thought…well…we don't need a baby to be happy. I thought your motherly urge would pass and there was no absolute guarantee that I couldn't sire offspring, just one man's word."

"One man's word? A DOCTOR'S WORD!" Clara was nearly screaming now. "Why wouldn't you believe a doctor. You mother said that you almost died with the mumps and—"

A fist banged against the wall separating them from the next compartment, and a muffled voice said, "Hey, keep it down!"

"Sorry," Pearle called back. He cocked his head at Clara with a frown of disapproval as he pointed to the seat.

"Don't you dare try to discipline me!" she whispered fiercely, the brown of her hazel eyes glinting gold.

Pearle sank back on the seat, canted his head back, and looked at the ceiling again.

The train whistle announced a stop. The conductor came along the corridor calling out "Warsaw. All out for Warsaw."

The silence between them stretched until the "All aboard!" was heard, and the train slowly moved out of the station. The clackity-clack sped up, and soon they were once again in the gently rolling countryside of northern Indiana.

Pearle still stared at the ceiling.

"Praying?" Clara asked with a biting cynicism.

"I was ashamed." Pearle's voice was quiet, but Clara heard the words and the pain within them. "I knew you wanted so badly to have a child," Pearl's eyes met Clara's, "and yes, I prayed. I didn't want to lose you."

It was Clara's turn to break the gaze. She put her hands to her face and massaged her forehead. She had prayed, also, every day since they were married. She had imagined the children so well that they were almost real to her – a boy named Samuel and a girl named Ruth. Now they were…dead. A sob caught in her throat. She would not cry! She had cried enough to fill a river, and it didn't change a thing.

Clara looked up. "Tell me the story. I want to hear it from you."

Pearle sighed deeply and sat forward. "I was in love with Winnie, since we were ten years old. She was all I wanted. When she was away from me, I felt empty. She made me feel strong and confident. I could even face my father's anger and his lash because there was Winnie. My father never liked me…maybe he didn't like anyone after the war took his leg. My mother tried to keep him civil, but the drink soon overpowered her badgering, and they began to live separate lives. It seemed to work for them. I didn't care. I avoided him as much as I could, and I had Winnie."

"Do you still love her?" Clara's voice broke on the last word.

Pearle looked up and into her eyes then. "No." His answer was strong and passionate. "No. That was over when she told me on our wedding day that she was pregnant. She and I had only…um—"

"Made love?" Clara's voice shook a little as she voiced the words.

"Only once. Two weeks before the wedding after a fight. She had been asking for it for several months each time we were alone. And I gave in. What could it hurt that close to the wedding? And there were the mumps which the doctor said had ruined me. So, I thought we would be safe." A weak smile crossed his face.

"On our wedding night, I noticed her little pouch of a belly. She had always been so thin with not one ounce of extra fat anywhere. I teased her about it, and she started to cry. I thought I'd offended her. It was the first time we'd seen each other naked. The more I looked at it, the stranger it seemed. I looked at her and said, 'Do you have something to tell me?' And she did."

Clara stood and went to sit next to him on the bench, not touching him.

Pearle glanced up and gave a wan smile. "So, she was pregnant. She tried to make out like it was mine from our liaison two weeks earlier, but that was ludicrous, but it suddenly made sense why she was so anxious for relations for those last few months before the wedding. I knew that it wasn't my child. She had betrayed me. And I knew at once whose it was."

His voice sounded pitiful as if he were reliving the sad event. "They had spent hours and hours together planning services and working with the choir, at least that's what she told me they were doing. I had tried to get her to stop seeing him, but she was as smitten with him as the other girls."

Clara reached over and patted his knee. He startled a bit, but then covered her hand with his. "That's awful. They tried to trick you into covering up their sin. Do you think that's why she married you?"

"I don't know. Maybe, but maybe not. Maybe it was because everyone was expecting it. Maybe because the 'Reverend' didn't want to get married. Maybe because…." Pearle's voice caught with emotion. "Maybe because she loved me."

"You didn't ask her?" Clara shifted in the seat so they could look at each other.

"No. Once she affirmed that she was pregnant, and I affirmed that it wasn't mine; I didn't have anything else to say. I just got up and left. I went home...it was late at night, and everyone was asleep. I gathered a few things and went to the train station. I had some money saved up for the new household, and I took that and bought a ticket to Milwaukee, a big enough town to find work and where no one would know me."

He paused and looked into his wife's eyes. "And you know the rest of the story. Two years at the School of Engineering in Milwaukee and apprenticeship in Racine and you."

"Why didn't you tell someone where you were going?"

"I couldn't. I couldn't speak. I ran like a cur with its tail between its legs. I am not proud of that, and I know that my father would never let me forget it. I'll never let MYSELF forget it."

They sat with their own thoughts.

"It's possible that we could still have a child," he said softly. "The doctor could be wrong."

Clara didn't answer.

"Val-par-ai-so! All out for Valparaiso!" the conductor called out loudly right outside their compartment.

"I love you, Clara." Pearle's voice was filled with emotion. "Please don't pull away from me."

Clara sighed and moved closer. The car was very cold. She arranged herself under Pearle's lap blanket and put her robe on top of them. He was warm and he put his arm around her, drawing her close.

She rested her cheek on the rough wool of his shoulder and sighed again. "I love you, too."

Pearle coughed. It was a deep and wet cough.

Clara looked at his pale face. "How are you feeling?"

"Like I got run over by the milk wagon."

"Are you warm enough?"

"Now I am."

In the kitchen later, after Ida had provided Pearle with a cup of hot chicken soup, and Clara had tucked Pearle into a warmed bed where he fell into a deep slumber, Ida held Clara's hand as she retold the story of the love triangle, and Mother Dye's revelation about Pearle's condition.

Tears leaked from the corner of Clara's eyes. "I don't know if I'll ever stop crying. I know he is not at fault. He can't help having been sick as a child, and I even think he acted nobly by leaving as he did and letting Winnie get the annulment. Can you imagine the scene if he hadn't? I'm just such an ungrateful rug to hold it against any of them...well maybe holding it against Father Dye is justified."

"Don't be too hard on yourself. It was a bitter pill to swallow. I know how much you've wanted children."

Clara dabbed at her eyes. "It's just...I knew something was amiss, but I thought it was me. He's been through so much and is still not as strong as he was before the fall. It was extremely trying in Akron between his father's disdain, Winnie fawning over him after breaking his heart, and me upset about the babies I'll never...," she sobbed, "have. I should never have pushed to meet his family. He went there for me, you know."

"Maybe, but for himself also. It must have been hard to have that knowledge hanging over both of your heads."

"I suppose, but I would have appreciated a bit more honesty before we stepped off the train in Akron."

Ida patted her hand and reached for the teapot, warming the cups that sat before them. "Here, have a little more tea. I'm going to start supper. The girls should be home from visiting Oma Wienke any minute. I know they will be so happy you are here."

Clara wiped her tears and took a long soothing breath. "Yes, I have to have a smile for them, don't I."

"If you can."

Ida stood and started pulling out pans from the cupboard and food from the icebox. This would be a simple dinner of open-faced, hot beef sandwiches with mashed potatoes, corn put up last summer and a rich carrot cake for dessert. Easy.

"Is Pearle's malady just exhaustion then?" she asked as casually as she could.

Clara sipped her tea before answering. "I don't know. I think it's a combination of exhaustion and symptoms still bothering him from the electricity. The doctor said that he might continue to have...um...challenges."

"Like what?"

"He's going blind." Clara dropped the statement into the conversation like a bowling ball on a lane dropped from an inexperienced hand.

Ida turned around slowly. "He's going blind? How long have you known that? What is he going to do?"

"We haven't known for long. It's slow and caused by a disease called cataracts where the eyes' lens cloud up. He will eventually have surgery to remove the foggy lens and wear the lens in his glasses. At least that's how I understand it. But it will have to get much worse before they try that."

Ida turned back to the preparations. "What else?"

"When he is fatigued or nervous, his heart can beat irregularly, and he'll faint or worse. He has learned to control that most of the time because he can feel it coming on, so he can sit down and rest until it passes."

"What is 'or worse'?" asked Ida not looking around.

"There is a chance that his heart could seize up when he has one of those episodes and he could die."

Ida turned and looked at Clara.

"His broken leg still pains him when he walks too much, but the worst thing is that the heat of the electricity burned his lungs, so they are weak and prone to pneumonia, colds, and influenza, any of which could be deadly." Clara was tearing up again talking about things that could be deadly for her beloved.

Ida went to her and put her arms around her from behind, the chair back a barrier to a full hug.

"Most of the time, he just takes it slow and easy, but when things get stressful, he needs more sleep and to rest more often, hard to come by in Akron with all his friends stopping by constantly."

"I bet." Ida went back to peeling potatoes.

Clara took another sip of tea and brightened slightly. "I did find out that he was a very popular young man! Which I expected he would be. He kept in touch with some of his friends when he broke it off with Winnie, stupid name don't cha think? They knew more about him than his parents did. You know he never wrote to his mother about the accident. I had to tell her about it."

Ida put the potatoes in a kettle with water and set it on the 'hot spot' of the stove. "Indeed. Men can be so strange, can't they, about what and who they tell things to. When we were first married, I thought John was keeping secrets from me, but I figured out that he just holds most thing close to his chest and tells only when he feels it's necessary." Ida used two forks to pull apart the left-over brisket which she put in a warm oven to heat. "Here make yourself useful, cut this loaf into three-quarter inch slabs."

Clara accepted the bread, breadboard, and knife. "Three-quarters of an inch? How will I tell that?"

Ida had never thought about how she could tell. "I guess, just make them thicker than usual."

"Right. Why are the girls at Oma's so long."

Ida opened the jar of corn holding a dish towel over the lid to get a grip. *Pop!* Ida smiled. "Good seal! It's become a tradition of sorts to go there for an afternoon of baking and reading while Anna and Frank do errands. Ma loves it and so do the girls. She's still got most of her wits about her, and the cooking lessons have improved Mamie and Edna's skills in the kitchen. Helen takes pride in taking something inspiring to read to keep everyone happy. This was the first time that Bobby went for the whole time. I hope he was good for them. Today they were to make carrot cakes for everyone."

"So, we'll be able to evaluate their baking skill with our own mouths." Clara had finished cutting the bread which she placed in a basket and covered it with a damp towel to stay fresh.

"Yes, you will."

Clara rose. "I'm going to go look in on Pearle. Maybe he'll feel well enough to come down for supper."

"That would be nice. You'll know when they get here."

Clara climbed a few stairs, but then stopped and turned. "Tomorrow is the New Year, right? I've lost track of time."

Ida stopped what she was doing and looked at Clara. "Yes, tonight is New Year's Eve. Another year gone."

Clara looked down at the steps below her. "Good. Let's move on!" And she turned and climbed the stairs leaving Ida looking after her.

***

DARKNESS COMES
AT HOLIDAYS

Chicago, Dec. 31.—As has been the custom on days preceding a holiday, Chicago groped its way about in the dark Wednesday. On the day before Thanksgiving and on the day before Christmas, the city was enveloped in murky darkness. Wednesday, the day before New Year's, clouds hung low over the city and for many hours after dawn was scheduled to appear, street lights were kept burning in all parts of the city. Every business house and office began the day's work by electric light. The weather bureau promised a lifting of the darkness before noon.

Akron Beacon Journal, December 31, 1913.

***

The wind was blowing up a storm outside and the cracks around the windows whistled an age-old song of snow and cold. The day had been gloomy, dark by 4:00 p.m. when the children came clamoring in with Helen carrying a nice carrot cake. John got home forty-five minutes later. Supper, for which Pearle had come down, was all about the children. By 9:00 p.m. everyone was in bed.

Ida lay awake looking at the ceiling. Her mind flitted from one thought to another without any expectation of sleep in the near future.

A crack in the plaster of the ceiling looked a bit like a typewriter or maybe a buffalo. Yes, surely a buffalo.

How could she see a cracked ceiling in the dark? She looked at the windows bright with falling snow. Could be a blizzard.

John didn't have to work tomorrow and a blizzard that would keep them all safely at home was just the thing.

Maybe she should take Bobby and make a trip to Denison in the new year. Could she take Edna also? Edna was a good little helper. That would be exciting.

The girls were growing up. Helen would be eleven, Mamie, ten, and Edie, eight, next year. John and she were middle aged now and possibly would soon be the oldest generation.

Should she talk to Clara about adoption, or was it too soon? What a crushing blow that must have been for her sister. All she has talked about since marrying Pearle is starting a family. Luckily, she didn't just sit around waiting—

The bedroom door creaked open, and a small face looked in.

"Mama," Mamie whispered.

"Mamie?" Ida whispered back. "Come in. What's wrong?"

"I don't feel so good."

Ida sat up on the edge of the bed and put her hand to Mamie's brow. It didn't feel especially hot. "What doesn't feel good?"

"My elbow and my knee." Mamie pointed her elbow at her mother.

Ida stood up and gathered up her house coat. "Let's go talk in the kitchen so I can take a look."

"Okay." Mamie led the way out of the room, limping slightly.

In the kitchen, Ida lifted Mamie up to sit on the table. She pulled up the left sleeve of Mamie's plaid flannel night gown and gasped when she saw her little girl's elbow, red and hot to the touch and twice its normal size. Ida moved the joint a bit and Mamie pulled away with a scowl. "That hurts."

"I bet it does. Is the other one like this one?"

"No but my wrist hurts on the other side, especially when I try to write."

Ida pulled the sleeve up to display the wrist and found the joint in the same condition. "Oh, Mamie. I'm sorry I didn't notice this sooner. You must always tell me when you get hurt."

"But Mama, I didn't get hurt. They just grew this way."

"Grew this way?"

"Yes, I noticed that they hurt and were hot and they just kept growing, till now."

"Well, we will have to see the doctor."

"Now?"

Ida smiled. "No, tomorrow...or...wait...tomorrow is New Year's Day...we'll see how you are in the morning and decide. I'm going to get you some aspirin and orange juice. She rose, retrieved a glass, and went to the back porch icebox to fill it. Coming back, she took down the aspirin powder and stirred in a teaspoon."

Mamie watched the process with squinted eyes. Her face blanched, her lips puckered, and her eyes filled with tears. "I don't want that. It's yukky."

Ida didn't answer but continued to stir. The powder wasn't cooperating; it was floating on top. She used the spoon to push the powder into the juice.

"Mama, I said I don't want that!" Mamie was no longer whispering.

"Yes, you do. It will make you feel better."

"No, it won't." Tears now trickled down Mamie's face.

"Yes, it will. I promise."

"No, Mama." Mamie's voice was choked with sobs.

"There, it's all stirred in. You won't even taste it." She tried to hand the glass to Mamie.

Mamie turned away.

Ida stirred. "I know you are tired, and you hurt. And this will help you to sleep because it will turn off the hurt."

Mamie hiccupped. The clock in the parlor chimed once. Mamie shuddered.

Ida put the glass down and put her arms around her child. "You know. Tomorrow your Papa doesn't have work, and I think we are going to be snowed in. Did you know it was snowing?"

Mamie nodded into Ida's bosom.

"Don't you want to be fresh with a good night's sleep so you can play tomorrow?"

Mamie nodded again. Her hand snaked out and took up the glass. She pushed back from her mother. Ida stirred it one last time, and Mamie drank it all.

After Mamie was tucked in and asleep, Ida returned to her own bed. A new challenge. Was the rheumatism back? What did that mean? Poor Mamie. Poor Pearle. Poor Clara. Ida sighed and turned over cuddling up to John's back.

In his sleep, John's hand came around and caressed her buttock, pulling her into him, but then he was back to snoring, a comforting sound that said, 'All is right with the world.'

Maybe that feeling was right. All WAS right with the world. They were all together, and tomorrow she would call the doctor. Mamie would be fine...she would.... And with that last thought, sleep took her.

Let 'er Rip!
(1914)

"Good afternoon, Mrs. Wienke. Hello, Mamie. How can I help you today?"

"Hello Doctor. Mamie has been having some problems with her elbows and knee—"

"And wrists and ankles," Mamie broke in.

"What kind of problems?" He addressed the question to Mamie.

She pulled up her skirt to display her knees which were swollen and red."

"Goodness! That IS a problem." Dr. Windmuller carefully touched the swollen joints asking, "Does that hurt?"

Mamie winced. "Yes."

Ida broke in, "Is it the rheumatism come back?"

"Maybe. Let's get you up on the table. I want to listen to your heart and look at your other joints. When did this come on?"

Mamie answered. "It started around Thanksgiving but wasn't too bad, but then since Christmas, it's gotten worse."

The doctor listened with his stethoscope and frowned. He pulled the earplugs out. "Have you been tired? More than usual?"

Mamie looked at Ida. Ida said, "Maybe. The girls keep an active agenda most weeks." She looked at Mamie. "What do you think?"

"I think so. It's hard to play when my knees hurt."

"Yes, I suppose it is." The doctor probed her neck, and Mamie pulled away. "Is there anything else besides the swollen joints?"

"W-e-l-l...." The word was drawn out and Mamie looked at her mother.

"It's okay. Tell him whatever you want." Ida held her breath.

"Sometimes I jerk."

The doctor's brows pulled together. "Jerk?"

"Yes, without meaning to. At first, I was just clumsy, but now I can't run well at all. My foot won't work quite right. So, I trip over nothing a lot. And when I'm just standing there, my hand will sometimes jerk up and down or side to side."

They all looked at her hand.

Mamie looked up. "It doesn't happen all the time."

"What do you think, doctor?" Ida asked.

"Hm." The good doctor rubbed his chin. "I think…that we will attack the swollen joints first. That will give you a bit more comfort. I have some ideas, but I need to call a few colleagues in Chicago and see if they have encountered these symptoms."

Mamie and Ida left the office with a regimen of regular aspirin four times a day and a note from Dr. W. stating that Marion Wienke should be excused from recess for the next two weeks, and an appointment to revisit the condition.

Ida felt uneasy about this plan, but Mamie seemed pleased especially about not having to go out for recess in the cold.

***

Ida, John, and the Wienke children watched the slowly passing windows as Clara and Pearle's train pulled away from Woodstock station. The day was bright and not overly cold as long as one kept moving.

Edna broke away from the group and ran alongside the train to the end of the platform. "G'bye, An' Clara,' she called out, hand stretched as far above her head as possible so her beloved aunt could see it wave. "Have fun."

Ida smiled. Her youngest daughter still had wanderlust left over from that early train trip to the wild west of Iowa. She had asked that morning if she could go with Clara and Pearle as they explored Minneapolis before dipping down to Denison.

Ida hoped Pearle was up to the trip. He had revived some under her care over the last week, but the constant motion of the train couldn't be good for a nervous condition.

Helen broke into her reverie. "Are we just going home now?"

"Your father," Ida looked at John, "needs to go to work." He nodded. "But I thought the rest of us could go up to the square and see if there are any after New Year sales going on."

Helen and Mamie smiled. Bobby grabbed the side of the baby buggy and bounced it back and forth, up and down for all he was worth, bouncing it toward the edge of the platform with the tracks below. John caught the handle and steadied the craft.

"Down," Bobby said, clear as day.

"Not right now." Ida took the buggy in hand and wheeled it to the ramp leading down to the parking lot. "You just settle down, young man. You can get out at the park."

Bobby squealed.

Edna covered her ears. "Why does he do that?"

"He's just excited to go to the park," Ida explained.

"It hurts my ears."

"He'll outgrow it just as you did."

Edna stopped. "I screamed like that?" Her sudden cessation of movement caused the others to pile up behind her.

"Oh, for heaven's sake," Helen circumvented the group and continued walking toward the square.

Ida looked after her. "Yes, all babies screech like that when they are excited."

"But did I?" Edna asked for clarification. She could NOT be considered 'all babies.'

Ida brought her attention back to her youngest. "Yes, you did," she said as she pushed the baby buggy forward. Everyone followed her lead.

Edna's bottom lip protruded slightly as she walked with her head down. "But I don't like screams."

"Screams are different when you make them yourself." Mamie let out a little yell. "Try it."

"No." Edna's voice was gruff. "And you can't make me."

"Yes, I can." Mamie reached out and gave Edna's shoulder a push.

"Stop it!" Edna's light blue eyes hardened.

"I can make you scream." Mamie skipped a few steps ahead and stopped and turned. Edna, who was still looking down, smacked into her.

"Stop it!" Edna's voice was louder as she pushed past her sister.

"Both of you stop it or we'll just go home." Ida had lost sight of Helen. She glanced back at John who was smiling.

"Noo-wa." Edna's eyes filled with tears. "I wanna go shopping." Her steps started to drag like she carried a heavy burden on her back. Her shoes scuffed along the concrete walk.

"Edna!" Ida had had enough. "Stand up and walk like a lady. Look at what you are doing to your shoes! Come over here and walk right next to the pram...hold Bobby's hand. That's right. And Mamie, you stop bothering your sister. You know better. Now. Where is Helen?"

The two girls straightened up and both shrugged their shoulders as if to say they weren't their sister's keepers.

Mamie stood on tiptoes and shielded her eyes from the low winter sun. "I don't see her."

"Here's where I get off," John said. Ida stopped and looked back at him. Still smiling. "Don't worry. Helen will find you."

"I hope so. Thanks for coming with us to say good-bye."

"Glad to. Now, you children be good for your mother."

Mamie put on a most angelic look. "Yes Papa."

Edna was still looking down at her scuffed shoes. "Yes Papa."

Bobby bounced in the baby buggy. "Papa!"

"I'll see you at supper for a report." John gave Ida a peck on the cheek and turned toward his office and day's work.

"Mama?"

"Yes, Dod...Edna."

"Mama, can we take Bobby to the park first? Then Helen will see us and find us."

"That's a good idea if there isn't too much snow." They continued up Main Street, crossed Cass Street and entered the park from the north. The paths had been shoveled, but the snow made berms at least three feet high on each side of them. All the better to keep Bobby reined in, thought Ida. She reached in and lifted the little boy out and set him down on his sturdy legs which started running before she even set him down. Edna and Mamie ran with him up the path. They made their way over toward the Donnelly sister's millinery shop.

While many of the stores on the square had been rebuilt in brick or stone after fires or other disasters, the Donnelly home was still a clapboard house on the corner across from the courthouse. The unmarried Donnelly sisters lived above and made beauty below. Ida considered whether she needed a new hat and decided she would wait. She had a few warm winter hats to wear, and she always liked the feel of a new hat in Spring.

The girls stopped Bobby at the west entrance, each grabbing a hand. Ida and the buggy caught up, and they turned back to the park heading for the stores along the south side of the square. As they crossed Van Buren, Helen caught up to them.

"Where have you been, young lady?" Ida tried to make her voice stern.

Helen didn't seem to notice. "I stopped in the *Sentinel* office and told them that Aunt Clara and Uncle Pearle came for a visit."

Ida stopped to window-shop. "That was nice of you, but I would very much like you to get permission before you just wander off like that."

"I didn't wander off, I walked purposefully up Main and turned left. You could have guessed where I was going if you had been watching."

"I was watching...somewhat."

"Nah. You were telling Mamie to stop bothering me." Edna shot Mamie a withering glance.

"You're right. Well, just tell me where you are going before you walk purposefully off, okay?"

Helen's nod seemed to lack conviction.

"I mean it, Helen!"

"All right, Mama, I'll report in and out."

"I will appreciate the effort. And thank you for giving the information to the paper. That was smart thinking."

"You're welcome. Can we go to Uncle Herman's store?"

The younger sisters joined in, "Yes! Yes!"

Bobby let out a whoop. Edna covered her ears. "Can you make him stop that?" she shouted.

Ida laughed at the chaos. " are having a 'Great Clearing Sale' today, so we might get bargains! Uncle Herman should be there so we can say 'hi.' And no Edna, I can't make him stop any more than I can make Uncle Herman lower his prices just for me. So, let's take advantage of his sale."

The contingent of Wienkes turned onto Benton street in front of the Church Block and proceeded toward Murphy and Doering's mercantile.

***

FOUR WOODSTOCK MEN
ENLIST IN U. S. NAVY

Herbert Towne, Dan Boyd, Ed Webster, and Boyd Cantrell are four Woodstock youths, who have recently entered for a four years' term of service in the United States naval service.

One other young man, Rasmus Rasmussen of Woodstock, joined the navy a few months ago, and is already assigned to service on the sea.

Woodstock Sentinel, January 3, 1914.

***

"John? Did you see by the paper that Ras Rasmussen joined the navy?" Ida rested the paper on the kitchen table without letting go of the edges.

John looked up from his breakfast of oatmeal and toast. Good for a cold day. "I had heard that at church. It was a while ago."

"Why didn't you tell me?" Ida continued to make eye contact.

John went back to the oatmeal. "I didn't know you knew the Rasmussens."

"I don't, but we should be including him in prayers at Women's Circle. Mrs. Rasmussen doesn't come to Circle, but still, we should include him." Ida looked back at the paper but didn't raise it for reading.

"True. I should have mentioned it to you."

"Do you know them?"

"I know the children. Well, Ras isn't a child anymore, but the other two…um…Maryloo and Pedro. At least that's what the other kids call them." John smiled.

Ida shook her head. "It's probably Mary and Peter. Why do children insist on nicknames—"

"Especially when they have good biblical names, right?" He spooned a mouthful of porridge and looked at her, a twinkle in his eye.

"Well…yes! What are the Mrs. and Mr. like?" Ida liked to make a personal invitation to Circle when she could.

"I've only talked to them once or twice. Seemed nice. Old country. Farmers from up McHenry way. I don't think the parents are members. The kids often walk in to town for church."

"Hm. You'll have to introduce me next time they are in church." Ida lifted the paper. "Anything else you aren't telling me?

John's spoon stopped halfway to his mouth as he considered. "I don't think so."

"As your mother would say," Ida tried for a German accent, "'Gut husband!'"

***

Trading in Their Sleighs

The McHenry Plaindealer says that it begins to look
as tho auto owners will be able to run their cars thruout
the entire winter. A number of local cars have been in
use daily since early last spring.

Woodstock Republican, January 10, 1914.

***

Ida, John, and Mamie sat in Dr. Windmueller's waiting room
with its straight-backed ladder chairs and unpapered walls. The
doctor had requested John's presence at the appointment, which
in Ida's opinion did not bode well. Mamie was excited about her
father taking part and was now sitting on his lap and telling him
about a book she had read for school titled, *Anne of Green Gables.*

"It's so good, Papa. This girl Anne with an e is an orphan and she is
adopted by these two old people who didn't have children."

John's eyebrows raised. "Indeed."

"They are brother and sister."

"The two old people?" he asked.

"Yes, but they adopt her, and she becomes their family, and she is so
happy and joyous and—"

"The doctor will see you now." The nurse's voice rang out into the
room.

Ida snapped to attention. Stood and motioned the others to do the
same. John stood still holding Mamie who didn't protest being carried at
all.

The doctor greeted them and motioned them to chairs. He leaned
against his desk and began. "So here is what I have found out. There is a
theory that rheumatic fever often stays in a person's system for years
after the first diagnosis. And it manifests in various ways. For girls it
often manifests in a malady called St. Vitus Dance, usually after the age
of ten. How old are you right now, Mamie?"

"Nine."

"Close enough. And it usually goes away by puberty, but not always.
Another manifestation of rhematic fever is heart disease. I've listened to
Mamie's heart, and she has a heart murmur."

Ida found her throat too dry to speak, but John asked, "What does
that mean – a murmur?"

"When I listen to her heart, there's an extra swooshing sound. It means that one of the valves of the heart isn't closing tightly when her heart beats, and blood is flowing backward for a moment making that sound. That won't, in and of itself, hold her back from a normal life, but it can become more severe over time, so we will need to keep track of it."

John cleared his throat. "Tell us about this Saint's Dance. I believe in the apostolic saints, but not like the Catholics do. What is it?"

The doctor smiled. "It has very little to do with Catholics. Some people believe if you touch or dance around the headstone of St. Vitus, you will be cured. The dance part comes from the muscle spasms that Mamie has already begun to experience. Those will, I'm afraid, get worse. Most often slowly and the symptoms diminish as puberty comes on."

Tears sprang to Ida and Mamie's eyes.

Mamie drew herself up. "What's pew-birdy?"

The doctor took a breath and looked a bit uncomfortable, being unable to look directly at Mamie.

Mamie's brows furrowed. She looked at her mother.

Ida slid to center stage. "It's when a girl becomes a woman, and the body starts to bleed each month."

Mamie's eyes grew round, and John blushed.

Dr. Windmueller regained control. "Mamie, it is when your body is able to have a baby, and yes," he looked at Ida, "there is a cycle that lets that happen. You don't have to worry about that now. It happens when you are thirteen or fourteen, so between ten and fourteen, it seems a body, after it has survived rheumatic fever, loses a little control and starts to jerk around, and we don't know why."

Mamie burst into tears and buried her face in her father's wool jacket.

Dr. Windmueller looked anxious and reached out to touch Mamie's back. "I know this is a lot for one so small to accept." He switched his attention to Ida and John who were looking dismayed.

John held Mamie close and looked Dr. W. in the eye. "What can we do?"

"Not much," the doctor admitted. "Keep a close watch and wait it out. We especially want to keep an eye on her heart to make sure it does not get worse, but even that we can't do much about at this point. Maybe in the future—"

"So, you are saying that we can do nothing but pray?" Ida wiped her eyes with her hankie.

"Yes, I guess that is what I am saying. I would try to keep Mamie involved in as much as she is able to do and pray that this passes quickly. We also need to do our best to keep her from other illnesses. Polio or Influenza could be deadly for her. I'm sorry that I don't have better news."

John and Ida walked home from Dr. Windmueller's office with Mamie between them. Mamie held each of their hands and both could feel the intermittent jolts of muscle spasm in her arms as they walked. The silence was deafening.

"I want to keep going to school," said Mamie.

Mamie was dragging her left foot along the snow covered walk, Ida noticed. "We'll try," she said quietly.

"Of course, you'll stay in school. We aren't going to waste a good mind," John said, sounding almost jovial. He swung Mamie up into his arms, and they walked a bit faster.

Mamie giggled, and Ida nodded.

"What's Influenza?" asked Mamie.

"I'm not sure," Ida hedged.

"Don't you worry about that. We will do our best to keep you safe," said John. He looked at Ida, and they caught each other's eye for a moment. She slipped her hand through his arm and leaned her head on his shoulder. And they walked the blocks to 365 Lincoln Avenue.

***

School for Women Voters

The idea of a school for the benefit of women voters has been taken up and committees to handle the matter have been named by some of the religious societies. Arrangements are expected to be completed soon for the holding of a public school, where instructions will be given to women concerning their new privileges, which have been granted them under the recent act of our state legislature. Schools for this purpose are being held in other cities and villages, and it is to be hoped that the women voters here will avail themselves of this opportunity to become acquainted with the method of voting and it might be added that they may be able to put some of the male voters to work to learn their duty in exercising their right to vote.

Woodstock Republican, January 21, 1914.

***

Personals

Albert Wienke of Woodstock was in Crystal Lake on business Saturday.

Woodstock Sentinel, January 22, 1914.

***

"John!" Al called out just as John stepped out of his office and waved from a half block away.

John's face lit up. "Well, look at who's come home to roost!"

"Oh, heck no! Beloit's treating us good." Al talked as he walked, closing the distance between them.

"Then why are you always wandering around McHenry County?"

Al grabbed John's outstretched hand and lowered his voice. "I don't mind taking Lincolns from Illinoisians whenever possible."

John slapped him on the back. "What brings you down?"

"We have a job over in Crystal Lake that I had to look in on and I thought I'd stop and see Ma before heading back."

"And instead, you bumped into me." John grinned, his words coming out in puffs of steam in the cold air.

"I was coming to talk to you about insurance."

"What about it…wait, come inside where it's warmer, and we can talk." John held the door and both men entered, removing their hats and coats, hanging them on the tree by the door. They moved to John's desk and sat on either side.

"So, what do you need?"

"One of my men fell at the job in Crystal Lake because, he says a ladder was broken and the supervisor knew it. He says that he is going to sue me even though I was miles away in Wisconsin."

"Sounds like you need a lawyer, not an insurance man."

"He and I have to come to an agreement. I'm waiting to see how bad the injury is. Broken leg. If it heals well, and he can work, I'll pay less than if it heals badly, and he can't work."

"Okay. But I still don't see how I can help."

"A couple years ago Wisconsin passed a law that says that I am responsible for the safety of workers working on my site."

"Okay, but this worker was in Illinois, right?"

"Yes, and so now the question is should I have workmen's compensation insurance in both Wisconsin and Illinois?"

"I would say it can't hurt, and I can help you with that."

"Thank goodness! What's it gonna cost me?"

They worked through the details with John looking through his portfolio of possible companies and policies, and Al doing a lot of groaning. Eventually, the two shook hands in agreement over a plan, and Al rose to go.

John held Al's coat as he bundled up. "How is your family? I know Ida will ask when she hears I saw you today."

"Evie is great. She loves school, especially music. She will be advancing to High School in the fall. She's already in their orchestra playing her violin."

"And Artie?"

"Artie is nearly as tall as I am and plays any sport he can lay his hands on. He especially likes baseball but also plays touch football and soccer. I'm anxious to get him into high school so I can attend real games. Another year or two for that. Maybe I'll settle down in Wisconsin if that happens. And Lucy is fine. Likes school, and if one can believe the teaching staff, is quite gifted."

"And Lena?"

Al looked at the floor before answering. "Lena is doing well. It's good that we have the in-laws nearby. I'm not sure what we would have done without her sisters taking over during the difficult times. She still has her ups and downs and on occasion it's hard for her to get out of bed, but overall, she's doing well with the children." Al laughed a humorless chuckle. "I spend a lot of time either corralling painters or at the saloon, so I miss most of the drama."

John shook his head looking down. "I'm sure they miss you when you are gone. At least you still got beer up there. Any talk of going dry?"

"A bit, but there are too many Deutschers to allow that to happen. Here too?"

"Maybe. But I think the women will be the determining factor. If they get to vote on the wet-dry issue, we will be dry."

"The German women won't vote dry."

"But the vast majority of the others will. Better stock your basement shelves. Will you stay over with Frank tonight?"

"I may. It will depend on what Ma wants. How is she?"

John chuckled, shaking his head. "As determined and stubborn as ever. She'll drink with you."

Al smiled and nodded. He pulled his trapper hat down and tied the earflaps under his chin. "Thanks, John!"

John put out his hand. "You're welcome. I'm glad we could find a policy that fit so well, and it gives you a reason to drop by occasionally."

"You betcha."

***

WEEKLY EXCHANGE ITEMS
Miscellaneous Assortment of News Items in Condensed Form for Busy People.

Plans are on foot for the erection of a magnificent crypt mausoleum in Oakland cemetery at Woodstock.

Over at the county seat they are still trying to decide the question whether or not hitching places should adorn the public park.

A Ringwood farmer lost a $50 bill in a Richmond store recently. We have not learned the name of the farmer, nor do we know whether or not he recovered the bill.

McHenry Plaindealer, January 22, 1914.

***

WILL TEACH TANGO

Beginning next Saturday evening, Mr. and Mrs. Conn will be at Stoffel's hall for the purpose of teaching the tango and other late dances. Instructions will begin at eight o'clock and continue until nine. Social dance from nine to twelve. Mr. and Mrs. Conn will be here every Saturday night until further notice.

Woodstock Republican, January 28, 1914.

Closing The Books Is Taxing

County Clerk Guy E. Still has broken the record this year in the matter of finishing up the tax books. Grover P. Chittenden, Mrs. Nettie Losee, Mrs. William Roth, Miss Lura Wandrack, and Miss Emma Charles were employed by County Clerk Still to work on the books this winter and last Thursday the books were finished, the earliest date of completion on record.

Woodstock Sentinel, January 28, 1914.

***

Woodstock's Finest

Our illustrious Woodstock policemen have supplied themselves with new overcoats with brass buttons. The officers now look like real "cops." And to make the job even sweeter, Woodstock's two police patrolmen will hereafter serve but nine hours. Heretofore they were required to be on duty twelve hours.

Woodstock Republican, January 29, 1914.

***

Scarlet Fever

There have been 23 cases of scarlet fever and many cases of scarlatina in Woodstock over the last few weeks. There have so far been five deaths.

Woodstock Sentinel, February 1, 1914.

***

February 2, 1914
365 Lincoln Ave.
Woodstock, Illinois

Dear Clara and Pearle,

I was so glad to get your letter telling us about your trip back to Denison and about Pearle's improved health. I agree that it is good that winter is keeping him at home for a while. How are you otherwise? Finding any good mysteries to solve?

We are as before. Everyone has been healthy this winter, which is very uncommon. Even Mamie has had only one bout with a cold. That's sure to change as Woodstock now is having a scarlet fever epidemic. They haven't closed the schools yet, but I'm keeping Mamie home for the cold months until I hear an 'all clear.' She isn't happy but seems resigned and is throwing herself into her studies. She is especially good with numbers and knows her times tables by heart and is working now on long division.

Helen, as you saw in January, is our little adult. She takes care of me as much as I take care of her. She is talking about trying to get a job...at 10 and a half years old...a job? The Sentinel needs a clean-up person, and she says it will give her a leg up when she wants to start reporting. Maybe so. Her studies come easily, and I think she's read every book in the library, so she has the time. We'll see.

Edie...yes, we are calling her Edie (pronounced Eddie...and I know it's a boys' name), but she insists. Anyway, Edie likes school better than last year. She has found her niche now that Mamie is out of her room...less comparisons, I suppose, at least for this year. She has such a good soul, but her temper gets the best of her sometimes (remind you of anyone?).

John is busy every day but Sunday and then church activities take over the day. I am refusing to cook a big meal on Sundays because I never know if we are going to all be here or all go our separate ways. So, we often have breakfast in the evening instead of supper. John says this will only get worse as the children get older. I hope not. Bobby and I stay home and take a nap. He is a good little boy, but also so active. I never knew how active boys are.

Do you know how to tango? They are giving lessons here and it sounds so intriguing. I'm not sure how I'd use the skill, and I doubt I could get John to go with me, but...still.... If you were closer, I'd suggest we go.

We got a big snowfall and so the sleighs are out in force now. One can hardly walk outside without hearing sleigh bells. I love that, don't you? I suppose it is the same in Denison.

Not much other news. Write and tell me what you are investigating; you know my only excitement is through your mysteries.

Love from all of us to you both,
Ida

***

A Dry County?

Every town in McHenry county with the exception of McHenry, Huntley and Union are very likely to be voted dry at the coming spring elections. The last time that Woodstock voted on the question the wets won out by 285 votes. The drys in the city feel quite confident that the woman vote will assist them in winning this time. North Crystal Lake, Crystal Lake, Harvard, and Richmond are other towns that will undoubtedly be voted dry. Marengo and Hebron are two of the towns that are already dry.

Woodstock Sentinel, February 10, 1914.

***

Sleighing Party

A number of young ladies from Woodstock journeyed down to Crystal Lake on a sleighing trip Tuesday and enjoyed a 10 o'clock supper at the Richmond House. Among those who participated in the fun were: Louise Gahlbeck, Clara Ladwig, Della Gimbal, Alma Gimbal, Ella Hoefs, Letah Wienke, Alice

Wienke, Bertha Steinke, Bertha Schnett, Martha
Gahlbeck, Ida Gahlbeck, Bessie Steinwart.

Crystal Lake Herald, February 19, 1914.

***

WOODSTOCK REDUCES NUMBER
OF SALOONS

The city council of Woodstock, at their meeting
Monday evening, passed an ordinance reducing the
maximum number of saloons to five. At present there
are eight saloons and three of these must retire from
business when the ordinance becomes operative, May
first. This ordinance provides further that all screens,
curtains, etc., must be removed from the windows, thus
placing the saloon, in appearance, in the category with
other business houses.

Since the passage of the above ordinance, a great deal
of discussion has arisen as to its effect upon the wet
and dry issue at the coming election. Rumor has it that
the above movement was originated by the "wets" to
mollify the "drys" in the former's effort to keep
Woodstock wet. From this movement it would seem
that the "wets" have attempted to "purify" the
business.

On the other hand, the "drys" claim that this is the
best possible move to ensure the defeat of the "wets,"
for the wets have acknowledged by this movement that
the city can be run, even though they reduce the
revenue by one-half from the saloons. The people will
now believe, so say the "drys," that the city can go one
step farther and eliminate the entire income from this
source. They also claim that the business cannot be
purified.

Again, it is claimed that this movement has divided
the forces of the "wets." It is reasoned that the saloon
men who will be denied their licenses will throw their
influence and that of their friends to aid the "drys," in

order to play even with those who expect to have their licenses renewed.

If the vote goes against the "wets," the city is likely to wait until they hear the decision from the Illinois Supreme Court as to whether the women's votes will count before closing any saloons. It's in your hands, voters.

Woodstock Republican, February 19, 1914.

***

ALL THINGS DENISON
By Clara Daring

It has been a quiet winter in Denison, but that is about to change. Ames College is bringing its second annual Short Course College to Denison beginning February 9th. If you didn't take part last year, make plans to do so now! Interest is growing in the rural areas around Denison so classes will be filling up quickly. And if you decide not to register, here are some of the things you'll be missing.

The classes are just like those taught at the Ames College, but shorter so all the good stuff is at the top of the agenda. Specialists from Ames and some from our own county will bring their expertise to our burg in lectures and demonstrations. Some topics will be corn class, corn and grain judging, school children's exhibiting, school children's corn, stock judging, domestic science with exhibit and free samples, and baby health. Some of the lectures will be held in the evenings for the working folks to attend. The school children will have an immense exhibition of work they have been planning all winter and a spelling bee will be held on Wednesday evening at the Opera House promptly at 7 o'clock.

Denison doesn't often get a chance like this to host such a free-wheeling extravaganza and invites all the surrounding communities to attend. I know I'm going.

Crawford County Courier, February 7, 1914.

***

STILL GROWING

F. R. Foreman of Woodstock has just issued a new directory for that city, which gives the county seat a population of 4,653.

McHenry Plaindealer, March 12, 1914.

***

ROEBUCK TYPEWRITER COMPANY

The stockholders of the Emerson Typewriter company held a special meeting in the offices of said company one day recently and adopted a resolution, changing its former name to that of Roebuck Typewriter company. The toolmakers employed at the factory have been busy for several months' past, manufacturing new tools with which to turn out a new and improved typewriter. A few of these machines will be placed on trial sometime next month and if satisfactory the plant will resume operations. The new machine will be a big improvement over that of the old and reports are to the effect that the Roebuck machine will compare with the best now manufactured.

Woodstock Sentinel, March 12, 1914.

***

BIG FORCE NOW ON BORDER

The orders for the dispatch of two more regiments to Texas will result in the assembling in that state of nearly 18,000 troops, 3,000 more than the entire force of the regular army which General Shafter led into Cuba.

Nearly 11,000 of these soldiers are in camp at Texas City. The others are scattered along the border from Brownsville, Tex., to Nogales, Arizs, the largest garrisons being maintained at El Paso, Nogales, Douglas, Laredo, Eagle Pass, and Brownsville, where the railroads from the United States enter Mexico.

Marshalltown Evening Times-Republican, March 12, 1914.

***

For Tax Collector

I will be a candidate for tax collector for the town of Dorr for a second term. I respectfully solicit the support of voters.

WALTER H. BROTT.

For Tax Collector

I will be a candidate for tax collector for the town of Dorr and respectfully solicit the support of the voters and friends.

A.P. BAKER.

For Dorr County

I hereby announce myself as a candidate for Tax Collector for the Town of Dorr, and respectfully solicit the support and endorsement of the voters of said township.

FRANK C. WIENKE, JR.

For Dorr County

I hereby announce my candidacy for the office of tax collector of Dorr township, and respectfully solicit the support of the voters at the usual township caucus to be held in March.

MRS. ROSE GODDARD.

For Dorr Tax Collector

I hereby announce my candidacy for the office of tax collector of Dorr township, and respectfully solicit the support of voters.

MRS. L. H. JONES.

For Dorr Collector

I hereby announce myself as candidate for tax collector for the Town of Dorr and respectfully solicit the support of the voters of said township.

E. A. ROGERS.

Dorr Tax Collector

I am a candidate for the office of tax collector for the town of Dorr, subject to the action of the voters, male and female, of said town at the annual election on April

7, 1914, and I will greatly appreciate the support and votes of the electors at the annual election where women can vote the same as men.

MRS. G. J. MILLER.

Woodstock Sentinel, March 19, 1914.

***

Frank Wienke was just about to go up to bed when he heard the fire siren from the city works begin to wail. His body tensed, and he realized that he was no longer a member of the Woodstock volunteers. At forty years and counting, he was tired. Having his mother, Sophia, live with them had worked out okay, but it also made his work at Oliver more important than ever. And now he had heard rumors about a shut down. He sighed. If he were laid off, how would they live?

Bbbbrringgg! The phone? At 10:30 in the evening? Frank rushed to the kitchen. It could only be an emergency.

"Hello?" He knew his voice sounded a bit panicky.

"Frank? We need Oliver's help. It's city hall."

"I'll call them up!" Frank hung up the phone and went to the stairs. His wife stood at the top wide-eyed with her robe pulled around her.

"Fire at city hall. I have to—

Anna waved her hand. "Go!" she finished for him.

He grabbed his coat and was out the door and running toward Oliver before he had it on.

The Oliver crew gathered minutes after Frank blew the whistle. The horses' steel shoes clattered on the brick paving as they reached the square.

A hundred people were milling around outside the city hall. Those evacuated, he assumed. They had been watching a wrestling match when the smoke appeared through the vent system.

Now smoke was billowing from every window and door of the building. Frank feared the worst. His experience said that the building could be a total loss if they didn't act quickly.

The men from Oliver got to work unrolling the hoses and connecting the pumper.

Frank approached one of the Woodstock volunteers. "Do we know where the fire is?"

The fire fighter looked at him with glazed eyes as if he were in shock and said, "In the building, I suspect." A rookie.

"What's your name, son?"

"James...uh...I mean...J-Jimmy."

"First fire?"

"Yessir."

"Okay. Stick by me. We need to figure out where the fire is in the building. The people are out. Now we try to save the building."

"Dunno. I just got here. Someone said there's nothing we can do."

"Buck up, man. We have a fire to fight! C'mon. Help me find that fire."

The new recruit followed Frank toward the building, and Frank's crew pulled the fire hose after them.

Frank called out over the hubbub, "Aim the stream at the basement. It's a good place to start. I'm going to try to get a look inside."

"Frank! Good to see you here." The captain of the volunteers led a group toward him. "We're going in."

"I'm with you." Frank turned toward the building and approached the main entrance. "Keep your wits about you."

The entrance was billowing hot smoke and the men, try as they might, were driven back into the street, coughing, and gasping for air.

"Not getting in this way," said Frank. "Let's go around back."

They tried three more entrances with the same results and gathered back in front to regroup.

By this time Frank had taken charge, being the most experienced of the fire fighters. He knew the interiors of the buildings around the square as well as he knew the layout of an Oliver typewriter factory where he worked. "There is one more door to try. Bring a hose to the furnace room door over on the side."

"That's for sure on fire," said Jimmy.

"Not necessarily. It might not have been the source of the fire, or it might have burned out already. C'mon."

Frank used his ax to break the locked door into splinters. No smoke, or not much smoke, billowed. The men waded into waist deep water – at least the plan to flood the basement was working – and opened the inner door bracing for the inferno. But the basement was nearly fire free.

Jimmy looked around. "Where is all this smoke coming from?"

Frank looked up. "It's in the walls." He made for the main stairs. On the first floor the smoke was thick. The hose men had followed them up. Frank looked at them. "Ready?"

They nodded.

Frank and the others used their axes to break through the lathe and plaster wall into the Police Magistrate's office. Smoke and fire belched out and the hose was used to extinguish the flames.

"And that's how we beat it!" said Frank to Jimmy.

They worked their way, yard-by-yard along the corridor. They approached the door that said "Library," hand-painted in script on the glass window. They could see fire dancing on the opposite side. Suddenly the window shattered, and fire flared out into the hallway. The firemen ducked for cover but brought the hose up to shoot directly through the window on the tons of burning paper. After fifteen minutes and many gallons of water, the flames ceased, and the men looked at the sodden mess that had been Helen's sanctuary.

Frank looked at the sodden mess that used to be library books and shook his head. "Total loss, I'd say."

A worn and now soaked Alice Through the Looking Glass lay on the floor amid smashed window glass. The word Library could still be read on the shards. A $20 picture is a journalist could get up her before the clean-up,

"Captain?" Jimmy was at his shoulder pointing upward. The upper floors were still billowing smoke.

Okay fellows, stop thinking about your warm beds. Let's get after 'er!"

The tired fighters pulled the hoses up to the second floor. After about four hours of inching through the building, knocking holes in the walls, and playing water over every surface, the smoke abated, and the fire was out.

Frank came out into the fresh air of the square and tried to breathe deeply. He was seized by a coughing fit that was eased only by some fresh water and a few more breaths. It was cold. His lungs seemed to be both burning and frosting at the same time. His outer gear was soaked and heavy as the moisture began to freeze. He had no idea where his coat was.

"Here Sir, put this on." Jimmy stood there holding open his coat. "You'll catch your death."

Frank smiled. "Thanks." He slipped his arms into the coat and buckled a few of the catches along the front.

"James, you did a mighty fine job tonight. I was proud to have you at my side."

"Thank you, sir."

A call came from somewhere in the park – a blow horn, "Free breakfast at the Rex!"

The weary men made their way across the square. Frank shed his outer coat, leaving it on the sidewalk with others and entered the restaurant.

"Frank! The man of the hour!" a voice called out and the men stood and applauded his entrance. He made his way through the crowd accepting handshakes and claps on the back.

Moisture was steaming off the men as they found chairs and dug into scrambled eggs with bacon and biscuits.

Frank looked around at these fine men. He would miss being in their ranks, but what a way to end his career as a fireman.

***

Library Losses

The library suffered the severest loss of any part of the building in the City Hall fire. Librarian Lura Wandrack informs us that every book contained therein is more or less damaged. Various estimates are given as to the value of the books, but it seems a fair figure would be around $5,000. Only $2,000 insurance was carried, and we understand that the board will make a claim for the full amount. The adjusters were expected to make settlement Thursday afternoon.

Woodstock Republican, March 20, 1914.

***

Young Frank C. Wienke, nephew of Fireman Frank, took the steps up onto his father William's porch two at a time. It was a cold night, and he was late getting home, so he would have to be quiet. He slipped the key in the lock and heard the click. Pushing open the door he was glad to hear that his oiling last week had gotten rid of the telltale squeak that had plagued his boyhood. Now that he was a man, he did not want to wake his mother or be greeted by his father's glower because of his late nights. Frank tiptoed through the living room toward the stairs.

William's cigar flared in the darkness. "Good evening my boy."

"Pa. What are you doing up so late."

"I could ask the same, but I know where you've been. I stayed up to hear the results. Do we have a Republican nominee for tax collector?"

Now excited, Frank sat down on the chair opposite—his mother's. He was smiling although he doubted his father could see the grin.

"Well, as you know there were several people running for the nomination. Seven of us."

"And four ladies. How was it to have women at the caucus?"

"Just fine. Uncle John kept it very professional. When someone made a joke about the perfume, Uncle John changed the subject and no one laughed, and so the rest of the night was very respectful."

"Good. So….?"

"I won!"

"Hurrah!"

"There were ninety women who voted, including the ones running. I think they all voted for the women. But the whole vote was, I think, about 650 votes. I got 215. Closest next was Mrs. Rose with 170."

"That's great! I knew you had a good chance. The name recognition and all those others splitting up the women's vote. And what's next?" William took a draw on his cigar.

"There are two ladies running from the Democratic side, so I'll be up against them in the election. Again, they will split the Democratic vote, if I can be lucky two times in a row."

"You will be. I'm sure of it. How is the shop shaping up?"

"Great. I might need your expertise next week. The buyer is coming in from Chicago, and I need to order the first stock of smokes. I'm thinking about stocking more than cigars. I'll let you know when."

"Fine. I will be interested in what he has to say. Maybe I can get a discount for my expertise."

"Of course, you can. One hundred percent discount." Frank was feeling generous.

"Don't throw your money away before it's earned. Ten percent will be adequate. Have you talked to your brother lately?"

"No. Not lately. Paper says he's been spending a lot of time in McHenry, but our paths don't cross much." Frank clapped his hands on his knees. "I'm going to hit the hay. You better finish that off and get upstairs before Ma wakes up."

"Ack, she can sleep through anything. G'night. Dream of winning big!"

Frank C. Wienke smiled again into the dark.

***

WOODSTOCK GOES "DRY"
BY 400

A memorable day in the history of Woodstock will always be April 7, 1914, for on this day, by the aid of the women's vote, the city of Woodstock was voted "dry," a condition which has not prevailed here for about forty years, some giving the date when the city was last dry as 1872.

Early in the morning the women were in evidence and continued coming in large numbers all day, and it was estimated that by 12 o'clock fully 600 had cast their ballot.

The final figures in Dorr township are as follows:

1st precinct—Wienke, 450; Mrs. Jones, 119.

Mrs. Miller, 133

2nd precinct—Wienke, 313; Jones, 206.

Miller, 248.

3rd precinct—Wienke, 354; Jones 117.

Miller, 282.

4th precinct—Wienke, 41; Jones 53; Miller, 31.

Total vote cast—2,490

Total wet vote—1,015 (Men, 778; Women, 472)

Total dry vote—1,415 (Men, 663; Women, 782)

Woodstock Republican, March 29, 1914.

***

The Passing of "Rube" Waddell.

"RUBE" WADDELL is gone. The amazing giant "southpaw" who pitched the Athletics to their first American League pennant in 1902 and until 1908 was the most notable figure of the national game has been knocked off the mound by the grim reaper.

Only one player—KELLY, the "$10,000 Beauty"—ever vied with RUBE in the popular furor he created wherever he went. The crowds flocked to the hotels where he stopped as they did to the grounds where he played. He lived for this adulation. He performed his best for the biggest ball crowds. He posed in the lobbies so that the "fans" might worship.

RUBE was many kinds of man—angler, trap shot, football player, actor, fire fiend, amateur barkeeper, prize borrower, practical joker, comedian, a sworn enemy of gloom, a joyous wastrel, a boy that never grew up—as well as one of the greatest of pitchers.

As a fire fiend, the lure of a blaze was irresistible. He joined several fire companies and made some daring rescues. The tuberculosis which carried him off dated back to an attack of pneumonia which resulted from his neglect to change his wet clothes after rescuing several persons from a fire at Hickman, Ky.

Thus, passeth GEORGE EDWARD WADDELL at the age of 37, a great pitcher and the king jester of the national game.

Inter Ocean, April 3, 1914.

***

Emil Wienke slouched up the front steps of Frank Wienke's house and wrapped softly on the screen door. He heard his mother's voice say, "I go," but it was Anna, Frank's wife who opened the door, inviting him in. His mother Sophia sat in a large wing-backed chair looking like a diminutive doll complaining that Anna should let her answer the door.

"I can walk to da door. You busy."

"Oh mother. By the time we got you up and started toward the door, the person on the other side would have given up and gone home. Don't worry, you do a lot to help me." Anna had spoken this looking at Emil rather than Sophia and now she smiled and raised her eyebrows in a somewhat frustrated way.

Emil took the cue. "It's me, Ma. Thought I'd stop by and see if you needed anything."

"What you doin' here? You not work any?" Sophia's words were slightly slurred due to the stroke that had laid her low the year before, but clear enough. "I don't need nottin'."

"Emil, would you like a glass of something? I have tea or lemonade or milk or—

"No nothing for me. Thanks, Anna."

Anna smiled again and retreated to the kitchen.

"Sometink's wrong." Sophia was looking at him critically. "You lost job?"

"Nothing's wrong, Ma. I'm fine. My workday ends at four."

"Sometink wrong. Look at your face."

Emil smiled and sat down in a chair to the right of his mother—her good side. "My face is fine, too. I just heard that someone died."

"Who died?"

"No one you know, but he was one of my...um...heroes, I guess. A baseball player named Rube Waddell."

"Mm."

"You probably don't remember him." Emil paused for a reaction.

"Mm. Maybe. Tell 'bout him."

"He was on the White Stockings team when they came here and played the Olivers...oh man...when was it? Ten years ago, now. Did you go to any of those games?"

Sophia waved her hand to shoo away the notion that she was a baseball fan. "I only go when you play."

Emil smiled at her and patted her hand. "That was a long time ago. Rube would do little trick things while playing. At that game, he called in the whole outfield and infield players to the mound, like he wanted to tell them something but then just left them standing around him, while he started pitching again. He struck out the next three players, basically saying that he didn't need them to win."

"They mad at him for dat?"

"I don't think so. They all knew he was a real joker."

"Mm."

"And boy howdy, could he pitch! You know he once pitched and won a fourteen-inning game and refused to give up the mound for a second game—it was a double header—and he won it after another nine innings. Unbelievable!"

"Mm. You play wid him?"

Emil laughed. "No, he was totally out of my league. I'm just sorry to see him go and so young."

Sophia shook her head and looked at her hands. "What he die for."

"TB. He was only thirty-seven years old."

Sophia nodded. "Turdy-seven. Bobby only tventy-nine."

"I know." Both sat for a moment with their own thoughts about the son and brother lost too young.

"You and Bobby always did like da baseball."

"Bobby didn't like baseball. He liked the Cubs!"

"Dat da name still call dem now?"

"Yup! After they won the World Series under that name, I don't think they will change it again." Emil looked out the front window at the waning light. "I sure wish Bob would have lived to see them win the series. Can you imagine his joy? He always wore his heart on his sleeve."

Sophia shook her head still looking down at her hands. "Ja. Bobby is gone eight years, but I will see him soon. Seventy-eight is too oldt."

Emil's head swiveled to her. "Ma? Why do you say that? Are you not feeling well?"

Sophia waived her right hand toward him, air escaping from between her lips. "*Fffft*. I fine but too oldt. It's soon my time."

Emil took her hand. "Well, let's not hurry it. We all still need you."

She looked at him. Her blue eyes were faded and watery with her left eyelid nearly covering her eye completely. Her wizened face was lopsided with the left sagging noticeably more than the natural aging of the right. She squeezed his hand. "You and your brothers don't need da mama anymore. *Ich bin nur eine Last. Kann kein Brot backen. Kann nicht Wäsch waschen. Kann nicht—*

"Ma. Don't talk like that. Maybe you can't bake bread or do the laundry but are not a burden None of us feels that way." He searched for words of comfort. "You are the glue that holds the family together. We won't know which way to turn when you're gone."

It was Sophia's turn to pat his hand. "You vill. I taught right unt wrong, and if vorried, ask your brothers. Sie mus take care each other."

"Ma—

"Go ask Anna if dar any coffee left. I bit dry."

Emil rose and took a step toward the kitchen, but then turned back. "I love you, Ma."

Sophia's face lit up with a lopsided smile. *"Unt ich liebe dich."* She made a shooing motion. "Go! Afore I die of tirst."

***

SALOONKEEPERS LOOKING
FOR PLACES

We are told that saloonkeepers of Woodstock, North Crystal Lake and Harvard are looking for new locations. A few of these men have already looked over McHenry, but whether or not any have decided to come here we have not learned.

McHenry Plaindealer, April 8, 1914.

***

Poison Berries

The six-year-old daughter of Mr. and Mrs. Harry Fishburn, residing near Woodstock, was found dead in the yard of the home on Wednesday evening of last week. It seems that the deceased, with two other children, had picked and eaten some red berries at the roadside, which is given as the cause of the child's death.

Woodstock Sentinel, April 8, 1914.

***

New Fire House

Woodstock is to have a new fire department building. The structure will be erected in the rear of the present city hall and will be two stories in height. The lower floor will be occupied by the fire department and horses, while the upper floor will house the driver and caretaker of the horses and department.

Woodstock Sentinel, April 16, 1914.

***

Eight-year-old Edna sat with her mother at the dining room table reading the paper. It was homework for Edna, assigned because she had gotten an 'Unsatisfactory' in Reading on her last report card. Ida and she had made a deal that they would read the paper twice a week on Wednesday nights and Saturday afternoons.

The older girls were in their rooms also 'doing homework.' Ida could hardly believe that Helen would be moving to the high school in two more years. How time flew.

"Did you know," asked Edie in a know-it-all voice, the facts are in the paper, of course, "that Woodstock is building a firehouse next to the city hall?"

"Why no." Ida had read the paper and knew of the plan, but she wanted Edie to tell her about it.

"Yes, it will have a place for the horses and fire de-part-ment," she sounded out the word, "downstairs and a house for the driver upstairs." Edie looked at her mother. "I would like to be a fire wagon driver. Maybe I could do that someday and live down on the square."

"That's a thought." Ida had glanced up to gauge the seriousness of this statement, but now bent back to her darning.

Edna went back to her reading. "Oh no!"

"What?" Ida hadn't noticed any distressing articles in this week's paper. The article about little Emma Fishburn dying from poison berries had disrupted last Wednesday's reading. Luckily, Edie didn't know her personally, but there were still tears. "What's wrong?"

"Someone doesn't like horses."

Ida hid a smile. "They don't?"

"No, here's a letter to the ed-ter."

"Ed-i-ter," Ida corrected.

"Ed-i-ter. Let me read it and then I'll tell you." Edie bent to the task with finger following the words on the page and lips moving as she read.

Ida noticed when she raised her head and looked concerned.

"Well?"

"Well, the letter says that the horses stink and the smell will come into the opera house and de-ter-ate..."

"Deteriorate. It means to make something get old or lose value or get in worse condition."

"It will make the opera house," Edna considered the options, "get in worse condition."

"Well, I suppose it would be displeasing if you could smell horse manure during a play, wouldn't it?"

"But they can't help it." Edie's voice had risen a bit in defense.

"Who can't help it?"

"The horses. They have to...to...poop."

"It is a dilemma, isn't it?"

"Yes. The letter says that the fire house should be put somewhere else away from the square."

"What do you think?"

Edna looked at the table. Thinking was hard work. She wished she could just play with her paper dolls now. She'd had enough of—

"Well?"

Edie looked up, looking surprised that Ida was still expecting an answer. She shook her head slowly. "I wonder if they will let us see the horses when we go to the square?"

"Maybe."

"If they told the letter writer that, maybe it would change his mind because they'd be able to make friends with the horses and not worry about them smelling."

"Maybe."

"I would go see them, and I don't care about the smell of horses. I think their house should be next to the city hall."

"Very good. I hope the adults think it through as well as you have."

"Can I stop reading now?"

"Yes." Ida wound up her floss. "I have dough rising. Do you want to bake some rolls for supper?"

"Yes!" Edie clapped her hands in glee. "Making rolls is one of my favorite things. And maybe a cookie and milk?"

"I think I can arrange that."

***

VERA CRUZ SEIZED TODAY

Washington, April 21. —Action by the army and navy of the United States to force General Huerta to salute the flag was held up early today through opposition in the senate to the form of the joint resolution approving President Wilson's purposes as it passed the house last night. A recess of the senate was taken.

It sets forth:

"That the state of unrest, violence and anarchy which exists in Mexico, the numerous unchecked and unpunished murders of American citizens and the spoliation of their property in that country, the impossibility of securing protection or redress by diplomatic methods in the absence of lawful or effective authority, the inability of Mexico to discharge its international obligations, the unprovoked insults and indignities inflicted upon the flag and the uniform of the United States by the armed forces in occupancy of large parts of Mexican territory have become intolerable.

"That the self-respect and dignity of the United States and the duty to protect its citizens and its international rights require that such a course be followed in Mexico by our government as to compel respect and observance of its rights."

"A joint resolution justifying the employment of the armed forces of the United States in enforcing certain demands against Victoriano Huerta.

Resolved, by the senate and house of representatives in congress assembled, that the president of the United States is justified in the employment of the armed forces of the United States to enforce the demands upon Victoriano Huerta for unequivocal amends to the government of the United States for affronts and indignities committed against this government by General Huerta and his representatives."

Forty-eight hours, possibly less, the United States government will have taken possession of the Mexican customs houses at Tampico and Vera Cruz.

Denison Review, April 22, 1914.

***

All Things Denison
by Clara Daring

The Bible says that as the end days approach there will be wars and rumors of wars, and that is exactly what has happened at the United States southern border. A seemingly innocent and accidental injustice has brought out the wolf in our country. Baring their teeth and howling in reprisal, our army, navy, and marines have rushed in to remind the Mexican government just what they are dealing with north of the border.

Your friends at the Denison paper believe that this action is what should have been long ago and that our forces should continue to put pressure on the Mexican government to "suppress the riotous conditions there." If this leads to war, they shout, so be it!

Across the pond in Europe, rumors of war are also running rampant. Good Kaiser Wilhelm is plagued both by illness and by a family of buffoons who would bring all of Europe into conflict. Luckily, the German Emperor is smart enough to tightly hold the reins so as not to let the warhorses stampede.

Does this posturing by the U. S. and Austria signal the coming of the last days? I hope not. War has its place, but its place is not in the twentieth century where peace and prosperity prevail.

Crawford County Courier, April 22, 1914.

***

Personals

Ray Wienke of Woodstock spent Sunday as the guest
of friends in McHenry.

McHenry Plaindealer, April 23, 1914.

MUMPS

Mumps have been quite general among the employees of the Oliver typewriter factory at Woodstock of late.

McHenry Plaindealer, April 23, 1914.

Hard-boiled Hens

A number of Woodstock women, after making a purchase of eggs recently have discovered that some of 'em were boiled and now they are wondering what farmers near Woodstock own the hens that lay hard boiled eggs.

McHenry Plaindealer, April 23, 1914.

***

GOOD ROADS

Supervisor P. A. Renie and Commissioners of Highways, Jos. Schneider, Charles Ackmann and Chris Fritz, were at Woodstock on Saturday afternoon to attend a good roads meeting and discuss the best improvements to be made on the roads. There seems to be a great awakening all over the land about having better roads and the local highway commissioners propose to be found in the front ranks.

Woodstock Republican, May 1, 1914.

***

Ida stood up from her squat position in the garden and ran the back of her hand over her forehead as her vision went black for a moment, but brightened and came back into focus with flashing lights. Goodness, she hated that feeling like she was going to swoon for no good reason. Just getting old. She'd be forty on her next birthday.

She looked around her garden. The vegetables were all in. It was a bit early, but she had a good feeling about the weather. The cold was gone if not the damp. Her daffodils and jonquils had been gorgeous this year, and the tulips were just about at the end of their bloom. She breathed deeply, feeling less dizzy. She could smell the turned dirt and the smell of cut grass from the Cooney's yard a house away. They were always the first to cut their lawn.

Ida looked at her gladiolas that were sending up shafts. They would be blooming by May 31, right on time. She had thinned them last fall and sold over a hundred bulbs to women at Circle, giving them instructions on how to plant them and what to expect. The way they had spread this spring, she would have more to sell in late summer. The tulips and daffodils could also stand thinning out or pushing back as they had taken up a row on the vegetable garden as they came back this spring. Ida smiled. In them was the constant struggle between utility and beauty.

She picked up the hoe to V another row in which to put the sweet corn. Putting her head down and her back into the effort, she again felt the dizziness descend on her, and she hung on to the hoe as a staff. Maybe that was enough for today. She would go sit and have a lemonade. It was almost time to start supper anyway. The sweet corn could wait a day.

She left the tools leaning on the old carriage house or shed as they called it now in such motorized modern times. They didn't own a horse anymore nor a surrey. Ida smiled thinking about how much John wanted an automobile, but it was far out of their reach at present. Seemed like they could walk everywhere they wanted to go in Woodstock and beyond that there was the train. If push came to shove, they could rent a horse and cart. So far, except for John's campaigning, there was no need to go even to McHenry or Crystal Lake. Woodstock had not only variety, but quality merchandise.

Ida listened at the stairs and heard the *vroom* of Bobby's small voice. He was awake and playing in his crib.

"Bobby?" she called up.

"Mama?" he called down. "Come."

She slowly climbed the stairs to the second floor. She was a little breathless from the climb. When did that start happening? Goodness. Getting old wasn't any fun at all.

As she rounded the corner into his room, Bobby greeted her with an ear-to-ear smile that would have melted the heart of the gloomiest person – not that she was gloomy. In his nearly two-year-old mind, he was almost ready for a regular bed, but she liked it, especially on a day like this, that he stayed put after waking up in the crib rather than coming downstairs alone. He had accomplished opening both the front and back doors on his own and could, at least in theory, disappear out the front while she hoed in the back. Now, she lifted him over the rail and set him down, and he toddled out and over to the stairs.

"Go backward," she said, "So you don't fall."

"Climb."

"No backward, like Edie taught you."

"Mama, climb."

"Mama will go backward too." She turned around and started crawling backward down the stairs. He giggled and followed suit.

They ended up sitting on the stairs that extended into the kitchen.

Lemonade. She was going to get lemonade when she came in. "Are you thirsty? Or hungry?"

Bobby touched his mouth and nodded.

"Okay. Pull up a chair, young sir, and I will find some cookies and lemonade."

Bobby went to one of the kitchen chairs and reached across the seat attempting to get a grip on the other side. It was a long reach for his short arms, but he was persistent. Ida found the lemonade in the icebox and poured a large glass for herself and a small glass for the boy. A few cookies on a plate and they were ready for afternoon tea.

Bobby whined a little. "Climb! Up!"

"You can't make it up?"

Bobby shook his head and scowled, his high forehead scrunching to almost nothing above his eyes.

"Are you mad because you can't climb up?"

He seemed to consider this, looking at the chair and then back at her again nodding. "Mad! Up."

Ida smiled at him. A new word. "Do you need help?"

That word he knew. "Hep up." He raised his arms above his head in the universal 'pick me up' position.

Instead of picking him up she pointed at the chair. "You try again, and I'll give you a boost."

"Booz?" His face was scrunched in confusion.

"Boost. I'll show you. You try."

Again, he considered. He looked at the chair. Then he took three quick steps, put his foot up on one of the rungs and threw himself across the seat flailing for purchase. Ida put her hand under his bottom and boosted him just a little so he could reach the opposite side. He grabbed the edge and pulled himself up onto the seat.

Ida clapped with delight. "There you go. What a big boy you are!"

Bobby turned around and sat solidly in the middle of the chair, squealed, and raised his arms in happy V just as his sisters had taught him. Then pulling his legs up under him, he got up on his knees, so he could reach the table, and grabbed one half of a cookie as a prize.

Ida sat down heavily at the table. She drank a long draw from her glass. Maybe she needed water, although it hadn't been hot out in the yard at all. If anything, it was a bit chilly. She liked it when the air was just a bit crisp and the sun a bit overcast. She leaned her head into her hands and rubbed her temples with her thumbs.

"Mama. Dink."

She looked up and held the glass so he could get a drink. His face puckered up and his brow again furrowed. She took the glass back and looked at him.

"Mad. Mama."

"Why?"

He shook his head. "Co-kie."

She handed him the other half of the cookie, and he settled back on his haunches to eat the sugar cookie. Was something wrong with the cookies? She reached for one and took a small bite. No, they tasted delicious. Rich vanilla and sweet sugar in just the right proportions.

As Bobby finished his treat, Ida offered him the glass of lemonade.

He pushed the glass away, almost knocking it out of her hand. "No! Mad. Mk"

"You want milk?"

He nodded.

Ida rose and poured a small glass of cold milk and offered it to him. He took it in both hands and drank it down, spilling only a dribble in the end.

Ida shrugged. She tossed the last of her own cookie into her mouth enjoying the soft texture of the center and the crunch of the edges. She swallowed and reached for her lemonade. Bobby's eyes got big as he watched the glass draw close to her mouth. Ida took a large gulp.

The lemon mixed with the sweet of the cookie to make the most awful sour taste. She felt every inch of her gums and tongue jump to, and she looked around for somewhere to spit, but then she caught sight of her son staring at her wide-eyed. She breathed in carefully, holding the vile concoction in her mouth, collecting her courage, and swallowed. Her face puckered and her shoulders raised to her ears as she tried to shake off the taste. Without meaning to, she uttered a strangled, "Ugh."

Bobby ventured a comment. "Mad."

Ida shook her head. "No, not mad, just surprised."

"Mlk."

"I agree cookies go better with milk than lemonade."

Bobby's arms shot up in another enthusiastic V! Ida burst out in laughter, much to Bobby's delight.

***

Local News

"Near Beer" parlors are to take the places of Elgin saloons on and after today.

A lively battle between a number of colored gents residing at Woodstock and Harvard and a few Harvard young men took place in the latter named city one day recently. The colored boys were taken to Woodstock, where a fine was imposed upon them.

The supreme court has affirmed the decision of Circuit Judge Charles H. Donnelly of Woodstock holding the Sunday closing barber ordinance of Marengo as invalid. The finding came as a result of a suit of the city of Marengo against a local barber in that city who operated his shop on Sunday.

McHenry Plaindealer, May 7, 1914.

***

Helen watched the caravan of horse and oxen drawn wagons circle the square – six in all. She had not seen such a display before. The colors of the canvas coverings ranged from white to light orange, the banners flowing from staff at the rear of each wagon. But it wasn't the wagons that made her stare, but rather the people who rode on their front benches. The dresses were in rainbow colors. Hair drawn up with feathers and tied with red and yellow and blue scarves.

The customers and merchants of Woodstock square came from the establishments and were drawn to the curb as if the circus had just come to town.

The children from the caravan had smudged faces and bare feet, and they ran here and there with their fathers' hats begging the small crowds for money.

As they approached her position, Helen reached into her pocket and put a penny into the hat. The little girl with the hat smiled at her and said, "*Va multumesc*. Tank you," and she ran on to the next person.

Helen felt John come up behind her and put his hand on her shoulder. She couldn't move. She wanted to know more.

"Who are they, Papa?"

"They are gypsies and not people that I want you to associate with."

She looked up at him. "Why?"

"They aren't...I mean, they don't...well it's hard to explain. They have bad...um...manners."

"Manners? The little girl said, 'thank you' for the penny I gave her."

"That's good, but I mean other kinds of manners."

"Like what?"

"You are too young to hear about that. Let's get on home."

"I want to stay. Are they going to put on a show?"

"I don't know. But we'll be late for dinner and Mama will be disgruntled with us. You don't want that do you?"

"No, but just a little bit longer."

The little girl had covered the north side of the square and was working her way back up the hill. She came close to Helen again and smiled. She held out her hat to John.

"Papa?"

John made a sound in his throat but reached for his coin purse.

"I like your bracelet," Helen said, pointing to the gold bobble on the little girl's wrist. The girl looked at the trinket and tried to hide it up her sleeve. John dropped a nickel into the hat.

"What's your name?" Helen asked.

The girl smiled and nodded.

John put his hand on Helen's shoulder and leaned down close to her ear. "She might not understand English."

"I'm Helen," Helen said, patting her chest. "Who are you?" She pointed at the little girl.

The little girl patted her own chest. "Elsa."

"Elsa. That's a pretty name." Helen considered what sign language might translate pretty name to Elsa's language and came up with no ideas, so she just smiled again.

Elsa did a little curtsy and worked her way toward the courthouse, playing the crowd. From the other side of the square there was a loud whistle and all the 'gypsy kids' (as Helen was calling them in her head) skipped away through the park. Elsa climbed up into the seat of the second wagon which had stopped in front of J. J. Stafford Furniture and Undertaking. She looked back. Saw Helen watching and waved. Helen raised her hand in farewell.

"Come on. We must go." John reached down and took her hand and led her away. The gypsy caravan circled the park once more playing music on pipes, drums, and tambourine dancing behind their wagons. She kept looking back until they turned the corner onto Throop Street.

"Papa?"

"Yes?"

"Where do the gypsies live?"

"They live in those wagons."

"Should we build houses for them?"

"They like to live like that."

"Do they?"

"Why yes. I've heard that they do. They travel from town-to-town begging and doing odd jobs and…. His voice trailed off.

"And what?"

"You don't have to worry about them. They take care of themselves."

Helen thought about that. She could take care of herself, but she still needed a house and her parents. For a while yet, at least.

***

Gypsies in Court

A band of gypsies wandered into Woodstock, Wednesday, and little attention was given them until the middle of the afternoon, when one of Woodstock's infant suitors rushed into the office of Police Magistrate Brown and informed him that one of the gypsy girls was wearing a gold bracelet that belonged to his sweetheart, the little daughter of Frank Inger. Police Magistrate Brown was a bit inclined to pass the matter up, thinking the boy was mistaken, but the youth was so insistent that he finally sent Officer Wilcox to the gypsy camp to investigate the matter. The bracelet was found on the arm of one of the little gypsy girls, and after some parleying, the whole band of gypsies was taken to the magistrate's office, where the gypsy girl said she found the bracelet on the street. The Inger child to whom the bracelet belonged admitted that she had lost it, but the gypsy girl wept copiously at the thought of giving up her find, and it was not until the Inger child's father was called in and agreed to let the little gypsy girl keep the bracelet upon the payment of a fine of $3 that the affair was settled, and everybody concerned made happy.

Woodstock Sentinel, May 13, 1914.

Announcements

I hereby announce myself as a candidate for the office of County Treasurer, subject to the decision of the Republican voters at the primaries, September 9, 1914, and respectfully solicit the support of my friends.

LYNN RICHARDS.

For County Treasurer

I herewith announce myself as a candidate for the office of county treasurer and solicit the support of my friends at the coming primaries.

JOHN WIENKE

Woodstock Republican, May 13, 1914.

***

"I see by the paper you're in the running again." Ida's voice was not critical but matter of fact. If John kept running, he was sure to win someday.

"Yes." John poured a glass of orange juice and sat down to a breakfast of eggs and ham. "No one else wants to run against Lynn Richards. We can't let a candidate run unchallenged. Everyone says he will win, but I'm hoping people vote for the underdog."

"Ah. I'm glad to see the gossip doesn't hold you back."

John smiled and reached for a piece of bread to eat with his eggs. His favorite way to eat eggs was to eat the white...not his favorite part...with bread, then break open the yolks and salt them and eat them separately...his favorite part.

Ida glanced at his Saturday attire. Good suit, white shirt with high neck collar and gold cufflinks. "Don't drop egg yolk on that tie."

John looked down at his tie. It was a favorite. Red and white stripes at an angle. Perfect for a day of pressing the flesh around the county. He picked up his napkin and tucked a corner into his collar.

Ida smiled. "I guess the gypsies are in town. Have they been in the office selling trinkets?"

"No, not yet. But we are off the square so they might not get to us. Too bad they can't come up with a better way to earn a living than begging."

"True. Let's see. What could they do? Vaudeville? Horse training? How to pick a pocket?"

John laughed. "Any of the above, I suppose. The other night, Helen was worried about where they made their homes."

"Under the sky." Ida placed her hands together in a display of prayerfulness.

John smiled. "It does sound close to God, doesn't it"?

Ida glanced at him with a rueful expression. "No. I was kidding."

"But don't you think it would be fun to sleep outside on a warm night under a blanket with the whole starry sky above you," John argued.

Ida's face lost all humor. "No. Are you thinking of joining the caravan? Don't tell me. You are going to buy a caravan wagon so you can go about the county making stump speeches from the tailgate and collecting campaign funds by our three girls running hither and yon with top hats." Ida reached for her coffee, smiling.

John kept his face straight. "Hey, that's not a bad idea."

Ida almost spit out the sip of coffee. She sputtered but managed to control herself.

"I don't think we could get Helen to do it, so we might have to enlist Bobby." A smiling John took a bite of his egg and a string of yolk fell from the fork and landed on the napkin. John looked down at it.

Ida smirked at the egg splotch. "Gotcha!" And took another sip.

"No, it didn't, because my gorgeous and smart wife stepped in and saved the day with a suggestion."

"Pshaw! I'm not gorgeous. But I am S-M-A-R-T."

"That you are."

***

Will Be a Strong Candidate

Lynn Richards has announced himself as a candidate for the office of county treasurer. He will undoubtedly be a hard opponent for anyone who comes up against him. For a number of years, Mr. Richards was in the office of the circuit clerk at Woodstock.

Crystal Lake Herald, May 14, 1914.

***

Personals

Ray Wienke of Woodstock visited among McHenry friends Sunday.

McHenry Plaindealer, May 21, 1914.

***

Running For Treasurer

John F. Wienke, Republican candidate for county treasurer, was in McHenry Monday afternoon, forming the acquaintance of the voters in this vicinity. Mr. Wienke is one of those big, good-natured fellows who make friends at sight and his visit here undoubtedly gained him a number of votes.

Lynn Richards, Republican candidate for county treasurer, made this office a welcome call on Monday afternoon. Mr. Richards is cashier of the Crystal Lake State bank at North Crystal Lake and looks like a live wire. He is well qualified for the job which he seeks and has the support of a large following of friends thruout the county.

McHenry Plaindealer, May 28, 1914.

Local News

A rattle snake with ten rattles was killed in a slough near Harvard one day last week.

An auto bus line has been established between the cities of Genoa and Sycamore. A charge of $1.00 is made for the round trip.

Crystal Lake's only saloon closed its doors on Thursday evening of last week and now the village as well as Nunda township is absolutely dry.

Beginning June 6 and continuing thruout the hot summer months, the employes of the Elgin National Watch factory will work but five days a week. This means Saturday off.

On account of the decrease in the sale of typewriters in Mexico since the present outbreak, the Oliver Typewriter company at Woodstock has been forced to lay off fifty men.

The city council of Harvard passed two new ordinances last week. The first relates to junk dealers in that city, who in the future must pay to the city $60 per year for carrying on their business, while the second prohibits the running of automobiles by persons under fifteen years of age, unless accompanied by their parents or guardian.

McHenry Plaindealer, May 28, 1914.

***

Ed Wienke and Frank Wienke met as they exited the 'Employees Only' door at the Oliver Typewriter Company.

"Well, Ed," Frank said, holding the door for his older brother. "Haven't seen you in a donkey's age."

"Frank. Yup, it's been a bit."

They walked down Wheeler Street toward 1st Street and on to Railroad.

"How's Ma?" Ed asked, hardly moving his lips.

Frank had to strain to hear him with the crowd of workers around them, laughing and joking, headed home for an evening's rest.

"She's doing well. She gets down about not being able to do what she used to do, but she gets up and dressed every day and is able to manage the stairs, although we do stay with her while she does that. I'm sure it feels like she gets babysat too much."

Ed nodded. "S'pose so."

They walked on.

"Did ya hear about the layoffs?" Frank moved on to another topic.

"Yup."

"Doubt it will be me or thee, right?"

"Yup."

"Last in, first out, right?"

"Yup."

They walked on, turned on Short street, and within a block reached Wicker where Ed would go to the right to his house and Frank would go left to his.

"Well, it was nice seeing ya," said Ed hand extended. "Say hi to Anna."

Frank shook Ed's hand with a smile. "Yup. And you to Kate. Good talk."

Ed smiled and waved over his shoulder as he turned north.

Frank looked after him. His brothers were so different from each other. Ed, the quiet thinker, William, the leader, Al, the gregarious neighbor, Emil and Charles, the hard workers, and John, the politician. Frank wasn't sure where that left him. It was amazing to think that they all came from the same loins.

Frank turned south, crossed the tracks and Washington Street to Dane Street. He thought about his own children, Ethyl, sixteen, Bessie, fourteen and his son Clayton, eleven, and wondered what they had been up to today.

Frank climbed the steps and heard a commotion behind the inner door. As he opened it, Clay rushed toward him saying, "Papa, papa, guess what!"

Frank hung his hat and jacket on the pegs by the door and looked at his son. "What?"

"No! Guess!"

"Um…the dog had pups."

"Noooo…we don't have a dog."

"Oh right. The cow fell in the well?"

Clay giggled. "Noooo, papa! We don't have a cow."

Bessie had walked up behind Clay.

"Oh yes, I forgot—

"We are all going to be in the Decoration Day celebrations," said Bessie.

"Bessssieee," Clay whined. "I wanted to tell him."

"You're too slow," said Bess.

Frank made his way into the living room and sat down. "Well Clay, tell me what you will all be doing. Good afternoon, Ma."

Sophia waved a hand in greeting.

"Okay. I will be in the sixth-grade chorus. And Ethyl will be playing with the high school orchestra."

"And Bessie?"

"And Bessie will—

"I will be singing with the high school Glee Club!"

"Besssieee! I was telling him." Clayton flopped down on the hassock at his grandmother's feet.

Bessie just smiled.

"Well, it does sound like a family affair, doesn't it Ma?"

"*Ja, sie sind alle sehr musikalisch. Singe 'Bleib bei mir'.*"

The children beamed. "We can do that," said Clay, and he started with a solid alto, "Abide with me fast falls the eventide…" Bessie came in with the harmony, "The darkness deepens…." Ethyl ran in from the kitchen and got up to the piano and accompanied them on the second and third verse, adjusting the key only a bit. When they finished with "Oh Thou Who changes not, abide with me." Anna, who had come from the kitchen to listen, Sophia, and Frank gave them a rousing 'hurrah.' All three children held hands and bowed.

Lyte, H. F. "Abide with me," 1847. *Evangelical Lutheran Hymn-Book*, 1912.)

"Tank you," said Sophia, wiping her eyes with a handkerchief.

"Oh, Oma, don't cry. We will always sing for you," said Clay.

"Yes, always," agreed the girls.

Frank rose and went to Anna and gave her a peck on the cheek. She put an arm around his waist as the children decided what they would sing next.

"We are so lucky, aren't we?" said Anna softly.

"Yes."

Anna patted his back. "Go get cleaned up while you listen. Dinner is almost ready."

***

FITTINGLY OBSERVED

Decoration day was observed in a fitting manner by Woodstock Post No. 108, G. A. R. and Woodstock Relief Corps, No. 223. Early in the morning members of both orders were busily engaged in placing flags in the cemeteries or gathering flowers with which to decorate the graves of the soldier dead, while Capt. Senger of Company G, Illinois National Guard, with his able assistants, decorated the stage in the city hall.

Services were held in the afternoon at the City Hall, and although different in form from any held in recent years, as there was no speaker, were very delightful and gave general satisfaction. The services were opened by the High School orchestra playing a patriotic melody in a very efficient manner. Commander Still welcomed the audience in the name of Post No. 108, and Mr. Burdick, chaplain of the post, read a prayer, followed by a selection by the High School orchestra, after which the High School Girls' Glee club sang, "Cover Them Over," in a very pleasing manner.

Mrs. Beatrice Cowlin, of Elgin, gave two excellent readings, which were favorably received by the audience. Lincoln's Gettysburg address was given by Frank Hurley in a manner which showed ability and power as an orator.

The pupils of the sixth grade sang two selections; a chorus of the fourth grade of the North Side school gave two numbers and the tots of the third grade gave a very fine flag drill. Numbers were all executed with so much skill and the pupils exhibited such ease and self-reliance that it not only reflected great credit upon them, but also upon the teachers who so carefully trained them—Miss Gericke and Miss Austin, for the North school, and Miss Cooney and Miss Carey, of the South school. The closing song, "America," was led by the High School orchestra.

After these services, the usual march to the cemetery was made, headed by Comrade George Eckert, marshal of the day. In the absence of the band, the drum corps of Company G dispensed martial music to the satisfaction of all.

Those in line were Company G, Illinois National Guard; Post No. 108 G. A. R., with Comrade Randall as the color bearer; Corps No. 223, W. R. C.; a detachment of the Spanish War Veterans, and about eighty children carrying flags.

The graves of 73 Civil war veterans and four Spanish-American war veterans were decorated.

Woodstock Sentinel, June 3, 1914.

***

Personals
Ray Weinke of Chicago spent Saturday and Sunday as the guest of McHenry friends.

Woodstock Sentinel, June 4, 1914.

***

Work on New Depot
A gang of men is tearing down the depot at Woodstock, the office and the men's waiting room alone being left. These rooms will be moved to one side for use while a new depot is being erected. As soon as the work is completed at Woodstock the same gang will come to Crystal Lake and tear down the old depot preparatory for building a new one.

Crystal Lake Herald, June 11, 1914.

***

Honorary President of State Suffrage is Jubilant

When the Rev. Olympia Brown Willis was interviewed this morning on the recent developments of suffrage both as to the decision of the supreme court of Illinois and as to the step taken by the twelfth biennial convening in Chicago, she was most enthusiastic.

She said, "The decision of the supreme court of Illinois is the greatest victory for equal suffrage. This will influence women, making them sure of what they now have and will also influence other states in the suffrage direction, and I hope it will influence Wisconsin so that we may gain the same privileges which are granted to Illinois women."

The resolution adopted at the biennial, she said, was equally find. "This," said the honorary president of the Wisconsin Suffrage league, "will have a vast influence on congress and all over the United States." She considers the federation very influential, and its influence will directly influence the women of the United States.

The Rev. Olympia Brown Willis denied the report that she was to leave Wisconsin for good. She said the home would be kept in Racine as long as she lived, but that she would probably spend most of the winters in the east with her son and daughter.

Racine Journal Times, June 15, 1914.

***

Ida sat down at the kitchen table for the ritual morning coffee and kuchen break. Two-year-old Bobby was already there with a fresh blueberry muffin on his tray. He reached out and tried to grasp it, came away with crumbs which he tried to get to his mouth, but succeeded in dumping most of them down his front.

"Wait. I'll break it up a little for you." Ida broke the top off the muffin and each resulting piece in half. "That should do it."

Bobby studied the chunks of muffin and bravely waded in. He accomplished the difficult job by squishing handfuls of the muffin into a small pillow that would fit into his mouth.

"You like blueberry muffins?"

Bobby nodded vigorously, his face smeared with blueberry and crumbs.

Ida picked up her own muffin, took a bite, and opened the *Chicago Tribune* which John had left on the table when he rushed out to his first appointment.

***

ASSASINATION OF HEIR TO AUSTRIAN THRONE
WILL TRAGEDY BRING PEACE FOR AUSTRIA?
Francis Ferdinand Has Been Disturbing Factor of Nation

New York, June 28. —[Special.]— It is difficult to discuss the tragedy at Sarayedo without laying oneself open to the reproach of the heartless. For while it is only natural that one should be stricken with horror at the brutal and shocking assassination of Archduke Francis Ferdinand, it is impossible to deny the fact that his disappearance from the scene is calculated to diminish the tenseness of the situation and to make for peace both within and without the dual empire.

"Indeed!" Ida said aloud, and Bobby looked at her. "Oh sorry, I should keep my opinions to myself. You're doing fine. Here, a little milk will make things go down easier."

She held a small glass for him to take a couple gulps. He smiled and milk streamed down his chin.

"Oh my, like father, like son. We are going to have to do a change of clothes before Papa comes home, aren't we?"

Bobby looked down at his shirt. "Wet."

"Yes, finish your muffin. We'll worry about that later."

"Wet!" Bobby was pulling at his shirt with vigor.

"It's okay, Bobby. Just eat your muffin. We'll change your shirt later."

"No. Wet!" said Bobby very clearly. His face began to cloud like a thunderstorm was just behind his eyes.

"Okay, wait." Ida got up, got a clean dish towel, and skinned the shirt off the little boy. She tied the dish towel, bib-style across his bare chest.

Bobby looked down at the dish towel, found it suitable for muffin eating, and went back to squishing muffin pieces.

Ida smiled. She didn't like wet clothes either. She picked up the paper and found her place in the article.

> To such an extent has Francis Ferdinand been regarded, both at home and abroad, as a disturbing factor, and as committed to forceful and extremely aggressive policies, that the news of his death is almost calculated to create a feeling of universal relief.
>
> Twice the archduke during the emperor's illnesses brought Germany to the very brink of war with Russia, and on three occasions also with Servia, while four years ago he adopted so aggressive a policy toward Italy that hostilities seemed imminent and were only averted by the timely recovery of the old emperor from his illness and by Wilhelm putting the brakes on both the military and political activities of his government.

Yes, Ida thought. Kaiser Wilhelm was the only one the Germans can trust to keep their economy strong and their country out of war. John had said as much last night when he blessed the Emperor during supper's grace and asked God to let Ferdinand's passing be a harbinger of peace.

> Even in Germany the possibility of his advent to the throne of the dual empire was viewed with

apprehension. For it was known there that he disliked
the idea of Germany playing first fiddle in the triple
alliance and relegating Austria-Hungary to a secondary
role. The fear was that Francis Ferdinand upon
becoming emperor would break away from the alliance
with Germany and throw himself into the arms of
Russia, although at St. Petersburg he was regarded as
personifying a distinctly hostile policy towards Russia.

Why would Freddy want to ally with Russia instead of Germany
with its long history and strong people? Russia was a cold Siberian
rock. Even someone like Ferdinand wouldn't choose Russia over
Germany. And that wasn't the main problem people had with him,
was it? Ida seemed to remember reading something earlier about
Ferdinand… oh…here we go…

> "…fell in love with his consort's lady in waiting,
> Countess Sophia Chotek, daughter of an Austrian
> diplomat of minor rank and member of a lower
> Bohemian nobility. When the king fired her because of
> these affections, Ferdinand became determined to wed
> her. It was only with the utmost difficulty that the
> emperor's consent to the match could be obtained.
> Indeed, it was only granted because it was believed that
> Ferdinand was doomed to an early death from
> tuberculosis of the lungs.

Yes! That was it. Not only was he inept when he acted as ruler,
but he wouldn't obey the rules of the crown. Europe is better off
without him.

Bobby banged both his hands down on his tray, causing Ida to
jump.

"Oh my!" Ida put her fist to the middle of her chest. "You
scared the devil right out of me!"

Bobby laughed. He had eaten most of the muffin crumbs and
had managed to pull off the towel bib. His chest was smeared with

crushed blueberries and muffin crumbs seemed to have made their way into his hair.

"Just let me finish this article, okay?"

Bobby started sucking his thumb while twirling a lock of his hair.

He's getting sleepy, thought Ida as she returned to the paper.

> Archduke Francis Ferdinand was the only prince of the historic and illustrious house of Hapsburg who ever visited the United States. He was over here some twenty years ago or so, at the time of the Columbian World's Fair in Chicago. But although every effort was made to make his visit pleasant, he failed to appreciate what was done for him.
>
> The archduke was quite the reverse of complimentary after his visit, where not openly hostile. It is no exaggeration to state that he had no friendly feeling whatsoever toward this country, and that he was indeed rather prejudiced against it, which might have influenced the policy of the dual empire towards the United States had he lived to take the throne.
>
> *Chicago Tribune*, June 29, 1914.

"Mlk!" Bobby demanded again banging the tray top.

Ida jumped again. "Don't do that. It scares Mama."

"Mama, Mlk!"

Ida held the glass for him. She put the glass down and looked him over. "Come on, Prince Charming. Let's get you hosed off. You never know when the emperor might visit."

***

TIME FOR A LINCOLN PARTY

Reno, Nev., July 18.—[Editor of the *Tribune*.]—The present political condition seems to be an opportune time to organize a people's party under the name of the Lincoln party, which should have to its slogan and the

first plank in its platform the saying of that great
American: "A government of the people, by the people,
for the people." A party that will stand for American
principles, American policies, and American
institutions. And for American citizenship as
exemplified in the life of Lincoln.

Such a party would be in line with the tendency of
the times and should be successful at the polls in 1916.
The opportunity is here and should be taken advantage
of. It may be many years before another political
condition affords the same opportunity.

H. G. Comstock
Chicago Tribune, July 23, 1914.

***

Millions of Men, Women and Children Helpless, Await Monarchs' Will.

WASHINGTON, D. C. July 30.—Several hundred
million men, women, and children in Europe—
particularly the millions in Austria, Germany, Russia,
and France—are groping tonight in utter darkness on
the brink of war. They know not whether they will be
plunged headlong tomorrow to destruction or
miraculously saved from the pit.

In their palaces, linked by telegraph wires, sit the
three monarchs, William of Germany, Francis Joseph
of Austria, and Nicholas of Russia, who hold in their
hands the destinies of the millions of people who have
no voice in the decision of peace or war. If these three
men know what those destinies are, they are not telling
the people. The palaces are silent, and the censorship is
on.

The meager information which comes out of Europe
today shows the overlords of the continent in their
Gargantuan game of political chess.

But though their life blood is staked upon the result,
the people are not even spectators of the game. They
merely know that somewhere, somehow, men are

deciding whether on the marrow the husband and father shall go forth with the sickle or the bayonet in hand. It was Nicholas' move yesterday, it is William's today, and it will be Francis Joseph's tomorrow.

Chicago Tribune, July 31, 1914.

***

"John? I thought you said that Ferdinand getting assassinated was going to keep the peace in Europe," said Ida.

John looked up. "Did I?"

They were sitting in the parlor, John with the *Chicago Trib* and Ida with her cross-stitching.

"Yes, you did."

"Hm. I must have lost my mind. You know what happened today, right?

Ida put her hook in her lap and looked at him. "No, what?"

"The stock market took a nosedive. American securities lost about $700,000,000 in value. The slide closed all the world markets except the New York exchange. It was the only market open for trade today."

"Why didn't you tell me right away. Are we destitute?"

"No. I don't have much riding on the market. Too uncertain. But it's bound to influence the price of things and who knows what will happen in Europe."

"What do you mean?"

"If I did say there wouldn't be a war, I amend that, with what I know now, to say there most likely will be a war, but we'll have to just wait and see."

Ida picked up her stitching. She was cross stitching the hem of pillowcases with bluebirds with ribbons in their mouths. Old crows with sickles in their mouths would be more appropriate. Or maybe little Indians beating on war drums instead of the bluebirds of happiness.

***

Local News

John F. Wienke of Woodstock, Republican candidate for county treasurer, was shaking hands with voters in town last Saturday.

McHenry Plaindealer, August 27, 1914.

***

LYNN RICHARDS FOR TREASURER

Lynn W. Richards, cashier of the State Bank of Crystal Lake, who is candidate for county treasurer, has been a well-known figure in the public life of McHenry county for many years. He is a son of the late Geo F. Richards, who served the county as circuit clerk for two terms.

Mr. Richards served as deputy circuit clerk for fifteen years, having been retained by our present circuit clerk Theo Hamer after he was elected to office. (followed by seven more paragraphs lauding Richards)

McHenry Plaindealer, August 6, 1914.

***

Local News

Woodstock's new depot will be ready for occupancy about the middle of next month.

Two hurdy-gurdy outfits, each carrying a monk, made visits to this village during the past week. They carried away a few of our nickels and dimes.

Rev. Karl Oestenkoetter, who has taken temporary charge of St. Mary's Catholic church in McHenry, is watching the war movements with the keenest of interest. He has three brothers who are now serving in the German army, and he is anxious to see the present trouble settled without going to a long and bloody war.

McHenry Plaindealer, August 6, 1914.

***

John perused the front page of the *Chicago Daily Tribune* EXTRA addition. He had picked it up from Ray's cigar shop before heading home to the normal tumultuous supper hour with the children. Sauerkraut and sausage was tonight's fare, with German potato salad and Bavarian cream pie for dessert.

After the children had retired to bed—Bobby—or homework—the girls—he had sunk thankfully into his chair in the parlor and opened the paper. The European war had come to fruition as the three-inch headline verified:

BRITISH-GERMAN CLASH IN NORTH SEA; MINE SINKS THE AMPHION. 131 MEN LOST.

The column stories were all about various parts of the war. Under **THE DAY'S WAR NEWS,** John read that the cable and telegraph services were "already more than half paralyzed" making it clear "the desperate character of the war." Thank God, Bobby is still a baby.

The British had voted for a second war credit of $500,000,000 and were ready to enlist 500,000 more soldiers. The Kaiser answered by calling on all Germans who were capable of bearing a gun to enlist in defense of the empire. One-upmanship at its worst.

In another story, Holland and Belgium had already been invaded by Germany, but were fighting back, with Germany taking as many as 8,000 casualties.

John put his head back against the chair. At that rate, how long can it last? How was this going to affect the prosperity of the United States or of Illinois or even Woodstock? He had heard a couple of men discussing "getting on the bandwagon" by selling food to the Europeans.

"It'll be hard to harvest wheat with the bullets flying overhead," one had laughed. "This is a golden opportunity for American farmers."

"You're right. And where are the guns and bullets going to come from? Seems like all they must fight with is pitchforks and penknives."

"If you're smart, you'll put your money into the munitions, while we ride it out. You could make a million."

John pulled the paper back up to eye level. There was one column, he suddenly realized, that wasn't about the war. The headline read:

DEATH TAKES WIFE OF THE PRESIDENT.
SLUMS SEND FLOWERS.
Both Houses of Congress Adjourn Sessions in Silence.
Washington, D. C., Aug. 6—Mrs. Woodrow Wilson, wife of the president of the United States, died at the White House at 5 o'clock this afternoon.

So that was why the *Tribune* had brought out an Extra Edition! "Ida?"

"Yes, John." Ida came from the kitchen wiping her hands on a striped dish towel.

"The President's wife died."

"What president? Surely you don't mean Wilson."

"Yes. Mrs. Wilson died."

Ida took off her apron, hung it over one of the dining room chairs, and came to the parlor. She perched on the edge of the davenport. "What happened?"

John looked over the story. "She had Bright's disease. Says she struggled with it for months. Remind me what Bright's is again."

Ida thought for a moment. "I believe it's the failure of the kidneys—what they used to call dropsy—and it is a very painful way to go. The treatment is as bad as the disease. How old was she?"

"Um." He scanned down the page. "It doesn't say. Maybe around fifty."

"Indeed. I had read a rumor that she might have been pregnant. She had missed a lot of social engagements. President Wilson is infamous for taking his daughter to events. I guess now we know why."

"She was pregnant at her age?"

Ida bumped his shoe with hers. "Stranger things have happened."

"I guess the President didn't know it was as serious as it was until this morning."

"What? Didn't know? How could he not know?"

"Article says he was taken to the red room—have you ever wanted to visit the White House?"

"No."

"Oh. Anyhow, the red room and the doctor '...in a broken voice, told him the truth.'"

"Do you think he was being lied to?" Ida had been known to keep John in the dark, away from all the gory details of medical situations. Men were often so emotional when faced with that kind of news.

"Don't know. The paper says, 'Mr. Wilson's face blanched, but he bore the shock well. He was informed the end was only a question of hours.'"

"Lord, help him."

"It says that he and the three daughters stayed at the bedside for…let's see…three hours after she was unconscious, and she died."

"I wonder if they prayed. Do you know if they are religious? Seems like a college president might not be."

"I don't know."

"Well, so it goes. There but for the grace of God go I."

John looked up, startled. "What? Do you need to tell me something?"

Ida smiled at him. "Nothing you need to know. I'm fine. The children are fine. Mamie has a check-up coming up in November, but she seems just fine. And that boy of yours is a bull. He is going—"

"To play football. I know."

Silence stretched between them for a few minutes.

"I love you, Ida. I want you to tell me if there are things wrong with the children or with you. I don't want to be surprised in the last hour."

Ida patted his hand. "Of course. I would never lie to you about things even if you were President of the United States. You aren't planning to run, are you?"

John laughed. "Not this week."

"Good. I have to finish up in the kitchen and…"

"And?" John's eyebrows rose.

"I'll always tell you."

***

War Declarations.

This is the record of Europe since July 28. The declarations in the general European war have been as follows:

July 28—Austria declared war on Servia.

Aug. 1—Germany declared war on Russia.

Aug. 4—Germany declared war on Belgium.

Aug. 4—Germany declared war on France.

Aug. 4—Germany and England declared war on each other.

Aug. 6—Austria declared war on Russia.

Chicago Daily Herald, August 14, 1914.

***

ONE MORE DAY TO REGISTER.
WOMEN GETTING BUSY.
Seventy Thousand "New" Ones Expected on Books.

Tomorrow is the only day for registration this year prior to the September primary, and all hands will devote the entire day to combing the country for the several thousand men and women who may be debarred from participating in the primary unless their names are enrolled.

Men and women, regardless of whether they registered in the spring, who have moved since then and are now not registered from their present addresses, must have their names enrolled again tomorrow. They must do this in person.

Women's registration is expected to be quite heavy, as this is only the third opportunity the new voters have had to get their names enrolled.

Chicago Tribune, August 18, 1914.

***

WEEKLY PERSONAL ITEMS

John F. Wienke of Woodstock, Republican candidate for county treasurer, was shaking hands with the voters in town last Saturday.

McHenry Plaindealer, August 22, 1914.

***

POPE PIUS X DIES
CRUSHED BY WAR
DEATH SHOCKS WORLD

Rome, Aug. 20—Pope Pius X died at 1:20 o'clock this morning.

Already suffering from bronchitis and a weak heart, the worry occasioned by the war involving all Europe brought on bronchial pneumonia, and the aged pontiff is a war victim as truly as if he had been struck down on the field of battle. He was ill for four days.

One great reform Pope Pius accomplished in his short nine-year reign, and it promises to be ever remembered in history. He proved that diplomacy in church matters is a thing of little importance compared with the direct teaching and preaching of the gospel to the poor.

By virtue of one of his documents known as the "Sapienti Consillio," the congregations composing the

Roman Curia of the Catholic church have been reformed and the American hierarchy has been accorded a recognized voice in the government of the church.

McHenry Plaindealer, August 27, 1914.

***

Roosevelt Assassin Insane

John Schrank, who attempted to murder Theodore Roosevelt in Milwaukee in the fall of 1912, by shooting him, has been declared hopelessly insane by physicians at the asylum for the criminal insane in Waupun, where Schrank is incarcerated. It is now certain that he will never be tried for the crime.

Woodstock Republican, August 28, 1914.

***

Lay-off Extended

Notice was posted at the Oliver factory Tuesday that work would not start Sept. 1, as planned, but that the lay-off would continue indefinitely owing to the military disturbances in Europe.

Woodstock Sentinel, August 31, 1914.

***

"Uncle John!" Young Frank Wienke greeted his uncle who had entered his cigar shop and set off the large bell that hung above the door.

"Can't sneak in here," John chuckled, looking up at the bell.

"You know how it is. Don't want to keep the customer waiting."

"I just stopped in for a *Tribune.*"

Frank smiled. "*Woodstock Sentinel* not bringing satisfaction anymore?"

"Well, not with the war on. *The Sentinel* is still a local paper for the most part. Nothing wrong with that, but I need to keep track of this war. Do you feel that way?"

"Hm…maybe a little."

"I need to know which side I should be on. I'm drawn, of course, to the German side, as is your aunt, no doubt you know—

"As are my grandmother and my other uncles and my father and…." Frank made a motion with his hands encompassing the whole of the city.

"Right. How can we not be? We have always had great respect for Kaiser Wilhelm. But I'm not sure about this whole invasion of other countries for what I see as 'no good reason.'"

"No good reason?" Another customer was drawn into the conversation. "How about the reason of securing the borders and keeping the riff raff out? What about the threat from Russia…do you know how big Russia is? Huge. And yet they want Germany's territory also. Or the threat from England. Don't they have the largest army? What can Germany do but fight the blockade? Ach der Lieber! No good reason? Don't be a stupid krauthead!"

Frank felt like he needed to intervene. The conversation had just degraded to insult. "Okay, okay. Let's not debate this here. I think you both are on the same side. Uncle John, I'd guess you would want to be on Germany's side, right?"

John did not want this debate at all. "Sure. My heritage is German and my wife's heritage. But I am an American, and I must speak for America. I'm not sure how the United States will fare in this war. I hope we don't feel obligated to enter on either side."

The man snorted, waved his hand in a 'no-use-talking-to-you' gesture, and went back to looking in the case at the cigar boxes.

John lowered his voice and said, "I just want a *Trib* tonight."

Frank smiled as he handed over the paper. "On the house."

***

OUTLOOK FOR FAIR
APPEARS BRIGHT

C. F. Jones, superintendent of privileges, reported on the amusements that had been arranged for this year. He gave a brief description of the performances to be given by the horses in chariot races, hurdle races, hippodrome races and fancy and sensational riding. He said that he had investigated all of the attractions that are to be brought here by the Clifton-Kelley Carnival company. They will have 11 carloads of riding devices and paraphernalia. Their carry-us-all or merry-go-around is a three-abreast horse affair and is larger and more attractive than anything ever seen here. Their motordrome, auto drome, tango shows, flea circus, minstrel shows, and free attractions are clean and very entertaining.

Woodstock Sentinel, August 20, 1914.

Local News

McHenry county produces more milk to the square mile area than any other piece of land in the world and stands third among all the counties in the United States, regardless of size. Herkimer county, New York, stands first, and one county in Pennsylvania stands second, while McHenry county leads the world per square mile.

McHenry Plaindealer, August 20, 1914.

***

Ida laid the open *Woodstock Republican* at John's place at the table. The exposed page held the campaign cameo of each candidate running for office in the primary. Each candidate had a heading of the office he or she was running for, a list of campaign positions, and a picture of the candidate, except one. John F. Wienke's picture did not appear on the page. She stood looking down at the page, shaking her head until she heard the back screen door bang, announcing her beloved husband's arrival for lunch.

She was ready for him. The egg salad sandwiches were made, with bread and butter pickles accompanying them on the plate. A cold slaw salad of cabbage and carrots with vinegar dressing sat ready for dishing. Raisin oatmeal cookies rounded out a healthy lunch.

"Hi, beautiful." John stood framed in the porch-kitchen doorway.

Ida blushed. "Oh, go on with you. Wash your hands."

He came toward her and took her forcefully into an embrace endowing her with a very lively kiss and let go. "Okay." And he turned to the kitchen sink.

Ida stood breathing hard. "What brought that on?"

John turned drying his hands on a kitchen towel. "You."

Ida considered folding over the newspaper. It could wait. She made a move toward the table, but John blocked her path. She giggled and moved to the side. He moved the same way. She giggled again. "Sit down," she said in her stern mother's voice.

"Yes, ma'am!" John sat.

He looked down at the paper, picking it up to examine.

Ida poured some cold tea in glasses and sat; her brow furrowed.

John bit off the corner of the sandwich that had been cut on the diagonal. "What's this?"

"Do you want some slaw?" Ida's voice was soft and, she hoped, enticing. Anything to distract him from the paper and back on her.

"Sure." He spooned some slaw onto his plate. "This looks good. I am hungry."

"I know," she cooed.

He was still looking at the paper. She knew he had noticed it was the Republican, one of only two papers that graced the Woodstock stands.

"Good publicity, no?" he said around chewing another bite.

"Yes." She cleared her throat although she doubted it helped. "Notice anything?"

"No. Should I?"

"No. What was that you were saying about 'hi, beautiful?'" She took a dainty bite of her sandwich.

He looked up at her. She felt the blood lift into her face. Maybe he will think it's amour.

"You must have left it here for a reason. This slaw is great!"

She sighed, resigning herself to the truth that the moment had passed. "Yes, I did."

"What?" His face looked blank.

"Look closely." Ida took a larger bite of her sandwich. It seems her allure was at an end.

"Oh. The pictures." He blanched and laid down his fork. "I'm the only one without a picture. Well, what do you expect from the Republican!" His flat hand came down on the table making the silverware jump.

"Shh." Ida's finger went to her lips. "You'll wake the baby."

"Oh. Sorry." They both sat quietly listening. Nothing.

"Did you put a picture in your packet?"

"No. They never have printed pictures." John ran his hand over his face. He had felt so good coming home after selling a large policy to Sears and Roebuck for their new factory.

"I'm sorry. I should have been helping you with this more." Ida suddenly felt like a very poor wife. She knew how important this was to him and yet she had held back from offering any help in his Don Quixote venture.

He looked at her. "It wasn't your fault that I didn't include a picture."

"Do you even know where a picture might be?"

"No."

"Well, there you have it." Ida felt like she was going to cry. No. I won't! This isn't about me. It's about my wonderful husband who would make a marvelous...what was he running for again? She glanced down at the paper. Treasurer. "You would make a wonderful treasurer. I will find a picture and you can take it around to the papers today."

She rose and started to climb the stairs to retrieve the box of pictures from the attic.

"No, come here." John's face was a bit ruddy, but his voice was calm. She obeyed.

He pulled her down on his lap and put his face onto her shoulder. She clung to him as tears, she didn't want to flow, trickled out and down her cheeks. She leaned down and found his mouth. The kiss was long and deep. He stood up, practically dumping her from his lap.

John held out his hand and Ida took it, and he led the way through the dining room to their bedroom, while the sandwiches dried up on their plates.

***

Women Can Vote For Four

Republican women can vote for but four candidates at the primary— Christopher C. Duffy, clerk of the appellate court, E. J. Murphy for state central committeeman, Arthur A Crissey for senatorial committeeman, and precinct committeeman. The name of the voter's choice for precinct committeeman is to be written in on all ballots.

Crystal Lake Herald, September 3, 1914.

**John F. Wienke
Woodstock, Illinois
Republican Candidate for
COUNTY TREASURER**

Less Taxes if McHenry County Receives Interest on the County Funds. Not Less Than 2 percent Will be Payed on All Daily Balances and Put in the Treasury if I am Elected to Office. Never Before Has Our County Received Interest on Its Money. This Money Would be put on Deposit in Banks Throughout the County.

**Vote For Me and Reduce Your Taxes.
Your support Respectfully Solicited
Primary Sept. 9, 1914.**

Woodstock Sentinel, September 3, 1914.

More Than Fair Fair

The fifty-first annual McHenry county fair at Woodstock is a record-breaker in all respects.

Woodstock Sentinel, September 3, 1914.

MUST HAVE GERMAN TYPES

Washington.—Every effort will be made by the United States government to reopen the way for importation of German dyes and chemicals, the lack of which threatens to throw a million American textile workers out of employment. Representative Metz of New York told Secretary Bryan that without these imported colors the government would be unable to print its stamps and currency, as the acid proof products of German plants could not be reproduced in this country.

Crawford County Courier, September 3, 1914.

LIABLE TO MILITARY DUTY
United States Has a Million
European Aliens

Washington.—Approximately one and one-half million unnaturalized foreigners, more than twenty-one years old, natives of warring European nations, are in the United States, according to the latest reports of the census bureau. Most of these undoubtedly are liable to military duty and many of them have gone forward to join the allies. Including women and children, there were 9,855,479 foreign-born in the United States who came from nations at war. That is about one-tenth of the entire population of the United States.

Crawford County Courier, September 3, 1914.

Revenue Tax on Luxuries

Washington.—War revenue legislation, to add $100,000,000 to the government's annual income, was considered at a conference between Secretary McAdoo, Democratic Leader Underwood of the house and

Chairman Simmons of the senate finance committee. It is generally understood that the plan for a tax on tobacco, beer, and liquors and possibly a stamp tax will be carried out. Such a bill's introduction in the house is expected to follow immediately a message from President Wilson asking for such legislation.

Crawford County Courier, September 3, 1914.

PRIMARIES NEXT WEDNESDAY CANDIDATES ARE ALL ACTIVE

Lynn Richards of Crystal Lake and John F. Wienke of Woodstock are the candidates for treasurer. Mr. Richards' friends predict that he will win. Mr. Wienke is saying nothing but keeps everlastingly busy seeking out the unsuspecting voter.

Woodstock Sentinel, September 3, 1914.

NEW TYPEWRITER TO BE CALLED "WOODSTOCK"

Roebuck Typewriter Company Changes to Woodstock Typewriter Company

At a meeting of the board of directors of the Roebuck Typewriter company, held in the company's office in this city at eleven o'clock Monday morning the name of the firm was changed from "Roebuck Typewriter Company" to "Woodstock Typewriter Company." The new machine will be called the "Woodstock."

A further description of the new machine to be placed on the market will appear in a later issue of *The Sentinel.*

Woodstock Sentinel, September 3, 1914.

***

Winner Declared

In the Richards-Wienke contest for treasurer, Richards was an easy winner, defeating his competitor by a big vote.

Other Republican winners were D. T. Smiley for county judge, he winning out over his opponent, B. F. Manley of Harvard by about two hundred votes. Guy E. Still, having no opposition, was again nominated county clerk. For county treasurer, Lynn Richards of North Crystal Lake won over his opponent, John F. Wienke of Woodstock, by about 1,100 votes.

McHenry Plaindealer, September 10, 1914.

***

Ida looked up from her embroidery as John pushed through the front door. "Hi there handsome," she called out.

His face looked anything but handsome this evening. Fatigue and disappointment etched his brow and drew down the corners of his mouth. But he attempted a weak smile in her direction as he hung his hat on a hook.

"Not such good news, I'd guess." She set aside her needlework and rose to give him a hug and a peck on the lips.

"No. Not good," he agreed. "But we knew who would win this one, didn't we? No surprise then."

"Yes, he was a formidable opponent. Are you hungry?"

"A little."

"Let's go have a sandwich and maybe a libation from the basement?"

"Sounds like a great idea." John's smile was stronger.

He went down to the basement while she pulled out bread, tomatoes, and leftover meatloaf along with plates and cutlery.

He returned with two brown bottles with swing tops. "We are down to only four more. I'll have to write Al for another case."

"Maybe we should go up to collect them. It would be nice to see Lena and the children. A little outing before school starts."

"I think that can be arranged.

"They sat at the table and snapped open the bottles. A little foam rose from the neck of the bottle. They clinked the bottle necks together and took a long sip of the cool homemade ale.

"Oh, that's good," said John. He took another gulp and sighed as he sat the bottle on the table.

Ida busied herself making the sandwiches—soft white bread, a thick slice of the cold meatloaf, and a slice of tomato. She placed the larger one in front of John. "There. That should make you feel better. When did you eat last?"

"Breakfast." John took a large bite and smiled. "I rove cold meatroaf samitches," he said around the food as he chewed.

"I know. They are better than the original hot meatloaf, aren't they?" Ida tucked into her sandwich also.

They ate in silence for a bit.

"There's enough for another if you still want more." Ida said as she swallowed her last bite.

He nodded and sipped his beer to wash down his last bite.

As Ida made the new sandwich, John finished the beer. "Want another? Since we are going to Beloit, we don't have to be frugal with them."

"No, you go ahead. I have plenty left."

John went down the basement stairs leaving the door to the kitchen open.

Ida finished the sandwich and put it at his place. He was taking a long time. She went to the door and called down, "John? Are you all right?"

"Oh sorry. Here I come." He came up the stairs two at a time. "I just stopped at the workbench for a moment, thinking."

They sat back down.

"What were you thinking?" Ida sipped from the bottle.

"Oh, nothing much. Just about what else the world needs that I could make."

Ida smiled. "You'll have to keep your eyes and ears open. It seems like it would be a good time to invent something to cheer us all up."

John took a bite and nodded. He chewed; his eyes hazing over a bit as he thought. He swallowed. "I could make something for the war."

"Yes, you could. But I'm not sure that would be quick and easy. And it might be dangerous if it was a munition. Maybe it should be something we can't get any more because of the war. Like dye."

John looked at her. "Dye?"

"Yes. Clara said in her last letter that money and stamps can't be printed without German dye. The government is trying to work out a way of getting dye, but with the war it is unlikely."

"I don't know anything about dye."

"Me either, but Clara says the first to go will be colored garments. We will only find black and white or maybe brown dresses and suits until the war is over. Even if the government gets dye from Germany, they will use it for the necessities to keep things running. The garment business will just have to find ways to do without."

John had been working on his sandwich as he listened, and he took the last bite.

Ida had warmed to her topic. After a sip, she continued. "Even children's clothes will only come in drab colors. Can't you just see all of us walking around as if in a photograph with no color? Of course, it might be pretty if it snows."

John was looking at her with a slight grin on his face. "That's quite a picture to think about. And what if the war carries on for years."

Ida looked up. "Years? Oh, I hope not."

"It may. Germany is pulling in Turkey with its huge army and the Allies are working on Italy. As much as anything to secure the Mediterranean. And I'm still not sure what they are fighting over. The Allies are fighting to hold back Germany, but are the Germans invading Belgium just to secure more land? Or improve their own security? It's very confusing. It's almost like everyone just wanted a war."

"Well, I don't understand any of it." Ida rose and gathered the dishes, stacking them in the sink. "I think we should sleep on it. Tomorrow is another day." She grabbed John by the hand and stood him up.

"That sounds like an excellent idea." He reached down and capped his beer and followed her to the bedroom where he was asleep thirty seconds after his head hit the pillow.

***

AN ALL-ENVELOPING COAT

A color combination of castanet brown and buff is this suit, with redingote enveloping the figure from the tips of the ears almost to the ankles. Peau-de-chamois facing the cuffs and high turnback collar give the note of buff, and the newest note in fashiondom is sounded in the Basque effect of the body of the coat. Modish button boots are worn with this costume.

Denison Review, September 10, 1914.

Congress Summoned

The small attendance in Congress has become such an evil that more than a third of the members have recently been summoned back to Washington, and a vote passed for suspension of pay in case of absence.

Denison Review, September 10, 1914.

***

Germans Send Money to Europe

Germans of Davenport and Scott county towns have already raised $7,273 for relief of their countrymen disabled in the great European war and for their orphans and families.

Denison Review, September 10, 1914.

***

German-Americans Close Session.

Columbus, OH.—The German-American alliance of Nebraska, which closed its annual session here, will try to raise $50,000 for relief work in Germany.

A celebration planned by Columbus for visitors was abandoned on account of the European war. The society passed a resolution against women's suffrage.

Crawford County Courier, September 11, 1914.

***

Tennyson, Indiana

Rev. and Mrs. William Calvin Cissna, of Wayne City, Ill., visited their daughter, Mrs. Joe Brown, and other relatives several days the past week.

Boonville Standard, September 18, 1914.

***

ILLINOIS STATE NEWS

East St. Louis.—The police have arrested a number of persons residing in the southern part of the city, both white and black, who are without visible means of support. The officers have been instructed to bring in everyone who could not give a good account of himself. This order is occasioned by the numerous reports of holdups that have been going on the last several days.

McHenry Plaindealer, September 24, 1914.

***

Local News

Richmond will not be given electric light conveniences the coming winter. The Public Service company, which was granted a franchise into that village last spring, has forfeited same and will not build its lines to that village for the present at least. The present money stringency has forced the company to stop all construction work on all lines.

Since the closing of the Oliver factory at Woodstock that city has lost a number of families.

A new band is to be organized at Woodstock in the very near future. Since the disbandment of the famous Oliver band that city has been without a music organization. The new band gives promise of being equally as good as the Oliver of old.

The McHenry County Poultry association will hold its annual show in the old Princess theatre building at Woodstock early in December.

The Woodstock Law and Order league wants to be given the credit for the closing of the blind pigs in McHenry county.

McHenry Plaindealer, October 1, 1914.

Oliver Typewriter Factory Will Reopen Monday, October 5.

Just as *The Sentinel* goes to press, we are requested by the Oliver Typewriter Company to state that the factory will re-open for work on Monday, October 5, at 7:00 a.m.

Woodstock Sentinel, October 1, 1914.

Business is Good

"Peace hath her victories no less renowned than War."

There is but little cause for complaint from citizens of this country—in fact, we should all be thankful that our lot has been cast in "Liberty- Loving America."

Business conditions are good, and we do not anticipate any immediate reversal of these favorable conditions.

We do not care to make extravagant claims, but we do and will continue to protect the interests of our customers in every way. Prices are still reasonable on most drugstore goods, but should slight increases become necessary from time to time we shall be glad to give customers a reason for such. Don't forget our slogan:

"Quality goods and right service at right prices."
N. H. PETESCH, DRUGGIST
PHONE 56-W

McHenry Plaindealer, October 1, 1914.

***

Methodist Parsonage
Wayne City, Illinois

The Reverend William Calvin Cissna looked at his pocket watch and fingered his luxurious horseshoe mustache. Four thirty. Where were they? Surely an hour to walk home from school was enough.

"William Calvin?" William Calvin's wife, Lenora, knocked at his study door. "Will you be wanting tea before supper?"

"No, thank you, Nora. I am hopeful that supper won't be too long in the future."

"No sir. I'm just awaiting the children."

"Fine. If they aren't here by 5 o'clock we will eat without them."

"Yes, certainly."

Nora closed the door and returned to the kitchen. With a furrowed brow, she looked out at the yard. The chickens were gathering near the hen house ready to be put up for the night. It would be getting dark by 5:30. And the cow needed milking.

She looked in the wood-burning cookstove and pulled out the beef roast, a gift from her cousin, Lafayette McCoy, who butchered a beef cow last week. It looked done. She cut into the middle and saw that the juice wasn't red. Perfect. She set it on the warming spot and turned to the boiling potatoes, testing one with a knife. A while more.

She hoped the children would hurry. What could have happened to them? It was a good three miles to the school. The Reverend had said that "a good man walking can make four miles in an hour." She wasn't sure she could walk that fast but still they were usually here by four o'clock, an hour after school let out.

She checked the potatoes again. Done. Draining them she added some milk and a bit of butter and mashed them right in the pan. The ears of corn had been done for a half hour but still lay in the warm water on the stove. A large loaf of yeast bread and butter was already on the table. So, all was ready. To drink, she would furnish coffee, perked and ready, tea and milk. Who could want more? It was a feast worthy of a king!

She set the table and brought the food forward and heard the mantle clock strike five. She went and stood at the foot of the table as the study door opened, and William Calvin stepped into the dining room.

"No sign of them?"

"No."

"Let us break bread. If they come while we are eating, they may sit down, but if we are done, they will go without tonight."

"But—

"No. They must learn discipline." Williams' eyes were hard like one of the snakes he preached about - ready to strike.

Lenora dropped her gaze. "I understand."

The Reverend sat down, and Nora followed suit. They bowed their heads low, and the Reverend began: "Oh God whose name is excellent in all the earth and Thy glory is evident in the Heavens above, who on this day did preserve our Church and our Nation and gave us deliverance from enemies who would make war without ceasing; we bless and adore Thy majesty. Create in us the

Spirit of Love and thankfulness to Thee, author of the universe, we humbly pray. Give this food Thy blessing as we replenish our strength to do Thy duty. And bring these wayward children home to our embrace. This we beg for Jesus' sake. Amen."

"Amen." Nora hoped that everything would still be hot enough to rate this blessing but sat straight in her chair waiting for the plates to be passed. Although who would pass them? The children were still not home.

"William, would it make things easier if I were to come sit at either your right hand or your left so we can share the platters with more ease?"

Will looked up and smiled. "That is a good idea, Nora. Please, come sit on my right. We will add a chair later, if necessary."

Nora moved to the chair on the right and began to pass the platters to the Reverend. She had been married to him for over forty years, and it had always been thus. They were well matched, and she had borne him nine children, and only two had died. Their first babe, Alvah Samuel, was stillborn, but she was told that was understandable as Lenora was very young, only sixteen, when he was carried. Nora sent up a quick silent prayer for her baby and also for their daughter Minnie who had died of the fever when she was twenty, just a few months after she was wed.

They filled their plates and began to enjoy the decadent meal. The juice of the meat was just at the right temperature and the potatoes and corn still melted the butter put atop them. Not much was said between them while they ate.

"Is there dessert tonight?" the Reverend inquired as he wiped his plate with a piece of bread.

"Yes. I baked an upside-down cake with some fresh peaches. I will clear up here and bring it in."

A back door creaking open indicated imminent homecoming. It closed quietly.

William and Nora looked at each other. It was unlike the children to be so quiet upon arrival.

"Hello," William called out. "Who's there?"

Lillian appeared in the doorway "Good evening, Father. Mother. I am heartily sorry that I was not here in time for supper. I was detained and didn't realize how late it had become. Please forgive me."

Lenora looked behind Lillian for her youngest, Roy, but could not see him in the gloom of the kitchen. She had only lit one candle before coming to the table. William Calvin was also trying to see around her. Roy was usually the loud one who pushed in and sat down without ceremony.

"Where is your brother? Has he gone to the barn?"

"No, sir." Still standing in the doorway, Lillian looked at the floor.

Ashamed? Will wondered. "What is wrong, girl? Come here this instant."

Lillian stepped into the room but didn't look up at either her father or her mother.

Nora could stand it no longer. She rose and in a shaky voice, "W-where is Roy? Did s-something happen to him?"

Lillian looked up at her mother. "Nothing that he didn't bring on himself. He's gone to join the army because of the war."

"He what!" William voice had changed to the one he usually reserved for the pulpit.

Lillian's eyes filled with tears, and she covered her face with her hands. "He left for Springfield on a freight wagon an hour ago." She sobbed. "I couldn't stop him."

Nora went around the table and gathered Lillian into her arms. "There, there," she said. "It wasn't your fault."

"But I was to keep him safe, and he me, right? He just… went," Lillian said into her mother's shoulder.

Nora looked at William Calvin who was examining his empty plate. "Father, is there anything you can do?"

William looked up at his wife and daughter. Their eyes were wide and expectant.

"Maybe. I will pray about it."

Nora nodded, but Lillian stiffened. "Oh, father, can't you do more than pray? He is so young, and they will send him to Mexico, and he will surely die. That's what I told him…that he was signing his death certificate. But he wouldn't listen. He just wouldn't listen." Again, she fell on her mother, sobbing.

Lenora's gaze was steady and unyielding. William stared right back at her. "Someone must get the eggs picked and the chicken's in. And there is the cow to be milked. I think dessert will have to wait until later."

The pastor rose and went to the kitchen where he pulled on a barn coat and galoshes. Lillian followed him, still in her outside clothing. They left together carrying a milk bucket and bucket of chicken feed.

Nora sighed. She cleared the table making a plate for Lillian which she put on the warming spot of the stove with a sack cloth over it. She took some hot water from the reserve on the stove and put it in the dishpan and rinse pan, cooling the dish water just a bit from the well water bucket.

Her hands lingered in the hot water as she looked at the dark window that faced the backyard. Her round face was reflected in it. Wire-rimmed spectacles surrounded her eyes. Her dark hair, streaked with white, was piled on top of her head as she had worn it all her life. Her double chin reminded her of how blessed their family had been. Never did they go hungry what with the donations of food from the congregation members, often instead of cash payment. Many children had given them lots of hands to have a large garden and livestock. No, they had never gone hungry. What would they do with only Lillian at home? This was just another challenge sent from the Almighty. When is a boy old enough to go off to war? Certainly, barely sixteen was too young. Although she had been a few months shy of fifteen when she married William. Maybe it would be good for him to learn discipline in the army. God knows, she had been unable to teach it.

Nora shook herself back to the task at hand. William Calvin would pray on it, and so would she. She prayed the old trustworthy prayer that never fails, "Thy will be done."

***

GUARD JAIL AGAINST MOB

Cairo, Ill., Oct. 13.—The county jail here was heavily guarded all last night in order to prevent a mob demonstration against a Negro accused of the murder of Eli Johnson, Saturday, but the mob failed to appear. Rumors of trouble were rife throughout the night. Everything was quiet this morning.

Woodstock Republican, October 13, 1914.

Men in Masks Lynch Gunman

Percy, Ill., Oct. 13. [special Quad Cities Times]—A quarrel over a cigaret which started Sunday night in Willisville, Ill., resulted in

A revolver duel.

The murder of one man.

The wounding of two men.

The lynching of another.

Last night the climax to the quarrel came when a body of masked men sprang from the sides of a country road, covered Sheriff Bresner of Willisville with revolvers, took from him his prisoner, Albert Ciazza, and poured a broadside of shots into him before the sheriff's eyes.

Ciazza, was an Italian miner, one of two brothers who engaged in the revolver duel with two American miners, Willis Adams, and Ben Cooper. The latter was wounded seriously. Ciazzi's brother was the man slain in the duel.

Woodstock Republican, October 13, 1914.

***

Kaiser Loses Four Warships

London, Oct. 19.—Four German torpedo boat destroyers were sunk off the Dutch coast by ships from the British fleet. The names of the ill-fated crafts are not known. The German crews, totaling about four hundred men, with the exception of 31 male prisoners of war, were lost, the war press bureau announces. The British loss was only one officer and four men slightly wounded.

Chicago Tribune, October 22, 1914.

British Cruiser is Torpedoed

London, Oct. 18.—A German torpedo cost England her seventh cruiser and 330 men, the British admiralty officially announced. The cruiser Hawke was struck by a torpedo from a German submarine and sunk in the northern waters of the North sea. The cruiser Theseus was attacked, but the torpedo missed its mark.

The press bureau issued a list of 71 survivors of 400 officers and men on the Hawke.

Chicago Tribune, October 22, 1914.

ALLIES WIN FIGHT
March to Paris is Halted

On the Battle Front, Via Paris, Oct. 21.—British warships, cannonading the German land forces, who had opened a terrific bombardment of the allies' entrenched position between Nieuport, on the Belgian North sea coast, and Dixmude, southward on the Ypres canal, repulsed the invaders by their flanking and enfilading fire.

The Belgians, fighting on their own soil to regain their country, dashed forward and in desperate counterattacks are said to have hurled the Germans back.

Chicago Tribune, October 22, 1914.

***

The Reverend W. C. Cissna rode his pinto pony into the Parsonage gate in Wayne City, Illinois. Beside him on an all-black gelding rode his youngest son, Evans Roy. William Calvin had figured to be gone for three days to retrieve his son, and his estimate held true. One day ride to Springfield by train, one day back by train, and one day to sort out his son's stupidity. His goal, as it always was, was to return by the Sabbath so that his congregation would not go unserved. And here they were coming in at five o'clock on Friday. He'd still have time to prepare a sermon. Maybe something on the prodigal son....

The Reverend had left on Wednesday morning at daybreak for Fairfield on his pony leading the gelding. It had taken the morning to ride the fifteen miles and find a place to board the horses, so they would be waiting for Roy and him in Fairfield upon their return.

He had caught the 1:00 train to Springfield, sitting next to a woman who was talkative. It was a pleasant trip, made even better by the fried chicken and biscuits in her hamper.

Once in Springfield, he found an inexpensive but clean boarding house for the night, rising the next morning to the complimentary breakfast served. He found the recruitment office without difficulty only a few blocks from the house.

Wiping his feet on the boot scraper to remove most of the manure and muck of the street, he entered the narrow door, and removed his hat. He smoothed his white hair back and stroked his mustache as he allowed his eyes to accustom themselves to the dim light and then approached the smiling uniformed man who sat at a small desk.

"Hi there, old timer. What can I do for you?" The man seemed pleasant enough.

"Good morning. I am the Reverend William Calvin Cissna, and I would like to see my son."

"Your son?"

"Yes, I understand that he volunteered a few weeks ago and that you accepted him into your numbers."

"I'm Lieutenant Herman Jones. I'll try to help you. If he volunteered weeks ago, I'm sure he would have gone off to basic training. We are in training to go to Mexico to fight Poncho Villa." The Lieutenant smiled.

"Where are the training grounds? I must speak to my son."

"I'm sorry but I can't tell you where they are training – gotta watch out for the anarchists."

William Calvin looked at him for a long moment. "Do I look like an anarchist?"

Lt. Jones blushed. "Well, no sir, you do not. I can tell you aren't, but they still won't let you in."

"Can you start by telling me if he has actually volunteered?"

"Surely, that I can do. What was his name."

"Evans Roy Cissna."

Jones wrote 'Evans Roy S—' "Could you spell the last name please."

"C-I—"

"Oh, with a C, I see." He laughed.

"Yes, C-I-S-S-N-A."

"Thank you, Mr. 'Kissna.'"

"Reverend."

"Reverend 'Kissna.'"

"Reverend Cissna; the C sounds as an S."

The lieutenant looked at his note. "But that's not the way it's spelled."

"OK, fine. 'Kissna,' it is. Can you look at your records and see if an Evans Roy 'Kissna' has signed up?"

Jones nodded and went to the backroom. Will sat down in a chair by the front window, hat dangling between his knees. If he couldn't find the boy with expedience, he'd take refuge in a rooming house tonight. He had a bit of money, but if he had to pay a bribe to get—

"Here we go," said Lt. Jones coming back in. "Yes, he did sign up about two weeks ago."

William nodded. "And how old did he say he was?"

Jones looked over the paperwork. "Let's see. Eighteen at his last birthday on May 14th."

"Mmhm. You see that's where you went wrong. He got the birthdate right, but he was fifteen on his last birthday." William Calvin sent a little prayer for forgiveness for stretching the truth.

"Fifteen?" A look of genuine concern scrunched the Lieutenant's face.

"Yes, fifteen. Do you normally take recruits that young, sir?"

"No. We don't. We'll take a recruit at seventeen if his father signs for him."

"I didn't sign for him."

The Lieutenant looked at the paperwork again. "No sir. No one signed for him. You see, when a recruit says he's eighteen, no one must sign for him."

"Mmhm. Now can I see my son?"

"But how do I know he's only fifteen?"

"Because I say so, and I am his father!" the Reverend's voice changed to his loud wrath-of-God voice.

Jones wasn't a big man, but he was a soldier. He stood his ground and stared at Will.

The Reverend sighed and changed course and brought his voice to a more controlled volume. "Are you a man of God, sir?"

"Yes, I am. I'm a Baptist."

"So, you understand that a minister is duty bound to tell the truth."

"Yes, sir."

"So, when I tell you that my son, Roy, is too young to enlist on his own, do you believe me?"

Jones looked again at the paperwork. "I believe I am going to have to refer you to Captain Reynolds about this issue. I am just a recruiter. Private Kissna is now the captain's problem...er ...responsibility."

"Fine. Where can I find Captain Reynolds?"

After a few more go rounds, William Calvin was given a handwritten note, signed by Lt. H. Jones so that he could see Captain Reynolds at Camp Lincoln on the north side of town.

As he walked toward the address, William Calvin was sure that he would be able to talk logic to the Captain. He still hoped that it would just be a one-night layover.

William sat in the anteroom of the Captain's office, looking over his good shoes. Besides the train ticket and the boarding house, Roy was going to have to pay him back for a new pair of shoes. The streets of Springfield were despicable. Deep with mud and horse manure, and even some slop bucket waste, he was sure. If one could stay on the boardwalk, shoes could be saved, but as he walked northward the boardwalks had disappeared, and he was forced to forage along in citizen's front yards to avoid the most of it.

The front gate of Camp Lincoln was impressive, and with the note from H. Jones, he had no trouble convincing them that he was not an anarchist and that they must let him in to see the Captain. He had been left waiting...at least there were chairs...for several hours, three hours and forty-eight minutes to be exact. He had been told that the Captain was on 'maneuvers with the troops, and he would have to wait.'

Will heard activity in the hallway, and a distinguished uniformed man came into the waiting room, walked right through without looking at him, and went through the door marked Captain James Reynolds. Maybe things were about to move forward, and sure enough after another twenty minutes, the young man who had told him to wait, came through that same door and said, "Captain Reynolds can see you now."

William Calvin stood up, but after sitting for so long, his foot had gone to sleep, and he limped a bit as he moved toward the inner door. "Are you alright, sir?" asked the secretary.

"I'm fine. Just sat too long. Foot's taking a snooze."

"Sorry for the wait," said a smiling James Reynolds. He was a tall man with a ruddy complexion and salt and pepper hair. "Please take a chair. What can I do for you?"

"I think I'll stand for the moment. Been sitting, enjoying your anteroom for too long. I apologize for coming without an engagement. My name is Reverend William Calvin Cissna, and I'm looking for my son. He ran away from home and enlisted in the national reserves last week."

The Captain stretched a hand across the desk. Captain Hamilton Reynolds, at your service, sir."

They shook a firm handshake.

"What is his name?"

"Evans Roy Cissna."

Captain Reynolds wrote "Evans Roy S...can you spell the last name for me?"

"Yes. C-I—

"Oh C, is it?"

"Yes, C-I-S-S-N-A."

"Kissna."

"Cissna."

"Hm. I heard that name before. We've had Cessnas in the troop before. Isn't there a Cessna Park?"

"Yes, there is, but it's Cissna Park, with an I."

"Yes, I see. So, Evans Roy Cessna."

William Calvin shook his head, smiled at the floor, and sat down as did the Captain. "Roy is fifteen years old, and I have not signed so him to join you. I would like to see him and take him home."

"Fifteen years, you say. Well, yes, let's get him in here. Corporal?" he called out toward a small office to the side.

The young corporal came through to stand erectly in front of the Captain's desk. "Yes, sir."

"Corporal do you know which barracks," he looked down at his note, "Evans Roy Cessna is in?"

"Cessna?"

"Yes, that's right, isn't it?" He looked at W.C.

"Cissna with an I." Will directed the answer to the corporal.

"Yes, sir. I know Roy Cissna."

"You do?" The Reverend sat up straighter in his chair.

"Yes, sir. Shall I fetch him?"

The Captain took back the conversation. "Yes, Corporal. Go fetch him."

"Yessir." The corporal saluted, turned on his heel, and hastily left the office.

"Can I interest you in a bit of libation, sir?" asked the Captain.

"No sir. My religion disallows me to enjoy libation of any type."

"I see. Would you mind if I had a small nip?"

"No sir. Be my guest. Will this take long?"

The Captain reached into the bottom drawer of his desk and brought out a bottle. He poured the amber liquid into a small clear glass. Will could smell the familiar odor of whiskey.

"No. As long as he's not on duty, they should be back in a few minutes."

Will nodded. Maybe he should have taken the Captain up on his offer by asking for a glass of water. He was a bit dry. He settled in the chair more comfortably as the Captain sipped his drink.

It was a well-turned-out young lad who came into the Captain's office twenty minutes later. He walked in and stood at attention in front of the desk and saluted. "Private Roy Cissna, reporting, sir."

William was taken aback. For the last year, they could hardly get a good suit on Roy of a Sunday, and here he stands decked out in a uniform that very nearly fits him with a hat down over his ears making a crisp salute to his superior. Is this my boy?

"At ease, Private."

Roy relaxed a bit but then noticed his father who had stood and come forward to touch his son's arm. "Roy."

"Pa...um...Father? What are you doing here? Did something happen?"

"Yes. My son ran away, and I've come to fetch him home."

All pretense of stature decorum had left the boy. His hands went to his midsection as if he had a huge pain in his stomach and his eyes welled with unspent tears. "But no...you...you can't...I'm...I'm...fine here. I like it and I'm getting paid. You can't just—

"Oh, but I can. And I will." His father's voice had become more severe.

William Calvin turned to the Captain. "What do we have to do to get him released?"

"How old did you say he was, sir?"

Will looked Roy in the eye and said with certainty, "He's fifteen."

"No, I'm not! I'm sixteen!" Roy spoke before he could stop himself.

The Reverend looked at Captain Reynolds, and he nodded. Seeing the exchange, Roy became very animated, turning and pounding the wall with his fist. He kicked a chair and collapsed into it.

The two men watched this display without comment. The Captain thought of reprimanding him, but could see that he was only a boy, just as the father had said. "Pretty slick trick. Your father is a very smart man. Yes, Reverend, we will release him, but we can't do it anymore tonight. Do you have a place to stay intown?"

"I stayed last night in Miller's boarding house downtown."

"If you don't mind roughing it a bit, we have a couple of basic rooms that are available for overnighting when we must. I could set you up with one of those."

"Much obliged. One less cost that my son will have to repay." He looked at his son who sat with his face in his hands. His hat, which had gotten pushed back during his antics, fell to the floor. He did not try to retrieve it.

The paperwork took most of the next morning, but by noon, William Calvin and Evans Roy were walking to the train station. They walked along in uncomfortable silence until Roy couldn't stand it anymore. "Why?" he said, stopping and turning on his father.

"Why what?" William was calm as a flat lake.

"Why did you have to come and get me? It was embarrassing. I could have passed for eighteen, and you wouldn't have had to worry about me anymore."

William took the boy by the shoulders, turned his son to look at him squarely. "Roy, you have always had it easy. You are your mother's golden boy. The one that makes her laugh when she wants to cry. But also, the one who makes her cry more than all the others."

"That's my fault?"

"I didn't say anything about fault, but you have been able to get away with much of what you have...um...pulled...without punishment or censure because of your personality and your good looks. It will not always be thus."

Roy snorted as color crept up his neck.

"You are too young to face killing another person even if it is in war. They told me that that troop was being sent to Mexico as soon as it was trained. You would be forced to shoot or be shot, and you are too young to have that on your conscience and too young to die. You'll just have to take my word for it."

"I could have—"

"I know you could have, but what would it do to your soul, boy? And what would it do to your mother? To your sisters? To your brothers? Or…" he hesitated, "or to me if you would have been killed. How would I have faced God if I allowed you to throw away your life? I prayed about it, and your mother prayed, and we both heard the same message from above. Go get him. So here I am."

"I am not a golden boy." Roy scuffed his feet on the boards like a pouting ten-year-old.

"Yes, you are." Will started walking again. He wanted to catch the train so they wouldn't have another night in Springfield. "I think I've just gotten tired. I've tried with all of you children to teach you discipline, but you have been the one where I feel I have failed. As the Bible says, 'Spare the rod, spoil the child.' Maybe I should have rodded you more. But your mother wouldn't hear of it. She was worried that your spirit would be broken."

They trudged across a muck filled street to the boardwalk on the other side. They stamped off their feet and scraped the bottom on the side of the walk as many others had done before them.

"Do you have any idea how upset your sister was when she had to come home and tell us that you had run away?"

"I didn't run away. You run away from something. I went toward something - a future." Roy pulled out a pack of cigarettes and lit one with a match struck on his zipper.

Will looked at him. "When did you start those?"

"A while ago. You gonna say I hafta stop smoking, too?" Roy stopped again, glaring at his father.

Will kept walking. "I should, but I know it will fall on deaf ears." The pastor wanted to cross himself to find strength, but Methodists don't do such papist things. "You can still plan toward the future. It's fine that you have spirit and the will to fight for your country, but not when you are only sixteen. I want you to stay in school."

Roy coughed, hacked up a gob of phlegm, and spit it on the walk. "I'll go back with you, but I'm not going back to school. I'll get a job."

"Doing what? What are you qualified to do without a diploma?" William felt a queasiness. He must convince this man/boy he'd seen in that uniform to stay in school.

Roy's head snapped around. "What does that mean? You think I'm lazy. You think I can't find a job."

"Yes, I think that without a high school diploma you are going to have trouble finding a decent job."

"Well, you just watch me then. I'll be making more than you inside of a month. I have skills you have never seen." Roy started walking faster to outpace his father.

William Calvin shifted to a quicker pace to try to keep up. Maybe this fight could wait. They would be home tonight, and he would have time to prepare a sermon. 'Thank you, God, for protecting my son. Now please, give him some common sense.'

***

Translated and Published in Crystal Lake Herald
A Letter from Germany

October 29, 1914
Schleswig-Holstein, Germany

Dear Cousin,

We received your letter yesterday and will answer at once. Our Willie is serving his country in the army and is at present stationed in France. Karl is still at home but has been called upon to enlist. He has not as yet received orders to go to the front.

The war that is raging now is certainly horrible. Killing thousands of soldiers on the battlefields is indeed bad enough, but more and most horrible is the murdering and atrocities committed by the Russians and Belgians upon our poor and helpless wounded.

Wounded soldiers that have been picked up on the battlefields have been found terribly mutilated by civilians. Last Saturday I met a woman from Tvenning, accompanied by her children, at the railroad station. She had been to Kiel visiting her husband, who had been reported wounded. On arriving at the hospital, she was informed that her children would not be allowed to see their wounded father. Upon entering the room, she found her poor husband with one foot shot off and both eyes gouged out by the mean people, who had tied both of his hands to his back and then had left him to his fate on the battlefield. A bullet through the head would have been a blessing to this poor sufferer.

The Russians have acted more inhuman in East Prussia. They have chopped off the hands of children, cut off the breasts of women and ripped their abdomen. Others they have driven into a large enclosure and then set the same on fire burning the children and women alive. Besides, the Russians have burnt and destroyed everything in their path. Contributions are being gathered for these poor people.

Today we hear rumors that England has declared war on Denmark. Pontoon trains are heading for the north. During the last two years a double track has been laid here Suppose the English intend to land their Hindoo troops at Schleswig-Holstein, who then probably shall commit such shameful deeds as the Russians are committing in the east. May God help us!

Willie writes from the battle front that if the civilians are decent our soldiers molest no one, but where they have found civilians shooting at them, they have shot down many and burnt their buildings. At Louvain and Liege; it has been terrible. Even children had armed themselves with weapons. Willie is now at Rhelms. Our soldiers have been in this city before but had to retreat. Willie is one of the men who are in charge of the pay and ammunition wagons, this wagon being one out of a train of 80. These men, however, must go close to the front, supplying the soldiers with

*ammunitions, cartridges, etc. They also have to pick up
the wounded left on the field. Willie writes that the
suffering seen on the battlefields is indescribable.*

*Our "Wilhelm" did all he could to prevent the
bloodshed, but he was forced to do it. Everybody loves
the Kaiser, for he does not even spare his own children,
for all his sons are gallantly fighting at the front. Our
crown prince himself on one occasion has acted as a
drum-major when the drummer was wounded.*

*Airships are flying over us constantly. You shall
hear that the killing in this vicinity has started. We are,
however, hoping for the best. No country can be trusted
at this time. Otherwise, we are all well.*

*We would like to have you come abroad to
visit us when this war is over.*

My best to you,
Your Cousin, J. F. Mugge

***

Hanna Triplets Move to Woodstock

Ida, Iva and Eva, the famous Hanna triplets noted
from coast to coast, have moved to Woodstock. Their
coming here has created more than usual interest for
these dainty little maids are something out of the
ordinary run of little girls. Their fame has spread from
the Atlantic to the Pacific and they have traveled all
over the United States and Canada. The sisters spent
one year on the road with Forepaugh's, two years with
Ringling's and one year with Gollmar Brothers,
completing their last tour on October 15 of this year.
The Hanna triplets were born in Buffalo, N. Y., eight
years ago. Half of their lives have been spent in travel,
and they have seen more sights during their short
public career than most of us do in a lifetime.

Ida, Iva, and Eva are so much alike that even their
own father sometimes makes a mistake in telling one
from the other. Iva is an inch shorter than the other

two, but all three register the same weight. They are of the fair type, with blue eyes and beautiful long, heavy hair.

Ida, Iva, and Eva started school Monday morning. They are enrolled in second grade in the Clay street building. They had attended school only six months prior to this time, and then they attended school in Chicago, completing the first-grade work. And hereafter until their education is completed, the big circuses will be deprived of the famous Hanna triplets as one of their star attractions, for from now on they are going to attend school regularly, just like other little girls who don't enjoy the unique distinction of "being triplets." The Hanna triplets are living at 918 Clay street. Their father is C. Hanna, a lineman with the Chicago Telephone company.

Woodstock Sentinel, October 30, 1914.

***

Youngsters Enjoy Hallowe'en Birthday Party

Miss Marion Wienke entertained a number of her little friends at a Hallowe'en party to celebrate her tenth birthday from 2 o'clock till 5 last Saturday afternoon. Games and the usual hilarity of a merry crowd of youngsters made the afternoon pass quickly, but before the little guests departed dainty refreshments were served.

Woodstock Sentinel, November 5, 1914.

***

"But why not!" Edie threw herself down on a kitchen chair, crossed her arms, and lowered her head and lips into a pout.

"I didn't say no, I said 'we'll see.'"

"That's the same as no." Edie mumbled into the collar of her smock. "Mamie got to."

"Well, yes, but it was a BIG birthday for Mamie this year. Her tenth." Ida was working on dinner. The ham was in the oven, and tonight, she was trying something new—split pea soup. A large kettle on the stove had the bubbling pea-green liquid thickening.

"Helen got to." Edie remembered Helen's birthday party well with games and contests and the beautiful cake. She got to help Papa with starting the contests with a "ready, start, go." It was so much fun. She didn't even get to go to Mamie's party. She and Bobby had to go stay with Oma Wienke and Bobby wouldn't take a nap, so she had to play with him the whole time. Edie raised her arms, not uncrossing them and brought them down on her rounded belly. "Humph!" she said.

Ida glanced up from cutting carrots for the soup. "Okay, that's enough. I will think about it. If not this year for sure on your tenth."

Edie didn't move. "That's more than two years."

"I know." Ida went back to her chopping. "Let me think about it."

Edie didn't move.

Ida glanced at her again. "Did you get to meet the triplets, yet?" *Chop, chop, chop.*

Edie raised her head an inch. "Yes."

"What are they like?" *Chop, chop, chop.*

"They all look the same." Her head came up a bit more arms, and the tension in her arms eased a little.

"Yes, I suppose they do. That's what triplets are. Sisters born all on the same day." *Chop, chop, chop.*

Edie looked up at her mother. "Like if Helen and Mamie and me were all ten years old and all born on December 13th."

"Well, yes. Then you'd be triplets." *Chop, chop, chop.*

Edie's arms relaxed, and she put her hands on the table reaching for the proffered mid-morning cookie she had been ignoring. "Why didn't you have triplets then?" she said around the cookie chewing.

"Don't talk while you are chewing. You'll choke."

Edie swallowed. "Why didn't you?"

"I didn't have any choice. God acts in mysterious ways. He wanted each of you to have your own birthday. And I think it's better that way and safer."

Edie took a swallow of her milk and carefully put the glass back on the table. "Why better? The triplets are famous."

Ida looked at her using the knife as a pointer. "But look there, you said 'triplets.'"

"They are triplets."

"But they never get to be known as their own person with their own name. They are always 'the triplets.' What are their names anyway?"

"Um, Hanna?"

"No. That's their last name, like Wienke."

"Oh yeah, I forgot. One has your name, Ida. And there is Eva and the last is...um...I can't remember...maybe it is Hanna." She giggled. "Hanna Hanna."

Ida smiled. "I don't think so. Have you talked to them."

"No. They sit by themselves and play with each other. We just look at them."

Ida stopped chopping and looked at her, a small smile playing on her face. "You look at them."

"Yes, they are very lookable. Sometimes they all turn to us and curtsy."

"They what?"

"Curtsy." Edna jumped down from the chair and curtsied low.

"Does your teacher think that's strange?"

Edie shrugged. "Maybe. She tried to make them sit in different rows away from each other but the small one started to cry. So, she put them all in a row."

"Small one?"

"Yes, one, maybe Eva is a little bit smaller. If they are triplets, how could that happen?"

"I don't know," Ida said. Amazing! She supposed she'd just look at them if she were in second grade also. "You'll have to find ways that they are different so you can tell them apart."

"Oh, we can tell them apart." Edna said in an offhand manner as she examined the last of her cookie. "They wear different colored ribbons in their hair."

Ida went back to her knife work. "I see. So, all you must do is memorize which name goes with which color. That sounds easy."

"I suppose. Can they come to my birthday party in December?" Edie's eyes were on her cookie.

"Sure." Silence. Then Ida turned to her laughing. "You little trickster!"

Edie's eyes were sparkling as she popped the last bite into her mouth.

***

Turkey's Action Looked For

London, Nov. 1. —It has been expected for weeks that, yielding to German pressure and promises, Turkey would break its neutrality and do some belligerent acts.

Six hundred German officers have arrived in Turkey since the war began. They brought siege guns, field guns and ammunition with them.

It is computed that Turkey has from 600,000 to 700,000 men ready to take the field. The German officers put the number at 900,000.

The menace of Turkey's action lies in the possibility of a "holy war" by Mohammedans against Christians. She undoubtedly will attempt to incite to revolt the great mass of Mohammedan subjects of Great Britain in Asia and Africa.

McHenry Plaindealer, November 5, 1914.

***

New Movie

"The Christian" is playing at the Woodstock Theater
this week.

Woodstock Sentinel, November 12, 1914.

***

Ida wrapped her arm in John's as they strolled home from the
movie along the quiet evening streets of Woodstock. "The movie
had an interesting story, don't you think?"

John looked down at her. "If one could follow what was going
on. I'm reading the headings and missing the action most of the
time."

Ida laughed. "Do you need a synopsis?"

"Here, let me try." They stopped under a streetlamp. "Boy
loves girl. Girl leaves to be a star. Boy goes to college—

"No. To a monastery to be a priest. Isn't that what all Christian
men do when they are thwarted in love?"

He smiled. "I doubt it. Anyway, he goes to the…the monastery
and can't stand being apart from her or doesn't want to be a priest
or maybe he becomes a priest, so he goes to the slum to feed the
hungry."

"Good! Then what?"

"In the meantime, the woman's friend becomes pregnant by a
lord, not God, but like an English lord, but he will not marry her."

"Right. See you get the story. Then what?"

"The woman goes and tells the man or priest or whatever
…how did they get back together anyhow?"

"I don't know. I think he couldn't stay away from her."

"The priest confronts the lord and says he must marry the girl's
friend because it's the Christian thing to do."

"Excellent! Now the hard part. It's cold. Can we walk and
talk?"

"Sure."

They took a few steps and John resumed. "The lord says no, and I'll challenge you to a bet on a horse race. If my horse wins, you'll marry her. If my horse loses, I'll marry her."

Ida stopped dead in her tracks looking up at him. "What? No! Although that makes as much sense, I guess."

"More I'd say."

Ida laughed. "No. The lord says 'No, I won't marry her; I'm marrying my rich American heiress,' and so John, that's the man, exposes the lord's affair with the girl. And Polly, that's the pregnant girl, dies of shame."

"Oh. Then how does Derby Day fit in?"

"After John tells the world, the lord swears revenge. Because he's rich and famous, the lord broadcasts to the world that this holy man, John, is predicting that the world will end on Derby Day, the biggest sports day in the land."

"How could you read that fast?"

Ida laughed. "Of course, this prediction sends all of Britain into a frenzy and everyone hates John even his best friends because he made the prediction that is causing riots in the slums. That is everyone except Glory, the love of his life."

John shook his head, chuckling. "That's just foolish. Who'd even listen to this nobody priest and why?"

"I think the idea is that they believe him because he is a Christian." Ida continued, "When the false prediction doesn't come true everyone is even more angry and John, poor soul, goes crazy."

"Oh, is that why he looked like that with his big eyes and hair standing on end?"

"Yes...as a matter of fact he is so crazy he goes to Glory's and tries to save her from her friend's fate by killing her."

"Fate? Getting pregnant? Stupid."

"No, remember Polly, the friend dies from a broken heart."

"Why is the girl...um...Glory...heartbroken?"

Ida walked a few paces in silence. "I'm not sure. Ah-ha! We have found a hole in the plot!"

John considered this, but then took up the story again. "In the end, Glory defends John in court and convinces everyone that it was not John, but the lord that caused the riots."

Ida jumped in to finish the saga. "And John snaps out of it and returns to his loving self and is acquitted of both trying to kill Glory and of making the prediction. Then Glory realizes that she loves John more than being on stage, and they live happily ever after."

"Hm."

"Now what do you think?"

"Stupid. These movies are not going to account for much if they tell stories like this one. What does being a Christian have to do with any of this?"

"It gave a reason for him to go to the monastery and the slums, there to meet Polly."

"No Glory introduced him to Polly. The whole monastery/slums thing was unnecessary."

"Perchance it was to make the movie longer."

John laughed, "Maybe you are right. But it also doesn't make sense that the whole of the slums and society would riot because one guy says the world will end on a certain date, even if he is a Christian."

"I'm not sure about that. People do get conned into believing that kind of thing when they are part of a religion, don't they? Maybe that's the moral of the story."

"What is?"

"Don't get conned by a Christian?"

"But what if it HAD been the end of the world?" John was still trying to make sense of the moral of the story.

"What if it had? We can't stop it. It's God's will. We should look forward to it, not riot because of it. I agree that the riots seemed unrealistic."

They walked a bit more then John made his final decision. "I can say that I did not enjoy the movie or the story. But I loved the discussion afterward. I wonder if Pastor Kaufman has seen this movie. I'm this close," he held up his hand with the thumb and first finger an inch apart, "this close to being offended by the title."

Ida laughed. "I bet many Christians come away feeling that way."

They walked on, turning onto Lincoln Avenue.

"I do like it when you take me for a night out," Ida purred.

"Me, too." He held her a bit closer and wished that they'd gone dancing instead.

**

LIQUOR CASE DISPOSED OF

Of all the "liquor cases" that have been fought out in the county court at Woodstock in the past few weeks, none have caused more interest than the case of the People vs. Adriale E. Cowlin, former Woodstock saloonkeeper, now operating a soft drink parlor in the county seat. Eleven counts in all were filed, and the jury, after being out four hours, brought in a verdict of guilty on seven counts.

To be specific, Mr. Cowlin was charged with selling a so-called temperance beverage called "Tonica," which the manufacturers, a brewing company at Indianapolis, Ind., claimed to be non-intoxicating, and therefore, salable in anti-saloon territory.

"We have just started on this cleaning up process," asserted States Attorney Joslyn over the telephone this afternoon. "We are going to put every blind pig and bootlegger in the county out of business."

McHenry Plaindealer, November 19, 1914.

**

Penny Tax for War

After next Tuesday, all people who send telegrams will have to pay just one penny more for any telegrams they send than they did previous to that date. This extra cent is going to find its way into the United States treasury and will be collected in accordance with one feature of the war revenue bill recently passed by congress to meet the curtailment of revenues brought on by the European war. It is not likely that this tax will hit Denison business men very hard inasmuch as there are not many telegrams sent out from the local telegraph office.

Denison Review, November 25, 1914.

***

THE DEMOCRATIC WAR (?) TAX

We desire to call the attention of our readers to this new "war" tax provided by congress. It's decidedly interesting and illuminating in regard to the astonishing manner in which the finances of the government are run. Don't laugh; the new "war" measure, when there is no war, is going to cost you more than you believe to be right.

Just think of the man who sells his quarter section being obliged to pay $75 "war" tax when there is no war. The "war" tax is the price paid for the administration that has brought on these psychological good (?) times. It's great. —Carroll Herald

Woodstock Republican, December 2, 1914.

Encouragement for Horse Breeders

The enormous number of horses to be bought in this country for war needs in Europe should encourage farmers and others to raise them more freely. Military experts are strongly impressed with the value of the horse. It seems likely that cavalry forces all over the world will be permanently strengthened.

Denison Review, December 2, 1914.

***

Local News

Nearly six hundred new books have been added to the public library in Woodstock.

The Borden Condensed Milk company is laying off hands at a number of its plants in Northern Illinois. At Chemung, where tin cans are manufactured, 12 young ladies and 25 men were laid off recently. The layoff affects the entire village.

Woodstock Sentinel, December 10, 1914.

***

EIGHTH NEGRO LYNCHED

Shreveport, La., Dec. 12.—The total of illegal hangings in this parish in the last year reached eight with the confirmation today of the lynching of Watkins Lewis, reported last night. Three of the eight Negroes who met death at the hands of mobs were hanged yesterday. Five have been lynched in the last ten days.

Watkins Lewis was taken from the Caddo parish jail shortly before midnight and put to death for his part in the murder of Charles Hicks, postmaster of Sylvester, La., for which crime Tobe Lewis and Monroe Dirden were lynched last week. Two other Negroes were hanged by a mob yesterday after they confessed to the murder of a farmer.

Seven of the eight Negroes were charged with murdering white men and one with attacking a white woman.

Marshalltown Evening Times-Republican, December 12, 1914.

***

Hoof And Mouth

It has been claimed that this cold weather will effectually kill the germs of the hoof and mouth disease. It is sincerely hoped that it has done that for the present at least. The disease has not appeared in this vicinity anymore, but the dairymen are taking every precaution to prevent extending its disaster among the cattle, hogs, and other livestock. The quarantine which had been placed east of Marengo was on Monday taken off, letting people pass along the highways east of Union.

Marengo Beacon/Republican, December 18, 1914.

***

DECEMBER RECORDS FOR COLD BROKEN

Twenty-Eight Below Zero In Central Iowa.

From Omaha, Neb. to the Atlantic coast, zero weather prevailed today in the wake of a cold wave which originated in Manitoba. Cold weather records were shattered in many places.

Some of the coldest places were Charles City, Iowa, 24 below; Waterloo, Iowa, 23 below; Peoria, Ill., 18 below; Davenport and Des Moines, Iowa, 15 below; St. Paul, 22 below; Green Bay, Wis., 18 below.

Telegraph and telephone companies reported many "cold weather breaks" due to contraction of wires.

Marshalltown Evening Times-Republican, December 26, 1914.

***

Local News

Beware. Whether you drive a team or a motor, the Town Council has limited the speed at which you can circle the Woodstock square and business streets to 10 miles per hour and 5 mph around the corners. Slow down or pay the fine.

Twenty-two horses were purchased from the Novelty Tye Barn on Throop Street by the British government to use as artillery horses in the great European war. Who said horses were going out of vogue?

Woodstock Sentinel, December 30, 1914.

***

News of the War

After reading the war bulletins, how nice it seems that ALL of the contending powers can win each day a continuous succession of glorious victories on all fields of battle.

Crawford County Courier, December 30, 1914.

News From Afar

George W. Vanderbilt, millionaire died March 6th in Washington; aged 52.

"The segregation of the negro employees in Washington is unworthy of the American government, and unworthy of the proclaimed ideals of the Wilson administration," in the opinion of the Muscatine Journal.

"Iowa is doing a great deal of talking and very little work on the Lincoln highway," observes the Clinton Herald.

"It is a pleasure to behold a defeated candidate shaking hands with the winner and not laying his defeat to sinister reasons," says the Boone News-Republican in characterizing Maurice Connolly as a good loser.

Crawford County Courier, December 30, 1914.

***

"Come in! Come in! Happy Sylvester!" Roger Kaufman's voice boomed. John, Ida, and Helen Wienke entered the over-heated house. A large wood fire roared in the fireplace and the windows were steamed up from the inside and several of the ladies were fanning themselves with paper fans. The sounds of New Year's Eve joviality were raucous.

"Here, give me your coats, boots over on the pile...we'll figure it out after midnight whose is whose."

The three Wienkes took off their coats and boots and waded into the crowded room.

"We brought these canned goods for donation," Ida said, handing the cloth bag to Blanche Kaufman after hugging her in a greeting.

"Wonderful. Happy Sylvester," said Blanche. "So glad you could make it. Help yourself to the punch and other goodies. The games will begin soon." She hugged Helen. "The children are upstairs, but you can decide to play with them or take part in the adult games."

"Thank you, Mrs. Kaufman. I was so glad to be invited." Helen curtsied.

Ida felt pride in her oldest daughter. "Go on then." She shooed Helen toward the stairs with her hand and turned back to Blanche. "Is there anything I can help with?"

"No, no. You are our guest. Just get yourself some punch and relax.... Oh hello, Mr. Nelson. It's so good to see you." And off she went, Pastor's most important ambassador.

Ida looked around. The room was filled with people from both the church and the town. Roger Kaufman had made a name for himself not only in Woodstock, but in the surrounding communities. She wasn't surprised to see the mayor and several aldermen, Judge Donnelly and his sisters, Eliza and Jane. What a wonderful gathering.

Ida made her way over to the refreshment table, just as a group of men including John stepped out to the back porch. To smoke, thought Ida. Well, better than hazing the hot air in the house with cigars. Helen had gone upstairs to see which 'children' were here and hadn't returned. A good sign.

A few hours later, Ida was feeling a bit tipsy. The *Glühwein* punch obviously had wine in it. She had won a game of anagrams and they were back to the Christmas tree, and she was to pull a slip from it and read it aloud to those gathered. Oh, my which one should she choose?

"Pull this one, Mama." Helen's arm went around her waist, and she steadied herself on her young support.

"When did you get so tall?"

"This one, Mama."

She did. She opened the folded slip and read to the room at large:

> "What is conscience?" asked the Sunday school
> teacher?
> There was dead silence from the class.

"Oh, you know," she said encouragingly.

"What is it that tells us when we do wrong?"

"I know," said the littlest girl in the class. "It's Grandma!"

The crowd reacted with polite laughter.

Ida hauled herself up to full stature and said, "And MY Grandma says that I have had too much punch!"

The crowd burst into robust laughter and some applause.

Helen led Ida to a seat.

"Why didn't they say the punch was Gluhwein?" Ida whispered.

"What do you mean?"' Helen whispered back.

"Never you mind. Where is your father?"

Helen looked around. "I don't see him."

"Go find him. I'm ready to go home."

"But it's almost midnight!"

"Then go find him so I can kiss him and go home."

Helen bustled away but met John at the dining room door.

Rev. Kaufman took center stage. "We are minutes from the new year."

Applause.

"I have asked my beloved wife, Blanche, to take us into the new year with a bit of Tennyson."

Blanche stepped forward "Let's all join hands."

Ida stood and grasped Helen and John's hands. She felt better just knowing John was beside her.

Blanche's clear alto voice began the countdown:

"Ring out the old, ring in the new,
Ring, happy bells, across the snow.
The year is going, let him go.
Ring out the false, ring in the true."

Roger's basso came in loud and joyful. "Seven, six, five, four, three, two, one, Happy New Year, Everyone!!"

The bells of St. Mary's began to toll along with a multitude of others, including Grace Lutheran, just down the block.

"Frohes neues Jahr"! Everyone sang out!

Some couples kissed and said a quiet 'Happy New Year' to each other. Acquaintances hugged and slapped one another on the back. Ida and John kissed and engulfed Helen in a hug.

"Nineteen fifteen is going to be a great year," John told them.

"Let 'er rip," said Ida.

**Clara Doering Dye
(Alias Clara Daring)**

William Calvin and Lenora Cissna

Keeping Cool
(1915)

Mamie knocked softly at her parents' bedroom door. "Mama. Bobby is awake and wondering where you are."

Ida groaned.

John rolled over and sat up at the side of the bed. "I'll go. Just a minute, Mamie. I'll be right there."

Ida rubbed her hand over her face. They hadn't gotten home until after one thirty from the pastor's party. "What time is it?"

"Six thirty. Go back to sleep. We'll be fine."

"But you need your sleep, too."

"I'm fine." He smiled and leaned down to kiss her cheek. "We'll make pancakes."

Ida's eyes opened wide. "Pancakes?"

"Don't worry. I bet Edna knows how. Just rest. It was a short night."

"Okay but come get me if something goes awry. Recipe is in the recipe box." She yawned and closed her eyes.

"Are Mama and Helen ever going to get up?" Edna sat at the kitchen table with John, Mamie, and Bobby. It was eight o'clock and the pancakes had been accomplished, albeit ranging from slightly undercooked to a bit charred. John had taken the blackened ones for himself.

"We had a very late night. We will let them sleep a while longer."

Bobby stuffed a handful of pancake into his mouth and chewed. John reached over and tore it into smaller pieces and offered milk, which was eagerly accepted.

"Why did you stay up so late?"

Mamie could answer this question. "They brought in the new year."

Edie's eyes were saucers. "They did?" Then she looked around. "Where is it?"

John chuckled. "All around you. The New Year is invisible but very real."

"Like God?"

"Well, I suppose, yes."

"What does it do like God?"

"Let' me see…I suppose it gives you a chance to turn over a new leaf."

Edie's face scrunched. "What does that mean?"

Mamie said, "It's like starting over, right Papa?"

"Sort of. It might not be a complete overhaul, but each new year we should each examine ourselves and make at least one resolution to do better."

Edie poked at the cold half pancake on her plate, both of which were precariously close to the edge of the table. "Res O Lu Shon!"

"That's a promise to yourself." John pushed the plate back a bit. "Like I will never miss church or I will be kinder to my customers or…." John tried to think of a resolution for an eight-year-old. "Or I won't get mad at my friends."

"Or I will lose weight," Mamie added.

Edie shot her a look. Mamie shrugged.

Bobby, who had almost finished a whole pancake, held up syrupy hands. "More, Papa." John reached for a cake and broke it into small pieces on his plate and poured syrup over it. Bobby smiled.

"What have you promised for this year, Papa?" Mamie asked.

"I haven't really thought about it. Maybe I should smoke fewer cigars."

"Nooo," Edie looked shocked. "I like the way they smell."

"I don't," said Mamie. "I like how a pipe smells."

John chuckled. "So, I should resolve to switch to a pipe?"

The girls giggled. Mamie said, "You won't do it."

"That's the thing with resolutions, most people can't or won't keep them. They sound great on New Year's Day, but a week later, like water down the drain. Forgotten."

Mamie's face was pulled together with lips pursed. "I promise that I will not miss any days of school."

"That's a good one," her father encouraged. "Edie?"

Edie was mesmerized watching Bobby build a wall with his pancake pieces, the syrup acting as mortar to hold it together, but now, she shook herself. "I promise not to...um...miss any days of school."

"That's MY promise. You have to think of your own promise." Mamie said a little bit too loud. "Maybe you should promise not to be so much of a pest."

Edie glared at her. "I'm not a pest, am I, Papa?"

"Well...um...no...um...," John stammered.

Edie turned her glare on him. "Am I?"

"No, of course not. And there's nothing saying that two young ladies can't make the same promise."

"What's this talk of promises?" Ida stood in the kitchen door, her eyes running over the scene. Two cast iron skillets were balanced on the edge of the stove, batter running down the outside. On the table, a plate was mounded with pancakes, enough to feed three families. In front of each person was a plate with half-finished cakes. Bobby had pancakes and syrup in his hair and surrounding him on the floor and an impressive pancake wall at the edge of his highchair tray. Edie's sticky finger marks could be seen on the tabletop. John in his pajamas was holding court from one end of the table, a smear of batter down his lapel. Mamie sat with hands folded primly in her lap, a syrup mustache gleaming on only her top lip.

"Mama!" Edie hopped down and came toward her.

"Wait, wait, wait. You are all sticky." She took her by the collar and turned her toward the sink. Grabbing the dish cloth, she wet it and handed it to the girl. "Wipe your hands and face."

"How do you feel?" asked John.

Ida once again looked around the room. "Wonderful!"

"Mama, did you make a resolution when you brought the new year in?" Mamie wiped her mouth on her sleeve and the mustache disappeared.

Ida poured herself a cup of coffee and sat down. "Let's see. I think I'll resolve to sleep later one day a week so that Papa can make breakfast, most likely it will be Saturday."

John blanched a bit and got up to refresh his coffee. The children were more enthusiastic.

"Yes, Papa. Let's do it!" said Mamie.

"Papa, you can make eggs next time," suggested Edie.

Bobby broke in, chanting, "Papa, papa, papa!"

John sat back at the table. "I think you have made a resolution for me also. I resolve to make breakfast on Saturday morning, with the help of my friends." He looked around the table. "So that my beautiful wife can get extra sleep."

"Yay!!" shouted the children and Ida.

Mamie went to John and hugged him. "You are the best Papa in the world."

***

Local News

A small army of men are now employed on the ice fields of Lake county. It is said that Lake county has some of the largest ice houses in the world and at the present time hundreds of men are given employment on the ice.

The Woodstock boy scouts delivered twenty-eight, fifty-pound and fourteen, twenty-five-pound sacks of flour to needy families in that city last week Wednesday.

The smallpox situation at Harvard is greatly improved, there being but only one case there at the present time.

Christmas was ushered in with the thermometer down to 10 below zero and the following day it dropped to 19 below zero. A number of water pipes were frozen.

Woodstock Republican, January 1, 1915.

1914 in Woodstock

The year just closed has seen many changes made in this city. These changes have marked vast improvements along many lines, and, perhaps to the minds of some, have caused a calamitous number of hard times. However, if a look backward is taken it will be seen that this city hasn't suffered so badly during the past year in spite of the fact that a few of our ever-present "hard time" criers have had us all ready for the scrap heap and the grave.

The first milestone set down in the city during 1914 was the passing of the saloons. At the option election on April 7, last, the suffrage vote put the town on the "dry" list by an overwhelming majority, and it was asked on every side, "How are we going to fill up the vacant buildings?" The buildings have been filled all but two or three of them, and these will doubtless be occupied again before many months pass by. The direct effect of the closing of the saloons has not been noticed owing to the general depression around the country. The hard times which may have been experienced thus far cannot be laid to the outgoing of the saloons.

The addition to the city of a new depot by the Chicago & Northwestern Railway Company was an improvement which has long been needed but which was realized only in the closing months of the year.

The paving of the outlying streets of our city was also included in the records of the work accomplished in 1914. This addition adds much to the beauty of Woodstock.

Woodstock, McHenry county, and the state of Illinois, all have experienced a rebirth of the Republican party. The winning of voters back to the old banner of the G. O. P. augurs a prosperous future for the Republican party. All seems to indicate that the Democratic ascendancy is about to end.

The advent of a new typewriter company into our city came during the year. The Woodstock Typewriter company purchased the plant and equipment, formerly occupied by the Emerson Company, and has started operations toward the marketing of a machine which ought to help stamp Woodstock as the Typewriter City of this country.

On the whole, we have prospered in this city during the year just closed. 'Tis true we may have felt a little depression but when it is taken into consideration that we are living in a land of peace we can justly sacrifice a little prosperity for the sake of continuing that peace which ultimately will make America the greatest nation in the world, and she will be so considered even by the great powers now being ravaged by the worst war in the world's history.

Woodstock Republican, January 1, 1915.

WILL OUST U. S. CONSULS

Washington, Dec. 30.—The German government has formally notified the American state department that American consuls in Belgium must be acceptable to the German military authorities, and that it is desirable that some of the consuls be withdrawn for the present.

Woodstock Republican, January 1, 1915.

U. S. MAKES PROTEST
GOVERNMENT ASKS BRITAIN FOR RIGHTS
AT SEA FOR ALL AMERICANS

Washington, Dec. 30.—The United States government on Monday dispatched a long note to Great Britain insisting upon an early improvement in the treatment of American commerce by the British fleet.

The document, constituting the strongest representation on this subject made by the United States to any of the belligerents since the outbreak of the war, was cabled to Ambassador Page to be formally presented to Sir Edward Grey, the British foreign secretary.

As the detailed point of view of the United States in numerous specific cases of detentions and seizures of cargoes had been set forth in a series of emphatic protests, most of which have gone unheeded, the communication was couched in general terms covering the entire subject of the relations between the United States and Great Britain as affected by the latter's naval policy, considered highly objectionable by this government.

Woodstock Republican, January 1, 1915.

ENGLAND FULL OF WOUNDED

London, Dec. 30.—England is becoming so full of wounded soldiers that some who have been so badly disabled that they cannot re-enter the service are being sent to South Africa for the convalescent period.

Woodstock Republican, January 1, 1915.

Personals

Stricken with pneumonia while on the desert that he knew and loved and rushed to a hospital at Los Angeles, Cal., in a vain effort to save his life, John Muir, America's greatest naturalist, father of Sequoia

and Yosemite National parks and discoverer of Muir's
Glacier in Alaska, died.

Woodstock Republican, January 1, 1915.

A Christmas for the Poor

Springfield.—The first organized effort on the part
of the capital city of Illinois to provide for its needy
poor at Christmas time was inaugurated and the plan
proved a success. A huge Christmas tree, standing 30
feet high and located in the courthouse square, was
laden with hundreds of gifts, which were distributed by
Santa Claus.

Marengo Beacon/Republican, January 1, 1915.

***

The back door banged, and Mamie and Edie rushed in, snow in
their knit hats and rubber boots. Ida looked up from peeling eggs
for 'stuffed eggs' which would be taken to the Women's Circle
meeting tomorrow. She went to them.

"Goodness. Mamie, your lips are blue."

"And I'm shivering," she said through chattering teeth.

Ida pulled two chairs over to the stove and opened the oven
door. She added a shovel of coal to the fire. The girls in the
meantime had shed their hats, scarves, coats, and boots on the
floor and were climbing up into the chairs.

Ida went to the bedroom and brought back two lap blankets,
one for each girl. She wrapped each of them with the blanket
around the shoulders and placed another chair in front of the
stove where they could prop their feet.

"There. Feel better?"

Mamie's voice shook as she agreed. "Ye-yes Mama-ma."

"How about some hot cocoa?"

"Yes!" The first word out of Edna whose eyebrows were
melting down her cheeks. She sat very still as if frozen in place.

Ida filled a pan with milk, reaching over the girls, put it on the
stove top to scald. From the cupboard she brought down cocoa

powder, sugar, and vanilla. She stirred the milk watching for the tell-tale bubbles around the edge that would tell her it was ready.

After removing the milk from the stove, she stirred in a drop of vanilla, a heaping tablespoon of powder and a teaspoon of sugar. Using the stirring spoon, she tasted it and added another teaspoon of sugar.

Ida filled three cups and passed two to the girls who were looking a bit rosier. She sat down at the table enjoying the heat being generated from within the oven and from the hot cocoa.

"How are you doing now?"

"Better," said Mamie. She sipped the cocoa and smiled.

"Much better!" Edie's shoulders had relaxed under the blanket. "It was really, really cold out there."

"Yes. The paper said that it wouldn't get above zero today." Ida opened the paper and pointed to the article. Neither girl turned their head to see. "Mamie, have you stopped shivering?"

"Almost. Where did you learn to put cold children in the oven?"

Ida chuckled. "From Oma Stoffel. She always put our feet in the oven when we came home cold. She didn't have a furnace and so it was always a little cold in the house."

Edie looked at her. "No furnace? How did you stay warm?"

"Well, we wore more clothes in winter, and we had fireplaces or stoves in each room, but we didn't always use all of them. It depended on how much wood we had to burn."

The little girls considered this. "Sometimes the school stove gets hot and glows," Mamie said. "Did your stoves glow?"

"Yes, they did. In fact, I remember best the stove that we had in the barn where you were born, Mamie. It glowed a bright orange but then cooled down fast, so it was always chilly in the barn. We had to get up and add wood halfway through the night."

Edie looked at Mamie with a grin. "You were born in a barn?"

Mamie looked at Edie with total sincerity glowing in her face. "In truth, it was a stable, like Jesus."

Edie was still smiling. "Where was the BARN?"

Mamie looked at Ida. "I think it was at Uncle Al's place."

"In Beloit?" Edie was aghast. "You were born in Beloit not Woodstock?"

Ida felt she better clarify. "Mamie was born in Woodstock. Uncle Al and Aunt Lena used to live two houses up Lincoln Avenue."

"They did?" Edie was flummoxed. "What happened?"

Mamie smiled at her. "They moved, silly."

"Why?"

"So, they could live in Beloit," Mamie said with authority.

"Did they want to live in Beloit?"

Ida laughed. Even she found it hard to believe that anyone would pick Beloit over Woodstock. "Aunt Lena's family, her sisters and mother and father, lived in Beloit. She wanted to be closer to them."

"But what about us? Didn't she want to be closer to us?" Edna's eyes filled.

"She wanted to be close to all of us. So, she lived in Beloit first and when she married Uncle Al, they moved to Woodstock—"

"Like you did from Racine, right?" Mamie sipped her drink.

"Right. And after they had lived here for a while they went back to Beloit." Ida's eyes welled up at the memory.

"So…." Edna's blue eyes cleared a little. "So, they will come back here again, right?"

"Maybe, but most likely not. Afterall, Uncle Al has his business up in Beloit, and Aunt Lena is happy there."

"Oh. I don't like it that they moved to Beloit." The final word came from Edie as she pushed her lip into a pout.

"Me either." Ida remembered the pain of that separation. "Me either."

***

CIRCUIT COURTS OPENS JAN. 11
Hon. Charles H. Donnelly Will Preside

Among the more important cases scheduled for this term are Fred Brendt of Harvard, indicted for murder; Richard Lissok, who burglarized the Wenninger meat market in Crystal Lake, and Peter Meyer of McHenry, who is in the county jail charged with larceny.

There are sixteen divorce cases set for trial for this term in court, thirteen of which have been brought for action by the "weaker" sex. Whether this disturbance in matrimonial affairs has been caused by hard times or through the "cussedness" of men will be determined at the hands of the higher court than the decrees promised in the front parlor.

Jurors for the January term are:

Grand jurors from Dorr Township: Albert Sahs, H. C. Doering, Lester Nogel, E. G. Griebel, Jay Compton, Wm. Wiley, Geo. F. Eckert, Frank Kapplar, W. H. Mann, Frank Kimball.

Crystal Lake Herald, January 7, 1915.

MINIER, ILLINOIS

Revival meetings are in progress at the Methodist church. Rev. Mr. Wm. Cissna, the pastor, is preaching.

Bloomington Pantagraph, January 7, 1915.

***

Local News

Wheat was reported on Monday as selling for $1.37, the highest price paid in forty years. The high price is caused by the European war.

This locality has been visited by another storm, and the farmers are well pleased with the splendid sleighing now present.

Down in Wabash county, Indiana, a schoolteacher who was trying to keep up with the procession was skidooed by the school board because he insisted upon

his pupils starting with p when they spelled 'taters.'
People down that way won't stand for these
newfangled notions.

Marengo Republican-News, January 8, 1915.

***

New Ambulance

J. J. Stafford & Son have purchased an ambulance for
conveying invalids to and from the hospital. The new
vehicle is a Cunningham make, easy riding, with a solid
mahogany inside, electric lighted, painted gray, and
equipped with all modern conveniences. The
ambulance has seats for two persons along the side of
the patient. Messrs. Stanford do not expect to put the
ambulance service on a paying basis but feel that in
providing the ambulance they are filling a public want
and this service will be of great comfort and
convenience to hospital patients.

Woodstock Sentinel, January 21, 1915.

"Your Uncle Fuller"

Sample of the stuff with which Billy Sunday
converted 13,000 and received $11,000 for it in Des
Moines:

"Oh, a lot of people have told me that if I did not
preach so plain against Unitarianism, I would have
gotten more money in Des Moines," he said. "You can
take your money and go to hell with it! I'll uphold Jesus
Christ if I have to wheel my trunk to Chicago. You bet
your life! You can't insult Jesus without getting the best
fight in your life from your Uncle Fuller" and he shook
his fist at the crowd as if determined to pound his
words home. --Des Moines Register and Leader

Woodstock Sentinel, January 21, 1915.

To Take Religious Census

Members of the Luther League of Grace English
Lutheran church on Friday evening of this week will

take a religious census of the North side of town. The data obtained will be shared with other churches. The pastor and also *The Sentinel* asks Northside residents to receive the census takers kindly and give them the information which they are seeking as the data obtained will be for the common good of the various churches.

Woodstock Sentinel, January 21, 1915.

***

Dinner was over and Mamie and Edie had been excused from the table, but Helen lingered. Bobby had had an early supper and was asleep.

John drank the last of his coffee and pushed back from the table, "Well! There's a paper that needs reading."

Ida smiled. "And a nap to be taken."

"Hush, woman." John chuckled. "You'll give Helen the wrong impression."

"Mama, Papa. Can you wait a moment?"

The adults both remained seated. "What's the matter, Helen?" Ida said with a look of concern.

"Nothing's the matter, but I would like to go with the Luther League to do the religious census tomorrow after school."

"No," John said and again went to get up.

Ida looked at John. "Wait a minute. What religious census? Why are our Luther Leaguers doing it? I don't know about this."

Helen switched into information mode. "Pastor volunteered our young people to go house to house on the Northside to ask some questions about people's affiliation with the church, whether Lutheran or other. The Luther League has agreed to do it tomorrow afternoon and next Saturday. That way they will cover the people who workdays and nights."

"No. You are not in Luther League yet. You are too young." John held his position.

"So, let me understand. You'll just knock on a door and ask the people's religion?" Ida was not sure what her position was.

"There are six questions. Only one asks their home church." Helen was not to be deterred.

"And what do the others ask?" Ida took a sip of her tepid coffee.

"Different things. Do they like to go to revivals? Were their parents the same religion? Um...do their children go to Sunday school or parochial school? I can't think of the others."

"John. I can't see why she couldn't do this. She is more articulate than most of the older children at church and much more social."

"No. She isn't old enough."

Ida looked at John. At his set face and drawn together brow. There was more to this than met the eye.

"Tell you what. Let your father and I talk, and we'll tell you in the morning whether it's okay or not. We need to think about it more."

"I said 'no'."

Ida patted his hand. "I know you did, but it won't hurt to explore the possibilities, right?"

John looked at Helen and stood up. "Don't get your hopes up, young lady."

Later, after Helen stayed to help her mother clean up the dishes, Ida sat down on the davenport and pulled out her stitching.

"What are you making now?" asked John.

"Still pillowcases. It takes a while for each one. I'm doing twelve. Six for us and six for the Circle raffle. Two in each set so they will have three sets to raffle."

"Nice. Are those bluebirds?"

"Why yes, they are."

"Not robins?"

"No, they have red breasts, but are blue above not brown."

"Mm. Pretty."

Ida dropped the hoop to her lap. "Okay, enough small talk. What is going on with this religious census?"

"It's a lot of hogwash. I don't want Helen associated with it."

"You think something the Pastor wants is hogwash?"

"I'm not sure that Pastor wants it, but the board does. One of the guys went to a conference in Chicago and came back with all these highfalutin ideas about growth. This census is just the first part. I'm sure Pastor isn't against growth, but I and some others are against proselytizing."

"Is that what they are doing with this census?"

"Yes. They are to go to a house, tell whoever opens the door that they are English Lutherans, and ask them questions and 'chat' about what Grace congregation has to offer."

"But Grace does have a lot to offer."

John brought one hand to his face and rubbed it and his bald head vigorously. "I know, but I think people will naturally hear about us and come if they want. If we recruit people, they will come FOR something and if it isn't offered, they won't stay."

"I thought the revival question was...um...interesting. Are we going to start holding revivals?"

John looked at her. "I don't know. John Paul seems to think that the way to grow is to give the customer what they want. Customer, can you believe that? Our parishioners are now to be customers. It's very disturbing."

"I can see that. What exactly does growth give us besides fuller pews?" Ida picked up the embroidery hoop again.

"Good question." John considered for a moment. "Well, I suppose longevity would be the primary answer. John Paul brought up the Universalists and how they didn't work at growth and have almost disappeared in Woodstock. So, stability comes from steady growth."

"I can see that." Ida thrust the needle through the broadcloth, folded the tail over, and secured the strand with her next stitch by catching the tail under the stitch. "But that Universalist church is still open. They just don't advertise much. In Racine we had a very, very good Universalist minister. Clara attended there a few times and liked it very much. I would think you would like that about them."

"That's the point. I do. We should not start publicizing our congregation beyond the time of events or topics of sermons. That should be enough. If people want to come, they know where to find us."

"And this census—

"Does just the opposite. It puts us in a position of pride where we say we will gather information for all the other congregations while we are slyly gathering information to draw people to Grace Lutheran. Everyone will see through that ruse, especially the Catholics."

"And our daughter—

"Sees this as fun and games with her friends. She does not see what the ramifications of such action might be."

"Like what?" Ida looked up. His words sounded ominous.

"Like having the door slammed in her face, which would be the mildest negative reaction I can think of. From there it gets more dangerous. We should never be sending children to do the work adults are afraid of. The board thinks that the doors will be opened wide because the children are asking. I don't want Helen anywhere near this danger." John's face was as serious as Ida had ever seen it.

"When you put it like that, I tend to agree. Especially if they will be out after dark. People are more likely to overreact when they are tired after a day's work or if the knock at the door interrupts their supper." She shook her head and went back to stitching.

"She isn't in the Luther League yet, and I think we should prevent her from engaging in this activity." John shrugged. "Maybe we could do something special for her to make up for it. A movie perhaps on Saturday?"

"With a friend, maybe? That's a great idea. I bet she would rather take in a movie than walk around in the cold knocking on doors." Ida felt pleased with the decision. She looked up with a smile, but her face fell. John was glowering at her.

"Great! Can I get back to my paper?"

Ida looked down and took another stitch. "Of course, your grumpiness."

"Harumph!"

Ida chuckled. "My beloved curmudgeon."

A small smile flickered on John's face as he brought the paper to eye level.

Helen, who had been eavesdropping from the front stairs, sighed. Looked like she wasn't going to be one of the census takers. But darn it all, she was old enough to do it, but Papa had made some good points about evangelizing, too. As quietly as she could she stood and made her way up the stairs to her room and closed the door behind her. This growing up was taking too long!

She flounced down on the bed. She wanted to scream, but she knew it would do no good. No reason to make things go from bad to worse. She knew Mama would back Papa on this one, but next time....

She pulled the pillow over her head. She was so tired of being a child.

**

Dogs and Cats Must Be Restrained

A quarantine notice has been issued by Assistant State Veterinarian W. W Lichity of Woodstock, ordering all owners of dogs to securely fasten them and keep them so fastened until further notice. All dogs running at large will be considered a nuisance and will be shot immediately. Sheriffs, deputies, constables, mayors of cities, presidents of village boards, town marshals and policemen have authority to kill at sight any dog, cat, rabbit, or squirrel found running at large. This order will be strictly enforced, as the animals may be carriers of hoof and mouth disease, and there is no necessity for their being allowed to run at large.

DELOS L. JAMES
County Agriculturist and Agent U. S. Dept. of Agri.
McHenry Plaindealer, January 21, 1915.

***

ATLANTIC AND PACIFIC OCEANS JOINED BY BELL TELEPHONE LINE

New York, January 25.—The completion of the long-distance telephone line between New York and San Francisco was celebrated today. First this city had speech with her California neighbor, 3,400 miles away. Then the wires that swing southward from New York brought Washington and San Francisco in touch. On down the coast to little Jekyll Island opposite Georgia, they carried the Golden' Gates greeting. To the North, Boston, the birthplace of the telephone, talked across the continent.

Woodstock Sentinel, January 28, 1915.

***

Keep Cool—It Is January

Keep your mind from getting fevered over the war talk. It is going to take more than the mutterings of a few disappointed contractors and jingoistic statesmen to start anything belligerent between England and the United States. If the owner of the Dacia wants to try a little experiment, it is his affair alone, and he will probably bear the consequences. This country cannot legally prevent him from his move and Great Britain feels that she cannot allow this defiance of neutrality to pass unchallenged. This does not, however, constitute ground for war or war talk. In times of peace, it would pass with the hundred other fine points of international relations into its proper court for settlement unnoticed. This is exactly what will be done now. The only difference is that war fever is prevalent and somewhat contagious. There is no particular reason for getting excited. Be reasonably and seasonably cool. It is January. Hence it ought not to be a difficult task.

Woodstock Sentinel, January 29, 1915.

***

He Didn't See His Shadow

The ground hog is at large. But he need fear no evil for he is in the good graces of the community, as he had decreed that "wintry blasts will so be past" and "the flowers that bloom in the spring, tra la" will soon peep from the highways and byways. As Mr. Ground Hog emerged from his winter quarters last Tuesday, there was no sun, so of course there was no shadow to frighten him back into hibernation, and he just gave one prodigious yawn, decided he no longer felt sleepy and started out to visit his old familiar haunts in this vicinity.

Woodstock Sentinel, February 4, 1915.

Woodstock Swept by Forty-Eight-Hour Storm of Snow, Rain and Sleet

The worst storm of the season swept Woodstock Saturday night, Sunday, and Monday. On Sunday morning the blizzard had abated somewhat, but toward evening its fury increased and Monday morning it raged at its height. Beginning with snow, it changed to rain, then the mercury crept down, and the rain changed to a blinding stinging sleet. The wind blew furiously, sidewalks were covered with a sheet of ice. Pedestrians were forced to take the middle of the road, and even there, walking was extremely difficult.

Telephone lines were crippled, particularly in the country and railroad schedules impaired, trains from the North being very late and making but slow progress, attendant with many stops, from station to station.

Dozens of extra linemen were called to work on the telephone lines and for some time it was impossible to make long-distance calls. Telephone service in town was not impaired but rural lines, in many places, were put out of commission.

Woodstock Sentinel, February 4, 1915.

***

"What does it mean when the groundhog doesn't see his shadow because he comes out in the middle of a blizzard?" Helen leaned on the snow shovel eyeing Mamie who was diligently digging a trench down the front walk to the street. The layer of ice on the top of the snow made the lifting heavy, but she was chipping away at it.

"I don't know. Is this a joke?"

"We can make it one." Helen resumed her work on the driveway that came up the west side of the house.

"Let's see," said Mamie, "It means that Spring will be plagued by cold weather and occasional ice storms."

"That's not funny." Helen shoveled in silence for a minute. "It means that the woodchuck got the date wrong on his calendar."

"That's not funny either," said Mamie, puffing a bit.

"It means that we will not have any Spring at all." Helen tried again.

"That's not funny, but true. It means that the ice age is coming back."

"That's not bad." Helen said, trying to be generous. "They might put that in the paper."

"Think so?" Mamie was always skeptical.

"How about it means that the rivers will be frozen all summer?"

"Mm." Mamie made a non-committal noise.

"Gee whiz, this is heavy stuff. Couldn't Papa do this when he gets home!" Helen panted.

Mamie stopped for a moment, too. "Mama says it will give him an apoplexy. And we wouldn't want that."

Helen didn't like thinking about losing Papa. He was getting old, but not old enough to die or to have an apoplexy. "That wouldn't happen. He is still very strong even with his bald head."

Mamie giggled. "There, I made it to the street. I'll come help you."

"Why are we doing the driveway?"

"I don't know. Papa always does."

"We don't have an automobile or a sleigh."

The girls leaned on their shovels.

Mamie thought of a reason. "We do walk up the driveway to the back door. All of us usually use the back door."

"Well then we need a path rather than a driveway." Helen said with authority. "We can't both work from this end on a path. Why don't you go up to the back porch and work your way down to meet me."

Mamie looked at her. "I guess that will work."

Mamie waded through the snow to the back porch and started making a path down the drive as Helen made a path up the drive. In very short order—it wasn't a long drive—they met each other on their paths, side by side, about three feet from each other.

"Oh, for heaven's sake," said Helen. "You came down the wrong side of the driveway."

"I did not. This one is closer to the house. See I even made a path over to the basement door in case someone needs to deliver something." Mamie pointed at the auxiliary path to the side of the house.

"Okay. Fine. I can fix this." Helen retreated about ten feet and started making the path curve instead of going straight.

Mamie saw the plan and did the same, and they met in the middle, their shovels clanging against each other.

"I think that's good enough. Anyone can get from the street to the front, side, and back doors."

At supper, John swallowed a bite of pork chop and applesauce and said, "Who did the creative snow shoveling today?"

Edie's head jerked up. "Creative?"

"Yes. The path does an S-curve up the drive. It's just wide enough for one person to walk to the front, side, or back door."

"We did, Papa. Mamie and I." Helen jumped in before Edie could say any more.

"I would have helped but there are only two shovels," Edie's face turned to a thunder cloud.

"Thank you for that work," said John. "After supper we will need to go back out and do a little touch up."

Helen slumped in her chair. "Oh, Papa, it was so cold. We barely made it back in the house. I thought we would freeze out there and be ice statues in the yard. Just tell us what we did wrong, okay?"

"No, we'll go out. It won't take long."

"Can I come, too." Edie was stirring her applesauce into her mashed potatoes.

"Sure. Mama can come too if she wants." John was smiling at Ida.

Ida shot him an evil eye. "I think Bobby and I will stay here in the warm house."

"Did we do it wrong, Papa?" Mamie was concerned because she had thought they did a wonderful job.

"Not wrong; just not complete."

Helen sniffed.

Edie threw a snowball at Helen, hitting her so snow went down her neck.

"You little rat!" Helen picked up a big piece of icy snow and lifted it over her head and flung it at her little sister who danced out of range. Helen picked up a shovel, "Come on. Let's get this over with."

John leaned on the second shovel with his audience in front of him. "We must remember that we are not the only ones using our walks."

Mamie chimed in. "We thought about that, so we made the path to the basement door."

"And that was good thinking. There's also the mailman who comes along the front walk from house to house. And Mrs. Cooney who walks Daisy past the house every day. And others who need to use the front walk for any number of things like going to the square to shop or going to work."

"Does that mean we have to cut a path through there too?"

"Yes, but more than a path. If two people are walking arm-in-arm…." He pulled Helen over to him, handing the shovel to Edie. He tucked Helen's hand in his arm, and they started walking one of the narrow paths. Both he and Helen walked in the snow.

"I see." Helen dropped his arm. "The path must be wide enough for two people to walk."

"Yes, at least for the walk in front of the house and up to the front door. Only the family uses the back door and delivery people the side so those can be single file, but it is still good to make them a bit more than just a shovel wide. It can be hard to keep your balance on a narrow path."

Mamie walked up the path swaying a little as she put her feet down. "It is hard. It kinda makes me dizzy."

"Right. So, we need to widen everything and make a nice broad walk along the front."

Helen picked up the shovel that Edie had dropped. "Papa, Mamie, and I can do this. Mama says you'll have an apoplexy if you shovel, and we don't want that to happen."

"Yes Papa. You go in, we'll do it." Mamie started shoveling along the front. The snow and ice were worse than in the afternoon.

"Thank you, girls, but let's trade off. When someone gets tired just hand off the shovel. It looks like we need to have three shovels."

"Four," said Edie, kicking at the snow.

They worked this way for about thirty minutes with Edie getting too cold and going in at about the fifteen-minute mark.

When they were finished, the three of them looked at their accomplishment and were pleased.

John dropped his shovel and grabbed Mamie's hand, tucked it in his elbow and walked along the front of the house, tipping his hat to a sleigh that came down the street. Then he did the same for Helen. They were all laughing and breathless as they went in the back door.

"Have you completed the lesson in creative shoveling?" asked Ida.

"We have," all three replied.

"And it was fun," said Mamie.

***

Local News

Ray Wienke of Chicago spent Sunday as the guest of friends in McHenry.

The Oliver Typewriter factory has just received an order for 500 nickel plated typewriters to be delivered to South America. Other orders are coming in nicely and the employees started to work ten hours a day on Monday. More days may soon be added.

Ski enthusiasts of Woodstock are making trips to the Bull Valley hill. Some of the boys are determined to become real jumpers and the stunts they pull off on their visits to the hill are most laughable, but highly enjoyable to those taking part in the sport.

Woodstock Sentinel, February 11, 1915.

***

COURT HOUSE RENOVATION

The rest room in the courthouse has been tastily furnished by Woodstock Woman's club and is now open to the women and children of McHenry county. The county board has had the rooms appropriately decorated and papered, and the Woman's club has furnished rugs, draperies, and furniture. The hangings and rugs are in a soft, restful green, and the furniture, consisting of easy chairs, writing desk, rockers and settees are in attractive green willow.

The place is particularly cozy and attractive and should prove a great boon to women shoppers and out-of-town business callers. In a secluded room at the side is a comfortable couch fully equipped with good bedding for the convenience of visitors who may be taken suddenly ill. A tiny room at the rear is to be equipped as a kitchen, with a small electric stove for cooking purposes.

The rest room has been furnished for the convenience of the women and children of McHenry county, who are welcome to make use of it when shopping or calling in Woodstock.

Woodstock Sentinel, February 18, 1915.

***

Personals

Hamilton Heald and Ray Wienke, of Chicago, enjoyed the dance at McHenry Saturday, and afterward came over to our city for Sunday.

Mrs. Herman Doering was in Chicago, Wednesday.

Ray Wienke returned early in the week to Chicago, after visiting his parents here.

Woodstock Sentinel, February 19, 1915.

Tax Notice

Tax Collector F. C. Wienke announces that he will be at his office 204 Main Street, Woodstock, Ill., each day

of the week except Thursday, when he will be in
Ridgefield, to collect the taxes for Dorr township.

Woodstock Republican, February 19,1915.

***

John slipped into Ray Wienke's Cigar shop. A line of seven
were waiting at the register most likely to pay their taxes. He
perused the cigars, selecting thirteen so he got one free and
picked up the *Tribune*. The line was down to five. He pulled up
behind J. J. Stafford, the undertaker.

Stafford turned and smiled at him. "Good evening, Mr.
Wienke."

"Good evening, Mr. Stafford. Congratulations on your new
ambulance. Is business good?"

Stafford sighed heavily. "Too good. We always lose many in
the winter and spring. The weather seems to be taking its toll."

"I suppose. My wife and daughters are worried about me
when I shovel snow. Mrs. Wienke is sure I will suffer apoplexy."

The hint of a smile creased the undertaker's mouth. "I've seen
it happen. You should take care."

The line moved a bit as one person shook the bell over the
door on the way out.

"We might come see you. Mrs. Wienke and I have been
talking about a new dining room table. Ours is fine for the six of
us, but if we have guests, there is no place to put the food."

"Indeed. Well, come any time. I will give you a merchant's
discount."

"How nice of you. You know I'm no longer a merchant."

"True, but I have been meaning to stop—

The line moved as two customers retreated into the cold
evening air.

"I've been meaning to stop and talk to you about fire
insurance. You know the Donnelly's and my establishment are
the only two wood frame buildings left on the square. Would it
be possible to insure them against fire?"

John smiled his insurance-man-come-calling smile. "Of course, it would. Please stop by anytime and we'll find a policy to fit your needs. The sisters Donnelly already have a policy although I should stop by and see if it is still up to date. The inflation rate is increasing the value of everything."

"Isn't that true? Of course, with their textiles and my wood supplies, I suppose we are an accident waiting to happen."

"Quite possibly. While I'm sure you and they are careful. Maybe one of our adjusters could come by and give some guidance on safety measures before the fact."

The line moved.

"That would be most kind. It was nice and profitable to speak with you, Mr. Wienke. I'm glad we found ourselves in this line together."

They shook hands and the line moved forward.

"Nephew."

"Uncle. How can I help you today?" Frank Wienke looked dapper in his brown vested suit and pumpkin tie. His hair was slicked back with grease as was the style. He, at least, still had some hair.

"First I want to pay my taxes and then I want to pay my mother's taxes and then I want to buy these fine smokes and this paper."

"A good plan." Frank looked up the amounts for J. F. Wienke and Sophia Wienke, and John proffered the full amount $731— $102 for the house on Lincoln Avenue and $629 for the rooming house.

"The cigars will be twenty-five cents and five cents for the paper." Frank rang the sale up on the register.

John handed over thirty cents and looked behind him at the line, now ten deep.

"You have a long night ahead of you." John took the proffered paper-wrapped cigars.

"I'll sleep well tonight." Frank smiled.

"That you will." John made the bell ring over the door as he left.

***

Motor Bus Between
Woodstock and McHenry

Ed White of Woodstock will operate a motor bus line between Woodstock and McHenry just as soon as the weather will permit regular trips.

McHenry Plaindealer, March 4, 1915.

***

Dorr Republican Caucus

The Republican voters of the town of Dorr are requested to meet in caucus at the polling place in the courthouse at Woodstock on Saturday March 20, 1915, at 1 o'clock p.m. for the purpose of placing in nomination candidates for supervisor, one commissioner of highways, one trustee of schools and pound master and transact such other business as may properly come before the caucus.

ROBERT McLEAN,

J. F. WIENKE,

A. J. MULLEN,

Town Committee

Woodstock Sentinel, March 11, 1915.

***

Bilton's Bunk

A Milwaukee saloon makes a bold display of this sign: "Notice—We're neutral. If you can't say a good word for the Germans, keep your d-----d mouth shut!" (Very succinct.)

"Why did Kate refuse at the party to sing, 'All That I Want Is Love?'"

"She refused because it wouldn't be true; she wants the vote also."

Woodstock Republican, March 12, 1915.

***

Sophia looked down at the page of the ledger. With her good right hand, she raised her lifeless left hand to lay across the book to hold it in place. Then she picked up the pen, dipped it in the inkwell and wrote:

13.April.1915   *Vermögenssteuer* $629

Emil had held out against the arguments of his brothers to sell Sophia's rooming house for over four years. "Managing it is all she has left," he said, and the others would grumble a bit but then give in to their youngest brother.

Sophia didn't actually manage the house, but rather she managed the money. She collected the rent – dropped off at Frank's house where she lived – and did the books. The money earned went into an account from which she paid repairs and other miscellaneous expenses like *Vermögenssteuer* (property tax). Emil did the rest: renting the rooms, overseeing the on-site 'manager,' shoveling the walks in winter, mowing what lawn there was in summer.

Sophia put the pen in the inkwell and closed the book. *"Nichts sicher außer dem Tod und den Steuern."*

Now Frank smiled. "Nothing for sure except death and taxes? What about a comfortable bed?"

"Ja. Now comfortable maybe, aber der Teufel wartet direkt von der Tür."

"Well, the devil won't get through the door. I locked it well. And maybe it's an angel that is waiting outside, not the devil."

Sophia shook her head. *"Wenn es einen Engel gibt, its es ein Wunder."*

"So, an angel waiting is a miracle, but the devil waiting isn't. That sounds pretty cynical, Ma." Frank searched his mind for the German word. *"Zynisch."* He liked stretching his brain by conversing in German. It kept him on his toes.

"Zynisch? *Pshaw!*" Sophia waved her good hand at him. "*Realistisch.*"

"You're right. You are a realist.

"*Auf Deutsch bitte.*" Sophia seemed to like it when he used German.

"*Du hast unser Leben immer auf das Wesentliche konzentriert.*" You have always focused our lives on the essentials.

"*Gut! Du wrist doch ein Deutscher sein.*" Good. You can still be German.

"*Was...Ich bin ein amerikanischer Deutscher.*" What? I am an American German."

"*Ja, aber vergiss das Vaterland nicht.*"

Frank laughed. "How could I forget the fatherland? You are here to always remind me."

Anna came in from the kitchen. "*Zeit fürs Bett? Die Kinder sind alle ins Bett gegangen.* The children went up to bed without a fuss. Let's see if we can get the Oma to do the same."

Sophia yawned. "*Ich bin fertig.*" I am ready.

Frank sat up on the edge of the bed. Something had awakened him, but he wasn't sure what. In haste Anna exited the bed and pulled her housecoat around her. She had heard it, too. Frank looked at the window - just getting light. Anna opened the bedroom door and came face to face with Ethyl who stood there, her ghostly face an apparition with tears streaming down her cheeks.

Anna reached out and gathered the girl into her arms. "Ethyl, what is it?"

Ethyl sobbed. "It's Oma."

Frank pushed past and went to his mother's room. Sophia lay on her back looking at the ceiling with unseeing eyes. He sat next to her on the bed. "Oh, Ma. No." He took her hand.

Anna came to stand behind him. She put her hands on his shoulders not saying anything but pulled him into her breast. They stayed like that for a long time as the truth sunk in.

Frank reached over and closed Sophia's eyes just as Ethyl, Bessie, and Clay came to the door. Anna had sent Ethyl to wake them. Bessie said, "Mama?"

Anna nodded.

Bessie said quietly to her siblings, "Just as I am." She hummed a C and Clay began in a high tenor. "Just as I am...."

Bessie and Ethyl joined with a beautiful harmony. "without one plea....

Ethyl had played and sung this song for Sophia last week and her Oma loved it. She took up the third verse with the others coming in. "Just as I am, though tossed about....

Anna joined in on the final verse. ...Oh, Lamb of God, I come, I come."

(Elliot, Charlotte, "Just As I Am," 1836. *Evangelical Lutheran Hymn-Book*, 1912.).

After a moment of silence, Bessie took a deep breath and began "Amazing Grace," Oma's favorite hymn. The other children joined in. "Amazing grace how sweet the sound...."

But it was on the fourth verse that Frank rose and holding Anna's hand signaled his children over. They stood in a circle hand-in-hand, Frank's bass balancing the higher voices:

When we've been here ten thousand years
Bright, shining as the sun.
We've no less days to sing God's praise
Than when we first begun.

"Thank you," Frank said, as he hugged each of his children. "That was beautiful. Oma would have loved it."

(Newon, John, "Amazing Grace," 1772. *Evangelical Lutheran Hymn*, 1912.).

"She did love it," said Clay, moving closer to the bed. "Look, she is smiling."

The others came closer. She wasn't smiling but her face looked so peaceful. She had been called home in her sleep. Frank put his arm around the boy. "I think you're right; she did love it."

Frank called Pastor Laufer of St. John's German Lutheran and the other six Wienke brothers. And those in Woodstock came at once. The brothers, wives and children had surrounded the bed as prayers and good-byes were said and they sang a few more of Sophia's favorite hymns.

John and Frank went to the square to inform J. J. Stafford's of the death and to select a casket. The undertaker would come and take the body to be embalmed so the funeral could be arranged at a suitable day and time without worry.

Lizzie Kate, Ida, Anna, and Etta commenced the duties that were left to the women of the family. Lizzie, Kate, and Ida removed Sophia's flannel nightgown and washed her body from head to toe and wrapped the body in a fresh flannel blanket but left the rest to the undertaker. Then they picked out the clothes she would wear in the casket. Her good black dress, hat, and gloves. Her softest chemise and underwear. Black shoes, well worn, but invisible at the showing and black stockings.

"Do you think we should find just a bit of color?" asked Lizzie.

They looked through her dresser drawers. They landed on red gloves and a beautiful red/orange and gold cameo brooch picturing a man and a woman under a tree.

Anna and Etta took on the job of covering the windows, stopping the clock in the parlor, and covering the mirrors as Sophia would have wanted. Anna found some black crepe in her material cabinet and Etta fashioned a door badge to cover the front door knocker indicating a house in mourning.

**

LIFE'S TRIALS ENDED
Mrs. Sophie Wienke

Sophie Sund was born August 21, 1836, near Demmin, in Germany. She was married to Johann Carl Friedrich (Charles) Wienke, while still living in the Fatherland. Two children were born to this couple in Germany, William, and August.

In the early spring of 1866, Mr. and Mrs. Wienke decided to join the long line of emigrants which was wending its way on the journey to the new country of freedom and opportunity in America, and with their family they came to this country to build their future home.

They first settled in Dundee, where relatives were located, but two years later they removed to Woodstock, establishing their home just west of this city.

In all ten children were born to Mr. and Mrs. Wienke, two daughters died in early childhood, while eight sons grew to man's estate as respected citizens of Woodstock. Of these, Robert, the second youngest, departed this life only a few years ago, Charles and Albert are now residents of Beloit, Wis., while William, August, Frank J., John F., and Emil J. live here.

The father, Charles Wienke, died in January 1885. His untimely death left the mother with the heavy burden of a large family to care for, but she was fully equal to the heavy task. With Christian fortitude and a staunch German heart, the mother brought up her sons as industrious God fearing and law-abiding citizens.

Fourteen years ago, she sold the old homestead and purchased a home on Washington street in Woodstock, but three years later she gave up housekeeping and took up her abode with her son Frank, where she continued to reside until her death.

The end came unexpectedly. During all of her lifetime, she had enjoyed good health, and her last illness, a stroke of apoplexy, had been taken in stride. She died peacefully in her sleep.

Mother is gone, she is weary and has gone to her eternal rest. Thus, we do look back over life's chasm, to the days when mother was our all. Mother is gone; but we remember her loving care, her kind sympathy, her every thought for our comfort. Mother is gone; little did we then know the long watching, the worries, the waiting and perhaps even the pinch of poverty, as we romped in and out of play, to school, or to do the little tasks, which then seemed irksome, but now we remember them with pleasure. Mother is gone; she gave her all for her children, they were her treasures and well did she guard them.

This mother, like many another, bereft early of the strong support of husband, had a heavy burden to carry. She struggled bravely on to successful completion of her life's work. And now, mother is gone—her children rise and call her blessed.

The funeral services were conducted Monday from the German Lutheran church, Rev. H. A. Laufer officiating. There was a large attendance. Six of the seven sons acted as bearers.

Besides seven sons, the deceased leaves twenty grandchildren.

Woodstock Sentinel, March 16, 1915.

***

MOTHER IS AT REST
Mrs. Sophia Wienke Enters Eternal Rest at the Advanced Age of 78 Years.
Beautiful Character and Fond Mother
Long Time Resident of Woodstock

Sophia Wienke was born Aug. 21, 1836, at the town of Hagelsdorf, Germany, and came to this country in 1866, taking up her residence in Dundee, Ill., and remaining there until 1869, when she moved to Woodstock, where she passed peacefully away at 1 a.

m. Saturday March 13, aged 78 years. The deceased was united in marriage with Carl Wienke, and this union was blessed with ten children, two daughters and eight sons. Her husband, two daughters and one son preceded her to the "Great Beyond," those being left to mourn are her sons, William, August, John, Frank, and Emil of Woodstock, and Charles and Albert of Beloit.

Mrs. Wienke was a devoted member of the German Lutheran church and a most active worker for its welfare. Her quiet Christian life endeared her to all who knew her, and her great love for her children was a beautiful example of Christian piety and motherly love.

The funeral took place Monday from the home of her son, Frank, on Dean street, at 1:30, and after a beautiful service at the German Lutheran church, the Rev. H. A. Laufer, pastor of the church, officiating, the remains were laid to rest in the beautiful Oakland cemetery.

The sad duty of the pall bearers was reverently carried out by the six sons of the deceased, and thus the last act of tenderness that could be shown to a loving mother was lovingly carried out.

A great number of relatives and friends were present at the funeral and the floral offerings were numerous and beautiful. Those attending from out of town included: Fred Schuett and wife, of Chicago; Mrs. Fred Zierck and daughter, of Dundee; Frank Zierck, of Elgin, and Carl Schuett and wife, of Elgin.

Card of Thanks

We wish to express our heartfelt thanks to all who kindly assisted us in so many ways during the illness and death of our beloved mother, Mrs. Sophia Wienke. For the beautiful floral tokens from the following orders, we are truly grateful: B.P.O. Elks, Royal

Arcanum, Woodstock Typewriter employees, Oliver type-bar department, and others.

HER SONS.

Woodstock Republican, March 19, 1915.

MRS. SOPHIA WIENKE
DEAD AT WOODSTOCK

Mrs. Sophia Wienke, who was well known in this city, died at her home at Woodstock last Saturday at the age of 78 years. She is survived by her sons, William, August, John, Frank and Emil of Woodstock and Albert Wienke at Beloit.

Belvidere Daily Republican, March 19, 1915.

***

"Now we can sell the rooming house," said Emil.

"Good," said William. "The money can go right into her estate then. It will make everything easier."

The family and others had gathered in the church basement after the funeral for a buffet dinner put on by the Ladies of the German Lutheran Church.

John joined the conversation, turning it away from money and estates. "She was a good old gal, wasn't she?"

The others nodded and grunted their agreement.

"A mind of her own," said Emil.

"That's for sure," Frank chimed in.

"A good mother," said Ed. The group nodded at the first words Ed had uttered all day.

"She's with Pa and Bobby now." Emil had been one of the pallbearers as had all the sons except William. William had carried a large blanket of carnations with a ribbon that said "Mother" as they climbed the hill to Oaklawn Cemetery led by the horse-drawn hearse.

"And Caroline and Doris," said William. The girls had not been spoken of often, having died in Germany and were buried there.

William and Ed had been toddlers when cholera took them both in the same week. In America, it had always been the eight sons.

"Yes. The girls," Ed said. "That's why we left Germany. That and to avoid military conscription."

Emil, who had heard very few stories of life before America, looked up questioningly. "Wasn't Pa was in the German navy?"

William took up the story. "Ja, and he didn't want to go back in – not even for the kaiser. But losing those two girls was more than Ma could take. I was only three when we crossed the ocean, but I remember Caroline. She had a braid down to her waist and crystal blue eyes.

"What about Doris?" asked Frank.

"I can't remember her, but Ma had a picture. What happened to those pictures?"

"I don't know," said John. "We'll have to look."

They all sat in silence for a while.

"Well," said William, slapping his knees and rising. "We best get back to work."

The others followed suit, mumbling in the affirmative.

Frank held up a hand to stop them from leaving. He raised his voice above the other conversations taking place in the room. "I...we...," his hand swept over his brothers, "want to thank you for this peaceful time of communion with each other. Our mother was a special woman, and we will all miss her. Thank you."

A murmur of agreement went around the room. And Sophia Wienke's sons headed back to work.

***

Shmile
Shmile and the vorld shmiles mit you.
Laugh, und the vorld will roar:
Howl and the vorld vill leaf you.
Und nefer come back anymore.
For all of us couldn't be handsome
Nor all of us vear fine clothes.

But a shmile vas not exbensive
Und coveres a vorld of woes.

Woodstock Republican, March 19, 1915.

***

LOCAL SHOPS NOW SHOWING EASTER GOODS
New Styles are Prettier Than Any Shown in Many Years

Sunday, April 4, is Easter Sunday. Everybody will want something new to wear. The old saying, "Get your Easter bonnet" means just what it says: Get your Easter bonnet. There is no proverbial turn to this.

Murphy & Doering also have a display worthy of special mention. One window shows a lattice work topped with flowers and the other is in the form of a bird arbor, also of lattice design. Millinery and spring garments are displayed.

Woodstock Sentinel, March 25, 1915.

Personals

Ray M. Wienke was home from Chicago on Sunday.

Woodstock Sentinel, March 26, 1915.

Knitting for Soldiers

A Clinton, Wis., man last week received a letter from his mother in Germany, in which she says she is compelled by the government to knit four pairs of socks per week for soldiers in the German army.

Woodstock Sentinel, March 26, 1915.

***

CLASS OF NINE TAKES VOWS OF CONFIRMATION
Impressive Ceremonies Held on Palm Sunday in Grace English Lutheran Church

A class of nine young people was confirmed at last Sunday morning's service at Grace English Lutheran church by pastor, Rev. R. C. Kaufman.

Rev. Kaufman talked very eloquently, and his words made a visible impression upon the large audience as the church was filled to its utmost capacity.

The confirmation rites were very impressive, and the class showed evidence of careful training and thorough instruction. The class was composed of the following young people: Misses Ebba Anderson, Clara Lorenz, Marie Kania, Henrietta Kania and Elta Schroeder; and George Lein, Harry Piske, William Anderson, and Peter Rasmussen.

On Good Friday night a class of adults will be confirmed.

Woodstock Sentinel, April 1, 1915.

Hikers' Club

The Office Hikers' club of the Oliver typewriter factory walked to this village one day recently. They returned to Woodstock by train.

McHenry Plaindealer, April 1, 1915.

***

LETTER SHOCKS PEACE WOMEN

Chicago, April 10.—Publication of the fact that Theodore Roosevelt had written a letter denouncing the women's proposed peace propaganda, caused a shock among the leaders here today. The letter reposes in the custody of Mrs. William I. Thomas, secretary of the Woman's Peace Party, and she refused to allow its publication.

The missive which aroused the discussion was sent to Mrs. George Rubelee of Washington. One report had it that the Colonel declared that pacifists in general constituted a "menace to the future welfare of the United States." No enemies of the republic, at home or abroad, are comparable in the extent of their menace with the pacifists at large in the United States.

Mr. Roosevelt characterized the feminine peace movement culminating in the forthcoming Hague conference as utter folly and advised the women that they would be much better employed if they stayed at home and minded their own knitting. A stern and aggressive stand taken by the United States to uphold The Hague conventions on the rules of civilized warfare, to which this country as well as the belligerents are parties, would be the most effective influence Americans can possibly exert to end the tragic conflict in Europe.

Marshalltown Evening Times-Republican, April 10, 1915.

***

GERMANY'S DYE MONOPOLY

London, April 5.—Correspondence of the Associated Press: Representatives are now in London for the purpose of bringing to the attention of the British government what is said to be a critical condition growing out of the threatened failure of the dye supply from Germany. Pressure is being brought to bear to keep the trade routes open for dye shipments from German ports.

It is estimated roughly that an annual output of $500,000,000 worth of silk, woolen and cotton goods manufactured in the United States can reach its finished state through the use of dyes made in Germany. Of these essential dyes there are now on hand only thirty days' supply, according to textile representatives. Three ships are at this writing in German ports loaded with dyes consigned to America valued at $6,000,000 sufficient to supply the American mills until August.

The war has disclosed a condition with respect to the American textile interest and its dependence upon Germany for dye which, while well known to the experts, will cause surprise in lay circles.

While progress in the United States has been slow in establishing the manufacture of colored dyes. Only one item, black dye, in America may be said to be independent, and if the German supply should be shut off entirely, America will literally be thrown into mourning. Variants of natural white, black in stripes and checks, will tend to break the funeral monotony.

Crawford County Courier, April 18, 1915.

ACCUSED DYNAMITER PARTLY ADMITS GUILT

Kansas City, Mo., April 17.—John Mulvahill, held by the police in Kansas City, Kan., in connection with the wrecking of the cooling plant of the Cudahy Packing company last Saturday night, denied he wrecked the building, but admitted he was on his way to dynamite another part of the plant at the time of his arrest.

Mulvahill, who is a laborer, asserts he was educated at Kings college, London.

I'm an Irishman," he said according to the police. "All Irishmen should oppose Great Britain in this war. The first nation to feel hunger will fall. I wanted to prevent the Cudahy people filling meat orders for English consumption."

Sioux City Iowa Journal, April 18, 1915.

***

Beer Most Animalizing

The following utterance has been made by the New York offices of the Home Life Insurance company:

"Of all intoxicating drinks beer is the most animalizing. It dulls the intellect and morals and feeds the sensual and beastly nature. Beyond all other drinks it qualifies for deliberate and unprovoked crime. In this respect it is much worse than distilled liquors. A whisky drinker will commit murder only under the direct excitement of liquor, a beer drinker is capable of doing it in cold blood. Long observation has assured us that a large proportion of murders deliberately planned and executed without passion or malice, with no other motive than the acquisition of property or money, often of trifling value, are perpetuated by beer drinkers."

McHenry Plaindealer, April 22, 1915.

WOMEN HOLD MASS MEETING IN CITY HALL

There was a fair-sized crowd in attendance at the mass meeting held in the city hall last Sunday afternoon, at which time Mayoralty Candidate, Geo. W. Conn, Jr., and Otto E. Seller, of Evanston made addresses on "Higher Citizenship" and the "Civic Duty of Women."

The meeting, while called primarily for the benefit of the women voters, was also open to the men, a number of whom were in attendance.

Much enthusiasm was aroused at the meeting, the speakers being repeatedly and vigorously applauded.

Mr. Conn spoke first, giving a brief but to-the-point talk. He emphasized the fact that the ballot is not a sacred right, but a privilege bestowed upon people who earn it, the three requisites being character, intelligence, and maturity.

Mr. Conn spoke of woman's interest in the most vital problems of public welfare and stated that he believed that a woman's public conscience tallied with her personal conscience, and that when public and personal conscience, in a general sense, became one and the same, there would be a great stride toward higher and cleaner politics. He spoke of women's devotion to the home, and he dwelt upon the fact that the home is the bed rock of the country.

Mr. Conn spoke briefly about the local situation, saying among other things that he, too, believed in paving the streets, but only to the extent that the pocketbook permitted without attracting the wolf too near the door.

"Concerning the wet and dry issue," he said, "you all know where I stand. I have been and am dry."

Mr. Conn's talk was enthusiastically received, and he was given a hearty round of applause.

Mr. Desmond next introduced Mr. Seiler who gave a very splendid talk on "Higher Citizenship." Mr. Seiler said he believes a woman has justified her place in politics by her deathblow to the saloons in America, and he further maintained that an interest in politics was not a matter of choice but a duty on the part of every American citizen. He spoke of the need for the highest types of citizens as active workers in politics, in order to eliminate the impurities and corruption, and make the controlling vote the vote of the higher-minded people.

"We do not need more laws, we have laws enough," said Mr. Seiler, "but we do need law enforcement and effectual administration."

Woodstock Sentinel, April 22, 1915.

***

POLITICS OUSTS CHIEF OF POLICE AND ELECTRICIAN

Tom Swale came to Woodstock as city electrician thirteen years ago. His appointment followed the failure to make good of several men who had been on the job during the first few years after the electric light system was installed here. Mr. Swale was first appointed by Mayor Walters, his first appointment being "on trial." "Tom" soon made good and demonstrated his ability to handle the Woodstock plant successfully. Since he has been here the plant has been extended and improved, new additional machinery has been installed and the powerhouse rebuilt and installed.

During the first years of electric lighting in Woodstock there were frequent breakdowns and shutdowns, but these have been entirely eliminated until now the electric light and power service in Woodstock is just as dependable as it can possibly be made.

Electrician Swale, like Marshal Bolger, has fallen from grace as the result of too much politics in Woodstock.

By a vote of the city council, it was decided to continue Mr. Swale in the employ of the city for another month until certain important work he now has charge of is completed. After that Mr. and Mrs. Swale will move to Beloit, his former home, and where his mother is now living. Until that time, "Tom" says he isn't going to worry about the future.

Woodstock Sentinel, May 6, 1915.

***

"Well, well, well. How far the favored have fallen." William Wienke held the newspaper a bit further away than he had when he was city engineer "It didn't take them long to eat that boy up. And now they can get some fresh meat to feast on."

"What are you talking about?" William's wife Lizzie had come into the room to hear only the end of the one-sided conversation. "Who is eating a boy?"

"Just a manner of speaking. Swale got fired from being city electrician." Will folded the paper and tossed it on the coffee table.

"Indeed. Are you going to apply for the job?" Lizzie's mouth twitched a bit.

"I doubt I'd have a chance at my age, plus I'm still not a certified electrician, which is what they want. Thing is, the 'trained' men know almost nothing about electricity. They may know the theory, but they don't know a black wire from a white one."

Lizzie chuckled. "Are wires different based on their color?"

"You bet they are, one is hot, and the other isn't. I've told you this before, haven't I?"

"Maybe but tell me again."

"You can get shocked by either wire, but they serve different purposes. The black one carries the electricity to the lamp, where some of it is used to make it glow, and the white carries the unused electricity back to the source. If you connect the black one where the white one should go the circuit won't work properly. If you disconnect the black, you will have no electricity running and no lamp glowing. If you draw too much electricity through the black one, it will melt or burst into flames. If you touch the black wire, you become a wire and the electricity runs through you and into what you are standing on, and you might die. If you touch both the white and the black, the electricity will flow from one hand to the other, frying your brain or your heart."

"Good grief, William. You are starting to scare me. Maybe I want to go back to lanterns and candles."

William smiled. "No, you don't. Done right, electricity is very safe, but you must know what you are doing and be careful."

"And Mr. Swale doesn't know what he's doing." Again, a smile threatened to break out on Lizzie's lips.

"Oh, I'm sure Swale may know what he's doing. Maybe that is why they are firing him. The new guy will be a certified engineer who may or may not know. Some electrical engineers know the theory behind everything, but they've never done hands-on work. They are nothing but supervisors. I doubt most could look at a job and say whether it was done correctly or not. I'm just glad I don't have to put up with those jugheads on the city council. They are the problem. One complaint and they have to find a scapegoat."

Now Lizzie smiled. She had heard Will say that so many times.

Will looked at her and smiled a bit sheepishly. "I never had a problem with Swale. My gripe was with the politicians, who know less than Swale or me, but feel that they can milk a man for all he is worth and just toss him aside when their goals are not met. They think they know how things should work. But they don't."

"I see. I'm glad to have such an expert on our staff here at the Wienke chateau." Lizzie leaned over and kissed William's cheek.

William smiled and said a sincere, "Thank you."

***

No Naturalizations

There will be no naturalizations at this term of court, owing to the fact that the judicial election occurs on the 7th day of June, which is less than thirty days following when hearings on naturalization cases should be held, i.e., May 25. The law provides that no hearings in naturalization cases shall be made thirty days prior to election. A term of court without any naturalizations is a rarity. All naturalization cases which ordinarily would have been deposed of all this term must now be held over until the September term.

Woodstock Sentinel, May 6, 1915.

***

Martial Law Troops Deployed

Victoria, British Columbia, is under martial law as a result of renewed attacks upon German establishments by mobs bent upon revenging the sinking of the Lusitania. A detachment of troops has been ordered there from Vancouver because further trouble is feared.

Chicago Livestock World, May 11, 1915.

***

Local News

John F. Wienke, special agent for the Illinois Life Insurance Co., and Eugene Nolan, special agent for the same company, of Woodstock, were in this city selling insurance Friday.

Marengo Beacon/Republican, May 15, 1915.

***

Local News

Ray Wienke of Chicago passed Sunday as the guest of McHenry friends.

McHenry Plaindealer, May 27, 1915.

Stores Will Close

The stores in Woodstock will close at 12:30 p. m. on Memorial Day, Monday, May 31, and remain closed until 4:00 o'clock. Reopening at 4:00, they will remain open until 6:00 o'clock, when they close for the remainder of the day.

Woodstock Sentinel, May 27, 1915.

***

LUSITANIA SINKING
Germany's Claim.

Germany blames unjustified attacks on neutral ships on carelessness or suspicious acts of the vessels concerned.

Germany charges Lusitania was armed.

Germany charges Lusitania was a British auxiliary cruiser.

Germany charges England ordered British merchantmen to attack German submarines.

Germany declares itself unable to regard British ships undefended British territory.

Germany charges United States laws violated in presence of explosives on passenger ship Lusitania.

Germany claims that the passengers were killed by explosion of ammunition in cargo bays.

Germany invites United States to end German submarine operations by securing change in British trade policy.

U. S. Position

United States holds Germany responsible for making mistakes.

United States has officially declared Lusitania left New York unarmed.

United States holds Lusitania was a British passenger ship not engaged in the service of the British government at the time she was sunk but engaged only in bar normal capacity of merchant service between New York and Liverpool.

United States holds only evidence that Lusitania did attack submarine would make this claim admissible.

United States holds laws of humanity and nations forbid attack on neutrals on merchant vessels on high seas.

United States holds American law regarding explosives on passenger ships never held to apply to rifle cartridges.

United States holds it cannot bargain in American lives or rights of humanity.

Chicago Livestock World, Monday, May 31, 1915.

***

Ida looked at John behind his paper. "Are you asleep?" It was almost bedtime. The children had all retired and the clock was about to strike nine o'clock. The parlor was quiet and cool as the furnace needed stoking.

John peeked out. "No. I'm reading one man's opinion that the sinking of the Lusitania will either take us to war or at the very least break our relations with Germany."

"Oh no. I haven't had time to catch up on the newspapers the last few days with serving at Women's Circle and getting ready for the end of the school year. So, the Americans are saying that there were no war munitions on that ship?" Ida picked up her crocheting. She was using her smallest hook to crochet collars for the new summer frocks she had sewn for the girls and herself.

"I guess so, although they are allowing that there might have been rifle cartridges on the ship." John had again retreated behind his paper but peeked out to see her reaction.

Her eyebrows raised. "Don't those fall under the category of 'munitions?'"

John lowered the paper to his lap. "I don't know. I would think they would be, but I agree with the President. Bullets have been sent by ship forever without question. To sink a ship and take all those American lives, because you 'think' there might be war materials on board is most likely an act of war and a slap in the face of American readiness."

"Are we ready?" Ida's face had taken on a scowl.

John ran a hand over his bald head and looked down at the crumpled paper. "We've been paying to get ready for two years. Think of all the war taxes Congress has levied. I hope we are ready. I've heard that many young people are signing up for service since the sinking."

"Aren't you glad Bobby is too young?" Ida cut the yarn and pulled the end through to tie off the last stitch.

"Well, sure. I'm glad he won't have to fight, but if he were old enough and wanted to go, I'd support that choice."

"I just hope that this war will end all wars as they are saying. Let them get it out of their system and settle down to a peaceful world. Then Bobby won't have to make such a decision." She flattened the collar out, measuring it against the material.

"We have five or six from the Grace congregation who signed up this last week, and you already knew that Ras Rasmussen had joined. If war comes, it will change those boys' lives forever."

"Especially if they are killed or captured or we lose."

"We won't lose." John brought the paper up to eye level.

"How can you be so sure? Everyone thought the European war wouldn't last more than a few months. It's been almost two years and it shows no sign of stopping."

The paper again collapsed to his lap. He locked his eyes on Ida's face. "We won't lose."

Ida continued to look down at her crocheting. "We could. You said that England couldn't lose with all their ships and volunteers and war bonds but look at how the Germans have attacked and sunk so many of those ships, and they have bombed the island, killing so many. They are about to lose, don't you think?"

A bit of pink had risen in John's cheeks. "No, they aren't. And it will be more likely they will win if the Americans join their side. If it looks like we are going to lose, I will sign up to fight."

Ida looked over and swatted his knee. "You will not. Over my dead body."

John's eyes never wavered. "I will. And I'm sure every able-bodied man in America will do the same. We will not lose."

"I'm going to hold you to that."

***

Delavan Factory's Loss

When the Lusitania was sunk by a German submarine, there was on board and went down with the ship, approximately $15,000 worth of goods made by the Bradley Knitting Co. of Delavan, Wisc. These goods had been sold to agents of the English government. The loss will doubtless fall on the transportation company.

Woodstock Sentinel, June 3, 1915.

Personals

Ray Wienke was out from Chicago over Decoration Day.

Woodstock Sentinel, June 3, 1915.

Uncle Tom Coming

When will the time come when "Uncle Tom's Cabin" will lose its charm to the rising generation. Judging by its present freshness, its alluring powers will be perennial. There is something in the skillful combination of the pathetic and the humorous that never fails to fascinate and the story that it tells of the suffering of the poor slaves appeals directly to the finest sensibilities of the human soul.

Such plays are better than sermons. They point to a moral and adorn a tale. They teach us lessons in thoughtfulness and charity. They impress on our minds the precepts of the Golden Rule.

Mrs. Stowe's book is one of the greatest books of literature, because it deals with questions of immeasurable human import, and the play itself is one of those simple masterpieces that can never die. If it does no more than keep alive the memory of the rise and fall of one of the greatest iniquities that history deals with, it was not written in vain.

Mort Steece's colossal Uncle Tom's Cabin company will appear here under the big tent Saturday, June 5.

Woodstock Sentinel, June 3, 1915.

***

Executor's Notice
Estate of Sophia Wienke, Deceased.

The undersigned having been appointed Executor of the last will and Testament of Sophia Wienke, deceased, late of the County of McHenry and State of Illinois, hereby gives notice that he will appear before the County Court of McHenry County, at the Court House in Woodstock in July next, at which time all persons having claims against said estate are notified and requested to attend for the purpose of having the same adjusted. All persons indebted to said estate are requested to make immediate payment to the undersigned.

Dated this 3rd day of May, A. D. 1915.

FRANK J. WIENKE, Executor.

Woodstock Republican, June 4, 1915.

Lusitania Survivor on Way Home

Charles T. Jeffery, president of the T. B. Jeffery company of Kenosha, who was one of the survivors of the Lusitania, lost a bundle of valuable papers in the water before he was rescued. The contract with the French government for autos was among the papers, but only one Jeffery machine was on the Lusitania.

Many false reports have been circulated concerning the affairs of the Jeffery auto company since the boat went down, among them was the story that three thousand trucks went down with the Lusitania, while the shipment was really made on the Transylvania, which arrived safely in port. Another rumor said that fifty German employees had been discharged from the auto factory at Kenosha because of suspected tinkering with trucks made for the French Government. These rumors are denied by the Jeffery company. —*Richmond Gazette.*

Woodstock Republican, June 4, 1915.

***

JANE ADDAMS IN ITALY

Rome, via Paris, June 10.—Jane Addams of Chicago, chairman of the special committee appointed by the women's peace conference at The Hague to visit the capitals of Europe in an effort to hasten the end of hostilities, has left Rome for Madrid, when she will go to France and Belgium. Miss Addams was received here by Pope Benedict, Cardinal Gasparri, papal secretary of state; Premier Salandra and Foreign Minister Sonino.

All the officials listened to her peace propaganda, but they gave her little encouragement. She was received with greater sympathy, however, at the Vatican, where the pope has labored to bring about peace, but even there, no secret was made of the fact that the present moment was not considered opportune for the labor Miss Addams was undertaking.

Marshalltown Evening Times-Republican, June 10, 1915.

***

Births

Born to Rev. and Mrs. Roger C. Kaufman on
Tuesday, June 8, 1915, a son.

Woodstock Sentinel, June 10, 1915.

Personals

Rev. R. C. Kaufman expects to be away at the
meeting of the Chicago synod at Maywood, Ill., from
June 11 to June 16.

Woodstock Sentinel, June 10, 1915.

***

"It is so nice to be back under your roof, Ida." Blanche
Kaufman lowered herself gently into a wooden kitchen chair clad
in a voluminous white caftan. She accepted a cup of tea and
reached for a sugar cookie.

"Blanche, you are always welcome here. I'm glad we could be
your port in a storm."

Blanche washed down her cookie with a gulp of tea. "You and
John are so good at furnishing safe haven for people."

"You are always welcome."

"You know Roger almost didn't go to the conference, but I
insisted. He gets so little time away from Woodstock, and it is
such a joy for him to be with his colleagues. We didn't know what
we were going to do. And you saved the day by offering your
home. Thank you, Ida."

"Pastor deserves a break now and again. I can just imagine
what a pleasure it is to spend time with like-minded fellows."

"Oh, they are hilarious or at least think they are. He has such a
good time with them." Blanche's large smile gave away the love
she felt for her erstwhile husband.

"Something it is hard to do with parishioners, I'm sure." Ida
put a bowl of freshly washed green beans on the table and sat
down with a paring knife. She took one end off, pulling the string

along the length of the bean, and popped the cleaned bean into a pan of water.

"I think you and John are the closest to like-minded people we have here in Woodstock."

Ida felt gratified at such praise.

A small voice sounded from the second floor. "Ah the naps are at an end. Let's see if they can entertain each other for just a bit longer," said Blanche. "Marguerite loves playing with Bobby now that she's a bit older."

"Being a year apart matters at this age but won't be anything when they get older." Ida's hands were on automatic, destringing the beans without having to think about it. "And now we will have three to play together." Ida smiled.

But Blanche frowned. "Babies are small for such a short time. We are so thankful for the clothes you passed down to Rete. She is into toddler sizes now. I will reuse what clothes I can for little Roger."

Ida stood up and offered a refill on the tea which Blanche accepted.

Ida sat down and resumed the de-stringing. "Let's see, today is Thursday. Pastor should be back on Saturday, right?"

"Right. Or maybe tomorrow."

"Pastor is going to preach, is he not, on Sunday?"

"Oh yes, and I'm sure I'll feel up to going to the service. I think, if I might, I will accept your wonderful hospitality until Sunday afternoon so he can work on his sermon on Saturday. He was talking about redoing an old sermon and if he does that then maybe he can come on Saturday?"

"Let's just see what happens. Sunday afternoon, all things being equal, would be very appropriate to return to the Parsonage." Ida had finished the beans. She covered the pot.

Blanche nodded and smiled.

"I'll go get the little ragamuffins," Ida said, rising. "Why don't you take your tea into the parlor?"

A little over an hour later, the back screen slapped open, and
Mamie and Edie bounced in.

"Is there anything to eat? We're starving," Edie called out.

"Edie is starving. I'm just a little hungry."

"There are cookies in the canister and milk in the icebox. You
can help yourself," Ida was in the middle of a row of knitting and
didn't want to lose count.

"I'll wait for supper." Mamie climbed the stairs toward her
room to change out of her school dress.

Blanche had dozed off on the couch and now aroused herself,
sitting up.

Rete looked up at her mother and smiled. "Mama." She stood
and toddled over to climb up in Blanche's lap.

"One hundred and five! There. I can stop now." Ida smiled at
her accomplishment. "I better get going or there won't be any
supper."

"Can I help?" Blanche slid the baby back to the floor and Rete
walked carefully over to Bobby and fell to the floor on her
bottom.

"No, no. I've got it all planned. Just sausage and sauerkraut
tonight with green beans and almonds. Everything boiled on the
stove top. You stay and watch the babies."

Blanche settled back against the couch and closed her eyes.
And baby, Roger Henry began to fuss in his bassinet in the dining
room.

"I'll bring him to you," said Ida. It was so nice having babies in
the house.

***

Cattle for Europe

It is reported that during the past ten days the
Chicago packers have been buying cattle to be shipped
to Europe on the hoof. By landing at French ports, it is
thought that live cattle can be shipped to points near
the army lines, and from there they are driven to the
points needed. It seems clear that the demand for beef

and meats of all kinds must be constant and increasing
as long as the war lasts, and apparently the war will last
for a long time.

Chicago Tribune, June 12, 1915.

***

WAR BABY STORY BLOWN UP BY REGISTRAR'S FIGURES

LONDON, June 11.—The war baby, as a big social
problem of the future, has come to an untimely end.
The registrar general's returns for the first nine months
of the war show the percentage of illegitimacy to be
just normal.

Scotland Yard, moreover, has issued a warning to the
public against subscribing to a charity described as "the
War Babies and Mothers' league." Established by Mrs.
Helen Best, by profession an electrolysis operator. She
says she started the league because she knew what was
bound to happen, and still maintains it is happening,
but fortunately there is no evidence to support her
fears.

Bishop Winnington-Ingram of London says the cry
has turned out to be a great delusion, that it was a big
bubble and now has exploded.

"Women generally had behaved well, but there are a
number of young giddy girls, excited by the presence of
so many young men in khaki, who caused mischief at
some camps," he said. "The troops set a remarkable
example of good behavior to the people among whom
they lived."

Chicago Tribune, June 12, 1915.

U.S. PLANTS BEGIN MAKING MODERN MILITARY RIFLES

New York, June 11.—American arms manufacturers
are just getting into the business of manufacturing army
rifles. All of the army rifles manufactured in the United
States up to the opening of the European war were

turned out in the United States arsenals. Private companies have just completed experiments which have evolved a type of gun which can be used in Europe.

One company in Connecticut has obtained a contract for 400,000 rifles to be delivered to allies early this summer.

The Savage Arms company of Utica, N. Y., is another company which has obtained large orders for a new military rifle it has perfected.

Chicago Tribune, June 12, 1915.

***

BAR WAR LIFE INSURANCE

New York, June 11.—The three largest life insurance companies of New York, the Mutual, the New York, and the Equitable, have virtually quit insuring persons who propose making any voyage to a belligerent country. It makes no difference whether they sail under the American or a foreign flag, whether the intended sojourn there is to be for a day or a year.

"We issue no insurance to any person who plans to go to Europe," was the information given at the Equitable offices today.

"We are willing to insure you, even though you admit that you intend going to Europe within the next two years," Actuary Hall of the Mutual Life said, "but we have inserted in our policies the special proviso that, should you meet death on your trip through war causes, such as having a German submarine sink your ship, you may collect no insurance, but we shall pay to your beneficiary the amount you paid as premium."

Chicago Tribune, June 12, 1915.

***

American Navy Falling Behind

New York, June 15.—George von L. Meyer, who was secretary of the navy in President Taft's cabinet, addressing the peace and preparation conference of the National Security League at luncheon to-day, asserted that the American navy is deteriorating, outlined the respects in which he believed such to be the case, and urged that investigation of the national defense and a comprehensive plan for the future should be made obligatory upon the next Congress.

Lack of battle cruisers, airships, armed aeroplanes, and men, lack of naval reserve of experienced men, lack of a comprehensive policy of national defense, lack of general public knowledge of the navy's condition, reduction of complements of some ships to man other and newer ships, and general unpreparedness on the part of the many battleships and other fighting units were enumerated as instances of naval inferiority.

St. Albans Daily Messenger, June 15, 1915.

***

"John, what happened?" Ida jumped from her chair and rushed to her husband's side. He was holding a handkerchief to his face and there was obviously blood coming from somewhere.

"Buddy nose. Hep me get out of my suit coat and shirt. I don't want to get more bud on dem."

Ida pulled the coat off while John leaned into the kitchen sink. She grabbed a kitchen towel and thrust it into his hands. "Look up, pinch your nose, and hold the towel there while I unbutton your shirt." She pulled the shirt off and tried to look at the damage.

"Did someone hit you?" she said as she pulled down the towel a bit, his face was starting to bruise.

"You should see de udder guy."

"Indeed. I cannot see you in a fist fight."

"You're right I didn't hit him. He hit me, and I pushed him off the walk and into the street. He sat in horse manure, and I walked away."

Ida shook her head. "When was the last time you were in a fist fight?"

"Years ago. Closest was your rescue from the ruffians that night a couple of years ago. I got a good punch in during that fight. This time I just pushed him away."

"It's better than hitting and missing. Let me see. Good. The blood is slowing. Do you think it's broken?"

"Maybe. I did hear a crack. Does it look crooked?"

"No. just swollen. You might have a black eye. What was it about?"

"I was walking home and as I turned on Tryon, this guy stepped out from a bush, and I bumped into him. I got a hold on his lapel to steady us and said, 'I'm so sorry. Excuse me" and backed away. He just looked at me, but when I tried to go around him, he stepped in my way. I could tell he was drunk. I decided that the best recourse was to step out into the street and just as I was going to do that, he hit me. I wasn't expecting it, and he knocked me back into the bushes which kept me upright. When he moved at me again, I just pushed him with all my might, and he fell backward, and I ran home."

"Why would he do that? To rob you?" Ida was dabbing at his bloody face with the corner of a wet towel.

"I don't think so. He said, 'Dirty German swine. Keep your hands off me,' right before he swung the first time."

Ida's eyes grew large with concern. "Had he been lying in wait for you?"

"No. I think he was relieving himself or something in the bushes and just happened to step out as I passed. Has it stopped bleeding?"

Ida looked and nodded. "Just about. Did you know him?"

"No. I didn't recognize him. But I'll surely know him if I see him again." John took the towel from her and held it protectively to his nose.

Ida smiled a bit. "I thought you knew everyone in Woodstock."

"I do. Thus, he must have been a vagabond. If so, I hope he moves on." John stood up and stepped into the washroom to see himself in a mirror. "Looks pretty straight to me. I don't think it's broken."

Ida raised her voice so he could hear. "But then how did he know you were German?"

"I dunno. Maybe I just look German." He came back into the room, raised his arms, and struck a pose showing off his muscles.

Ida chuckled and leaned back assessing her husband as he sat at the kitchen table in his undershirt. "Maybe. It just seems odd."

"He yelled some other things from his seat in the street. I could hear him ranting as I hurried away."

"Like what?" Ida ran the white shirt under cold water.

"Go ahead and run you filthy old Jew. I know where to find you."

She whirled to face him. "What? Why would he say that? You aren't a Jew."

John's turn to chuckle. "I know that, and you know that, but a person passing through wouldn't have known that. If I look German, I probably look like a Jew also."

"Do you have Jews in your family?" Water was dripping from the shirt to the linoleum.

"Not that I know of. You?"

"Heavens no! My mother is turning over in her grave." Ida noticed the drip and put the shirt in the sink to soak, wiping up the drips with the bloody towel which also went in the cold water.

"Yes, mine too. I never asked her about Jews, but we are Prussian so it's unlikely. And you are more likely to have a Romanian in your line."

"Romanian? Do you mean Roma? Do you think I look like a gypsy?" Ida's voice was slightly shrill.

John smiled. "Just as much as I think I look like a Jew."

Ida went back to scrubbing at the blood stains. "Well anyway you better go put on a shirt before the girls see you. They are going to be shocked enough at your face. No need to expose them to those fine German muscles."

John came over and put his arms around her from the back. "I'm okay. I was just surprised. It won't happen again."

She turned. "I hope not. You only have three white shirts."

***

BRYAN IN PLEA TO U. S. GERMANS

Washington, D. C., June 11.—William J. Bryan tonight delivered the third of his broadsides on the controversy with Germany.

In a statement addressed to the German American citizens, Mr. Bryan urges that they do everything within their power to help maintain peaceful relations between this country and their fatherland.

The former secretary tells the German Americans that it is absolutely wrong and inhuman, and that Germany cannot offer any excuses to the civilized world for the sinking of Lusitania, which can in any way condone the offense.

"I am glad to repeat in public what I have often said in private and would have said in public before but for the fact that it would not have been proper for one in my official position to do so—namely: that in case of war between the United States and Germany—if so improbable a supposition can be considered—German-Americans would be as prompt to enlist and as faithful to the flag as any other portion of our people.

"Knowing that the president desires peace, it is your duty to help him secure it, and how? By exerting your influences to convince the German government of this fact and to persuade that government to take no steps that would lead in the direction of war."

Marshalltown Evening Times-Republican, June 17, 1915.

WHITE SOCKS

White socks are now in fashion for men. The people of the southern states, several months ago, commenced wearing white cotton. ...American manufacturers have never learned to make dyes that would stay put. Such dyes have always been imported from Germany. At the present time, Germany is not making dyes but is engaging in filling up graves and using quick lime on the dead. Germany being busy with other matters, the helpless manufacturers of America are making white socks for men. Gentlemen sit around the club, displaying their ankles in their white socks, not knowing that they are proclaiming one of the weaknesses of the great republic. It is a pity that this great, rich country has not attended to details; has not looked after small things. This country affords every known material for the manufacture of dyes. Yet we have been importing them. Germany has been able to make them cheaper. There being no tariff, Germany has held the market. Germany has furnished Great Britain with her dyes and an effort to organize a great company for the manufacture of dyes in Great Britain has failed. When men were asked to buy stock, they replied that the British demand for British dyes was only temporary, and that after the war, Germany would make dyes cheaper and better than the same could be made in Great Britain.

These lessons ought to sing into the hearts of the American people. This country should not be dependent upon Europe for anything, not even for a music teacher. When the next European war breaks out, we should be able to laugh at the warring countries.

Marshalltown Evening Times-Republican, June 17, 1915.

Flag Day Observed

Monday was flag day and Old Glory was displayed at the entrances or in the windows of every business house in Woodstock while private residences in all parts of the city likewise exhibited the national emblem. It was indeed a gratification to see the spirit of patriotism so keenly aware, which is as it should be.

Woodstock Sentinel, June 17, 1915.

***

WOMEN PASTORS WILL SAVE CHURCH, SHE SAYS

San Francisco.—Men have fallen down on the job as ministers and women must take their places in the pulpits if the church is to be saved. This is the opinion of Universalist Rev. Olympia Brown of Kenosha, Wis., president of the Federal Suffrage association of the United States, which is in convention here.

"We must encourage our girls to study for the ministry," the Rev. Mr. Brown told the convention. The men have been lured away from their duties as misters by ping pong, tennis, and pink teas. Today there is more brawn than brains in the pulpits; the women must become preachers.

"Many of our ministers are influenced by rich men in their churches and are afraid to attack child labor, white slavery, and other evils and some clergymen are ruled by society cliques and do not dare offend the society women who are members of their churches by extending a helping hand to the poor people who drop into church on Sunday morning."

Neenah Daily Times, July 20, 1915.

***

"Come on, Papa. We HAVE to go right now." Mamie grabbed John's hand and pulled him toward the front door. "Helen is already out there."

"Just slow down a bit. I want to make sure Edna doesn't want to come out with us. If Helen is on the porch, you may go out with her."

"I'll wait for you." Mamie yelled up the stairs, "Edie, are you coming or not?"

"I'm coming. I just had to find my ear mufflers in case it's too loud." Edie ran down the stairs to the front door.

Mamie snickered, and Edie shot her an evil eye.

"Ida, we are off!" John called out to the kitchen.

"I'm right here. And if you don't all stop yelling, you'll have a grumpy three-year-old to take with you. Now scat!"

Edie opened the front door. "I've never been up this late. It's after ten o'clock, you know, and I'm not even tired."

John herded the girls out onto the porch where Helen was waiting, her eyes on the sky. "See anything?" he asked.

"Maybe." Helen pointed northward over the houses across the street. Through the trees there was a slight glow.

"Let's walk up toward Uncle Frank's house. We should have a clear view over the typewriter factory." John suggested.

The four of them started walking and Mamie slipped her hand into John's as they walked two blocks up Lincoln and right on Pleasant Street. As they turned the corner the whole sky to the north came into view.

Edie, who had been running ahead a few yards, stopped in her tracks. Her mouth made an O as she gazed at the sky. A bright green glow moved across the sky streaked with white, the black sky showing through beyond it every now and then.

"The Northern Lights," said Helen in case anyone was wondering.

They stood with no one moving for a minute or more, staring at the production.

John was the first to come to his senses. "Let's go on to the corner on Washington where we can see more of the sky."

The entourage moved slowly down the block to the corner and the whole sky was green, but in motion. Flowing from left to right, swirling around, and shooting over their heads.

Edie pulled off her ear mufflers. "There isn't any noise. How can that be?"

"I've heard of the Northern Lights, but this is the first time I've ever seen them. You usually must go further north, I think," John tried to answer.

Because seeing the lights, should they appear, was a class project, Helen had read up on the subject. "It has to do with rays from the sun that are made up of invisible electrically charged particles that come into our air at very high speeds. Our air tries to slow them down and the friction causes the colors."

John stared at her. His daughter outshone the Northern Lights. "Good grief. How'd you learn that?"

"Miss Carter explained about it, and we had to read the article in the Encyclopedia Britannica that explained it. I'm not sure I still get it completely, but that's why. It's called the solar wind."

Mamie's eyes were shining with wonder. "Solar wind?"

"Yes," Helen continued. "Only a few particles get through usually and so we don't see them, but at times, we get bombarded with a lot and our poles, the north and south poles—

"Where Santa lives?" Edie was now interested in this explanation.

Helen looked at her, "I guess. The poles are magnetic and suck the particles to them. They burn hot coming through the air and as they cool off, they give off different colors of light."

"Looks like they all are green tonight," Mamie said.

"Then Santa would be right under the lights, right?" Edie said looking at her oldest sister.

"I suppose at the pole the whole sky would be swirling light," said Helen. "I think Miss Carter said that if it was green light then the particles are crashing into oxygen like we breathe."

Mamie and Edie snapped their mouths closed just in case they were breathing in the light.

"It can still get in your nose," Helen reminded them.

Edie looked down at her feet. "How long are we going to stay here? I'm tired."

"Just a bit longer," said John. "This will be a sight you will remember all your life, Edie. Let's not rush it."

***

Northern Lights Visible

Did you see the Northern Lights Wednesday night? It was a glorious night, the heavens being illuminated with a beautiful green glow, streaked with white. From 10 p. m. to about 12 p. m. it was most brilliant, gradually fading away after that time.

Woodstock Republican, June 18, 1915.

***

Bilton's Bunk

The carmen in Chicago strike and the fight is on. If the soldiers in Europe would strike, the fight would be off.

Woodstock Republican, June 18, 1915.

POLITICAL PRAYER MEETINGS

It is a sad day for Christianity when the church bells call the communicants together for a political prayer meeting. Such gatherings mark the high tide of religious political fanaticism, put bitterness into the lives of men; fan the flames of class hatred and destroy Christian influence in the community. The spirit actuating such meetings is anarchistic, un-Christlike and dangerous to both church and state.

Woodstock Republican, June 18, 1915.

***

Probate Court Proceedings
Estate of Sophia Wienke. Inventory filed and approved.

Woodstock Republican, June 25, 1915.

***

Personals
Ray Wienke of Chicago spent the first of the week as the guest of McHenry friends.

McHenry Plaindealer, July 8, 1915.

***

Ida's eyes popped open. She had been asleep, but she could smell him. Cigar smoke, sweat, and wet wool wafted from him as he crossed the room. She heard the rustle of his buttons being undone and his clothes being thrown off. She lay as still as she could and hoped it would be over soon, so she could slip easily back into dreamland. His weight on the side of the bed made her roll slightly toward the middle. He was—

She sat bolt upright clutching the coverlet to her bosom. "Good Lord, John! You're naked."

John, she hoped it was John, made a manly chuckle as he reached for her and tried to gather her into his arms. She had on her nice, dotted Swiss nightgown. "No, you'll rip it." She slid away from him out of bed and stood looking toward him in the dark room.

"Come here, milady," he growled. "I have a secret to tell you."

She pulled the nightgown over her head and slipped back under the covers.

"Have you been drinking?" She held him at arm's length, sniffing.

"No! I have not! I'm offended if you think it is only with liquor that I would engage your affections."

"Then what has brought this on?"

He cuddled up to her side. "You are sleeping with the newest member of the Woodstock City Council."

Ida made a small gasp and threw her arms around his neck. "Well, what do you know! They have finally come to their senses and elected the best man for the job."

"And no campaigning was necessary. Bane of my existence."

"The girls are going to be so excited. Should we go wake them?" she said in jest.

"No. They'll keep 'til morning."

"I'm proud of you," she said into his neck.

He didn't answer.

***

Personals
Mr. and Mrs. H. C. Doering, Edward Meyers and H. H. Bosshard and family motored to Brown's Lake and enjoyed very good fishing Sunday.

Woodstock Republican, July 16, 1915.

Notice
Hereafter all automobiles are strictly prohibited from entering the Oakland Cemetery. By order of THE CEMETERY BOARD.

Woodstock Republican, July 16, 1915.

Petty Thefts Annoy Automobilists
Several complaints have been heard regarding petty thefts from autos which have been left by their owners on the public square while they were transacting business. Too bad. Have a heart.

Woodstock Republican, July 16, 1915.

***

WAR AND ITS CAUSES
"MARCH OF THE GERMAN EAGLES"
Over 400 People Hear Stirring address at Crystal Lake's Concordia Hall

The illustrated lecture delivered at Concordia Hall Tuesday evening by Rev. George Schutes, under the auspices of the Deutscher National Bunde of Crystal Lake, was well attended. Rev. Schutes delivered his address in German, the great majority of the audience being conversant with that language. The address was delivered in a forceful manner and interspersed with good, clean wit and humor. Stereopticon pictures of actual scenes on the battlefields, fac-simile Belgian documents and famous war cartoons were of intense interest to the audience. A portion of the proceeds will go to the support of the German-Austrian Red Cross Society. Citizens of Cary, Algonquin, Huntley, McHenry, and Woodstock were present.

Woodstock Sentinel, July 22, 1915.

***

All Things Denison
By Clara Daring

This reporter is in receipt of a speech given by one Reverend George Schutes in German under the auspices of the Deutscher National Bunde of Crystal Lake, Illinois. I know many of us have been baffled about the war in Europe: how it started, who is fighting whom, how it will ever end.

Rev. Schutes begins by stating that the cause of the war was Servia hiring assassins to kill Archduke Francis Ferdinand in a plot to move Europe toward pan-Slavic control.

To say this more clearly, Russia has for over 100 years maintained a doctrine of Slavic rule of eastern Europe. Since the archduke was against this plan, the Servs murdered him. Austria, of course, took offense and were ready for war. Russia stepped in and told Austria to keep her hands off Servia, but

Servia was also readying herself for war by drawing up troops to the Austrian and German frontiers.

Here the Kaiser stepped in to insist on peace, but it was too late, the Russian Cossacks crossed into the East Prussian provinces, pillaging, and sacking as they went.

My question is "What would you have done if attacked in this manner?" Germany declared war on Russia.

France joined their ally Russia, mobilizing troops and bombarding German towns from the sky. When Germany went through Belgium in the hope of stopping the French attack, it was a signal that England should also join the fray on the Allies' side. So, there you have it: the world at war. And which side will America join if it comes to that?

Rev. Schutes calls on Americans not to forget that Germany is fighting England, the country that our colonists fought to gain independence. He also points out the fact that more German Americans fought with the Union in the Civil War than any other nationality. So, he is surprised that the sympathies of America do not lie with our longtime ally, Germany. And so am I.

Crawford County Courier, August 1, 1915.

EUROPEAN TRAVEL HALTED BY WAR; OCEAN PATHWAY DESERTED

New York.—A quarter billion dollars of good American money will be kept in this country this year on account of the war. There will be at least that much saved by the inability of the public to travel to Europe. Last year the steamship companies received in fares alone approximately $83,000,000, carrying eastward and westward more than 1,200,000 passengers. A conservative estimate fixes the amount spent by this traveling army at close to $192,000,000 making the total amount spent for European travel $250,000,000.

There will be no exodus to Europe this summer, however. The Great Green Way of the Atlantic is as lonely as New York's Great White Way on a summer Sunday night. This is the time of year when the rush across the ocean begins. Uncle Sam is holding back the tide by refusing to issue passports, and on the other side of the ocean the Kaiser's submarines prove an obstacle.

Woodstock Sentinel, August 1, 1915.

CHOICE FARM For Sale in Sargent County in Southeastern North Dakota

VIEW OF THE SE ¼-19-130-56

A choice quarter-section one mile from station, all under cultivation, 15 acres clover and timothy, new set of buildings, artesian well, water piped into the house, nice grove of large trees, yards fenced—a must be seen to be appreciated.

You can buy this land direct from the owner, who will give you low prices and easy terms. If you have any idea of buying a farm, it will pay you to see me at once.

J. F. Wienke, Agent
WOODSTOCK, ILL.

Woodstock Sentinel, August 1, 1915.

***

Ida listened, but still no Bobby. He was getting to be a very good sleeper. Maybe it was because the girls were out of school and so weren't getting up as early. Whatever the case, she enjoyed this time in the morning alone with John.

Ida took a sip of coffee, turned to the next page, read, and let out a little gasp. "Since when are you a real estate broker?"

John was famous for not telling Ida everything he had his fingers in so she was less surprised than she might have been.

John chuckled. "A very small real estate broker with only one client."

"Explain."

"Remember when the Manns left Woodstock for the west? You wanted to buy their gramophone."

"Yes, I remember."

"They got a land grant in North Dakota. All they had to do was improve it, and they did. They built a house, dug a well, and fenced pastures. It's cold there in the winter, but they get lots of rain for crops and are close to towns and the railroad."

"Sounds perfect. Why are they selling?"

"Not they. She."

"Oh no."

"Yup. Mr. Mann got the grippe last winter and after months of trying to improve, they came on the train to Minneapolis, and he was diagnosed with tuberculosis. The doctors told them that they needed to move to Arizona. They went back, packed up and moved."

"And he died?"

"He died a month ago. Mrs. Mann doesn't want to go back to the farm, but she does want to see if she can get any money for it. Since it was a homestead, and they improved it, it can be sold. But who would want it? Way out there in the middle of nowhere. She wrote to me and asked if I would act as her agent and advertise it in the paper here. So, there you have it. I am now a real estate agent."

"You are just full of surprises, John Wienke." Ida kissed him on his bald head and started clearing the table.

"Ma-ma!" Bobby's voice was emphatic coming down the stairs.

"I'll go," said John. And he took the stairs two at a time.

Real estate agent. Ida liked the sound of that. Better than insurance man, but then insurance had put bread on the table for quite a while.

After a few minutes, John came down the stairs with a giggling son, a diaper draped over his bald head.

Ida laughed. "I was just thinking that you are a man who wears a lot of hats."

***

Help Keep Woodstock Clean

Stringent rules have been made by Mayor A. J. Olson and Dr. A. B. Smith, health commissioner, and copies of the new ordinance have been passed and distributed in every house in the city. The need for some better system of garbage disposal has been evident for a long time, and with the approach of hot weather (unfortunately a long time approaching) the health of the city was a matter demanding prompt action, if disease was to be warded off. Every place in the business section must have an air-tight garbage container or procure one within ten days of the publication of the ordinance. Owners of lots are asked to keep them free from rubbish of every kind and remember that every empty can is a direct invitation to the deadly disease carrying fly to come right in and have a good time.

Woodstock Sentinel, August 6, 1915.

PROCEEDINGS OF CITY COUNCIL
Woodstock, Ill., Aug. 2, 1915.
Regular Meeting

A. J. Olson, mayor, presiding.

Aldermen Dygert, Eckert, Gaulke, Green, Pratt and Wienke were present at roll call, constituting a quorum.

Woodstock Republican, August 6, 1915.

***

FARMER ARRESTED
MUST CUT THISTLES

In performance of his duties as thistle commissioner, Ed LaBree of Harvard recently found it necessary to arrest a farmer living near that city, who refused to have the thistles on his farm cut or to permit Mr. LaBree to do the work, says the *Harvard Herald*.

"When the farmer in question made threats of personal violence, Commissioner LaBree reported the matter to Sheriff Wandrack and the latter took the offending farmer to the county seat.

LaBree didn't press charges, but the Sheriff pressed the issue, and the thistles were cut.

"Co-operation on the part of farmers who have had Canada thistles on the places will help in their eradication and it is the only thing to do, because working in concert is almost sure to attain the object sought.

Woodstock Sentinel, August 12, 1915.

***

Personals

George Moriarty of Detroit spent Friday evening with his family in this city while the Tigers were sojourning in Chicago prior to tackling the Sox in the series.

Woodstock Republican, August 20, 1915.

Special edition of Woodstock Republican honoring Woodstock Business Men and Farmers of the Community

Murphy & Doering

Murphy & Doering's dry goods store is one of the oldest in the city. The present manager, H. C. Doering, has been affiliated with the dry goods business for the last fifteen years. After several years of successful business of his own on Cass street, he bought out the interest of John Mullen, deceased, in the firm Murphy & Mullen in 1910. He has devoted a great deal of untiring energy to this business and has a well-established trade which finds bargains in goods of real quality at his store at all times. Under the direction of W. J. Sheahan, a large grocery stock is housed in the basement, and this department also enjoys liberal patronage.

Frank C. Wienke

Frank C. Wienke has been in business in this city a little over a year. Mr. Wienke is the owner of the cigar store located at the upper end of Main street, where he has established a fine business in cigars, tobacco cigarettes, pipes and Butterkist popcorn. He is also the Dorr township tax collector and takes care of this business at his Main street store.

Woodstock Sentinel, August 20, 1915.

THE INTERNED GERMAN SAILORS

Caught in Hampton Roads, forced to submit to internment at Norfolk, required to live aboard their ships, the officers and men of the German converted cruisers Prinz Ettel Friedrich and Kronprinz Wilhelm have transformed their vessels into comfortable homes. On the ships more than 600 men are living contentedly. Their contentment is attributed to the efficiency of German methods and to the generosity with which they are treated by the United States navy department and naval officers. As few restrictions as possible have been placed upon the interned crews, and reasonable requests have been promptly granted.

The cruisers, formerly transatlantic liners, with commodious cabins and expansive decks, have been cleared of all evidence which usually marks the warship.

About two hundred men are daily granted shore leave. In the case of enlisted men and noncommissioned officers the leaves of absence can be granted by the commanding officer of either cruiser. These leaves never exceed 12 hours. All leaves specify that the men thus quitting the ships must not leave the jurisdiction of the Norfolk yard. This includes the ports of Norfolk, Portsmouth, Newport News and Hampton, as well as Old Point Comfort and the seaside resorts.

It is no uncommon sight to see German sailors on the streets of Norfolk or at the seaside resorts. They have received the nickname "Sissy," because of the peculiar caps they wear, with ribbon streamers falling almost to their shoulders. The peculiar baggy manner in which the blouse is worn, with the protruding large white collar, a relic of pinafore days, and the numerous rows of brass buttons adorning the uniform make them easily recognizable.

When on shore leave, the principal amusements of the German sailor are sight-seeing, social drinking, and as a negro would say, "orating" with German Americans, of whom there are a considerable number in Norfolk.

In the evening, the German sailors are to be found at the rathskellers of the various hotels or the beer saloons. Men granted shore leave use American money. The sailors have been instructed not to attempt to spend the German coin on shore. Thousands of people in the Norfolk region now have German coin luck pieces for the pocket. Many persons visit the ships for the purpose of securing a German coin for this use.

Early after the internment, the sailors of both cruisers were lined up by their officers and given instruction that in conversation off ship strict neutrality must be observed. They were urged not to talk of German aspirations, of German successes, and above all warned to avoid bragging. They were warned that such conduct would probably lead to difficulties with those who favor the allies and would mean punishment and withdrawal of shore liberty. These instructions have been rigidly adhered to by the German sailors.

Marengo Beacon/Republican, August 20, 1915.

***

NO TAX - NO BEER

Mason City, Sept. 2.—Here is a new holding. In order to be a good citizen, you must pay our poll tax and thus show your interest in the government. In this case, it is going to work, for the foreigners do not like to pay poll tax, but they do enjoy their beer, and Beer Censor Mason will hereafter withhold beer shipments from foreigners who will not show their poll tax receipts. While the new ruling is meant to help in the collection of poll tax among the large number of foreigners, it will apply to Americans as well. "Pay your poll tax if you want your beer" is the adopted slogan.

Marshalltown Times-Republican, August 20, 1915.

***

SINKING OF ARABIC STARTLES WASHINGTON
SUBMARINE ACTION ADDS TO GERMAN CRISIS WITH U.S.

Washington, D. C., Aug. 19.—President Wilson is awaiting further advice concerning the sinking of the Arabic before he makes up his mind whether the attack on the vessel today was an act "deliberately unfriendly" to the United States.

In official quarters it is admitted that the attack, without warning, as it is claimed in London, comes within the scope of President Wilson's last declaration to Germany respecting the sinking of the Lusitania. The president said:

"The value which this government sets upon the long and unbroken friendship between the people and the government of the United States and the people and the government of the German nation, impels it to press very solemnly upon the imperial German government the necessity for a scrupulous observance of neutral rights in this critical matter. Friendship itself prompts it to say to the imperial government that repetition by the commanders of German naval vessels of acts in contravention of those rights must be regarded by the government of the United States, when they affect American citizens, as deliberately unfriendly."

Chicago Tribune, August 20, 1915.

***

Ray Wienke stepped into his brother's cigar shop and saw no customers. Good. "Frank you here?"

"Yes. Oh, hi there— What's happened? You're white as a ghost. Here, sit down." Frank retrieved a glass of water from the back room and handed it to Ray. Even at twenty-three, Ray was still the more emotive of the two brothers.

Ray took a gulp and looked at Frank. "I was just in an automobile accident. I'm fine, but Martha Richards is dead, I think."

Frank's face blanched. "She was in the car with you?"

Ray didn't look up from examining the half-full glass. He took another sip. "No, I was with Dotty Lemmer…she was driving."

"Dotty? Does she know how to drive?" Frank's voice was a bit higher than usual. At thirty-three, Frank thought he had seen it all, but no one that he knew of had been killed on the square before.

Ray looked at Frank and offered the water. "It wasn't her fault. Miss Martha stepped right in front of the car. We hit her full on. Dotty didn't even have time to put on the brakes."

"Goodness." Frank accepted the glass "Miss Martha was quite a gal. She worked for the Governor; you know." Ray nodded. Frank held up the glass, and they said in unison, "May she rest in peace." Frank drained the glass and took it to the back room for refill.

Ray called after him. "I don't want Pa to know. He hates automobiles."

Frank returned with the glass and a confused look on his face. "He does? He's never said that to me."

"He hates everything new. I'll never hear the end of it."

Frank patted his shoulder "He'll see it in the paper."

Ray moaned, rubbed his face with his hands, and reached for the water.

"Just remind him that you weren't driving. Poor Dotty."

"It won't matter. I was letting a girl drive. Yes, Dotty was very upset. The doctor they called for Miss Richards was going to give her a sedative, I think." Ray didn't look up but rolled the glass in his hands watching the water slosh.

Frank leaned back against the counter. "Were the two of you alone?"

"No, her folks were in the back seat." Ray's voice caught just a little.

"Well, there you go." Frank clapped his shoulder again, going for jovial. "What can he say if it was their car, and they let their daughter drive? It wasn't your business to object."

Ray shrugged his shoulders. "That's true. Do you have anything else to drink? Maybe a shot of whiskey?"

Frank shook his head. "Woodstock is dry. You know that."

"I know that, but in Chicago, I can always find a drink." Ray tried a small smile.

"See, there is where you went wrong! This is Woodstock, not Chicago." Frank noticed that Ray's hands were shaking. He took the glass from Ray's hands, sipped, and offered it back.

Ray waved the glass away. "Never mind then." He got up and took a hesitant step toward the door.

"Where are you going?" Ray set the glass on the counter and put his hand under his brother's arm for support, just in case.

Ray shrugged. "To catch the train for home. That's where we were headed in the car."

"You'll not be headed home this evening, young sir." Frank took off the white apron that designated him as the man in charge. "Ma would kill me if I let you go off by yourself. Remember how she always said, "You boys stick together," at the fair or wherever. Have you already talked to the police?"

"Police?"

"Yes, didn't they call the police over as soon as the accident happened?"

"Well, yes, but I didn't talk to them. What could I say that Dotty couldn't say?"

"Looks like we need to go to the station first. And then we can talk about where you'll be sleeping tonight."

Ray offered a weak objection. "I have classes tomorrow, you know."

Frank turned the sign to 'CLOSED' in the window. "We better wait and see what the police have to say about you leaving. In the meantime, I'm going with you, so you don't jump the first train to the city. You need me."

Ray pushed Frank's shoulder. "I don't need you. I can go two blocks without your help."

"Yes, you do. I'm better than a long draw of whiskey."

Ray laughed a little at that. "Are not! More like a long draw of lukewarm milk." Frank playfully pushed his shoulder.

The bell over the door jingled as Frank closed it from the sidewalk.

***

FATALITY AT WOODSTOCK
WOMAN HIT BY AUTO

Miss Martha Richards of Woodstock, for many years a prominent christian worker, was struck and instantly killed by an automobile driven by Miss Dorothy Lemmers on last Monday evening.

The Lemmers car was proceeding slowly, Miss Lemmers and Ray Wienke occupying the front seat. Mr. and Mrs. G. W. Lemmers, parents of the young lady, were in the rear seat. The accident occurred on the principal business street, in front of the city hall.

Miss Richards was crossing the street from the park toward Bartlett's store. She had just avoided one car and in doing so stepped directly in front of the Lemmers car which could not be stopped in time to avoid the collision. She was thrown to the pavement, the injuries sustained by the fall causing her instant death.

Miss Richards was for many years a governess in the home of former governor, Richard G. Oglesby, and is said to have practically reared the former lieutenant governor, John Oglesby. She was in Chicago a short time ago to visit the elder Mrs. Oglesby.

This calamity greatly horrified her many friends in Woodstock, as she was well-known throughout the city. She was a daughter of Jefferson Richards, deceased, who, years ago, resided on a farm north of Marengo.

Miss Richards is survived by two sisters, one Miss Mirella, with whom she lived in Woodstock, and the other, Miss Fedella, who for years was connected with the U. S. Treasury department at Washington, D. C., but who of late has made her home with her brother Milton Richards in the state of Washington. A brother, Frank Richards, lives in Arizona.

Woodstock Republican, August 27, 1915.

***

Wilson Has Demanded an Apology

President Wilson, having deliberated over the loss of American lives in Falaba and Gulflight cases, deliberated no longer.

He sent a note to Berlin in which he demanded an immediate apology for the attack on the Lusitania, an offer of repatriation, and assurances that such attacks without warning would not be repeated.

Chicago Tribune, September 2, 1915.

***
TENNYSON, INDIANA
Garrison Reunion

Rev. Elza Cissna, of Ill, preached a splendid sermon here Sunday night.

The descendants of Isaac and Nancy Tennyson Garrison held their third annual home coming at this place, Sept. 5. Caleb J. Lindsey, of Boonville, and Rev. Everett Cissna, of Mores Hill College, were the speakers of the morning, after which a spread was enjoyed in McDonald's Grove. Rev. William Cissna, of Wayne City, Ill., and Hon. Thos. Lindsey, of Evansville, spoke in the afternoon and a musical program was rendered. About 300 relatives and as many friends were present.

Boonville Standard, September 10, 1915.

***
ADMINISTRATION ADMITS
BENEFICIAL EFFECTS OF THE WAR

Washington, Sept 22.—Directly reversing the statements of Secretary of Commerce Redfield that revival of American industry was not due to war orders, the department of commerce has just given out a statement concluding with the assertion that "surveying the whole field, it may justly be said that the world's conflict has been of unmeasured value to American industry as a whole."

Denison Review, September 22, 1915.

***
APPOINTMENTS ANNOUNCED
MINISTERS FOR THE COMING YEAR
NAMED AT FINAL SESSION OF
CONFERENCE

At the closing session of the Southern M. E. conference at Mt. Vernon on Monday, the appointments were announced for the year. Among them: Iuka, supplied by Wm. Cissna.

Mount Carmel Daily Republican-Register, September 28, 1915

Luther League Convention in Woodstock

Over 500 young people were in attendance at the twenty-first annual convention of the Luther League of Illinois, held in Woodstock recently. Delegates from all parts of the state were present, and speakers of more than statewide renown addressed the audience.

Crystal Lake Herald, September 28, 1915.

***

Lenora Cissna put the last pie pan in the wooden crate and turned in a circle scanning the kitchen counters and cabinets for any item forgotten. She had had only two weeks to vacate the Parsonage in Wayne City to move to the Parsonage in Iuka, Illinois, eighteen miles north.

It had always been thus. The Methodist Episcopal church liked to rotate its ministers so every fall, they gave out new assignments. They had been lucky to have been in Wayne City for almost three years. The church had grown under William Calvin's hand. So, now they were off to the village of Iuka where the church was not thriving. The village might be too small to support the church, but there were farms surrounding the village where the pickin's should be easy.

Roy came down the stairs and into the kitchen with two crates of clothes and a suitcase. "That's it for upstairs."

"You sure?" Nora didn't know why she said it. She would check the whole house before they rode away.

"Yup. Well, except for Lillian's room." Roy was smiling slightly.

"Why haven't you done Lillian's room?"

"She says she doesn't need my help. She says she'll bring it all down. She's feeling sorry for herself. I told her that she was the

sorriest thing I'd seen all day." Roy grinned as he moved the
suitcase to the other hand.

"I'm sure that helped." Lenora looked at him above her glasses.
"Okay. Roy take that out to the wagon and come git these last
things from the kitchen. I'll go talk to her."

Nora laboriously climbed the stairs to the upper bedrooms—
five of them. She took her time going through each one, opening
drawers and closets.

Lillian sat on the bed, surrounded by several crates, a hat box,
and clothes tied up in a sheet. The crates were full of books and
other academic detritus, a stuffed dog named Buford that Roy had
won at a county fair, two landscape pictures in thin frames, three
pairs of shoes, a winter purse and coat, dungarees, and rubber
boots. Lillian sat with legs splayed and a far off look in her eyes.

"Lillian?" Nora tried to say it softly, but Lillian jumped in
surprise as if she'd been a million miles away.

"Mother?"

"It's time to go. You got everything? You've double checked
the closet and bureau? Under the mattress and bed?"

Tears welled in Lillian's eyes. "Yes, I have. Isn't it sad that at
seventeen, my whole life can be put in two crates and a hatbox? I
was just sitting here contemplating the future when I won't have
to move every few years. My senior year is being cut in the middle.
I must make all new friends, if that is even possible and try to
come up to or down to the standards of the new school. It isn't
fair."

"Aw honey, think of it this way. This is the last time you will be
forced to do this. By this time next year, you'll have graduated and
off to college. So, if we move, it will be without you."

"Yes. I know. I just…I just wish I could have finished school
here. I have such nice friends and I love the teachers, except for
Mr. French who I never have to take again. Isn't there anything
we can do?"

"You've asked me that every day for the last two weeks and I
again say, we can do nothing about it. This is the life of an ME

minister's family. We go where the church needs us. I'm sorry it has made you unhappy. Let's get your things downstairs. We can sing as we ride toward Iuka."

Lillian stood up. "Is Roy coming with us?"

"For now. He may have a new job over near Geff. If that happens, he will move closer there and find a room."

Lillian picked up the hat box and handed it to her mother. She took one of the crates for herself and they descended to the first floor. "I'll throw the clothing bundle down to you," she said to her mother as she ran back up the steps.

The bundle came bouncing down the steps and Nora hefted it up on the table. Lillian came with the second crate just as Roy came in, grinning. "You still have more? The wagon is plum filled up. Looks like we'll have to leave these things behind."

The two women looked at him without reaction. Nora picked up the crate and handed it to Roy. "Looks like these things will have to go in your seat then, Mr. Smarty-pants. You'll just have to walk along behind."

"Oh, come on. Can't you take a joke?" Roy took the box and headed for the door.

Lillian followed close on his heels. "No right now, I can't take a joke. I'm being forced to leave all my friends."

"I am too," he whined.

"Pshaw! You don't have any friends."

"I do too."

"Name one...."

Their voices faded as they left the house and walked toward the wagon.

Nora watched them go. So close. They had always been so close, but also, they knew just how to get the other riled up. Maybe that's how it is with sisters and brothers.

Nora wished she knew her brothers and sisters better. Her father had died in Tennessee, a victim of the Civil War, and her mother had died of a fever before she was eight. She was taken in by a family with no children, and it had taken her years to remake any connections to the McCoys or the Garrisons. They still seemed more like strangers than kin.

Maybe the older children saw these last two like that. Eleven years separated Chelso from Lillian and Roy, so the older children had been out of the house when Lillian and Roy were born. Roy had gotten almost no brotherly attention.

Two of Roy's brothers, William Everett and Elmer had followed in their father's footsteps into the ministry. How Lenora loved her 'preacher boys.' And Roy's sister Mary Massie was turning into a street corner preacher for temperance. Can preaching run in the family?

Lenora pulled herself out of her reverie. It was time to go, or they wouldn't make the eighteen miles to Iuka before dark. At least they had just had a dry spell so the road should be passable. Dusty, but passable.

William helped Lenora up into the front seat and Lillian and Roy climbed into the second seat with the bundle of clothes between them and the hat box on Lillian's lap. Lilliam wrapped a kerchief around her face and tied it in the back. The dust was going to be awful. Nora looked back at her and nodded approvingly. It was just part of being a preacher's daughter.

***

War Pictures Good

"The German Side of the War" drew crowded houses at the Princess theatre last Friday evening, the *Tribune* war pictures being the highest order of excellence. One was enabled by the pictures shown to get a very fair idea of the nature of the war, its horrors being depicted as well as its glories. The pictures shown represented the stern reality of the big conflict and brought forcibly home to spectators the unspeakable tragedy of war and the blessing of peace.

Woodstock Sentinel, September 30, 1915.

***

ALLIES WIN BATTLE

London, Sept. 28.—The greatest victory for the allied arms since the battle of Marne has crowned the first move of the great Franco-British drive to hurl the Germans from France. Almost a year to the day since that great battle, which marked the end of the German advance into France, General Joffre and Sir John French have hurled their legions at the German line with a violence for which they have been months in preparing.

In the two days since the great allied offensive began, the French and British have captured 20,000 unwounded prisoners.

The German war office admits the loss of ground and the retirement of the Germans for more than a mile over a wide section of the front.

The losses on both sides are reported to be fearful. Thousands of bodies are lying unburied for more than 100 miles.

McHenry Plaindealer, September 30, 1915.

Americans Defeat Japanese

Tokyo, Sept. 25.—The baseball team of the University of Chicago defeated the Waseta university team Friday afternoon by a score of 5 to 3 in the opening game of the series. Thirty thousand persons watched the game.

McHenry Plaindealer, September 30, 1915.

U. S. TROOPER KILLED

Brownsville, Tex., Sept. 27.—One American soldier was killed, the captain commanding the Americans was wounded and the post office and general store at Progresso, Tex., were looted and burned on Friday when about eighty armed Mexicans crossed into Texas and attacked a small detachment of Troops B and C, Twelfth cavalry.

All the Mexicans, with the exception of 17 killed and 18 prisoners, have recrossed into Mexico under the protection of several hundred troops on the other side of the border who kept up a heavy fire to cover the crossing of the Mexicans.

McHenry Plaindealer, September 30, 1915.

British Liner is Torpedoed

London, Sept. 17.—The Harrison liner Chancellor, a British ship, has been sunk by a German submarine. Part of the crew is reported missing among them G. W. King of New Orleans, an American, who was assistant Marconi operator on the liner.

McHenry Plaindealer, September 30, 1915.

Swedish Steamer Torpedoed

Kristiansand, Norway, Sept. 25.—The Swedish steamer Forsvik, 1,107 tons, has been sunk by a German submarine. The crew was saved. The ship was carrying a cargo of coal through the war zone.

McHenry Plaindealer, September 30, 1915.

News Brevities of Illinois

Peoria.—With thirty of the forty-eight delegates present, representing sixteen German societies of central Illinois which form the Peoria branch of the German-American alliance, resolutions were adopted protesting against local banks participating in the proposed billion-dollar loan to the allies; to petition for an extra session of congress to establish an embargo against the shipment of munitions of war. In the meeting, President Wilson was assailed as an autocrat by several speakers who condemned his foreign policies.

McHenry Plaindealer, September 30, 1915.

***

Ida put her head down on her arms. She was at the kitchen table, but just now she felt overwhelmed by the bad news in the paper. John had been in McHenry on business and had brought the *Plaindealer* home because it seemed to have more war news in it than the Woodstock papers did.

How were they ever going to get out of this mess in Europe? The best news she'd read in the last dozen articles was that the U.S.A. baseball team had beat the Japanese team. How could the world be at war and still play baseball?

She thought she heard a knock at the front door; a soft knock as when the hand knocking has a glove on. She stood up and floated up the stairs and down into the foyer. She looked through the window and saw three men in black coats and top hats waiting for the door to be opened. What in the world?

The first one knocked again. He looked amazingly like the pictures of Kaiser Wilhelm she had seen on plates.

She took a deep breath and opened the door a foot or so. "Ja?"

The Kaiser took off his hat. *"Guten Tag, Frau. Wie geht es dir?"*

"Guten Tag. Mir geht's Gut."

"Dürfen wir reinkommen? Als Deutscher, der in Amerika lebt, haben wir einen Vorschlag für Sie."

Ida knew her German was rusty, but she understood every word: Might we come in? As a German living in America, we have a proposition for you.

"Darf ich eure Namen erfahren?" Might I know your names?

"Kommen Sie, Frau Wienke. Ihr wisst sicher, wer ich bin. Und das sind meine Kameraden. Ich bin auf allen Tellern und Münzen." Come now, Mrs. Wienke. I'm sure you know me. I'm on all the plates and coins.

"Wie heißen deine Kameraden?" What are your comrades' names?

A good-looking man with the bluest eyes Ida had ever seen stepped forward. He had a longish face with a nicely trimmed beard and mustache.

"My good lady, I am King George the Fifth of England, your humble servant." He clicked his heels and did a half bow.

Ida did a simple curtsy and said, "How do you do?"

"Very well, mum. Thank you."

The king stepped back, and another handsome bearded man stepped forward. He had a receding hairline, and his dark hair was wispy when he took off his hat. His black eyes were piercing as if he was the devil looking into her soul. He reached for her hand and bowed over it. *"YA Nikolay Vtoroy Alexandrovich Romanov."*

Ida again curtsied. *"Dobryy den.' Rad poznakomit'sya s vami, tsar' Nikolay."* Very nice to meet you. Goodness, she knew Russian also.

"Zakhodite." Won't you all come in? *Willst du nicht alle reinkommen.* Please sit down. Would you like something to drink?

"Bier," said Wilhelm.

"Vodka," said Nicholas.

"Maybe some tea with a bit of cream and a teaspoon of sugar," said George.

Ida left the parlor to get the drinks. Should she call John? Why were these men here? How did they get here? Shouldn't they be in their own countries while war is being waged? She went in the icebox and grabbed the jar of baby gherkins from last summer's garden and brought the drinks and the pickles to the parlor.

Each man took his libation. She had brought a cup of coffee with cream for herself. They all took a sip except for Nicholas who threw back his vodka in one gulp and plucked a pickle from the jar and practically inhaled it.

King George set his teacup on the coffee table. Those blue eyes shone with excitement. "Madame, we come to you for help. We are in a war where there seems there can be no winner. We will all," and here he included the other men with a wave of the hand, "be losers if the war goes on. Men and women and children are dying at such a rate that we may wipe out the whole population of England, of Germany—"

"Ja," said the Kaiser.

"...and of Russia."

"Nyet!" said the Czar.

"Now Nicholas we are not going to start this again,' said King George in his beautiful, accented English. "We are all in this together, and we agreed this fine woman was our last hope. Did we not?"

The Czar's eyes blazed. He hit the end table with a fist. "VODKA!"

Ida reached into the pocket of her apron and pulled out the Vodka bottle, poured the glass a bit fuller this time, and set the bottle next to the pickles in front of Nicholas. She would have to explain to John what had happened to the vodka when he got home.

"Okay. Let's continue." The King turned his eyes on Ida. "As a German living in America, you are in a very special place to be a peacemaker."

Ida's hand flew to her chest. "Me? I don't know anything about politics or the war."

"Exactly," said the King.

"Tochno," said the Czar.

"Gewiss," said the Kaiser.

Edward nodded to the others. His eyes came back to Ida. "You know nothing, so you are perfect."

"To do what?" Ida was getting a bit tired of this beating around the bush.

"To solve the mystery of the missing link."

"M-m-missing link?" Ida stammered.

"Ja!" said the Kaiser.

"Da!" said the Czar.

She wanted to laugh right aloud at these three handsome bearded men sitting in her parlor. She looked from one to the other. They could be brothers; they looked so much alike. They were all looking at her expectantly, as if she would reveal the holy grail.

Maybe it would come to her if she just started. "The...the...missing...um...the...missing link is—"

The back screen door slapped. Ida sat bolt upright and looked around. She was in the kitchen.

The girls swept in with much chatter and activity. Ida wanted to go to the parlor to see if the Kaiser, the King, and the Czar were still sitting on the edge of their seats waiting for her answer.

"Mama? Are you okay? You look strange." Edie stood at her shoulder. "Are you going to get snacks? I have a lot to tell you about school today."

"I'm…um…fine." Ida removed her glasses and rubbed her face. "Yes, yes. Of course. Snacks." The children were hungry; ending the war would have to wait.

***

Competition in Caskets

Messrs. Merwin & Pierce, furniture dealers at Woodstock, have completed a finely equipped, modern dust-proof casket room, which will display fifteen caskets in such a way that their full length may be seen.

Crystal Lake Herald, October 7, 1915.

***

NEW YORK LETTER

Neutrality has some contradictory moods. For example, the shipment of arms was excused on the ground that Germany alone being prepared for war, an embargo on munitions could be interpreted as of direct assistance to German militarism. At the same time nothing was done against the shutting off food supplies for the civil population of Germany though such failure was admittedly being of direct assistance to the Allies. Now today the great war loan is excused rather cynically on the ground that the Allies need money to buy foodstuffs. In other words when Germany wanted food it could not have it, but money was given to England and France to buy food.

According to Dr. H. Barringer Cox, he has invented a contrivance that can be wrapped about a man under his waistcoat, so he can be his own wireless station, sending and receiving messages as he walks. Next!

The grave and weighty Court of Appeals sat up suddenly this week when two women appeared before the bench, where none, but men have ever stood and broke the precedents of a century. They were the first women lawyers to argue a case before the state's court of last resort.

Woodstock Sentinel, October 7, 1915.

***

PROCEEDINGS OF CITY COUNCIL
Woodstock, Ill. October 4, 1915
Regular Meeting

Alterman Besley, Dygert, Eckert, Frame, Gaulke, Green, Pratt and Wienke were present at roll call, constituting a quorum.

Woodstock Republican, October 8, 1915.

***

Personals

George J. Moriarty has returned from a successful season with the Detroit Tigers, who landed second place in the American League.

Woodstock Republican, October 15, 1915.

***

ALL THINGS DENISON
By Clara Daring

Iowa suffragists met, 500 strong, at the annual convention of the Iowa Equal Suffrage Association, which was held in Des Moines last week. The group as a whole regretted the defeat of the suffrage amendment in New Jersey, but many said that they were not surprised.

The defeat dampened the spirits of the delegates, who were asked by the leadership to keep the faith.

"I do not believe the defeat of the amendment in New Jersey will in any way injure the cause in Iowa," said Miss Flora Dunlap of Des Moines, president of the state association, in opening the convention, "While the defeat is very much to be regretted, I do not think eastern sentiment is as far advanced for suffrage as western sentiment. This election will not be the last one and people will be *educated*."

That is, in this reporter's opinion, an interesting twist on the sad news. I approached Miss Dunlap to see what proof she could provide for claiming that western sentiment for the women's vote was stronger than eastern. She points as proof to the fact that a number of the western states have already allowed suffrage for women in local elections, and some have even included state elections. These include Wyoming, Utah, Colorado, Idaho, Washington, California, Oregon, Montana, Arizona, Kansas, Alaska, and Illinois. None of the Eastern or Southern states have done so.

It does seem, looking at that list, that women's rights are being supported better in the west than in the east. However, a state does not have the power to allow women the right to vote for the President of the United States. An U. S. Constitutional Amendment is the only way to make women's suffrage the law of the land.

We have every right to be proud of our western states. And now Iowa has a chance to join them.

Crawford County Courier, October 20, 1915.

***

HUNT MEXICANS

Brownsville, Tex., Oct 20.—Posses and about 1,000 United States troops today continued to patrol the border, where a train robbery occurred Monday night.

The killing of ten Mexicans captured by posses yesterday failed to allay fear of more trouble, because posses claimed they had not captured the leaders. No trace of Luis de la Rosa, the head of all the bandits, has been found.

Ten Mexicans yesterday paid with their lives for alleged complicity in Monday night's wrecking of a St. Louis, Brownsville & Mexico passenger train on the outskirts of Brownsville, the killing of three Americans, and the wounding of four others.

Four Mexicans were hanged from trees at various points and four others were shot.

Crawford County Courier, October 21, 1915.

***

WILSON GIVES THANKS

Washington, D. C., Oct. 21—President Wilson today in a proclamation designated Thursday, November 25th as Thanksgiving day, called attention to the fact that the United States has been at peace while most of Europe has been at war.

"We have been able to assert our rights and the rights of mankind without breach of friendship with the great nations with whom we have had to deal," said the president.

"It has long been the honored custom of our people to turn in the fruitful autumn of the year in praise and thanksgiving to almighty God for his many blessings and mercies to us as a nation. The year that is now drawing to a close since we last observed our day of national thanksgiving has been, while a year of discipline because of the mighty forces of war and of changes which have disturbed the world, also a year of special blessings for us."

Denison Review, October 27, 1915.

***

WEEKLY ITEMS

The Woodstock Sentinel will be delivered to subscribers by carriers in that city in the future. Quite metropolitan.

McHenry Plaindealer, November 5, 1915.

***

WEARING OF WHITE
GENERALLY URGED

New York, Dec. 13.—More than 1,000 textile mills in this country, with more than 100,000 workingmen, are either out of commission or else on part time in consequence of the stoppage of dye shipments from Germany.

The dye famine is affecting postage stamps and bank notes as well as woolen, cotton, and silk fabrics, leathers, soaps, perfumery and even candy. The hosiery manufacturers are the only ones that have managed to make an extensive use of American dogwood dyes as substitutes for the German laboratory colors. Consequently, proportionately fewer hosiery mills are closed than any other line of textiles.

Manufacturers have been trying to persuade costumers to wear white goods, which accounts for the unprecedented vogue of white stockings and white shirts and dresses. A concerted effort is underway to swing fashion toward whites and grays for every kind of use.

Crawford County Courier, December 14, 1915.

CRETONNE TOQUE

An Out-of-the-Ordinary Millinery Creation in a Season When Velvet and Hatter's Plush Predominates is this Close-Fitting Toque. The Material Used is a Cretonne; This is Sewn on the Close-Fitting Frame, Which is Shaped to Form a Cone on the Left Side, and Dropped on the Right, Where it is Knotted and Left to Hang Loosely. A Band of Dyed Racoon is the Only Trimming.

McHenry Plaindealer, November 21, 1915.

***

FORD ADMITS PEACE EFFORT IS FAILURE

Turns Expedition over to Women.

Christiania, Norway, via London, Dec. 24.—The Norwegian liner Bergesfjord, with Henry Ford on board, sailed for New York this morning. Mr. Ford stated before leaving Bergen that the peace expedition would continue under the auspices of the Women's International Peace Association.

Henry Ford's departure from Europe apparently marks the termination in its original form of the most novel of the many movements undertaken to end the war.

After The Hague conference, Mrs. Rosika Schwimmer, one of the most prominent women at the Women's Peace Conference, came to the United States to continue her work for peace. She went to Detroit to see Mr. Ford, and it was reported that it was she who suggested to him the peace expedition.

Before the peace ship reached the other side there were reports of dissension among the peace delegates. He made his departure secretly and most of the delegates, when they left for Stockholm, were ignorant of the fact that he was not to go with them.

A Copenhagen dispatch says: "Before leaving, Mr. Ford gave a check for 1,000,000 kroner (about $270,000) to finance the expedition. He left because he recognized that it was impossible to make headway."

Marshalltown Evening Times-Republican, December 24, 1915.

***

M. E. Parsonage
Ioka, Illinois
Christmas Day, 1915

"Thanks, Pa." Roy Cissna opened the brand-new, store-bought jackknife he had received as a Christmas gift from his parents. He tested the blade against his thumb and saw the thin line of blood come to the surface. It was sharp!

W. C. smiled. Roy had been good to his word. He had not returned to high school, but he had landed a job at the Herrin mine near Fairfield. He was making a good wage at the mine, but the work was heavy and dirty.

Lillian opened the present from her parents – a nice hand knitted white sweater. "Oh, how lovely. Did you knit it, Mama, or did one of the church ladies?"

Lenora smiled. Her daughter knew her well. "Mrs. Robertson made them for the bazaar sale. It just looked like you."

"Thank you so much." Lillian took off the plain gray shirt jacket and replaced it with the sweater. "It fits."

Lenora looked her over, "Well, I should hope. I believe you've stopped growing. Looks right smart, doesn't it, Will."

"Yes, very nice."

"Open yours, Pa."

W. C. looked down at the two brown paper packages in his lap. "Which one?"

"The largest one. And no guessing," Lillian said.

Both Lillian's and Roy's eyes were glued to their father as he slipped the string off the side. "I bet it's a—"

"No guessing!" Roy and Lillian said together.

William pulled the gift from the paper and looked at its front cover. "A book. I would never have guessed. It's a thick one. *Jesus The Christ* by James E. Talmage."

Roy said, "Just got published. You're ahead of all the preachers in the county." Roy's effort and money had procured the book, mail order, from a shop in Chicago.

William was looking through the table of contents, nodding and smiling. "Looks like there are some good sermons in here."

"That's what we thought too," said Lillian.

"Very nice; very nice indeed." He seemed happy with the gift.

While he was examining the book, Lenora had been lifting and shaking her larger package also. "Do I also have a book?"

"Open it, Mama," Lillian always found it more fun giving than receiving.

Nora untied the twine and opened the package. "Yes, a book. *Spoon River Anthology* by Edgar Lee Masters. What's it about?"

"I'm not going to tell you; you'll just have to read it," said Lillian.

"When I have time."

"You'll need to make time for this one." Lillian was insistent.

Lenora put the book on her lap and folded her hands over it. "Thank you, children."

"Who is this other one from?" asked William.

"Me," said Lenora.

The Reverend pulled the string off and opened the small one inch thick, three-inch by three-inch box. "A tie." He looked at Nora who was smiling. "I hate ties."

"I know, and you won't buy one. But there are times when you must wear one. I'm ashamed of that old brown knitted tie you always fall back on so here is a smart one."

He pulled the black tie from the box. It was a soft silky material. He held it up and stretched it out. "What kind of tie is it?"

"It can be worn three ways. You can tie it as a usual tie down your front. Or it can be tied into a bow tie…there's instructions. Or if those don't suit you, it's good enough that you could wear it in what they calls an ascot."

"An ascot. Well, I'll be. And such a striking color."

Nora smiled. She hoped he was joking. "It's difficult to get colors other than black, white or brown right now."

"That might be, but I like it…black. It'll do for funerals as well. Thank you. Go ahead and open your last one. It's something I picked up in Springfield when Roy and I were there." He looked pointedly at his son.

"Why that'd be months ago. You was thinkin' about me and Christmas months ago?" Nora was touched.

Nora's box was very nearly the same size box as the tie had come in. "Looks like I get a tie also. You got a book, and I got a book. Now you got a tie and I..." She opened the box, "And I got a set of beautiful hair combs. How lovely. Are they ivory?"

"Yes. I almost got you diamonds, but I thought these were more appropriate for a minister's wife," said the minister, a brief smile playing on his face.

"Yes, much more appropriate. When would I ever wear diamonds? I love them." She paused, gazing at the pearly white of the combs. Tears suddenly filled her eyes.

"Good, I'm glad...but, Lenora, why tears?"

"I miss the children. Remember back? How they would all pile in here. We made pallets on the floor for sleeping and took up two pews at service." She looked at Roy and Lillian. "You two were just babes in arms. They always brought so much laughter." A tiny sob shook her shoulders.

"Oh Mama." Lillian crossed the room to hug her mother.

William rubbed his forehead with a free hand and laid the book aside. "Let's pray for them."

"Yes, please," said Nora.

Lillian nodded.

Roy opened and snapped the largest blade of his pocketknife closed. He again pulled the blade out—

"Roy?" William was looking at him.

"Yessir." Roy snapped the blade closed one last time and laid it aside.

William held his hands shoulder-high, palms-up and the others followed suit. He closed his eyes and began.

"Gracious father. We come to you on the day of your son's birth to ask your blessing for our children who are far from us this day. I shall call them by name as I know many people are joining me in prayer today for their prodigy.

"First for Alvah Samuel, our firstborn, and his sister Minnie who we know are abiding with you by your grace.

"We pray also for those who are preaching the Word today to their own flocks: William Everett, Elmer Hedden and Mary

Elizabeth. Let their words bring the Good News to all who hear them.

We pray for Unia and Chelso, who have gathered their families near them. Bless them as they work to keep food on their tables and God in their hearts.

"And lastly gracious Lord, I ask your blessings on those gathered here. Lillian and Roy who are quickly attaining adulthood. Keep them on the path of righteousness for Jesus name's sake.

"And my dutiful life companion, Lenora, for whom I thank you. May our lives be deserving of your grace. In the name of the risen Lord and Savior, Jesus Christ. Amen." He lowered his hands, opened his eyes, and saw his beautiful family. "Peace be with you," he wished them his voice huskier than usual.

The room was silent while everyone lowered their arms and opened their eyes.

Lenora looked around. "Merry Christmas to all."

"Merry Christmas, Mama, and thank you for the gift." Lillian hugged herself in the new sweater.

Roy cleared his throat. "When we gonna eat?"

Lenora got up. "No rest for the weary. Be ready in about an hour. Remember the McBrides are joining us. It's their bird."

Roy grinned. "Is Ginny McBride coming?"

"I assume so. Why?" Nora looked at her son curiously.

"Just wonderin'."

***

TO SEIZE ALL GERMAN MAILS

Washington, Dec. 28.—The allies, it is explained here, intend to seize and examine all mail passing between the United States and the European neutrals, which is intended, it is believed, to Germany.

The action is based on an article in The Hague convention providing that the immunity from seizure of mail shall not apply to mail "destined for or proceeding from a blockaded port."

Marshalltown Evening Times-Republican, December 28, 1915.

***

LABOR PEACE COUNCIL HEADS INDICTED ON CONSPIRACY

New York, Dec. 28.—Congressman Frank Buchanan, of Illinois; H. Robert Fowler, former congressman from Illinois; Frank S. Monett, former attorney general of Ohio; David Lamar, Jacob C. Taylor, President of Labor's National Peace Council; Franz von Rintalen, a German agent; H. B. Martin and Herman Schultels were indicted by a federal grand jury today for conspiring to ferment strikers in American munitions factories.

All of the indicted men except Lamar and von Rintelen are officers or former officers of the peace council, which the government charges was founded by von Rintelen to bribe labor leaders to call strikes in munitions plants for furtherance of German propaganda in this country.

Marshalltown Evening Times-Republican, December 29, 1915.

***

Women's Peace Movement Dead

The peace movement of Henry Ford seems to have exploded within the last few days. To those familiar with state affairs his attempt from the start seemed chimerical and dreamlike and what others knew in advance he found out by experience. It is not the first time that a dreamer has associated himself with a collection of other dreamers for the purpose of carrying out what may be considered a meritorious object and failed in the results because of a want of a practical mental grasp of the true situation.

Mr. Ford and his party were not made welcome after they crossed the Atlantic. They should have known this

fact before they started and should have avoided the
loss of time and expense of making the trip. This great
leader is now returning to the United States no doubt
convinced that the peace of Europe is not to be
restored through the efforts of an automobile
manufacturer. He has succeeded, however, in
advertising himself, and it may be that he will regard
that as sufficient compensation for the effort he has
made, and the expenses incurred. He and his party will
be looked upon in the future as dreamers and while
their sincerity may not be questioned, they will not be
regarded as visionary.

Denison Review, December 29, 1915.

***

SCARLET FEVER EPIDEMIC
GRIPPING GERMANY

LONDON, Dec. 27, 2 a. m.—A dispatch to the
Exchange Telegraph company from Amsterdam tells of
a serious scarlet fever epidemic in Germany, extending
from Bromberg to a number of villages in Posen,
where the sickness is unusually acute.

All military hospitals which have been requisitioned
to deal with the epidemic are crowded and the
government measures have proved altogether
inadequate.

The Bromberg garrison is so overrun with disease
that it has been evacuated by one entire regiment.

Chicago Tribune, December 27, 1915.

KAISER'S ILLNESS GRAVE, REPORT IN
SWITZERLAND

LONDON, Dec. 26.—Alarming rumors, probably of
an exaggerated nature, are being circulated in
Switzerland today concerning Emperor William's
illness according to the Zurich correspondent of the
Exchange Telegraph company. The rumors state, says

the correspondent, that the emperor's condition is causing anxiety in Berlin.

Chicago Tribune, December 27, 1915.

***

Day's News Condensed

One hundred five-pound cans of milk powder, equivalent to three tons of milk, were packed by the citizens' committee for food shipments to be sent by registered mail from New York to German and Austrian babies.

A Lusitania widow and her three children became the exception to the rule laid down by President and Mrs. Wilson that they would receive no visitors during their honeymoon in Hot Springs, Va. The first caller was Mrs. Herbert Stone, the daughter-in-law of Melville E. Stone of the Associated Press.

A dispatch from Zurich, Switzerland, says: "Emperor William, who is suffering from a suppurating phlegmon in the neck, has been given some relief, his doctors have resorted to lancing."

The planet Venus, rather than Mars, is inhabited, in the opinion of Dr. John A. Brashear, noted Pittsburgh astronomer. He told the Pan-American scientific congress dense atmospheric pressure surrounding Venus made it probable the planet teemed with life.

Woodstock Republican, December 31, 1915.

NUMBER OF GRIPPE CASES DOUBLED IN LAST WEEK.

Washington, D. C., Dec. 30.—The whole country is in the throes of a grippe epidemic, according to the advice received by the United States public health service.

The situation is rapidly becoming serious. The officials of the public health service estimate the number of grippe cases has more than doubled during the last seven days.

"The epidemic," Dr. W. C. Rucker, assistant surgeon general, said, "is not confined to any one locality. It is spreading through all of the larger cities and out into the country. Grippe is traveling almost as fast and as far as people travel. It is not improbable that every train, every street car, and every public conveyance that runs is carrying grippe germs to one or more groups of persons."

Officials of the public health service declined to report on the request of the New York health commissioners that nose and throat operation be suspended during the present epidemic.

Chicago Tribune, page 12, December 31, 1915.

***

"John, did you see the article on page twelve about a grippe epidemic? Is that the same as the Influenza? I'm not sure what to make of it." Ida was just coming to the parlor after cleaning up the supper dishes and doing a bit of prep for New Year's breakfast – pecan cinnamon sticky buns and fresh squeezed orange juice. It was already nine thirty; two and a half hours until the New Year.

John dropped the paper to look at her. "What do you mean?"

"What do you mean, what do I mean?" Ida sat on the sofa and started looking in her embroidery bag for the cross stitch she was working on.

"I mean, what about it? Yes, it is the same as Influenza."

Ida pulled out an embroidery hoop and looked at him. "Well, do you think it's right to see it as an epidemic when it is just out east?"

"I'm not sure it's just out east. How'd you get that idea?" John pulled the paper to eye level and paged forward to find the article.

Ida watched his progress. "Doesn't it say that the New York health officials are dealing with it?"

"No. The first sentence says, 'The whole country is in the throes....' And, that it is traveling fast. So yes, I'd say it's serious."

Ida felt a bit of panic building in her chest. "Then why was it hidden on the twelfth page?"

"I'm not sure how newspapers make the decisions about what page a story gets. To me it should have been more front and center, but maybe they are concerned with a panic."

"Maybe. More likely, if they put it on the front page, they'd have to bump one of their precious war stories." Ida kept her eyes on the paper.

John grunted in agreement from behind it.

"What do you think they are afraid of?" Ida's hands clinched and the embroidery needle poked her thumb. She brought the punctured phalanx to her mouth.

The invisible John behind the paper said, "I don't know. Stock market crash perhaps—"

Ida pulled her thumb out of her mouth so she could speak. "What! Because of the flu? Like the Titanic, then? Hold back the story until the rich people can get their money out of the market?"

John's voice seemed calm about the situation. "Or maybe everyone would go rushing to the doctor or accost the druggist."

Ida shook her head. A drop of blood dripped onto the edge of the cloth. "Doesn't it bother you when the papers tell a terrible story but don't give any guidance as to what we can do about it? I read that story, and I felt like we are all doomed." She dabbed at the red splotch and another drip joined it. She put pressure on the wound with her index finger to stop the bleeding.

John chuckled. "Maybe we are all doomed by one thing or another."

Ida's cheeks had gained some color. "Oh, don't say that. If it's not the war in Europe, it's Mexicans invading from the south or plagues of one sort or another coming from the east. And now the anarchists are attacking innocent people on the streets. By the way how's your nose?"

"Better, but there isn't a blame thing we can do about any of it. If it makes you feel better, I don't believe the Mexicans will attack the southern border. That war seems to have faded away some."

Ida checked to see if the thumb had stopped bleeding. It hadn't. She pressed her fingers together again. "But the war in Europe hasn't faded away. Every article I read seems to be warning that we will soon be in it."

John finally lowered the paper. "Yes, I think it will take a miracle to keep us out of it. But Ida, what are you really worried about?"

Ida thought for a minute, checking her thumb. The bleeding had stopped.

"I'm thinking about the children going to school. Should I let them go until the first flu case is found in the county? Or make them stay home? Should I pull Mamie out right away? But then if the other two keep going, they could bring it home to her anyway. Should I make them all stay home so we are safe?" Ida felt a wave of dizziness pass over her. She shut her eyes and rode the wave until it petered out.

She laid her stitching aside. "The war news is everywhere, all the time, and everyone is talking about it. But the flu is a direct threat to our children that we might be able to do something about, but they relegate it to the twelfth page where no one will see it. They make a statement about it spreading like wildfire but give no guidance about how we might protect ourselves and our children."

Ida's voice took on a more strident tone. "With the war, at least, they tell us a few things we can do like give money to the Red Cross or knit socks or wear white or pray for peace. But then something like the flu, they say not a word. I find that very frustrating."

"I can see that." John raised the paper back to reading level.

"So, what do you think?" Ida was looking at the paper again.

"About what?"

"John! Aren't you listening?"

John let his arms and the paper fall into his lap. "Of course, I am. You are worried about wearing white socks." John pulled the paper back up to hide his smile.

Silence.

"Right?" He peeked out with one eye.

Ida sat with her forehead in her hand. She was close to tears.

"Ida?"

"What?" she snapped but didn't look at him. The dizziness was back.

"I think we will hear if the epidemic comes to Chicago, and we can pull the girls out of school as soon as we hear that. You don't have to be so worried about it right now."

Ida looked up. "But Mamie—

"But no one. It isn't here yet if it's coming at all. As for the war, again we can do nothing except pray for peace and pray that America can stay out of it. You and I are little specks in the Universe. We have little importance to the ones waging the war. We have no sons to give at this time."

Little did he know. Ida looked up and into his eyes. "You know. I had a dream the other day that the kaiser, the king and the czar came here and sat in our parlor to ask me how to stop the war. They don't know what to do except keep fighting, and they asked me to tell them the secret of how to stop the killing, because if they keep killing hundreds of thousands of people, soon Europe will run out."

"What did you tell them?" John sounded intrigued.

"I didn't know what to tell them. I woke up before I had to say anything, but I think I might have said... 'Gentlemen, the first thing you have to do to stop the war is to stop fighting. If you were able to join forces to come to Woodstock to ask me what you should do, then you can also join forces to stop the fighting and sit down and talk it out."

John laughed. "Too bad you woke up."

Ida smiled. "It was so real. The Czar drank all your vodka."

"I don't have any vodka."

"See?"

John laughed again and got up, put the paper on the coffee table, and sat next to her. "I think we are both feeling a bit helpless and a bit afraid of the future. I know I am. The papers are full of things that we can believe and things that challenge the imagination. Or maybe I should say, make the imagination soar. Maybe we shouldn't put so much credence in it."

"But how can mothers protect their children without the facts? I can't stop reading the paper. I would be lost in the wilderness."

"I know." He shifted a little closer to her.

She moved her stitching to the arm of the davenport and looked at him. The specks of green in her hazel eyes reflected the light of the Christmas tree. "This time of year should be happy. Tonight, we move into a new year, get a new start, but instead it's dark and dreary and frightening. Maybe we need another baby."

John pulled back. "Another...another baby?"

"Yes. When Blanche was here with her little ones, I felt more at peace. There was much to do because the little ones need so much care, and of course, two toddlers and a woman lying in with a tiny baby was work, but it was happy work for a few days."

"You don't think it's happy around here?"

Ida shrugged. She knew she was acting like Edna.

John considered. "Well, I'm game for trying for a baby, but I think it might be too late for us to have another."

Ida shrugged.

John smiled a little. "Helen might leave home if we had another baby."

Ida looked up. "No, she wouldn't. She is as loyal as the day is long."

"Is she a senior in high school yet?" Now John was smiling.

"Not officially." Ida's mouth turned up a bit.

John slid over next to her and put his arm around her, and she cuddled into his shoulder. They sat for a few minutes like that, feeling the comfort of the embrace.

"Another baby," said John. "How old would we be when another baby graduated from high school?"

"I would be a young fifty-nine-year-old," said Ida.

"And I would be an old sixty-four-year-old."

"That doesn't seem too bad, does it?" Ida looked up at him.

John seemed to not have an answer, but then, "My father died when he was fifty-four years old."

"I know. My father was only forty-nine." Ida closed her eyes and felt the draw of sleep. "Do you really want to wait for midnight this year?"

"Um...I just assumed that we would." John's face creased with concern. "Are you feeling all right?"

"I'm just so very tired. I think I'm going to go to bed. The New Year can bring in itself." Ida tucked her stitching into her bag.

"I think that is a very good idea." He pulled her close and gave her a long kiss. "Happy New Year, my girl. May the new year be filled with happy surprises."

"That's my hope also. But I have a nervous feeling about 1916. I believe that you and I are more important to the world order than you think. I'll be ready if those three handsome gentlemen return for advice."

John smiled. "Who better could they ask?"

Ida gave a sniff of incredulity.

They continued to sit in this long embrace that calmed the nerves and renewed the spirit. The year to come might be filled with challenges, but as long as they had each other and God, they would be fine.

"You still awake?" Ida pulled away slightly.

"No. Shall we turn in?"

"But you are so comfortable a pillow," Ida purred.

Ida put her head back on his shoulder. "Let's just stay here and tell each other about the year past until we hear the bells."

"Okay. The biggest thing that happened this year was that we lost Ma," said John.

"Yes. She was quite a woman. I will especially miss her humor."

John chuckled. "Yes, she was the queen of the one liners, wasn't she?"

"And after the stroke she was quick to damn the louts whoever they may be. I wonder if that always happens after a stroke."

"I have no idea, but it was funny. I hope the Lord thought so, too." John shifted a little. His foot was going to sleep.

"I'm sure He did. I know you will miss her baking. She taught Edna quite a bit about baking during their afternoons together."

"I hope the girls will remember her well."

"They will. We won't let them forget."

John kissed the top of her head. She was the last of that generation to leave us, wasn't she? We are the old timers now."

Ida laughed. "Don't you tell the children that. They already see us as old fogeys."

"Maybe we are."

"Speak for yourself, Miles Standish. I'm as modern as a Cretonne Toque."

"A what?"

"You know. I showed you the picture - that hat – in last week's paper."

"That dunce's hat?" John burst out laughing. "You are not THAT modern. I like your flowered bonnets much better than that one even if they are old-fashioned."

"You think my hats are old-fashioned?"

"Of course not!" he answered a bit too quickly. "I'm the one who is old-fashioned."

Ida laughed. "I believe we are both—"

The bell of St. Mary's began to toll heralding the New Year.

"Oh!!" said Ida.

John leaned down and kissed her properly on the lips.

"Happy New Year. We made it!" she whispered.

"That we did."

John and Ida looked at each other and considered their next move. She smiled. He smiled. And they settled back and stretched full length on the davenport, Ida spooning into John's embrace. John pulled the red, brown, and cream-colored crocheted Afghan from the back of the davenport and spread it over them. Maybe sometime in the wee hours, they would awaken, their forty-year-old bones screaming in protest, and trundle off to a proper bed…or maybe not. Maybe Edna, their early riser, would come down and climb in with them, and jabber them awake. Maybe Clara, in search of her first cup of tea, would wander in and then reverse course, red-faced to see them so and retreat for another hour of sleep. John smiled. Tempting fate in a new year. Anything could happen in 1916. He felt Ida's body tight against him but threw away the idea of making "another baby" tonight. Only time would tell the path they would take His eyes closed against the lights of the Christmas tree making circles on the walls.

Printed in the USA
CPSIA information can be obtained
at www.ICGtesting.com
JSHW031722160823
46613JS00002B/150